"SINGLE BLACK FEMALE"

"The hilarious antics of the main and secondary characters made this book an enjoyable read."
—Rawsistaz Reviewers

"I found this book to be an excellent read."
—T. Rhythm Knight, APOOO Book Club

". . .well written and interesting novel with a strong and sympathetic protagonist."
—Elizabeth Ridley, Writer's Digest Magazine

"There are serious issues covered in this book which is one of the reasons it's such a good book."
—WZZA Radio
Tuscumbia, Alabama

"This is a great book."

—PCG Literary Marketing
Marietta, Georgia

SINGLE BLACK FEMALE

CARRIE CARR

♠

SINGLE BLACK FEMALE

AUTUMN GIRL PRESS

SINGLE BLACK FEMALE

Copyright © 2005 by Carrie Carr

Autumn Girl Press
P.O. Box 1424
Chicago, Illinois 60690

ISBN: 0-9766964-1-X
Revised Edition
Second Printing: July 2005

Library of Congress Control Number: 2005927925

Printed in the United States of America

A Note from the Author

Several years ago, I decided to spruce up my life with a little excitement, knowing exactly what was needed--romance, and lots of it. Armed with a positive attitude, I ventured into the world of personal ads. My debut novel, *Single Black Female*, mimics my own amusing experiences and fictionalizes the consequences of falling helplessly in love with a married man.

I understand the frustrations of searching for that special guy, and it is my hope that women will be entertained and inspired by my novel and realize that all roads can lead to happiness whether you are single or married.

Carrie Carr

Now and then we are compelled to do what is right, what we must, what we should. But . . . in the darkest hour, in the depths of our hearts, we are driven to follow our truest desires, despite everything and everybody.

CHAPTER ONE

ARE YOU THE ONE for me? This sweet single black female can stimulate your mind, make you laugh and arouse your passion. Let's meet in the Land of Imagination where all our dreams come true and no one is ever forgotten.

Let's connect on the phone, meet for coffee, exchange pleasantries, and get to know each other. Who knows? I may be exactly who you're looking for.

Optimistic, curious, petite single black female, just turned twenty-nine, in search of warm, open-minded and adventurous male for . . .

Cinnamon Brown longed for an intimate relationship especially just now as she slouched comfortably in her twin-sized bed, writing her personal ad. She sighed because for minutes on end she labored over the perfect words. She wanted to attract a good man, and she didn't want to sound silly or amateurish, though this was her first time at such an endeavor.

After several attempts, she balled up her drafts and tossed them onto the hardwood floor, which she interpreted as a sign to postpone the idea until a later date.

Her goal in placing an ad was twofold: to dispute the myth that personal ads were for losers, and to find Mister Wonderful. Knowing he was out there somewhere, she refused to abandon the idea without at least exploring it. Her life had become uninteresting and it was time to make a change.

When she actively dated back in the day, she slept with two men and she was not bragging about either of them. Her greatest wish then had been to win the affections of men and that was pretty much it, except it never quite worked out that way. And it didn't take her long to realize it was the illusion of closeness and affection that encouraged her. After all, she was in search of something--Love. And for all her efforts, the only things she acquired were a tainted ego and frustration. Lots and lots of frustration.

Upon discovering that sex was not affection nor love, Cinnamon shied away from dating and remained celibate. She even purchased a gold wedding band, which she wore on her right finger to symbolize her decision.

Her plan was to take a break from men and write a book about all the self-improvement material she studied over the years, a sort of compilation encompassing everything she learned. Well, two years passed and no book existed. Though it sounded like a novel idea at the time, it just never happened.

Things were different now. She was ready to make a connection with the right guy.

After sipping the last of her lemon tea from her ATA coffee mug, she clicked off the lamp on her marble night table. The night air from the open window circulated the room, and she scooted down in the bed and pulled the bulky black and white striped comforter up to her neck. With just a glimmer of light shining in from the street, she stared into the darkness.

Many nights she heard the chitter-chatter from the other units, but this night she heard none.

This moment of stillness was well deserved. For the past three days, she catered to more than one hundred passengers on a noisy plane. And she savored the silence.

After reciting her nightly prayer, she wondered how long it would take to meet Mister Wonderful, and how many dates she would have to endure before she met him.

An optimist at heart, she knew he was out there, and it was just a matter of time before she found him.

Upon waking the next morning, Cinnamon brewed her peach tea, her daily and nightly ritual. Since giving up cigarettes two years ago, water, herbal tea and decaffeinated coffee became her new practice.

Cinnamon was a size six with eye-catching almond-shaped eyes and perfect teeth, after wearing braces as a young girl. Having worn chemically straightened hair for seven years, she recently cut it off and now wore a short curly afro with the sides nicely tapered. Eventually, she planned to grow it shoulder length and wear one of the many natural styles for black women, but that would happen later down the line. For now, her short wavy hairdo suited her fine.

En route to Unabridged Books, two blocks from where she lived, she wore her jeans and pristine sneakers, intending to be there for a while.

Cinnamon resided in a middle-class gay populated area on Chicago's north side known as Lakeview. And it was the place to be. Everything she needed or wanted was within walking distance, which was perfect, seeing as she didn't own a car nor did she want one. She chose to invest her money in mutual funds instead.

Cinnamon entered the dimly lit bookstore. It was Saturday and it was packed. She roamed the aisle of her favored Psychology and Self-Improvement section. Even as a teenager, psychology always held an interest to her, studying it and sharing with others everything she learned.

Moments passed and Cinnamon lifted a book, *Feel the Fear and Do It Anyway*, from the shelf, then kneeled down on the floor and thumbed the pages. Right as she skimmed the table of contents, a man approached her, wanting to pass.

"Excuse me," he said in a delicate voice.

She quickly stood and stepped aside so that he could pass.

"Thank you," he said.

When he passed by, she perused his beaten leather jacket and cream-colored complexion. He could easily pass as white, but because of his wavy dark hair she could tell he was black. His potent cologne lingered in the air as she continued to scan the pages of the book.

Suddenly, she felt someone watching her. As she slowly lifted her head from the book, she saw the same guy from before poke his head from behind the shelf.

He was so obvious, she couldn't help but smile.

It didn't take him long to approach her. "Hello."

"Hello," Cinnamon said, wondering how someone so tall could have such a soft-spoken voice.

"Sorry about that," he said. "I suppose you saw me watching you?"

"It was kind of hard not to."

She adored his dimpled cheeks. He appeared to be around her age, maybe a year or two younger, and his face was flawless.

"What are you reading?" he asked.

She flipped to the front cover to remind herself. "*Feel the Fear and Do It Anyway.*"

"What kind of fear are you trying to feel and why do you want to do it anyway?"

She tried to keep from laughing but she couldn't. "I never thought about it like that."

"I'm Noel." He extended his hand and they shook. She watched his gaze scroll her body.

"I'm Cinnamon."

She liked his initiative. And he was witty and friendly too. Though her position with the airline required she possess an assertive personality, she sometimes found herself bashful in a more personal setting.

"You live around here?" he asked.

"Uh huh."

"And this is how you spend your Saturdays?"

"Sometimes."

Noel was about to dash away. "Excuse me, will you? I see some friends of mine."

"Sure."

Not only was he charming, but he was a real cutie. As a matter of fact, he was too cute and all she could think about was that he might be gay. But if that were the case, why did he show her so much attention?

Noel conversed with his friends and returned to Cinnamon. "I'm back," he said, as his tiny silver earring dangled from his earlobe. He stood against the bookshelf, seemingly relaxed, with his arms at his side. Cinnamon watched him watch her. "Can I help you?" she asked playfully.

"Just watching."

She laughed, continuing to thumb the pages. "So you're just going to stand there?"

"I wouldn't have to if I could convince you to have coffee with me next door."

"Now?"

"Can you think of a better time?"

"I don't know, I have this book to read and all."

"I could buy it for you."

"No, I couldn't let you do that. I don't even know you."

"Sure you do. I'm Noel, remember? We just met."

She smiled. "You know what I mean."

"Well, you could put it back on the shelf and I can't make any guarantees, but I'm almost positive it will be here when you get back."

"You're a real problem solver, aren't you?"

Noel stepped to her. "So shall we dance? I mean shall we go?"

Cinnamon hesitated, then said, "I guess you talked me into it."

"I guess I did."

The robust aroma of freshly brewed coffee greeted Cinnamon at the entrance of Café Classico. As she and Noel made their way in, the cappuccino machine buzzed from behind the counter. People in jeans and sweaters swarmed the café on this gloomy fall morning. Some read. Some wrote. Others talked with one another.

After Cinnamon ordered tea and Noel ordered coffee, they convened at a table that faced Broadway Street. She removed her suede jacket and draped it on the back of her chair.

"I'm glad you agreed to come with me," he said. "But I have to tell you, I don't usually do this."

"You mean pick up women in bookstores?"

"Oh, I do that all the time. I just don't usually pick up beautiful ones."

"You're too kind, Noel. You didn't pick me up, did you?"

"I'm afraid so."

"I feel so cheap," Cinnamon said, smiling.

"It'll pass. Anyway, you seemed like someone who needed to be picked up."

"Excuse me?"

He chuckled. "I'm sorry. That came out wrong. What I meant was you seemed like someone I would enjoy talking to. Am I right?"

"You're asking me?"

"Yeah," he said. "Do you think I would enjoy talking to you?"

"You tell me. Are you enjoying talking to me?"

Noel didn't answer right away as he gazed into Cinnamon's eyes. "Very much."

Cinnamon sipped her tea, trying to ignore the fact he was staring. She set her cup down on the table and smiled. "You're staring."

"Am I? I'm sorry. So what do you do, Ms. Cinnamon?"

"I'm a flight attendant."

"I bet you look really professional in your uniform."

"Besides hitting on women in bookstores, what else do you do?"

"I hit on them at grocery stores, libraries and churches."

"Very funny."

"I do a little temp work and I also take pictures."

"Of what?" she asked.

Leaning toward her, blushing, he said, "Anything and everything."

Noel was all personality, charm and wit. He was the kind of person she could be around all the time. He seemed to take notice of the wedding band on her right finger. "So where's your husband?"

"Huh?" His question caught her off guard.

"It's not a trick question."

"What makes you think I have a husband?" she asked.

"Doesn't every woman?"

"No. Not this woman."

"Any boyfriends floating around?"

"None of those either," Cinnamon said. "I'm single."

"Why is that?"

"Why is anyone single? They want to be, I guess."

"Not everyone," he said. "Why the ring then? You're trying to ward off us wolves?"

"Maybe."

"Why would you want to do that? Keep men at bay?"

"You ask a lot of questions," Cinnamon said.

He disregarded her comment and eased back in his chair. "You know, they say if you wear a wedding band and you're not married, you never will be."

"I'm not superstitious, well, not really anyway."

"How really then?"

Cinnamon sipped her tea, savoring the peppermint flavor. "I have only one superstition and that's dating married men. Outside of that, I'm not superstitious at all."

"Married men? What's that all about?"

"It's a long story."

"Give me the short version."

"Let's just say my two sisters didn't have the best luck dating married men. As a matter of fact, they had some pretty rotten luck."

"Like what?"

"Nothing I care to reveal at this time."

"But you will tell me?"

"Maybe one day." Cinnamon finished her tea. "And in reference to the comment you made about me never marrying, I might marry or I might not, but for sure it won't have anything to do with this ring."

"You never know." He paused and moved his chair closer to the table. "So no boyfriend, huh? I find that hard to believe."

"It amazes me when people say that," Cinnamon voiced with conviction. "Did it ever occur to you that I could have just broken up with my boyfriend this morning? In which case, I wouldn't have had a chance to find another one."

"Did you break up with your boyfriend this morning?"

"No, but that's not the point."

"What is the point?" he asked.

"The point is . . ." She smiled, wanting to maintain a warm and friendly atmosphere. "The point is a woman is allowed to exist in this world without a man by her side."

"She is?"

"Yes, she is."

"Excuse me," he said. "I didn't know you felt so strongly about this topic."

"Do you always have a woman at your side?"

"No, but that doesn't mean I wouldn't like to."

Twenty minutes passed.

Cinnamon slid her cup to the center of the table and scooted her chair back. "I should be on my way. Tea always stimulates my senses for reading, especially on a cold day like today."

"Would you mind if I tagged along?"

"Well . . ."

"Okay, okay, I won't push. I know when I'm not wanted."

Cinnamon laughed, admiring his dimpled cheeks. "I didn't say that."

"I'm just kidding. Can I call you sometime?"

"You don't have a problem asking anything, do you?"

"No. So can I call you? I can assure you I'm not a sex offender, heroin addict or an ex-convict."

"Are you sure?"

"I have references and everything."

Cinnamon smiled, knowing from the start she definitely wanted to know him better. "Maybe I could call you."

Noel scribbled his number on a napkin and handed it to her.

"Noel Green. Cute name."

She stood up, slipped the napkin into her jeans' hip pocket and slid her arms into her jacket.

"When can I expect to hear from you?" he asked.

"Soon."

"You promise?"

"Yes, I promise."

"Sometime this year, right?"

"Definitely this year."

Cinnamon exited the coffee shop and returned to the bookstore. Though fortunate to have met such a fun person in Noel, something about him was too right or maybe not right at all. He was perfect, absolutely gorgeous, kind, witty, charming and full of adventure. Was she that lucky or maybe not lucky at all?

Only time would tell. She regretted not giving him her telephone number. Now she was faced with the task of calling on him, something she would rather not do. But it was too late now.

Sooner or later, she would call upon him and discover the mystery of Noel Green.

Chapter Two

Sunday morning Cinnamon relaxed in her ivory kitchen. Her *Sunday Tribune* and *Chicago Reader* lay spread out on the table, with the movie section and personal ads smack dab on top.

In a cheerful mood, she listened to her much loved Bob Marley CD, which resounded from the living room stereo system. It was her favorite track, "Is this Love," which always sent happiness through her veins.

When she could, she attended First Community Church, but today her lazy mood persuaded her otherwise.

While the cool air coursed throughout her apartment, she scanned the *Chicago Reader* movie section. But nothing captured her interest. She would have liked to see a juicy love story but the really good ones were few and far between.

Many times Cinnamon skimmed through the personal ads section of the *Chicago Reader*, finding it amusing and sometimes even comical. As she glanced over a hundred ads, it was obvious many people, males and females, were looking to couple. Her position with the airlines did provide an avenue to meet different people, but they were mostly from other cities. Since she postponed placing her own ad, today she considered responding to one.

What kinds of people placed personal ads?

She browsed through the Males Seeking Females section and then glimpsed at the Females Seeking Males section and compared the two. She wondered about the women in search of men.

Were they just like her?

Were they outgoing?

Smart?

Shy?

Most of all, what did they look like?

Were they pretty?

Tall?

Short?

She flipped back to the Males Seeking Females section and scanned the various ads. It might be embarrassing to respond. Men would question why she felt a need to answer a personal ad, theorizing that just because a woman was somewhat attractive meant she was never without a date.

That theory did not prove true at all.

At a loss for companionship, Cinnamon sighed. The only thing she disliked about her job was her consecutive days off and not enough to do. She wanted to call her best friend, Arri, but Arri spent most of her time with her boyfriend. Arri was either with him, chasing him, or trying to win him back.

Then Noel leaped to mind. When he gave her his number, she planned to call, just not so soon.

Loud dance music vibrated in her ear when Noel answered the phone. "Just a second," he said before he turned down the music and returned to the phone. "Sorry about that."

"You know who this is?" Cinnamon asked.

"I know your voice, Cinnamon. I was hoping you'd call."

"I said I would."

"Yes, you did."

"Is this a good time?" she asked.

"It's always a good time," he said. "As a matter of fact, you just made my day."

Did he really like her or was he just a big flirt?

"Are you always this . . . this complimentary?" she asked.

"When I have reason. I don't meet attractive women every day. I see them but I don't meet them. So what can I do for you? Or better yet, how can I serve you?"

"You are all personality. You know that, don't you?"

"I do. What can I say? It's a curse."

"I just wanted to say hi and see what you were doing."

"Did you want to do something later?"

"Like what?"

"Drinks, dancing?"

"You mean like a nightclub?"

"You could call it that."

"I'm not too big on nightclubs."

"And why is that?"

"I'm not a nightclub person. And the music is always too loud."

"You'll like this place. It's probably not like anything you're used to. The crowd is different."

"What does that mean?"

"You'll find out. You want to try it?"

Though pressured, she did want to know him better. After a quick mental debate, she said, "Okay, but if I don't like it, I'm not going to stay. Okay?"

"Oh, but you will."

"You think you really know me, don't you?" she asked, admiring his certainty.

"I know I do."

Before ending the call, they planned to meet at eleven that evening.

Back at the kitchen table, Cinnamon tossed down her lemon tea and returned her focus to the personal ads. This time she would conquer her fear and respond. Unless she tried it, her questions would never be answered. She would never know how successful or unsuccessful meeting through the personals could be. And if her meetings didn't work out, she could always chalk them up to learning experiences.

After reading over the many ads, two fancied her interest.

What would you think if I brought you candy? I am a SBM, 32, 5'9", supportive and able to appreciate the best in you. I enjoy a good laugh, art galleries, museums, music and all sports. I am seeking a SBF, 25-38, who likes to have fun. She is looking for a lasting friendship. @91660.

SBM, 30, spontaneous, and energetic, 6'2", 180 pounds. I'm not looking for love but I am looking for females, single, black, white, Asian, or Hispanic. Good friends who'd love to have fun, dancing, camping, traveling, dining out, and health clubs. I am an actor and have a model look. Believe me. It doesn't go to my head. Let's be special friends. @91654.

Both ads appealed to her because they emphasized friendship, which was exactly what she sought. She left a brief message on the nine-hundred number for both men, including her phone number, noting that she sought friendship more than anything else. While in the midst of her second message, her doorbell rang, but she continued with her message before answering. She approached the intercom near the door and learned it was Arri, who lived only six blocks away.

Whenever Cinnamon returned to town, there was always some drama going on with Arri. Either Arri had a scheme in the making to garner more attention or a wild escapade to blab about. And it always, but always, stemmed from E-r-i-c, her boyfriend, a.k.a. her one true love.

She and Cinnamon had known each other for years, practically growing up together. Their biggest common interest was books. Only Arri liked to read romance novels, magazines and tabloids, whereas Cinnamon favored psychology, religion and spirituality.

At the front door, Cinnamon waited for Arri to tower down the hall.

"Hey, you," Cinnamon said as Arri approached. "What crisis brought you over?"

"I wanted to see you."

In Cinnamon's living room, daylight seeped through the closed mini-blinds, which reflected off the shiny floors and polished furniture. Except for the mushroom white director's chair, every piece of furniture was a lustrous black.

Arri moseyed through the door and quickly cleared herself of her coat and worn out leather bag and tossed them onto the plush sofa. Arri was an administrative assistant for Harris Bank. She was almost six feet tall, twenty-seven and the slimmest of the slim. Her thick auburn hair, which she wore in a ponytail, loomed halfway down her back. She was pale and because of her beige press powder, she emerged even lighter. Her long knit lavender dress draped sensuously over her shiny boots. With purple being her color of choice, it was more of an obsession. It was her boyfriend's favorite and she relished wearing it, even basked in it.

Never quite comfortable indoors wearing boots or shoes, Arri quickly removed her boots. She folded her arms and cuddled her forearms. "It's cold in here."

Cinnamon closed the window then headed toward the kitchen. Arri made a beeline right behind her and slumped down into the kitchen chair, sitting on top of one folded leg.

Cinnamon brewed a fresh pot of coffee, then sat across from Arri. Arri stared down at the floor and sighed, her face void of her usual zest.

"What's wrong?" Cinnamon asked.

Arri lifted her head and yawned. "I didn't get much sleep last night."

"Oh, what's that all about?"

"Eric asked me to do something that really bothered me."

"What? Put him on a higher pedestal?" Cinnamon laughed. "Isn't the one he's on high enough?"

"I'm serious, Cinnamon."

"I know you are. I'm sorry, but I couldn't let that one pass."

"He doesn't want me calling him in the morning before eleven anymore."

"What, you think he has someone over at that time?"

"That's what I'm thinking."

Cinnamon stood, seized two coffee mugs from the cabinet and set them on the table. "Did you ask him about it?"

"No, because he'll just say I'm paranoid. Then in addition to that . . ."

"There's more?"

"He must be going through some kind of phase or something," Arri said. "I don't know what it is, but he also doesn't want me wearing pants anymore, at least not when I'm with him."

"What is he, the master or something?" Cinnamon questioned with a twisted mouth.

"Then if that's not enough, he wants me to have those acrylic nails put on."

"Now he's really tripping."

"Tripping is right."

Cinnamon leaned against the counter, facing Arri. "I hope you told him where to go."

Arri raised her shoulders, seemingly riddled with ambiguity. "Well, I couldn't say no."

"Because?" Cinnamon asked.

"You know."

"No, I don't know. Tell me."

"Because I don't like saying no to him."

"I don't see why not," Cinnamon said with a bite in her tone. "He's not the only man in this world."

Though Cinnamon was never as wretched for affection as Arri, still a part of Cinnamon lived inside Arri. She understood Arri's dire longing to feel special because she used to be Arri and she shared Arri's heartache.

"I just don't want to miss out on what I have coming," Arri said.

"From whom? From Eric?"

"I've invested a lot into this relationship, and I don't want to miss what I have coming." Arri stood, about to pour the coffee when she noticed it wasn't ready. "I missed out on a lot growing up and I don't want to miss out again."

"Missed out on what?"

"I missed out," Arri stated firmly as she returned to her chair. "That's all I'm going to say. I know I shouldn't have to do certain things for people to like me, but . . ."

"No buts. You shouldn't have to act a certain way or do a certain thing for anyone. Not even Eric. You don't have to do these things for him."

"I know I don't *have* to."

With all the tact Cinnamon could round up, she asked, "Don't you think Eric sometimes takes advantage of you though?"

"No," Arri said, shaking her head. "I don't. I enjoy doing things for him. Most of the time anyway."

Cinnamon closed her eyes. She pitied Arri for allowing Eric to have such power over her. "The more I hear about Eric, the more I can't stand him," Cinnamon said. "And I know it's not right to feel that way about anyone, but Eric makes it very easy for me. He's manipulative. And selfish."

"That's just the part you hear about."

"What part haven't I heard?"

Arri stood and filled her and Cinnamon's cups with coffee.

"He's passionate, funny, confident. And he's always in control."

Cinnamon listened but she did not speak because it was useless. He was Arri's guy, almost perfect in Arri's eyes and that was that, regardless of what he may have asked of her, or even demanded of her.

Arri blew on her coffee, then sipped it down slowly. "So you want some overnight company?" she asked smiling.

"I'd love to have you over, but I made plans with this guy I just met."

"You met somebody? Good for you."

Arri shifted her cup to the side, slumped over, and laid the side of her face against the table. "I'll just go on home. Alone. By myself. And cry."

Aware of Arri's plea for sympathy, Cinnamon gently stroked Arri's head. "You know I'd much rather spend the evening with you than an outsider. Why don't you come with us?"

"No. No. I don't feel much like socializing."

"I'll get together with Noel some other time," Cinnamon said.

"No. Don't break your date on my account." Arri lifted her head. "I'll be okay. Maybe."

"If I go, you'll cry about it the rest of the week."

Though eager to connect with Noel, her friend needed her more and she was forced to cancel.

"I need to write some things in my journal," Arri said as she strolled into the living room. Cinnamon followed and watched Arri crash onto the sofa and take her journal from her bag.

"Do you still write in that funny code you invented?" Cinnamon asked.

"Every day."

Paranoid that someone might stumble upon her journal, Arri created her own made-up written language, a blend of French words, Spanish words, Chinese symbols and shorthand. Every time Cinnamon even gazed at it, it brought on a migraine.

Cinnamon stood over Arri, watching her scribble in her journal. "What are you writing now?"

"Just how I feel about what happened with Eric and me."

"Will you read me something?"

"Sure. From what day?"

"Any day. Just pick any day at random."

Arri flipped through the pages.

"Pick an interesting one now," Cinnamon said.

"All my entries are interesting." Finally, Arri found one. "Okay, here's one. I wrote this about two months ago when Eric was out of town. Dear Journal, I have been missing Eric all week. I find myself sometimes sitting at my desk at work fantasizing when I should be working. This morning on my way into the office, I happened to be on the elevator with nine white men, all dressed in suits. The only thing I could think about was doing all of them. I am in heat!"

Not sure she heard Arri correctly, Cinnamon didn't speak immediately, then she laughed. "I can't believe you wrote that. Did you really write that?"

"Did I paint the picture of horniness or what?"

"Honey, the picture is painted, wrapped and ready to be sold."

"That's what I'm talking about," Arri said.

"Read me something else," Cinnamon said, her eyes gleaming with curiosity.

Arri flipped through the pages. "Okay, here's something that's on the other side of the spectrum. Are you ready?"

"I'm ready. No, no, let me sit down for this one." Cinnamon quickly buckled down on the sofa and prepared herself.

"Dear Journal, if I were a color, I'd be blue, if I were a number, I'd be zero, if I were a fruit, I'd be spoiled and if I was alive, I'd be dead."

An extended silence cast over the room as Cinnamon consumed Arri's entry. "You have to be kidding me. It doesn't really say that, does it?"

"That's what it says."

"But it's so dark . . . and gloomy. When did you write that?"

"A few weeks ago."

"Is there anything in there about me?"

"Of course."

"Will you read something to me?"

"Absolutely not."

After changing for bed, Arri and Cinnamon rested their backs against the headboard, the ceiling light casting down on them. Via remote, Arri flipped on the television, muting the sound, then scanned the channels until she reached the cable channel E.

For thirty minutes, Cinnamon listened to Arri babble on and on about her darling Eric Lyles as if being paid to do so.

"So this is the infamous bed where nothing ever happens," Arri said with a devilish giggle.

Not the least bit amused by Arri's comment, Cinnamon stared at the television and nibbled on her already bitten down fingernails. She perused the white wall in front of her and reflected on her life. "Arri, do you ever get lonely sleeping by yourself?"

"Eric is with me most of the time and when he's not, I don't think about it. Do you?"

Cinnamon nodded her head in deep thought. "Sometimes I do. There are times when I wake up in the middle of the night and I think someone is sleeping next to me."

"Sounds like a hot dream."

"No, that's not what I mean. I don't know what I mean."

"Well, I do," Arri said. "Girl, it's time for you to get some. Okay? That's all that is. How can you be celibate like that anyway?"

"When you're not involved with anyone, it's not hard."

"But still, don't you think about it? Even if I weren't involved with Eric, my desires wouldn't disappear."

Cinnamon scooted down in the bed and turned away from Arri. "Well, I'm not like you."

"It's just weird that you've chosen this for yourself," Arri said. "Me, I would never choose celibacy. Never ever because I'd go to pieces."

"How would you know, you've never gone without."

"And don't want to either."

Cinnamon sat up and turned to Arri. "Do you really enjoy sex that much?"

"Yes."

"I mean really enjoy it."

"Yes."

"Do you have. . . ?"

Arri made a shape of an O with her fingers. "Do I have the big O?"

"Yes, do you have those?"

"All the time."

"Really?" Cinnamon asked. "Do you even know what an orgasm is?"

"Yes, I do, thank you."

"And you really have them?"

"Why is that so hard for you to fathom?"

"Fathom?" Cinnamon questioned. "When did you start using words like fathom?"

"Oh, shut up," Arri said.

"I read that most women don't have orgasms," Cinnamon said.

"Well, I'm not most women."

Cinnamon flew to Nashville the next day and didn't return to Chicago until later that week. She stepped through the front door of her darkened one bedroom apartment and pulled her tote bag over to the walk-in hall closet. While she hung up her coat, her weighty sack flopped to the floor. She then grabbed her tote bag and headed into the bedroom. In the pants section of the closet, she hung up her dark uniform and slipped out of her navy shoes.

In the front room, a message awaited her on her answering machine. Though most people switched to voice mail, she refused to pay a monthly fee for something she could own.

The message was from a gentleman named Joseph. In his brief message, she detected a slight stammer, but not enough to discourage her.

First she would prepare her lemon tea, then she would return his call. After she dialed his number, she hung up before he answered. Clueless, she didn't know what to expect.

What would she say to him?

How would she start the conversation?

She stared at the phone for a few seconds, released a breath of uneasiness and dialed his number.

A gentleman answered and in the background she heard a classic James Brown song, "Papa Don't Take No Mess."

"May I speak to Joseph?"

"This is Joseph. Who is this?"

"This is Cinnamon. I'm returning--"

"What did you say your name was?" he questioned.

"Cinnamon. I answered your personal ad."

"I know who you are now. I left you a message--A message on your answering machine."

"Right. So how are you?"

"I'm okay. So you got my message today? I called you yesterday."

"I just got back today."

For a moment, Cinnamon couldn't think of anything to say, then she asked, "What do you do, Joseph?"

"I work for a newspaper--newspaper downtown," he said, his breathing rather heavy as if in a hurry. *The Chicago Tribune.*

"Do you live in the city?" she asked.

"Yep, Rogers Park. Do you want to meet for lunch or dinner?"

"You don't waste any time, do you?"

He chuckled. "So would you like to get together?"

Though she didn't want to sound superficial by asking about his appearance, she needed to know. "What do you look like?"

"I'm about five feet nine. I have a mustache, black hair. So would you like to meet so we can--we can get to know each other in person?"

"Um. . . I guess."

With no prior plans to meet this quickly, she was eager to connect the voice with the face. They agreed to meet the following weekend at Bennigan's on South Water and Michigan.

His stammer could have easily deterred her from meeting with him but it didn't. He could very well be a great date. For years, she wholeheartedly subscribed to the Karma principle and if she held his stammer against him, someone might one day prejudice her as well.

Romantic instrumental music played from the stereo while Cinnamon dressed for her date Saturday evening. She loved instrumental music, found it relaxing and uplifting as she envisioned herself lying on a crystal-sand beach surrounded by beautiful blue water.

Standing in front of the bathroom mirror, she swiped dark earthy red blush against her cheeks, then applied bronze light lipstick to her full lips. As she glamorized herself, she was really feeling this dating scene. Up until this moment, she forgot how much she missed dating, the fun of it all. It being some time since her last date, she cherished this day, having plans to meet a potential companion.

Her cream-colored pants fit loosely around her tiny waist. With her two-inch heels, she stood five feet, six inches tall. After picking out her short afro, she inserted her gold loop earrings. She sprayed her much adored Cool Water Woman perfume on her ankles and wrists. In an effort to make a good impression, she exerted much effort dolling herself up. And she hated to think her efforts would be in vain.

With that unsettling thought in mind, she left for the restaurant.

Cinnamon flounced through the revolving doors of Bennigan's restaurant a few minutes late, choosing not to appear eager. Right away, she encountered the evening crowd waiting to be seated. With the blaring conversations, she could barely hear herself worry.

She and Joseph agreed to meet at the bar, informing each other what the other would wear. On the lookout for a gentleman wearing a grey suit, Cinnamon veered toward the bar and didn't see anyone fitting Joseph's description. With her eyes on the entrance, she stripped off her coat, placed it on the bar stool next to her and sat down.

While lingering, her eyes searched the room, periodically returning her focus to the entrance of the restaurant. Just as she felt a knot in her stomach, which was a sign of disaster, she pinpointed a gentleman with an oily forehead coming from the men's room.

Oozing disappointment, she blinked twice.

Could that be him?

CHAPTER THREE

THE GENTLEMAN FORGED TOWARD Cinnamon, wearing the worst outdated garage sale clothes she'd ever seen. "Cinnamon?" he questioned.

"Yes."

"I'm Joseph," he said loud enough to wake the dead.

"Hello, Joseph."

His grey polyester pants rose two inches above his shoes, and his receding hairline added abuse to his broad and greasy forehead. He reeked of barbecue sauce which she found odd until she noticed a stain on his banana yellow shirt.

Overcome with fear that all eyes were on them, she quickly asked, "Would you like to get a table?"

"I'd like that," he said with an open-mouthed smile.

The waiter seated them at a booth in the back, which was just where Cinnamon wished to be. In the back and out of sight.

Joseph reached into his pocket, pulled out a Godiva candy bar and handed it to her. "I got this for you."

"Thank you."

Joseph possessed a giddy smile that never left his face. "You like--you like chocolate, don't you?"

"Sure." Though she detected a slight stutter over the phone, it seemed much more pronounced in person. She could have kicked herself for impulsively agreeing to meet with this man.

What was she thinking?

As she reflected on the disastrous evening to come, she thought it would be amusing and even funny if it was happening to someone else. But that wasn't the case.

She was now stuck for at least two hours.

In the back of her mind, she contemplated excusing herself to the ladies' room and not returning, but she couldn't do that. A cruel stunt like that might come back to haunt her one day.

Abruptly, Joseph dismissed himself from the table, leaving his wrinkled suit jacket behind. As he drifted toward the men's room, Cinnamon noticed the stitching in his grey pants appeared sewn from the outside, with white thread.

Oh, no!

While awaiting his return, she realized he neglected to mention his stubby build. But it was her fault for not asking the right questions. One being, are you normal?

Though next time she might do things differently, how would she deal with this time?

On his way back to the booth, he bumped into a waiter who carried a tray of water glasses. Cinnamon's head dropped in embarrassment.

Luckily the tray did not fall.

Joseph reverted back to the table and barreled into the booth, seemingly amused, glad, happy or something. For some reason, the smirk on his face was never ending.

Not sure what to do next, Cinnamon held up the menu, pretending to skim it. Upon lowering it, she found Joseph eying her like he was some evil doctor in a horror movie.

The silence between them unnerved her as she fished for something to say. With no desire to converse with him, she didn't know how she would make it through dinner.

Then out of nowhere Joseph commenced singing to himself. "Papa don't take no mess--I love James Brown. You like James Brown?"

"I like him."

"Papa don't take no mess--You know that song?"

"I've heard it."

"You like sports?" he asked.

"Not really." She drank down her water and eased back in the booth, wishing she was somewhere else, anywhere else.

"What about gymnastics? You like gymnastics?"

"They're okay."

With that same stupefied grin, he leaned forward and whispered. "Can you do a split?"

"What? What kind of question is that?"

He avoided her question and instead chuckled like a cartoon character and slurped his water. "I drink two quarts of water a day. My doctor says it's good for me."

"That's nice."

All the ads to choose from in the paper and she ended up with him.

"Anything you want to ask me?" he asked.

"Not that I can think of at the moment."

Cinnamon knew little about him and desired to know even less.

Soon the waitress approached, ready to take their order. "What can I get for you this evening?"

Uncertain whether she would be staying for dinner, Cinnamon said, "I'm still looking."

"Take your time."

As soon as the waitress stepped away, Joseph said, "I know what I want already. I want the chicken fingers." He chuckled for no apparent reason and would not stop.

"What's so funny?"

"It's a surprise--what do you want to do after dinner?" he asked.

"I really hadn't planned on anything else."

He chuckled again and she would have done anything to turn him off, including smacking him.

"What are you laughing at?"

"Ah, nothing. Would you excuse me? I have to go to the men's room."

"Sure."

Joseph left the table and returned soon afterwards. Without delay, he began again with the questions. "Can you dance?"

"Yes, I can dance." Quickly, she changed the subject. "Tell me about your work, Joseph."

"There's nothing to tell." He eased back, seemingly relaxed without a care in the world. "You can call me Jojo. My friends call me Jojo."

Cinnamon associated the name "Jojo" with a drunken bum, and she refused to use it, especially in public. "I like Joseph better. Have you always lived in Chicago?"

"Uh huh. My mother and I have lived here all our lives."

As Cinnamon rested her hands on the table, Joseph noticed the ring on her finger and literally jumped from his seat. "You're married?"

"No, I'm not married."

"'Cause'--cause I wouldn't want to have dinner with someone who's married. You're not married, right?"

"No, Joseph, I'm not married."

"Good, 'cause I'm very interested."

"Did you say you lived in Rogers Park?" she asked.

"Yep. Maybe you'd like to come over sometime. My mother is hardly ever there. She spends most of her time at the *chuch.*"

"The what?"

"The *chuch.*"

"Oh, the church," Cinnamon said. At this point, Cinnamon was just asking questions to keep him from asking questions. "Did you drive here?"

"Yep. You want to see my car? I got a really good deal on it. It's right outside."

"That's okay."

Joseph rested his arms on the table, stretched out in front of him. "Have you ever met anyone through the personals before?"

"No, this is my first time."

"I have."

She could see why.

Abruptly he stood and stepped away from the table. "I'll be right back."

That was it.

Cinnamon could not and would not endure an entire dinner with a man who obviously couldn't control his bladder, not to mention his absurd curiosity. Though she did her best to play it through, she refused to continue, despite her best intentions.

While Joseph used the men's room, she clutched her coat and purse and dashed out the door. Once outside, she hailed a Checker taxi. No doubt, Joseph would contact her again, but that was okay. She would deal with that issue when the time came.

The taxi driver made a screeching u-turn in front of Cinnamon's high-rise building on Lake Shore Drive. Before going inside, Cinnamon hustled a block to the corner store and purchased chamomile tea, needing to unwind from her weird encounter.

Inside her apartment, the autumn air from the half-opened window flowed through the living room. Cinnamon sat snug on her sectional sofa, her legs crossed as she tossed down her tea. She relived her unforgettable date with Joseph, his stutter, his ridiculous laugh, and his senseless questions. For certain, she should have gotten to know him before agreeing to a date. In any event, she suspected she might have better results if she placed her own personal ad.

Sunday morning Cinnamon trotted less than a mile to the neighborhood church. After abandoning her life-long Baptist beliefs, she adopted a non-denominational faith. At First Community Church, women were allowed to wear pants, which Cinnamon liked. Her casual attire brought on a lax mind set, rendering church a welcomed practice rather than an obligation.

On this particular Sunday, Cinnamon found it strange that the pastor would speak about adultery, never before hearing him address the subject.

So why today? For sure, it was definitely a sign of some sort.

After her hour-long service, Cinnamon returned home. As she approached her front door, she heard the phone ringing. She quickly unlocked the door and raced inside.

"Hello," Cinnamon said.

No one responded, but she heard James Brown music in the background and immediately knew who it was. Joseph.

After greeting the caller twice, she hung up.

Suddenly, the phone rang again. This time it echoed even louder, almost frighteningly. She stood motionless waiting for the answering machine to click on. Finally, the message came through. She recognized Arri's voice and picked up.

"Hey, Arri."

"What's with the call screening?"

Cinnamon exhaled a breath of relief and eased down on the sofa, still wearing her coat. "I had the weirdest date last night and I thought it might be him."

"Him? Who is him?"

"Joseph, this guy I met last night."

"Did you tell me about him?"

"No, but I will. Not now though."

"Oh, come on, tell me now," Arri insisted.

"I'll tell you later."

"No, tell me now."

Cinnamon sighed and then laughed. "You are such a baby and if you must know, I answered a personal ad."

"Where? When?"

"About a week ago."

"You didn't. Did you? Really?"

"Yes, really."

"What was he like? I always wondered about the people in those personal ads. I don't think I could do it though. I'd be too scared."

Cinnamon listened to Arri babble, wondering when Arri would realize she was conversing with herself.

"Cinnamon?" Arri said.

"Yes, Arri."

"Tell me about Joseph."

"You seemed to be enjoying the conversation with yourself so well I didn't want to interrupt."

"Tell me about Joseph. Hold on a second, will you?"

Arri clicked over to her other line. Moments later, she clicked back over. "It's my sweetie. I'll have to call you back."

As always, when Eric called, everything and everyone else went straight out the window.

Cinnamon's decision to place a personal ad weighed lightly on her mind. After her infamous date with Joseph, she wasn't so sure she could do it again. But on the other hand, she couldn't stop now.

Determined that Mister Spectacular was somewhere out there, she continued as planned. This time, though, she would do things completely different. Before agreeing to meet anyone, she would learn as much about him as she could.

For twenty minutes, Cinnamon scribbled on her notepad, trying to compose something original, yet accurate. After several drafts, she came up with:

I dreamed about you last night. You were tall, sexy, affectionate, independent and in dire need of a playful, frisky, intelligent thirty-something black female to share indoor and outdoor activities with. Please no smokers or drug users.

While she addressed the envelope to the *Chicago Reader*, it dawned on her that she failed to hear back from the second guy for whom she left a message before. Obviously, he was not interested.

While enjoying a Doris Day movie on AMC, the phone rang. Joseph no doubt.

With no intention of talking to him, Cinnamon muted the television and waited for her answering machine to pick up.

"Cinnamon, this is Joseph."

Raising two clenched fists skyward, Cinnamon howled, "Shoot," while Joseph's message continued. "What happened to you last night? When I came from the men's room, you were--you were gone. I hope you're still interested. I thought maybe--maybe you'd like to have dinner again, my treat. If you're still interested, give me--give me a call, otherwise I'll call you. This is Joseph."

All the while Joseph's message played, Cinnamon cringed in disbelief.

How could he possibly think she was still interested?

In an effort to relieve the shock of it all, she powered on the stereo and out-poured the mellow sounds of Pat Metheny.

Thirty minutes later, she heard the phone ringing underneath the music. She quickly lowered the stereo volume and waited for her answering machine to pick up.

"Hello there, Cinnamon. This is Thomas. You responded to my personal ad a couple of weeks ago, and I'm doing you the honor of returning your call. Sorry it took awhile for me to get back to you, but I have been swamped with calls. You were next in line. I hope we can get together soon. I have engagements all this week straight through the weekend, but I do anticipate having some free time the following weekend. I'll give you a call then. Don't worry, I'll get back to you."

In silence, Cinnamon suffered through his message.

What made him think she was in line for a date?

While she mused over his arrogance, she heard a knock at the door and she jumped, still a little on edge after the disturbing message from Joseph.

With caution, she approached the door. "Who is it?"

"Who do you think?"

Immediately, she recognized Arri's voice.

"Hey, honey," Cinnamon said. "How did you get up here?"

"I came in with these two fine men. You know they were gay, right?"

"No, I don't know that."

Arri peeled off her coat and flopped down on the sofa. "Why is it always so cold in here?"

Cinnamon closed the window and huddled next to Arri.

"I tried to call you earlier," Cinnamon said. "But I got your voice mail."

"Yeah? Where was I?"

Cinnamon laughed. "How should I know? You should listen to yourself."

Arri stripped off her boots and threw her feet upon the sofa. "That must have been when Eric was over."

After Cinnamon brought Arri up to date on her fiasco with Joseph, Arri said, "That's why I would never meet anyone through the paper. I always wondered what kind of people placed those ads. Now I know."

"I don't think Joseph accounts for all the people who place and respond to personal ads. He's just one person."

"That one person is enough for me," Arri said.

"Well, I refuse to believe that everyone out there is a Joseph."

"Why else would they be placing ads?"

Arri's putdowns annoyed Cinnamon. What made Arri think she was so much better than everyone else?

"Maybe they just have trouble meeting people and don't like going to bars."

"Anyone who places or responds to personal ads is a desperado."

"So I guess that means me too then. After all, I did respond to Joseph's ad."

"No, I'm not talking about you."

"That's not what you just said."

"I meant the men," Arri said. "I was talking about the men, not the women."

Arri would certainly try to take back her remark now, realizing she inadvertently insulted her best friend.

Chapter Four

"So only the men who respond to personal ads are desperate, is that what you're saying?" Cinnamon asked.

"Yeah, that's what I meant."

"You are so full of it. This is a perfect example of how judgmental you are."

"I am not. I just express my opinion."

Cinnamon's anger stirred. "Your opinion is judgmental. You think everything is always one way. Every person, everything, and every situation is different, Arri. You can't just clump them all together."

"Okay, okay," Arri said, holding up her hands in defeat.

"You can't just tag everyone in the personals as losers. Otherwise you will find yourself criticizing a lot of people."

"I said okay," Arri said. "I'm sorry. What more do you want?"

It irked Cinnamon that Arri flustered her over such trivial things, but she couldn't help it. Overly opinionated people rubbed her the wrong way. It was her weak spot and she could only remain silent for so long.

An hour passed and Cinnamon and Arri drove down Broadway Street in Arri's lilac Honda.

The sky was dark and the air was cold. Even late in the evening, people in Lakeview populated the walks like lunch hour on a Friday.

On Belmont, Arri headed toward the park while the music on the radio played an old Al Green tune, "Love and Happiness."

In need of fresh air, Cinnamon rolled down the window halfway.

"Are you crazy, it's cold out there!" Arri yelled.

"It's stuffy in here."

"It's not that stuffy. Roll that window back up."

Cinnamon rolled up the window, then unzipped her jacket. "Any juicy stories to share?"

"Not really."

"No special request from Your Greatness?"

Coming up on a red light, Arri changed the subject. "You are really into those how-to books, aren't you?"

"Why?"

"I was reading this article about how a woman can make a man fall in love with her," Arri said. "It talked about love languages, the same thing you told me about. So I was wondering, do you think it's possible to make a man fall in love with you just by speaking his love language?"

"I believe there are certain things that may steer him in the right direction but no guarantees, and I don't want to sound negative or pessimistic about your endeavors but usually for those tactics to work, it needs to be with someone new."

"You don't think it would work with Eric?"

"Probably not. Your relationship with him has already been established, but of course there are some things you could do anyway."

"Like what?" Arri asked enthusiastically.

"Well, from what I have gathered, men really like women who like themselves, the same with women. We like men who like themselves."

"We do?" Arri questioned.

"Yes, we do. So if you can show Eric how much you value yourself, that might possibly enhance the relationship. Of course, if you establish this in the beginning, all the better but it's not too late now. The only problem now is that Eric already has an opinion of you and if you change it, you run the risk of. . ."

"Of what?"

"Well. . . He likes you the way you are, so if you should somehow stop being that person, he might like you more or less. It could go either way."

"That's really interesting."

Arri reached the park and crept onto the lifeless lawn, then shut off the engine, leaving the radio on. As Cinnamon gazed out the window, she witnessed a man walking alone, immediately bringing Joseph to mind. "What if this guy, Joseph, keeps calling me?"

"Eventually, he'll get the message."

"If leaving him in a restaurant didn't give it to him, I don't know what will," Cinnamon said as she nibbled on her fingernails.

Arri smirked as if she had something devilish up her sleeve, then said, "I thought about responding to an ad once."

"Really? When?"

"It was awhile back when Eric and I were having problems."

"You are something else. You know that."

"I said I thought about it. I never said I did it. And if I did, I would only be interested in meeting men of another race."

With raised eyebrows, Cinnamon's eyes shot to Arri. "Really? Who? Hispanic, white--?"

"Just white men."

Engrossed in the conversation, Cinnamon turned off the radio. "I never knew you had a thing for white men."

"I'm surrounded by them all day at work."

"Still, I never knew that was your thing," Cinnamon said. "Why haven't you ever dated any of them?"

"I just figured after the physical attraction wore off, there would be nothing left."

"What are you talking about?"

"We're different," Arri said. "We come from different backgrounds."

"And?"

"And, I don't think we would have much in common."

"You don't know that."

"Yeah, I know it's possible," Arri said. "But the bottom line is lust. That's how I see it."

"I don't know where you're getting your information, but you can have just as much in common with a white man as you can with any other man."

"And then there's this new manager at my office I have my eye on," Arri said. "He always makes small talk with me and one day he even complimented me when I wore my hair down."

"See? It could happen."

"Yeah, but I don't think it's too cool to date people on the job."

"Says who?" Cinnamon asked.

"Like you would date someone you worked with?"

"I would. If I really liked him, I'd do it in a heartbeat. I'm not trying to downplay Eric or anything. Though it's true I don't like the man, but I have to say, it would be great to see you date someone else."

"No chance of that happening too soon because as long as Eric and I are together, I'm his exclusively."

"I was afraid you were going to say that. Anyway, since you're in such an unveiling mood, I have something for you. I recently placed an ad in the *Chicago Reader*."

"After what happened with that guy? What's his name?"

"Joseph."

"Yeah, him. Are you sure you want to go through that again?"

"I'm not going to let one bad experience with Joseph make me close-minded."

"It should."

"I'm sure there are some good people out there," Cinnamon said. "Look at me, I'm placing an ad and I think I'm a pretty good person. Besides, this time I'm going to get to know them before setting up any dates."

"I hope you specified no crazies," Arri said.

"Actually, I did. I said crazy people need not respond."

"No you didn't."

"Of course I didn't. I said I was looking for a special friendship."

"Cinnamon, you know everybody is looking for more than friendship."

"Not everybody."

"I hope you know what you're doing."

After sitting at the park for forty-five minutes, they headed over to Arri's apartment on Pine Grove.

Arri lived in a three-flat complex on the second floor. As soon as Arri inserted the key into the door, her two cats inside meowed as if expecting her.

Immediately upon opening the door, the charcoal colored cats charged toward the hall before Arri stopped them.

Both full-grown felines were named after Arri's boyfriend: Eric and Lyles, Eric's first and last name, which proved one thing. Arri was in love and if it wasn't love, it was obsession.

Arri and Cinnamon stepped inside. The dull hardwood floor creaked with their every step.

"I'll be right out after I feed the kitties," Arri said as she dashed into the kitchen, almost tripping over the scattered two-inch heeled shoes.

In the front room, romance novels flooded the apartment to no end.

Cinnamon endeavored to locate a slot on the grape-colored futon not shrouded with cat hair, newspapers or junk mail. She brushed down the futon, not understanding how a person who wore such fine clothing could keep such a disorderly and grubby apartment.

Before Cinnamon could sit down, Arri returned, holding one of her cats against her chest.

Cinnamon yawned and covered her mouth. "I was going to stay awhile but I'm getting kind of tired."

"Okay, I'll talk to you when you get back in town."

Arri escorted Cinnamon to the front door. "But before you go, let me ask you this. If you happen to connect with someone in the paper that you really like, are you going to have sex with him?"

"You act as if I'm a virgin."

"Only because you've been living the life of one."

"Well, that may change sooner than you or I might think."

"Well, I won't believe it until I hear all about it."

"And you might hear about it real soon."

"If you say so," Arri said.

"And I do say so."

"Well, okay then with your bad self."

The alarm clock sounded at 5:30 a.m.

Cinnamon showered and prepared for her nine o'clock flight to Miami, her second favorite city, Orlando being number one because it was the land of Universal Studios, the all-time place to be.

Usually she rode the Orange line to Midway Airport, but this particular morning, time was not on her side and she hailed a taxi. She was almost out the door when she remembered her personal ad, making sure to mail it on her way out. During her ride to the airport, she relived her recent conversation with Arri. It being awhile since Cinnamon dated seriously, Arri seemed almost certain Cinnamon had lost her groove. But Arri was wrong. Cinnamon was ready for new adventures, new experiences and new men. And when the time came, along with the right man, everyone would know just how completely ready she actually was.

The temperature was a comfortable seventy-three degrees in Miami.

With a twenty-four-hour layover, Cinnamon indulged herself with some beautiful sunshine. After she checked into the Days Inn, she changed into her jeans and sandals, longing to enjoy every minute of the warm weather.

She strolled through the park toward the beach, her bag and beach towel underneath her arm. A warm breeze swept across her face and she closed her eyes for a second, savoring the moment. The fresh air flowed through her curly afro and it felt great. She advanced closer to the water, and the children's laughter surrounded her while the hot sun beamed down on the crowded beach. She dug into her bag for her sunglasses, then slid them on.

Before she stepped upon the sand, she removed her sandals and shoved them into her bag. The sun warmed her spirits with each breath. She admired the females on the beach, all the same, yet all different. And she understood. She understood why men were so drawn to them. They were so beautiful.

Why did such beautiful women allow men to mistreat them so?

It seemed like an epidemic. What was it about women that made them so driven for a man's love? Was it inborn or did society play a factor? She concluded it was inborn. What else could explain the man craze? Cinnamon used to think society programmed women to need a man's love, but now that she was older and wiser, she concluded otherwise. Women seemed to be born with an innate yearning for a man's love. That proved evident not just with Arri and Arri's desperate attempt for Eric's love but with so many women. And it wasn't just the women with the absent or unloving fathers either. It was every woman she knew, even the ones with the most loving father-daughter relationships. If Cinnamon could acknowledge this need in herself, it might aid her in future relationships. Then again, it didn't have to always be that way. Women could be different. Arri could be different. Cinnamon could be different.

Cinnamon reflected on her past, rethinking all the reasons she fell in love with men. It was never because he treated her so well but because of superficial stuff. He was witty. And funny. And smart. And ambitious. And of course, he was cute and fun. Garbage. Just plain garbage--in love with someone because he's sexy. Things were different now and Cinnamon vowed to herself that the next time she fell in love with anyone, it would be for the right reason.

Because he treated her so well.

Back in Chicago, a message awaited Cinnamon on her answering machine.

"Hey . . . Remember me. Your pal, your ace boon-coon, Noel. It's Monday, eight o'clock. When you get a chance, call me. I'll wait patiently."

Listening to Noel's message brought a smile to her face, one of the joys of coming home.

Following Noel's message was another.

"Cinnamon, this is Joseph."

The second she heard Joseph's voice, she exhaled a sigh of irritation as the message continued. "I'm still interested. Call me. This is Joseph."

Why was he still calling? And how long would he continue to call?

With annoyance streaming through her, she rewound the tape on the machine. After dismissing Joseph from her head, she returned Noel's call and made plans to see him on the weekend.

Though already having mailed off her personal ad, she liked to keep her options open with Noel.

CHAPTER FIVE

ONLY A WEEK ELAPSED since Cinnamon first met Noel and she awaited his arrival with high hopes.

Really digging this dating scene, she appreciated every nuance of it, from the preparation to the anticipation.

As she beautified herself, she kept tabs on the time. Concerned Noel might arrive before she was good and ready, she skittered from her bedroom to the bathroom, the heels of her boots clacking against the floors.

After dabbing on her favorite Cool Water Woman perfume, she polished what little nails remained after wearing most of them away.

Right on time, Noel met her in her building's lobby.

His familiar Musk cologne greeted her warmly. "Well, hello," he said as he flaunted his same habitual stare as when they first met. "You're looking captivating this evening."

"Thank you." She gazed at the raised collar of his leather jacket, dangling earring in his left ear and the five o'clock shadow on his face.

In Noel's spotless Intrepid, fully stocked with a sunroof, CD player and alarm system, they traveled downtown to 600 North Michigan Theaters and saw a Matt Damon movie, which they both enjoyed.

As they exited the theater, Cinnamon stuffed her hands into her pockets.

"What's next? Are you hungry?" Noel asked.

"Not really. Let's have a drink."

"I don't know, Cinnamon. Women usually lose control when they drink around me. They try to tear my clothes off and do all kinds of dirty and perverted things to me."

"That's a fantasy of yours, isn't it?"

"Pretty much."

"I kind of thought so."

At the Westin hotel lounge on the Magnificent Mile, Cinnamon and Noel made their way through the crowd. Past the bar, they treaded across the oatmeal colored carpet, then descended three steps into the sunken dining area. Nearly every seat was taken, but luckily they found a small table by the window only a few feet from the pianist who performed tenderhearted melodies.

As Cinnamon shed her jacket, she looked up with favor at the sparkling crystal chandeliers hanging overhead.

"I love these hotel lounges," she said. "Don't you? They're so elegant."

"Is this where you bring all your *mens*?"

"No, only my very special ones," she said playfully.

"I'm so flattered."

The waitress approached their table, preparing to take their order. Though Cinnamon seldom drank, she was feeling good this evening and decided to go for it with one of her favorites. "I'll have a Long Island iced tea."

"Same for me. That's a pretty potent drink," Noel said. "Are you sure you can handle it?"

"I'm sure."

"So what's it like going from city to city all the time?" Noel asked.

"When I first started, I loved it. I anticipated every trip with excitement, but now, just like everything else, after awhile the excitement fades."

"I'd love to do that, travel all the time."

"Don't get me wrong though," Cinnamon said. "I still enjoy it, just not as much as I used to. Anyway, tell me about you. I know you're a photographer."

"A freelance photographer."

"So what kind of pictures do you take?"

"You name it. Modeling pictures, weddings, family portraits. Just about anything, but the bulk of it is for actresses and actors."

"What about nude photography? You do any of that?" she asked.

"Every chance I get."

"No, I'm serious."

"I'm serious."

"I just thought since you freelanced, you would probably be open to just about anything."

"I couldn't have said it better myself."

The waitress brought over their drinks and set them on the table.

"What else do you do?" Cinnamon asked.

"I go to bookstores and pick up flight attendants."

"And how much does that pay?" she asked smiling.

"Not much."

"And you live in Evanston?"

"That's right," he said. "Did I tell you I had a roommate?"

"No."

"Yeah. We got a great deal on a house for rent up there."

Cinnamon silently slurped her drink from the straw, trying not to appear too shocked. "Who is we?"

"Are we jealous now?"

"No, nothing like that. I just asked."

"His name is Aaron if that's what you're worried about."

"It must be nice always having someone there to do things with."

"It's not bad," he said. "But it does have its disadvantages."

"Like what?"

Sidestepping her question and changing the subject, he asked, "You've been in Chicago all your life?"

"All my life."

"What about your family?"

"They're here too, but I don't see much of them. We talk every once in a while."

A mist fell over Cinnamon when she spoke of her family, mainly because she wished they were closer, regretting they weren't.

Noel set his drink down and eased back in his chair. "So still no boyfriend, huh?"

"That's right. What about you?"

"What about me?" he asked.

"Do you have a girlfriend?"

"Maybe. Maybe not."

"So the truth finally comes out."

Noel laughed and picked up his drink. "Seriously, in answer to your question, no, I do not have a girlfriend."

"You say you don't but you probably do."

Noel was the guy she could hang out with and tell all her secrets to, but not the one to become intimately involved with. She perceived him as someone always on the run with too many friends, too many things to do and too many secrets.

Noel continued. "I'm serious. I don't have a girlfriend."

"I'm supposed to believe you now?"

"I know I kid a lot, Cinnamon, but I'm serious this time."

"Uh huh. To be honest, Noel, I really don't care."

"So it's like that?"

"Just like that," she said as she turned from him.

After a relentless silence, Noel slid his hand on top of hers, stroked it lightly. "I really like you, Cinnamon. You're intelligent and I know you're smart because you read a lot. And I won't even mention how pretty you are."

Cinnamon glanced around the room as if looking for something or somebody. "Is it cold in here or is it the snow from your mouth?"

"This is not a line. I mean that."

"Yeah, yeah, yeah."

Noel finished his drink. "When we leave here, you want to check out that club I was telling you about? You did promise."

"I did not promise."

"So you want to check it out?"

"I don't know. The thought of a crowded noisy club doesn't exactly excite me."

"You said you'd try it. We'll only stay for as long as you like."

Cinnamon and Noel embarked upon the darkened Voyeur dance club, which was fire-hazard crowded. Men of different nationalities loitered in front while the dance music blasted onto the streets.

Noel and Cinnamon weaved through the crowd, past the dance floor and toward the back. Cinnamon's mouth hung open as she watched men embrace one another.

Then it hit her.

She was at a gay bar and moments would pass before it completely sank in.

Cinnamon stood against the wall, checking out the scene. "This is a gay bar, isn't it?"

"What do you think?" Noel asked.

"I think it is."

What struck her was how lavish and loose the men appeared, not inhibited in any way. Never before setting foot inside a gay bar, she was ignorant of the lifestyle.

"Why would you bring me here?"

"I thought you might like it. It's a pretty cool place, don't you think?"

"Why would you even want to come to an all-male bar?"

"I like the music."

She studied Noel, trying to figure him out, but she couldn't.

He clasped her hand and headed toward the dance floor. "Come on, let's dance."

Cinnamon resisted and subtly snatched her hand away. "I don't want to dance in here."

Already out of place just being there, she chose not to draw any unnecessary attention to herself.

Noel grasped her hand again and proceeded toward the dance floor. "Come on. It'll be fun."

"No, it won't," she said in a whisper. "This is a gay bar, not a straight bar."

"We're all the same here, Cinnamon."

"Can't I just watch?"

"You can do that on the dance floor. Just one dance, please, and then we'll go. I promise."

Though reluctant, she didn't peg Noel as one to give up easily. At least if she danced with him, they could leave soon after. She wrapped her purse strap over her body, grasped his hand and followed him into the sea of dancers. Though it would be difficult not to stare, she made a huge effort not to.

Twenty-five minutes passed and she soon realized everyone was into his own thing and showed no interest in her and Noel. She found herself feeling the music, her groove kicking in and she ended up dancing a lot longer than she expected.

She wiped the perspiration from her forehead. "All of this dancing has made me thirsty."

Noel led her to the bar and ordered drinks.

"So this is one of your hang-outs, huh?" she asked as she fanned herself.

"Something like that."

As much as she hated to admit it, she was having a fantastic time.

On their way home, Cinnamon was engulfed with curiosity. This whole concept of cruising the bars sparked a fuse inside her she didn't know existed. And she couldn't stop thinking about it. Though clubbing was not new, it never fancied her up until now.

A whole new world was opening up to her, a world of different and interesting people she might not otherwise meet outside the club scene, especially since she was cooped up inside her apartment most of the time.

In the past, she frowned on people meeting in clubs, but she now realized that meeting someone in a club was just as good as anywhere else.

With the wheels turning, she considering inviting Arri to join her for a night of clubbing but then decided against it. She wished to experience the whole shebang alone and see what it was like to frequent a singles bar *a la carte*, the cornerstone of the single life. And if she really wanted to stir things up, she would frequent a reggae bar, something she meant to do forever. Only this time, she would really do it. And soon.

Soon after leaving the club, Noel pulled up to Cinnamon's high-rise, shifted the gear into park and turned off the motor.

"I enjoyed myself," Noel said. "I'm really glad you came with me."

"It was different but fun."

"You don't need any help upstairs, do you?" he asked.

"I'll be fine, but thank you for asking," Cinnamon said as she unfastened her seat belt.

Before Cinnamon could open the door, Noel wormed his hand underneath hers.

It was time to spill the beans about how she felt. But before she could, he moved toward her and leaned in to kiss her, and just as their lips almost met, she turned away. "I should go."

As she stepped out of the car, a cold wind whistled past her. "I'll call you," she said.

Eventually Cinnamon would be forced to admit her true intentions for Noel.

She was just glad she didn't have to do it that night.

Cinnamon showed up at Arri's apartment for her weekly visit.

Arri, having just emerged from the bath, wore a thick towel around her body as water trickled down her legs onto the floor.

"I'll be right out," Arri said as she veered back into the bathroom.

Cinnamon found an uncluttered area on the futon, sat down and crossed her legs. She looked past the 8-1/2 x 11 inch photograph of Arri and Eric on the end table until her gaze reached the dozen *Nation Inquirer* magazines banked against the wall.

Did Arri actually read those magazines? Or was she just collecting them?

Arri soon returned wearing a rose-colored bathrobe. She cuddled one cat in her arms like an infant. Cinnamon failed to differentiate between, Eric and Lyles. Possibly not even Arri could tell them apart.

Arri rested on the lounge chair across from the futon, petting the head of Eric or Lyles.

"I finally went out with that new guy," Cinnamon said.

"You like him?"

"I like him as a friend."

"You like everyone as a friend. You enjoyed his company, didn't you?"

"Of course," Cinnamon said. "But I'm talking about more than that. I'm talking about physical chemistry. And I don't get that with him, though he is exceptionally attractive."

"Physical chemistry? Why should you care about that? It's not like you want to sleep with him."

"Maybe I would if he was the right guy."

"I don't think you know what you're looking for, Cinnamon."

Arri's cat suddenly sprung from her arms onto the floor. After Arri wiped the cat hair from her lap, she headed into the kitchen. Cinnamon veered close behind, bringing Arri up to date on her adventures with Noel.

"How is it he can get you to go out, but I can't?" Arri asked. "I've invited you to Excalibur more times than I can count and nothing."

"It was a spur-of-the-moment thing."

While Arri gathered the dishes from the table and placed them into the sink, Cinnamon slouched down in the chair across from the garbage container overflowing with empty cat food cans.

"What sign is Noel?" Arri asked.

"I have no idea. What will that tell you anyway?"

"Ask him next time you see him."

"Yes, mother."

"And why would he take you to a gay bar?"

"That's the same thing I asked him. He told me he liked the music."

"You believe that?"

"I don't know. What are you thinking?"

"I'm thinking that he went there for more than just the music."

"Yeah, I was a little suspicious myself."

Arri stood with her back against the sink, her hands at her sides. "I could sure use a drink and a cigarette."

"You don't smoke, Miss."

"Sometimes I do."

"Since when?" Cinnamon asked.

"Since Eric started working my nerves."

"How could you start smoking after it took me years to quit?"

"I had to do something," Arri said. "Either it was cigarettes or drugs. One or the other."

"This is a classic example of a dysfunctional relationship. You know that, don't you?"

"I do," Arri said. "Anyway, don't worry about it, it's just a temporary thing."

"That's the same thing crack heads say after they sell their parents' TV--it's just a temporary thing."

"Enough about the cigarettes, okay? You know how bull-headed I am," Arri said as she poured herself a glass of water.

"What's Your Majesty up to now that he has you turning to chemical substances?"

"Chemical substance is kind of harsh, don't you think?"

"Not when it comes to you and Eric."

"Anyway, I haven't seen Eric in a few days." Arri pulled out the chair and drooped down into it. "He's been at his mother's a lot."

"That doesn't sound like Eric," Cinnamon said. "He usually only visits her on the holidays, if then."

"I know but he's been helping her rearrange furniture or something, something like that."

"You think he's fooling around," Cinnamon asked.
"I thought about it, but. . . I think I believe him."
So much into Eric's clutches, with a convincing argument, Eric could convince Arri that the Pope was black.

CHAPTER SIX

CINNAMON PERFORMED HER BI-MONTHLY ritual of removing the books from the shelf, and giving the shelf and books a thorough dusting.

When the phone rang, her first thought was: it's Joseph.

No longer would she avoid his calls. Regardless of how cold or harsh she might sound, she would convince him that she was just not interested. With that in mind, she picked up the phone.

"Hey, stranger," the caller said.

Not recognizing the voice, she asked, "Who is this?"

"Forgot me already? This is Noel. The one you haven't called in a week."

Relieved, she said, "Oh, hi, Noel. I've been meaning to call you."

"Sure, you have. I left you a couple of messages. I started to think you had blown me off."

"Nothing that extreme."

"What then?"

"Well, you know I'm out of town a lot and all."

"Yes, I am aware of that, but you're in town now."

Not having an excuse for him, she said nothing.

"I'm not going to give you the third degree. I'll forgive you this time but only because I like you."

"I like you too."

"You don't have to say that," he said.

"No, seriously, I mean it."

"Then prove it."

"Prove it?"

"Why don't you let me pick you up later and we can see a movie or something."

"Today isn't good for me," she said.

"Because?"

"I don't know. I was just planning on staying in today."

"All right. I'll let you off the hook today but you'll owe me."

Cinnamon laughed, never tiring of his wit. "I'll give you a call later this week."

That afternoon when Cinnamon checked her mailbox, she was thrilled to receive the information about her personal ad. Immediately, she recorded a greeting on the nine-hundred number, revealing bits and pieces of her personality as well as the kind of man she sought.

Maybe this time she would find what she wanted.

Cinnamon worked straight through the Thanksgiving weekend. When she returned home, she eagerly checked her personal ad voice mailbox for messages.

Twenty-nine men called. And two women.

One particular gentleman, Roman, appealed to her because he recently relocated from Boston. Before calling him, she made sure to have pen and paper on hand. Getting to know people first was an important lesson learned from Joseph.

After dialing Roman's number, the phone rang four times before a man answered.

"May I speak to Roman?" she asked with her pen poised over her pad of paper ready to jot down pertinent information.

"This is he."

She heard running water and dishes clacking in the background. "Is this a good time?"

"To whom am I speaking?" he asked.

"This is Cinnamon. You left a message on my voice mailbox."

"Oh, hi. Actually, I responded to two ads. Did yours say something about sweet as candy?"

"That was me." Because he was up front about responding to other ads, she wrote *honest* on her notepad.

"I like your voice, Cinnamon. That's why I responded to your introduction. You have a really sexy voice."

"Thank you." Little did he know, flattery would win her over every time.

"Is there anything you want to ask me?" he asked.

It was as if he read her mind. "What made you respond to my ad?" she asked. "I mean before you heard my voice."

"I was impressed with your statement about friendship. That's what I'm looking for as well, especially since just moving here."

They both seemed to want the same thing and she liked him right away.

Roman continued. "It's not that I have problems meeting women, just not the kinds of woman I'm looking for."

His proper voice signified intelligence so she wrote *intelligent.* "What kind of woman are you looking for?"

"Well, first of all, I don't like the club scene, so I'm not looking for a party girl."

"I'm not much of a party person myself." She wrote *does not like clubs,* then continued. "What side of town do you live on? You don't have to tell me your address."

"I'm north. 6000 North."

"By yourself?"

"By myself."

She wrote *independent.* "What do you do?"

"I'm a paralegal."

She wrote *paralegal.* "Is there anything you want to ask me?"

"Why don't you just tell me anything you want me to know?"

"Anything?" she asked.

"Anything."

"You already know I'm twenty-nine and I'm a flight attendant. And I placed the ad because I haven't met the kind of person I'm looking for either."

"And what kind of person would that be?"

She hesitated, wanting to articulate her words just right. "Someone intelligent, ambitious, independent, humorous but not silly, kind, compassionate. And fun."

"I see you have given this some thought."

"I have."

"Do you have any children, Cinnamon?"

"No. No children."

"Tell me something else."

"I'm a homebody. I read a lot of psychology, go to church and see lots of movies."

"I wouldn't consider myself a homebody, but I do like to spend time at home," he said. "I also go to the gym and hang out with a buddy of mine now and then. . .Could you hang on a second? I'm going to get the other phone."

"Sure." She wrote *works out.*

Roman soon returned to the phone. "It's funny that you should say you read a lot of psychology. That's a big interest of mine also. That's one of the reasons why I write. I'm fascinated with people."

"What do you write?"

"Sports, murder, sex. My specialty is eccentric people."

"You can write all about my friend, Arri, then. She gives the word eccentric a fresh new meaning." She wrote *interested in psychology/writer*, then asked, "Is this a short story you're working on?"

"Actually, it's a novel. My second one."

"I'm impressed. Are you published?"

"No, but that is the plan. Maybe one day I'll let you take a look at one of my works in progress."

"I'd like that," she said. "I initially set out to write a nonfiction book. It was supposed to be a compilation of all the self-improvement books I read."

"Sounds like a great idea."

"Yeah, it did to me too except it never happened."

"So when am I going to get a chance to meet the face that's connected to this beautiful voice?"

Even with good feelings for him already, it was still too soon to engage. "I'd like to get to know more about you first."

"That's understandable," he said. "What else can I tell you?"

"You can describe yourself if you don't mind."

"Let's see. I'm about six feet, slim build, but well toned. My hair is short, faded in the back and on the sides. Is that good enough?"

"That's fine." She wrote *six feet, slim build* and *toned.* "Do you want me to describe myself?"

"I already know you're slim and average height. I can wait for the rest."

"Well, that's mighty big of you."

"Not really. I trust my instincts and I have good feelings about you."

"Now you're making me nervous. I'd hate to disappoint you."

"No chance of that happening."

"Okay, Roman, it was great talking to you."

"Same here. And thanks for returning my call."

"Let me give you my number just in case you want to reach me."

She would definitely speak to him again. And soon.

Winter was on its way.

Brutal gushes of wind swept past Cinnamon as she came from Jewel grocery store. Four plastic bags of groceries weighed her down, two in each hand.

She approached her building and to her surprise saw Noel standing in front after not having seen him since their night at the bar.

His perfect complexion and curly hair made him easy to recognize.

"What are you doing here?" she asked with a zealous smile.

"I wanted to see my girl. Can I help you with some of those?"

"Thanks." She handed him two bags. "This is a treat."

Once inside Cinnamon's apartment, Noel hung up his coat while Cinnamon delivered the grocery bags into the kitchen.

"I'll be out in a minute," she said.

When she returned to the living room, she found Noel skimming through the books on the shelf. "I was just noticing all of your books arranged by height. You're very organized."

"See anything you like?" Cinnamon asked as she flopped down on the sofa.

Noel turned to face her, smiled. "Very much."

"I'm referring to the books, silly."

"Oh, the books? No. Not really." He stepped to the window, peaked through a slit of the closed mini-blinds. "What a beautiful view. As far as I can see is water."

"I like it too," she said. "So what made you stop by?"

"You don't call nobody, and I wanted to see your pretty face again." He joined her on the sofa, scooted unusually close.

"Why are you sitting so close?" she asked.

"Because I'm trying to figure you out."

"I think you can figure me out without sitting so close."

"So what is it?" he asked. "I'm not married."

The moment of truth arrived.

She skirted two inches away from him and quickly considered what she would say. "I just want to be friends, Noel, and I think you know that."

"I sort of figured that. But I was hoping that maybe down the line things might be different. Do you think that's possible?"

"Anything is possible, Noel. You know that."

"Well, that's good enough for me. And just for the sake of satisfying my own curiosity, what happened with your sisters and these married men that has you so afraid?"

"You don't want to know."

"I wouldn't ask if I didn't."

After debating whether or not to give away her family's history, she said, "To make a long story short, my older sister, Kim, was infected with AIDS by a married man."

"Are you serious?"

"Very serious."

"And the other one?" Noel asked.

"Actually, what happened to my younger sister, Nickie, is a little funny, tragic, but funny."

Noel laughed as if preparing himself. "I can't wait to hear this."

"My younger sister, unbeknownst to her, was in love with a cross dresser and he stole her entire wardrobe. And when I say entire wardrobe, I mean entire wardrobe, pantyhose, bras, everything."

"You're making this up."

"No, this really happened. So as you can see I'm a little uneasy with married men."

"Yeah, but those could be isolated incidents."

"It doesn't matter. In my heart, I know it's wrong to date someone else's spouse because no good can come from it."

"I guess. But I have to admit, that's funny and I'm still not sure I should believe you."

"Believe me 'cause it really happened."

"You're all right, Cinnamon, you know that? And I'd like for us to continue to hang out as friends, of course. Can we do that?"

"We can."

Cinnamon couldn't picture her relationship with Noel progressing beyond friendship, but she didn't believe in the word *never*.

"Good, because my evening is free," Noel said. "What do you want to do?"

"Whatever you want."

"How about a movie?"

"Sounds good."

"What should we get?" Noel asked. "Comedy, action, something x-rated?"

"Yeah. Let's rent that last thing."

His eyes glowed with enthusiasm. "You're serious?"

"No. I'm not."

He stood and stretched out his arms. "For a moment there, I was about to get excited."

Cinnamon and Noel returned from the video store with the movie, *Showgirls*. She was about to insert the DVD when her phone rang.

"What are you doing?" Arri asked.

"Guess who's over here," Cinnamon asked in a whisper.

"Who?"

"Noel."

"The guy who took you to that club?"

"That would be him," Cinnamon said.

"I got to see this guy. I'm on my way over."

Cinnamon joined Noel on the sofa as they prepared to watch the movie.

"My friend, Arri, is going to stop by. You don't mind, do you?"

"Didn't trust yourself alone with me, did you?"

"Sure didn't," Cinnamon said. "I was planning on doing all sorts of nasty things to you."

"Do tell."

"I'm just kidding, Noel."

"I'd love to meet one of your friends," Noel said as he leaned toward Cinnamon and moved his face to hers. "We'd better smooch now before she gets here."

"Do you ever quit?"

"You know I'm kidding. You just told me you wanted to be friends."

She picked up the remote control and aimed it at the television.

"Okay," he said. "No more jokes. I promise."

Sixteen minutes into the movie, Arri showed up and hastily brushed past Cinnamon. "Where is he?" She unbuttoned her coat and made her way over to Noel, Cinnamon lagging behind her.

"Hi. I'm Arri. You must be Noel."

Noel rose to his feet and extended his hand. "That's me."

"Well, since the two of you have met. . ." Cinnamon said.

As soon as Noel sat down, Arri swung her coat over the sofa and joined him.

Cinnamon slid the director's chair away from the wall and dropped down into it.

"Cinnamon, come sit next to us," Noel said as he slapped the sofa next to him.

"No, that's okay. I don't want to crowd you guys."

Cinnamon glanced over at Noel, then ogled Arri. "You're not smoking today?"

Before Arri could answer, "You smoke?" Noel questioned.

"Not really."

"That's good because you are much too beautiful to ruin your skin with cigarette toxins."

"What?" Cinnamon questioned, crinkling her eyes. "Since when did you get so political about cigarettes and all of their toxins?"

"I'm political about everything," he said. "I thought you knew that."

Arri changed the subject with an elevated tone in her voice. "So what are we watching?"

"*Showgirls*, courtesy of Noel."

"Isn't there a lot of nudity in this film?" Arri asked.

"Yes," Noel and Cinnamon said in sync.

Noel glanced at Arri and then Cinnamon as if contemplating. "Don't you ladies try anything with me now. I'm a gentleman."

Arri looked to Cinnamon and laughed.

"I thought you said no more jokes," Cinnamon said.

"Okay, okay, I couldn't help myself," Noel said. "I'm surrounded by two gorgeous women and I must say I really like that lipstick, Arri."

"Thank you, Noel. What sign are you?"

"Does it matter?"

"Arri, no one is interested in that stuff but you," Cinnamon said.

Arri shrugged and flipped her hand at Cinnamon.

"Do you want to date me?" Noel asked.

Arri turned to him, didn't answer.

"Don't pay any attention to him, Arri. He likes to shock people."

"No, seriously, what signs do you like?" Noel asked.

"I like all of them."

"No, you don't. That's why you asked so you could see if I fit the profile."

"So are you going to tell me?" Arri asked.

"No, I want to keep you in suspense."

Around ten that evening, after half-watching the movie, Cinnamon escorted Noel to the door and said her goodnight. She then returned to Arri in the front room.

"What do you think?" Cinnamon asked.

After removing her boots, Arri swung her feet upon the sofa. "He's gay."

"You think?"

"Oh, yes."

"You really think he's gay?"

"Granted he doesn't look it, but that fluffy voice of his. And then him hanging out in that bar because he quote, likes the music, end quote. I don't think so."

"But he likes me."

"I didn't say he didn't like you. I'm just saying he likes men too. Trust me, I know what I'm talking about. He's probably bisexual, which is just like being gay."

"Bisexual?"

Cinnamon shielded her mouth with her finger, meditating on Arri's words. "I don't know, Arri, going to that club doesn't really mean anything. I went there and I'm not that way."

"It's different for women. What a shame though, he's a cutie, nice body too. . .Where did you meet him?"

Cinnamon laughed because her friend was predictably funny. "I told your butt seven hundred million times that I met him at the bookstore."

"Right, right."

"If something doesn't have anything to do with your cherished Eric, you just take it in and blow it right out, don't you?"

"I just forget sometimes."

In a daze, Cinnamon stared at the entertainment center, intrigued by the possibility of Noel being bisexual.

Snapping out of her trance, Cinnamon said, "It really doesn't matter one way or the other. We're just friends anyway."

With a whole new world of interesting people manifesting before her, namely Noel and Roman, Cinnamon couldn't wait to venture out into the nightclub scene alone and grasp the true essence of the single life.

Chapter Seven

It was Saturday night.

Cinnamon planned to visit the Wild Hare reggae bar, which she discovered in the *Chicago Reader*. The Wild Hare was the hot spot of reggae, all the more reason to call it Cinnamon's place. For the special occasion, she even rented a car. Though she always planned to frequent a reggae bar, it never happened. Tonight would change all of that.

The cool sounds of Bob Marley echoed throughout her apartment as she stood in the bathroom applying her makeup. The luminous ceiling light cascaded on her brown skin. She layered her blush and eyeliner, then finished with her glossy iced toffee lipstick.

All ready for her evening's adventure, she skipped into the front room, smiling as she fantasized about her night to come. Then suddenly an unsettling image occurred to her. This time she would be entirely on her own and not have Noel at her side to talk to. But it was okay because she anticipated this night for days now and the suspense overwhelmed her. She would soon be in a club filled with people who loved reggae as much as she did. And the idea absorbed her in all its glory. There would be live music and already she could feel the excitement.

It was a quarter after eleven when she left her apartment and made her way north on Clark Street. Arriving in Wrigleyville in her rented pearl white Ford, she didn't bother hunting for a parking spot. Instead she cruised into the public parking lot next door to the Wild Hare.

Cinnamon shifted the gear into park, turned off the engine and chewed on her fingernails.

Was she really going to go through with this?

For two minutes she sat in the car with the window halfway down. She gazed at the people as they entered and exited the parking area, consuming bits and pieces of their conversations. Even in the cold of winter, people gallivanted outside as if it were a hot summer day. With the motor off, she felt chilly. So not to be pegged as a voyeur, she blew a breath from her mouth and stepped from the car. After paying the twelve-dollar cover charge at the outside booth, she headed inside, wearing navy dress pants, a pink sweater and leather jacket.

A full-figured woman working the door smiled at Cinnamon as she presented her I.D. and already she felt welcomed. Though this place was much smaller than she expected, the music boomed as she experienced the Caribbean energy almost instantly. Something about reggae music just made her feel so damn good.

New Vibration, the five-member band burst with vigor onto the elevated stage while Cinnamon maneuvered her way through the crowd of white people, black people, Hispanics and Nigerians. Somebody for everybody.

A concentrated cigarette stench permeated the dark room and for the first time in a long time, she craved a cigarette. Though she recently frequented a club with Noel, one infested with cigarette smoke, she hadn't once fancied smoking. Then again, she probably wasn't as nervous then as she was this evening. It took her years to quit smoking and she was not about to return to such an addictive habit just because she was a little nervous.

Cinnamon continued through the mass of bodies, noting the dreadlocks, afros, and extension braid hairstyles. And she felt right at home.

With the music sweeping, the band popping and mostly everyone sporting a natural look of some sort, this was the place to be. All she needed now was a drank, not a drink, but a drank. But she wasn't sure she was quite ready for one just yet.

Luckily Cinnamon found a seat at the bar and eased down on the bar stool, all the while remarking the pictures on the wall of yesteryear performers, Bob Marley being front and center. Two songs later and more relaxed, Cinnamon unzipped her jacket, released her purse from her shoulder and tucked it in her lap. The eye-catching couple next to her with the undersized dreadlocks captured her attention and she thought she might perhaps desire that style some day.

The energetic sounds continued to thrive and Cinnamon longed to rise to her feet and roll her hips in unison with the beat but was too shy to do so.

The band broke down the music to a light drum, which seemed to captivate everyone's attention. The lead singer, wearing jeans and an African smock, was as tall as the average woman but his presence demanded attention as he asked the crowd, "Anyone out there in love?"

The crowd roared with a rigorous noise. "Yeah," they screamed.

Cinnamon remembered what it was like to be in love and so much she wished she could have been included in that *grand yeah.*

The band leader continued. "I want to talk to you about love tonight. Is that all right with you?"

Pandemonium at its finest. The crowd followed his lead and screamed, "Yeah."

"Back in the day, long time ago, I didn't know anything about love. And was too busy for love, didn't have time for love, didn't want to love and I have to tell all y'all something tonight. Are you ready?" The band plowed into a song, "Make Time for Love."

Cinnamon sprung to her feet, and the crowd went ballistic, clapping hands, stomping feet. His words obviously struck a vein with the group and they seemed very vocal in expressing themselves.

Cinnamon clapped her hands with everyone else, not being able to remain silent any longer. Then it hit her--why she liked reggae music so much. It spoke about what was real, what was true and most of all what was in her heart. Captivated by the moment and the song, out of nowhere, Cinnamon felt someone touch her shoulder.

"Would you like to dance?" the man asked.

Cinnamon turned around to face a tall, dark chocolate man with piercing hazel eyes and a shiny bald head. Instantly, her jaw dropped, and three little words flashed in her head: Mmm-mmm-mmm. He looked to be in his early thirties and must have been the finest man in the bar if not in the city of Chicago. He wore a black turtle-neck sweater and held a beer in hand.

"Hello," Cinnamon said as she scrutinized him inch by inch.

"Hi. Would you like to dance?" he asked again.

Still in shock after laying eyes on the black prince before her, she said, "No, thank you."

"Would you mind if I joined you?"

"No, not at all." Flattered and happy to have met someone, this fine someone, Cinnamon glanced at his dark skin, admiring it so much she yearned to touch it or maybe even lick it.

The cat inside her needed to come out sometime.

He benched down next to her. "I'm Mitchell."

"I'm Cinnamon."

"Are you here by yourself?" Mitchell asked.

Cinnamon nodded with a subtle smile.

The band performed a Bob Marley song, "Waiting In Vain," and Cinnamon couldn't help but rock her shoulders to the beat. Already she felt a buzz and she had yet to have her first drink.

"Are you sure you don't want to dance?" Mitchell asked.

The powerful romantic beat surged through her and she realized it was time.

"Okay." Cinnamon stood and wrapped her purse strap around her body.

Mitchell gulped down his beer before setting the bottle on the bar. He then led her onto the dance floor and she felt a tingle inside. Having met this fine, fine man and revving it up on the dance floor, she wanted to pinch herself.

Cinnamon allowed her eyes to openly linger on Mitchell's slick shoulders. He was much taller than she was. And she liked that, oh, how she liked that.

Thirty minutes passed and more people flooded the bar, causing Cinnamon to feel more and more like a sardine. But she did not mind.

Mitchell swayed his body toward hers, their hips almost grinding. He seemed to trail her every move and she soon realized that allowing him to dance this erotically would surely lead her to trouble. Casually, she stepped back from him and shouted over the loud music. "Is it always this crowded?"

"On a Saturday, yes. Aren't you warm in that jacket?"

"I'm starting to get kind of warm." Cinnamon wiped the sweat from her forehead. "I need a rest."

Mitchell led her off the dance floor and over to the bar.

"What do you want to drink?" Mitchell asked.

"Coke," she said, removing her jacket.

Cinnamon was about to go into her purse when Mitchell said, "Don't worry about it, I have it."

"Thank you." Cinnamon fanned herself with her hand.

The bartender handed Mitchell their drinks and Mitchell handed Cinnamon hers.

"Thanks again for the drink," Cinnamon said.

"Is that all you drink?"

"What do you mean?"

"Non-alcoholic," Mitchell said.

"No, not always. Every once in a while I'll have a Long Island iced tea."

"So I guess it's all or nothing with you."

"You could say that."

Mitchell liquored down his beer. "No boyfriend tonight?"

"I don't have a boyfriend. What about you? No girlfriend tonight?"

"No, no girlfriend for me." Mitchell studied her as if he knew her. "I've never seen you here before. Do you live around here?"

Cinnamon could barely hear over the music. "Lake Shore Drive actually, not far from here."

"Do you ever go anywhere else?"

"Anywhere like . . . ?" Cinnamon asked.

"Any other clubs?"

"No, not really."

Mitchell excused himself to two of his friends, one male and one female near the entrance. Upon his return, he said, "My friends and I are getting ready to head over to another club. You want to come with us?"

"Where is it?"

"On Broadway, not far from here."

"Okay," Cinnamon said. "I'll follow you in my car."

After just meeting him, she didn't dare let him disappear from her that easily.

Cinnamon trailed behind Mitchell, hoping the night would end as exciting as it began.

Already, she visited her first reggae bar alone and danced with the sexiest man alive. Now she was on her way to another club. Inside, she screamed with excitement.

Coming out tonight proved to be a good move as she discovered sparks in herself she never knew existed.

For sure she would remember this night. And this man.

At Lemar's Place, Mitchell paid the ten-dollar cover charge for the both of them, then proceeded inside. With his hand connected to Cinnamon's, he spiraled through the cluster of people.

Over one hundred people danced to the ear-splitting music as the familiar cigarette stench saturated the air. But Cinnamon was not inclined to smoke this time. Her inclinations lay elsewhere, lusting to know anything and everything about Mitchell.

After they checked their jackets, they approached Mitchell's four friends, three women and a man.

"Everybody, this is Cinnamon. Cinnamon, this is everybody."

"Hello," Cinnamon said.

Everyone greeted Cinnamon.

With as much alertness as she could muster, Cinnamon pretended to appear interested in Mitchell's friends' conversation, making eye contact with them as they spoke of people she did not know.

"We're going upstairs," Mitchell said as he led Cinnamon over to the bar. "I'll see you guys later."

Mitchell dug into his pocket and pulled out his wallet before ordering a beer. "Can I get you anything?"

"No, thanks," Cinnamon said.

His burnt brown complexion was a dynamite contrast for his crystal-like light brown eyes and she so much enjoyed the view.

It was already 1:30 a.m. and Cinnamon's weary body longed for sleep. She covered her mouth and yawned.

"You're not getting sleepy on me, are you?" Mitchell asked as he slid his wallet back into his jeans pocket.

"I'm okay."

Though tired, Cinnamon summoned the stamina to play this night through for all its worth.

Upstairs, in the corner, they found a rundown mini-sofa, which appeared to have been put to use many nights. The music on the second level was a lot less penetrating, which created an atmosphere for friendly conversation.

When they crashed on the sofa, Mitchell snuggled close to Cinnamon, so much that someone passing by might make them out as an intimate couple.

"Are you sure you don't want anything to drink?" Mitchell asked.

"I'm sure, but thank you."

With Mitchell sitting so snug, his hand on her knee, Cinnamon felt a little uneasy. Trying not to show it, she turned away.

"Why do you keep looking away from me, Cinnamon?"

Cinnamon turned toward Mitchell and smiled. "I'm just a little nervous."

"I like looking at your face. You have a nice face."

Cinnamon smiled to herself, reveling in the sound of Mitchell's silky and soothing voice.

He fondled the inside of her hand and gently stroked her fingers. Enjoying the warmth of his hand against hers, her heart pounded. It was as if he knew what felt good to her. Panting on the inside, Cinnamon absorbed the longggggg silence between them. And as much as she liked having Mitchell touch her hand, it scared her. She was torn between asking him to stop and never stopping, the passion inside too intense to overpower. After a few minutes, Mitchell released his hand from hers and she could finally loosen up. But before she could relax entirely, Mitchell grasped her fingers and gently embraced them as if communicating some message. "Your fingers are so sweaty. Does it bother you when I touch your hand this way?"

"No, not really."

But it did bother her because she was leading him on. Nevertheless, she relished the moment too much to stop herself.

"What do you do, Mitchell?"

"I'm a nine-to-five man, a social worker. . .Why haven't I ever seen you before at any of the clubs?"

"I don't come out much."

"This must be my lucky night then."

Mitchell rested against Cinnamon's shoulder, then rubbed his head against her forearm, not saying a word. He was a bold man, but it was okay because he was just as sweet as he was bold.

"You smell good," Mitchell said. "I like your perfume."

"Thank you."

Glad that Mitchell could not perceive the astonishment that lurked inside her, she brainstormed for something to say. But nothing sprung to mind. Instead, she envisioned him kissing her, seemingly the next logical thing to do and more importantly, what Cinnamon cried out for him to do.

Absorbing the idea, Cinnamon slightly shifted her body back, feeling a shiver of arousal just being near him.

This moment was unreal.

Not only had she just met a superior guy, but here she was cuddled up with him on a frumpy sofa.

What could be better than that?

Mitchell's head rested against her chest as they embraced each other's presence, saying absolutely nothing. Never before was she so in tune with someone whose closeness she could enjoy without so much as one word of conversation. Cinnamon closed her eyes and recapped her night's adventure. Because everything happened so fast, her brain was just catching up. But it didn't matter how she arrived at this point, just that she arrived.

As time passed, more and more people left from upstairs. Cinnamon and Mitchell were the only two who remained.

Mitchell lifted his head from Cinnamon's chest and in a whisper asked, "Can I ask you something?"

"Sure."

"Never mind."

Seconds elapsed and Mitchell turned to face Cinnamon again as he massaged the palm of her hand.

Having just met this man, knowing little about him, it wasn't right to cuddle with him this way. But the more wrong it seemed, the more she liked it.

"Cinnamon, would you like to come home with me?" Mitchell blurted out.

Caught off guard and completely taken aback, Cinnamon asked, "What did you just ask me?"

"I want you to come home with me," he said, continuing to stroke her hand.

"I just met you."

"And I just met you. I want to stay with you all night."

Having played this game long enough, it was time to go home. "I can't do that."

"Why not?"

"I just can't." Just considering the idea frightened her and made her curious at the same time.

When Cinnamon heard footsteps coming closer to them, she was relieved to see three of Mitchell's friends walking toward them.

"There you guys are," Mitchell's friend said. "What are you two doing back here?"

"We're minding our own business," Mitchell said.

The two other ladies appeared to have been up for days.

"We're getting ready to go," Mitchell's friend said.

"Cinnamon and I will be leaving soon. I'll talk to you guys tomorrow."

After Mitchell's friends left, he asked, "Are you sure you don't want to come home with me?"

"I can't do that."

"But I don't want to leave you."

"That's very sweet," Cinnamon said as she stood and straightened her pants.

"I wish I could at least drive you home, but you have your own car," Mitchell said. "After we get our jackets, I'll walk you to your car."

Through the corridor and down the stairs, she and Mitchell straggled along as if they were the only two people alive.

"Are you going to let me call you?" Mitchell asked.

"Sure," she said, not letting on just how much she wanted him to call her.

She tried to kid herself into believing he would make a good friend when in actuality he was definitely more-than-friend material.

From the bar, she grabbed a cocktail napkin and wrote down her telephone number. As she handed the napkin to Mitchell, she spotted Noel at the end of the bar, talking to a tall hairy man. And the first thought that leaped to mind was what Arri said about Noel being attracted to both men and women. Cinnamon was about to step over to him, then decided not to.

Outside, she and Mitchell approached Cinnamon's Ford Focus.

"Are you going to be okay going home?" Mitchell asked.

"I'll be okay." Cinnamon opened the door, climbed inside, started the engine and rolled down the window.

"Are you sure?" Mitchell asked. "It's no trouble for me to trail you home in my Jeep."

"No, that's okay. I'll be fine."

Mitchell leaned inside the car and kissed her cheek. "I'll call you soon."

Cinnamon rolled up the window, switched the gear into drive and blushed all the way home.

It was a night to remember.

Cinnamon stepped through the front door at two forty-five in the morning. As tired as she was, her face was still glowing in elation. Without delay, she washed her face, brushed her teeth and slipped into her nightshirt. On her knees, she said her nightly prayer, climbed into bed and fell immediately asleep.

A short time later, the loud ringing phone awakened Cinnamon from a deep sleep. With one eye open, she glanced at the lighted dial on the clock, having just closed her eyes not more than twenty minutes earlier. As she reached for the phone on the night table, she accidentally knocked her Bible to the floor.

"Cinnamon, did I wake you?" Mitchell asked.

Her eyes widened with joy. "Oh, hello, Mitchell. I was so exhausted I went straight to bed when I got in."

"I'm not going to keep you up, I just wanted to make sure you made it home okay."

A calm silence, then Mitchell said, "I should--"

"Should what?" Cinnamon asked.

He didn't speak right away, then said, "I wasn't completely honest with you this evening about me not having a girlfriend."

"Oh, so you do have a girlfriend?"

"Actually that part was true. I don't have a girlfriend. I have a wife. But we're separated."

In shock, Cinnamon rose to a sitting position, her eyes boggled as her lips formed the word *wife*. "A wife?"

"But we're separated."

"You have a wife," she asked again as if she hadn't heard him.

"I know you're probably disappointed."

"I'm just a lot surprised but I'm glad you told me."

"Cinnamon, don't be upset with me. My wife and I live separate lives and will probably file for divorce soon."

"Probably?"

"Definitely."

"Well, I must say you sure let the air out of my tires."

"I apologize but I wanted to see you again and thought I should be up front with you."

"I appreciate that, but I don't date married men. Thanks for your call."

It was unlike Cinnamon to behave so cold-heartedly, but there was no sense in giving him false hope.

It seemed their love affair ended before it even began.

And though she only met him once, once was all that was needed to make a lasting and spectacular impression.

Three messages awaited Cinnamon Sunday afternoon when she returned from church: one from Roman, one from Arri, and one from Mitchell. With no intention of returning Mitchell's call, she scribbled down his telephone number anyhow. Already having given him the low down on married men, she discerned no reason to repeat herself.

She continued with her plans to Arri's, dying to brag about her fiasco with Mitchell. Even though it was now over, it was just too exciting to keep to herself.

When Arri answered the door, Cinnamon was in awe at the person before her. Arri was barefoot and her bathrobe hung half open. She appeared to have just awakened from a deep sleep and her tangled hair resembled a playground for cats.

"Oh, hi," Arri said before she headed toward her bedroom.

Cinnamon closed the front door and trailed behind her. "Have you been in all day?"

Arri climbed into bed and munched on Hot Stuff potato chips.

Cinnamon clicked on the ceiling light. "Turn that light out," Arri yelled.

Arri was obviously in some type of funk.

When Cinnamon switched the light back out, the only light that remained emanated from the television. The television was tuned to *The Dating Game* reruns, the volume loud enough for the dead.

"Why is the TV so loud?" Cinnamon asked. "Are you going deaf?" Cinnamon lowered the volume on the TV, then took off her coat and eased down onto the bed. "What has you so down? What am I saying? The only thing or shall I say the only person who can affect you this way is Eric."

Arri didn't answer right away. Instead, she continued to munch on her potato chips, then said, "I called you this morning. Where were you?"

"I went to the late service this morning."

Boiling with excitement, Cinnamon crawled upon the bed and dusted the potato chip crumbs to the floor. "Boy do I have a story for you."

"I'm listening. What do you have to tell me?"

Upon studying Arri closely, Cinnamon could tell Arri had been crying. "You've been crying, haven't you?"

Arri remained silent.

"What's wrong?" Cinnamon asked. "I know it has something to do with Eric."

"Eric broke up with me last night."

"Really? I'm sorry."

Arri commenced to comb her fingers through her frizzy hair. "Space. He told me he needed his space."

"That was his reason?"

"That's what he said," Arri said, her lifeless body leaning against the headboard. "The sun doesn't shine on me anymore."

If it weren't for the pitiful expression in Arri's eyes, Cinnamon would have laughed at Arri's statement. But she couldn't. Her friend was in too much pain.

"I was so upset last night," Arri said. "I had to take something to help me sleep. I was going to kill myself but decided to cry instead."

Cinnamon wrapped her arm around Arri and gently patted her shoulder. "I'm so glad you chose to cry instead. And you shouldn't keep using that stuff. Eric isn't worth it. No one is."

Arri was all-too comfortable taking over-the-counter sleeping pills to relieve any kind of stress or heartache.

"I keep thinking about what you said about looking for something positive to come from everything, but I can't see it. I just feel so alone without him."

"I know."

"How is it that you can be with someone who is so wrong for you but when they leave, you are so hurt?" Arri asked. "Eric is so wrong for me. I know that. I have always known that, but I didn't care. I wanted him anyway and I couldn't let him go." Arri masked her face with her hands, sniffed a few times then wiped her eyes. "I know he doesn't love me but it is so hard for me to accept it because I so much want him to."

Dispirited babbles wailed from Arri's uncontrollable cries as she gasped for air. With her nose running and eyes watering, it seemed her sobbing would go on forever.

CHAPTER EIGHT

"I'M SORRY TO BREAK DOWN like this, Cinnamon."

Cinnamon nabbed a Kleenex from the dresser and handed it to Arri.

A large silence fell over the room as Arri wiped her eyes and nose, staring into space, seemingly lost in Never Never Land. "What's the best way to kill yourself?"

Cinnamon mused over Arri's words for all of three seconds and decided to play along. "Can you get to the roof?"

"Why?" Arri asked.

"Just answer the question. Can you get to the roof of this building?"

"I think I can, but the door is locked."

"Can you break it down somehow?"

"I guess."

"Okay, here's what you do," Cinnamon said. "After you break down the door, slowly walk to the edge. Don't look down though 'cause you might change your mind. Then take a deep breath. And jump."

With a smile, Arri's eyes shot to Cinnamon. "Forget you."

"You started it."

"I'm not going to kill myself. I just like talking about it sometimes, a way of exorcizing my demons."

"You and Eric will probably get back together anyway. You always do."

"I don't know," Arri said. "But I am feeling a little better today."

"After the way you were just crying?"

"I always feel better after I cry."

"Me too," Cinnamon said.

"You? When do you cry?" Arri asked.

"I have my moments."

"There's still a thorn in my heart though," Arri said. "But I guess I'll live."

"Yes, you will."

"No, I won't," Arri said, shouting as if purposely contradicting herself. "I want him back."

Cinnamon laughed, totally amused by Arri's theatrics. "Excuse me, but are you flipping out? I just want to know."

"Help me, Cinnamon. How can I get him back?"

"I don't know. You can't make him be with you."

"I don't want to hear all of that," Arri said. "Just tell me what I can do to get him back."

Arri leaped from the bed, her eyes glowing as she spun in Cinnamon's direction." I know what you can do. You're close to God. You can pray and ask God to bring Eric back to me."

"What? I know you're not serious."

"You'll do that for me, won't you?"

"No."

Arri collapsed on the bed next to Cinnamon. "Why not?"

"Because I don't feel right about you and Eric."

Arri kneeled on the floor and clasped her hands together. "Please, please, do this for me. Please, Cinnamon, please, please, please, pretty please, please, please."

"Why can't you ask God yourself? You know how to pray."

"I'm not that close to God. He may not hear me, but I know he'll hear you. You're a good person." Arri rested her head against Cinnamon's leg, scaling it like she was a kitten. "Please, Cinnamon, do this for me. Please. Please. Please."

Overcome with Arri's desperation, Cinnamon couldn't say no. "Okay. Okay. I'll ask God to bring Eric back to you, if it's in your best interest."

"Thank you." Arri rose to her feet and kissed Cinnamon on the mouth. "I feel so much better now. When are you going to do it?"

"I told you I'd do it."

"But when? Do it tonight."

"Yes, mother," Cinnamon said. "What makes you so sure God wants you to be with Eric?"

"God knows how much I love Eric."

"Arri, believe it or not, sometimes loving someone is not enough reason to be with them. You're just attached to him."

"But my Sagittarian instinct tells me he's the one."

"Didn't you just say he was wrong for you and you always knew it?"

Arri didn't answer right away, then said, "I may have said that but. . ."

"I can't wait to hear you explain this one."

"But I want him anyway. Okay. There, I've said it."

Cinnamon moved out of the way as Arri stripped the sheets from the bed.

"This is going to work," Arri said. "I just know it."

"Since you're feeling better and all--"

"You won't forget to say that prayer, will you?"

"No, I will not forget and will you stop asking me? You're starting to wreak havoc on my nerves."

"I'm sorry. Just don't forget about that prayer."

Cinnamon couldn't do anything but laugh. Her friend was obsessed and nothing else could be said.

After Cinnamon shared with Arri her night out on the town with Mitchell, Arri said, "First the nightclub and now Mitchell. What has gotten into you these days?"

"I'm just having a little fun," Cinnamon said, glowing with enthusiasm. "We danced all night, cheek to cheek, and had a rootin-tootin good time."

"Did you say cheek to cheek?"

"I most certainly did. But there is one small problem though. He's married."

"I wouldn't exactly call that a small problem."

"He says he's separated."

"Doesn't matter."

"I know that and you know that but my heart doesn't know that. And you should see this man, Arri. Oh. My. God. I'm telling you this is the kind of man who is so fine, when you're in his presence, you just find your panties coming down all by themselves."

Smiling, Arri said, "I have never heard you say anything like that before."

"That's because I've never seen a man as fine as Mitchell. I'm telling you he makes Denzel Washington look like Snoop Dog."

"Oh, I have to see this man. Sounds like you're planning on seeing him again. Are you?"

"Of course not."

"Why don't I believe you?"

"You should," Cinnamon said. "I have no intention of seeing a married man whether he's separated or not."

"I don't have to remind you what happened to your two sisters who got involved with married men."

"No, you don't."

"That's not what it sounds like to me."

"I don't care what it sounds like," Cinnamon snapped.

"You don't have to get all funky about it."

"I'm sorry, I didn't mean it like that." Cinnamon watched Arri tidy up the room and pick up the clothes from the floor. "There is one other small problem," Cinnamon added.

"What's that?"

"I did give him my telephone number, but this was before I learned he was married. Maybe we could be friends. Who knows?"

"You keep thinking that."

"I know what you're thinking," Cinnamon said. "Trust me, it's not like that. It was just one night of fun."

"You say it but I don't think you mean it."

Arri headed into the kitchen and Cinnamon followed. After Arri filled the dishpan with water, she soaked the cups and silverware. "You know what I'm thinking?" Arri asked.

"No, but I wish you'd tell me."

"I've known you for a long, long time, and met several of your boyfriends. We've even gone on a couple of double dates, and I have never ever seen you this excited about anybody, much less after only one date."

"That's true."

"And I'm thinking that despite the fact that he's married, you're not going to let him go, are you?"

"I already let him go."

"Okay. So you don't think it's possible that he's the one even though he's married?"

Cinnamon speculated, contemplated and deliberated for all of a split second. "No," Cinnamon declared. "It's not possible. Because if he was, he wouldn't be married."

"You don't think so?"

"No, I don't."

True, Cinnamon never met anyone like Mitchell, anyone who pushed her buttons the way he did. But so what. It didn't mean anything. Mitchell was a sweet and adorable man and it was no wonder she responded the way she did. Any woman would. Arri was just trying to put a bug in Cinnamon's ear, but it wasn't going to work.

Before going to sleep that night, Cinnamon said a special prayer for Arri as she promised despite her belief that Eric was totally wrong for her.

Cinnamon and Roman finally made plans to meet for lunch after conversing on the phone for over two weeks, and she eagerly anticipated their meeting. Convinced she and Roman would make a connection, she put off calling any of the other men who responded to her ad until after she met with Roman.

For her date, she wore her ankle-length black skirt and fire red cashmere sweater, black and red being one of her favorite combinations. The only other colors that came close were navy and white.

As she polished her short nails, she resolved to do away with her wedding band because it was causing way too much confusion in this dating game.

At Bennigan's restaurant, she would wait for Roman near the revolving doors at one o'clock. She knew she might tempt fate by meeting him at the same place she met Joseph, but what the hell. Bennigan's was a cool place.

It was Roman's lunch hour and she made certain to be on time.

On the corner of South Water and Michigan Avenue, Cinnamon stepped from the 151 Sheridan bus.

The sky opened up and snow pelted from above. As she waited to cross the street, she watched an array of people rushing in different directions.

Upon her approach to the restaurant, she spotted a towering thin gentleman waiting outside. Suspecting he was Roman, she stepped to him. "Roman?"

"Cinnamon? I thought that was you."

After her unforgettable meeting with Joseph, she didn't know who she'd meet, but she was pleasantly surprised. And relieved.

Roman extended his hand and they shook. "It's nice to finally see you."

"You're so formal," she said.

Roman was a little thin for her taste. He looked about thirty-three or thirty-four and wore tiny wire-framed glasses, which made him look clever. She admired his professional image in his dark tailored suit and though he wasn't what she would consider attractive, he wasn't bad looking either.

"So what do you think?" Roman asked. "This is the person you've been talking to on the phone for two weeks."

"What do I think?"

"Am I as ugly as you thought?"

Cinnamon laughed, enjoying his sense of humor. "I didn't think that."

"I'm just kidding. Shall we go inside?"

"Most definitely."

They spurred through the revolving doors and made their way through the congested lobby. As people continued to enter, Cinnamon was constantly bumped at the shoulder.

Taking hold of Cinnamon's hand, Roman led her away from the door. "They should be calling us for our table soon."

"I guess everyone in the Loop decided to have lunch here today," Cinnamon said.

"It seems that way, doesn't it?"

The hostess announced the Richardson party and Cinnamon and Roman were seated at a table near the window, facing Michigan Avenue.

"Let me help you with your coat," he said.

Roman helped her off with her coat, then draped it over the chair next to her.

After they ordered drinks, Cinnamon stared across at him, admiring his glasses. She liked his look, having a thing for men who wore glasses.

"You didn't tell me you wore glasses. They're cute. They make you look smart."

"It's a hoax," he said. "I just want people to think that."

"But it's not true?"

"No, it's not."

"I bet it is true."

This was their first meeting, and already she felt very comfortable with him as if she'd known him all along.

"I envisioned you differently," Roman said.

"What do you mean?"

"Well, voices can be deceiving. You sounded so nice on the phone, I didn't think you would match your voice."

"Thank you."

"You're a very pretty woman. I wanted to say that the moment you stepped toward me."

"Thank you again."

"Why would a pretty girl such as yourself need to place an ad in the paper?"

Cinnamon hissed. "Everyone says that."

Roman shot down his water, then set the glass back on the table. "Who is everyone?"

"Everyone. Everyone thinks that a half-way attractive woman always has it easy."

"That's not true?" he asked.

"No, it's not. It's not always easy to meet the kind of people I want to meet."

"What kind of people do you want to meet?"

"I want what everyone else wants," she said.

"I'm listening."

Cinnamon grinned, resting her arms on the table. "You're going to make me do this, aren't you?"

The waitress delivered their drinks.

"In answer to your question, I'm not going to make you do anything," Roman said. "But I would like an answer."

Cinnamon sipped her iced tea. "Didn't I mention what I wanted in my ad?"

"Probably, but we're here together now. It's different."

"What was the question again?"

"You're stalling but I'll repeat it anyway. Tell me about the kinds of people you want to meet."

"People in general or in a mate?" she asked.

"In a mate."

"Okay. Let's see. What's important to me? Intelligence, a sense of humor, smart, ambitious, affectionate, sweet, sensitive, generous, compassionate and someone who speaks my love language."

"What language is that?"

"Well, everyone responds differently to different stimuli."

"I like the sound of this already. Please continue."

"Well, there are five love languages. There's service, that's the language of getting coffee for someone, running someone's bath water, cooking for someone, that sort of thing. Then, there are the words of affirmation--'I love you', 'you're beautiful', etcetera. And then there's physical touch. I don't have to explain that one."

"Please do," he said.

Cinnamon continued. "Physical touch is stroking someone's hand, kisses, hugs, any kind of physical contact. Then there's gifts, that's the flowers, the presents, the cards,

the candy. And the last one is. . . I forgot what the last one is.
. . Oh, and the last one is quality time. And that's spending
lots and lots of time together."

"This is very interesting but I like all of those things."

"I'm sure you do," she said. "We all do. The thing is that
there is one or two that really do it for us. I mean really do it
for us."

"Do what?"

"You know," she said. "What really turns us on and makes
us feel loved. I like all of those things too, but what I like most
of all is someone who spends a lot of time with me and the
gifts. I love the gifts."

"That does it for you, huh?"

"Yes, it does."

"So what's my language?" he asked.

"I would guess that it's probably words of affirmation. I
could be wrong, but you would probably respond very well to
words, good words, complimentary words and sexy words."

Roman fanned himself, displaying a faint smile. "You
better knock it off, girl. This is a family restaurant."

She laughed, celebrating his unique wit.

On a scale of one to ten, Roman was a good seven.

Chapter Nine

"How did I get lucky enough to meet someone like you?" Roman asked as he gazed into Cinnamon's eyes.

Cinnamon raised her glass of iced tea to her mouth, trying not to expose how wonderful he was making her feel.

"I would think being on the road all the time, you would meet all kinds of men."

"It's not as easy as that, but I have met a few."

Roman rubbed his chin as if pondering some profound question. "I know this is probably none of my business, but have you gotten many responses from your ad?"

"I received some."

"Some as in ten, fifteen?"

"Some."

"Have you gone on many dates?"

"Actually, you're the first," she said.

"I like the sound of that."

After lunch, Cinnamon pulled out her compact mirror and applied her lipstick to moisten her lips.

"That's a nice color on you," he said.

"Thank you."

A soft silence hovered over them. Cinnamon absorbed the moment, concluding that their meeting was officially a success.

"I still can't figure out why you're not involved with anyone," Roman said. "Can you answer that for me?"

Before she could answer, the waitress approached and gathered their dishes from the table. "Can I get you anything else?" the waitress asked.

"Hot tea," Cinnamon said.

"More coffee."

The waitress stepped away and Cinnamon found herself once again admiring how sharp Roman looked in his glasses. "Why didn't you tell me you wore glasses?" she asked.

"Because people always picture you differently when they know you wear glasses. I wanted you to see me. I'm still waiting on an answer to my question."

"What question?"

"Why aren't you involved with anyone?"

"I don't know."

"There's something about you."

"What's that?" she asked.

"I haven't quite figured it out yet. But there's something more to you though, much more."

"Like what?"

"I don't know yet," he said. "Something mysterious."

"There's something mysterious about all of us."

"I mean something really mysterious. Haven't you noticed how some people you meet are so easy to figure out? I mean you know what they're about right away and then there are others you have to really get to know."

Cinnamon rested her elbow on the table, her hand underneath her chin. "I think I know what you mean."

"Everyone has their own little secrets," he said.

"That's right, they do."

"I'm sure there are things about you I'll probably never know," he said.

"What does that mean?"

"There isn't anything you could ask me that I wouldn't or couldn't answer." Roman leaned forward. "But . . . I bet there are things you wouldn't dare disclose to me."

"That's not true."

Not taken by the direction of the conversation, she changed the subject. "So what kind of law does your firm practice?"

Roman calmly dodged her question. "So it's not true, huh?"

"What?" she asked, pretending not to know what he was talking about.

"What I asked you before, about not disclosing anything personal to me."

"Oh, that. No, it's not true."

Before Cinnamon could continue, the waitress brought over their beverages.

"Well, let's see how untrue what I said is," Roman said as he added cream to his coffee and stirred it. "How long has it been since you've been involved with anyone?"

Unprepared to answer his question, she reached for her tea and dipped the lemon peel inside the cup.

"You don't have to answer if you don't want to," he said.

"It's been awhile," she said. "That's all I can say."

It was really none of his business, nor did she need to explain herself, especially to someone she just met.

"How long is awhile?" he asked.

"Just awhile."

"And why is that?"

"I don't know," she said, slightly irritated.

"That's interesting that you say you don't know, because it makes me wonder if you just don't want to tell me."

It was like he could see right through her.

"Were you in love with this guy?" he asked.

"Who?"

"The last guy you were involved with," he said, easing back into his chair.

Slightly irritated, Cinnamon shifted her body back and threw her hand up. "I feel like I'm being interrogated here."

"You're right. I apologize for all the questions. So were you in love with this guy?"

"I thought we put an end to the questions," she said kindly.

"This is the last one. I promise."

"The truth is I don't know if I was in love or not. Were you in love with your last girlfriend?"

"Very much."

"What happened?"

"I was in love with the familiarity of it all, but we didn't connect anymore."

Engrossed in his words, she said, "I just made the same statement to my friend the other day. She is in love with a man totally wrong for her and she swears they should be together because she loves him."

"Haven't you noticed how some people always end up dating the same type of person?"

"Uh huh."

Absorbed in his psychology, she could have gone on for hours talking to him, especially since he stopped with the questions.

After Roman finished his coffee, he asked, "What do you have planned this afternoon?"

"Nothing special. I'll probably do my laundry and catch up on some reading."

"I enjoy talking to you, Cinnamon."

"I was just thinking the same thing."

He signaled to the waitress. "I'm going to ask you something I probably shouldn't."

Right away, Cinnamon tried to prepare herself.

"Will I see you again?"

"Of course, but why is that something you shouldn't ask?"

"Because I put you on the spot and sometimes when people are put on the spot, they are not totally honest."

"That makes sense."

"How are you getting home in this weather?" he asked.

"The bus."

"I'll put you in a cab."

"No, that's okay. You don't have to do that."

"I insist. After all, you did come downtown to meet me."

He was a true gentleman.

Roman paid the bill, then helped Cinnamon with her coat. "I think this meeting went well," Roman said.

"I do too."

Upon reaching the outside, Cinnamon raised her coat collar and stuffed her hands into her pockets. It stopped snowing but a murky slush concealed the walks.

"Wait here by the door," Roman said. "And I'll get a taxi for you."

Roman stepped to the curb and flagged down a Flash taxi. As the taxi approached, Roman signaled for Cinnamon.

Cinnamon rushed over, careful not to slide on the sleety snow. "Thank you," she said, smiling as she climbed inside. "This is very nice of you."

Roman handed Cinnamon a twenty dollar bill, then closed the door.

As the taxi pulled off, he yelled, "Call me."

Hot chocolate was just what Cinnamon required after coming in from the cold. She tuned the television to the Discovery Channel while she lay stretched out on her sofa, staring at the lines on the ceiling. She listened to the buses screeching to a stop outside her window as the wind whistled.

She chanced on a wonderful guy in Roman and was very pleased, so much that she chose not to meet anyone else.

All the same, however spectacular, her lunch date lacked the thrill she experienced in Mitchell's presence--the warmth of Mitchell's hands, his mysterious stare and his impeccable charm. And she couldn't help but wonder if she might ever see him again.

Later that afternoon, Cinnamon prepared her laundry, separating the darks from the lights and then the lights from the whites.

When the phone rang, she immediately recognized Roman's voice.

"Are you reading?" he asked.

"Actually, I was getting ready to do the laundry. I was thinking about you."

"I didn't think you'd say that," he said.

"Why not?"

"I just didn't. You surprise me, Cinnamon. What did you think when you thought about me?"

"How nice it was meeting you, how much I enjoyed our conversation."

"That's all?"

"What did you want me to say--that it was a fabulous afternoon?"

"That's more like it. Are you still wearing that black skirt?"

"Why?"

"I just like to picture you when I'm talking to you. Red and black looks good on you. I happen to be a big fan of those two colors."

"Really?"

"If you ever come to my place, you'll see for yourself."

Quickly changing the subject, Cinnamon said, "I'm actually wearing a sweat suit and it's not very enticing."

"What color?"

She laughed, amused by his curiosity. "It's blue."

"I want to see you again. Real soon."

His directness enchanted her. Sometimes timid herself, an aggressive someone was just what she required.

"Are you still there?" he asked.

"I'm here."

"What about this weekend?"

"This weekend I'm working," she said.

"That's too bad. Okay, well, we'll work something out next week."

Upon disconnecting from Roman, Cinnamon invited Arri over for dinner, wanting to blab all about her first date with Roman.

In preparation for Arri's arrival, Cinnamon ordered Arri's favorite Chinese dish, Pepper Steak and Shrimp Fried Rice, leaving it on the stove to keep warm.

When Arri arrived two hours later, Cinnamon was in her room, folding her laundry on the bed.

Arri wore a violet mini-skirt highlighting her shapely long legs, her hair styled in a French braid.

"Do you ever get tired of purple?" Cinnamon asked.

"This is my lucky color." Arri posed in front of the full-length mirror, examining her body from every angle. "Do you think I'm getting fat?"

"Arri, please."

"No, I'm serious." Arri slid her hand up and down her stomach. "My stomach is bulging a little, don't you think?"

"You have no stomach, Arri. Trust me. It couldn't be any flatter."

"Yes, I do." Inhaling, Arri pulled in her stomach, then released it. "That's why Eric didn't want me. I'm fat."

"If you were any thinner, I wouldn't be able to see you. Your food is on the stove. Now get away from that mirror and go eat something."

Arri emerged from the kitchen with enough food on her plate for three people. She dropped down on the bed and stuffed her mouth with food. "Did you ever say that prayer for me?"

"Yes, I did."

"When?"

"A few days ago."

"I know we're going to get back together now. I just know it."

"Has he called?"

The question subdued Arri's mood so much that she stopped eating. "No, he hasn't."

"I'm surprised you haven't called him."

"I wanted to, but. . . I just said forget it. I'll wait for him to come back to me. I do miss him though."

Arri rose to her feet and set her plate on the dresser. "I'll eat the rest of this later."

"You guys will get back together," Cinnamon said as she continued folding her laundry. "You always do."

"I feel a depression coming on," Arri said, then exhaled a long breath. "Let's do something."

"Like what?"

"I don't know. Anything, because if I stay here, I'll get depressed."

"Okay, let me put the rest of these clothes away."

Arri carried her plate into the kitchen and returned wearing her coat.

"That was fast. I guess you want to go now."

"Can we? I just don't want to stay in thinking about Eric anymore."

Arri waited by the front door. Cinnamon came from the bedroom still wearing her sweat suit and having slipped into her rubber boots.

"I know you're not wearing that," Arri said.

"What's wrong with what I'm wearing?"

"You're wearing a sweat suit and boots?"

"Yeah," Cinnamon said. "What's wrong with that? It might snow tonight, and I don't want to mess up my shoes."

"You look like you stole something or about to steal something."

"Who cares? I'm not trying to meet anyone."

"Wearing those boots," Arri said, "You definitely won't. As a matter of fact, you might get arrested."

"Good, I always wanted to get arrested."

In the hallway, Arri waited while Cinnamon locked the door.

"It's not enough that you dress the way you like," Cinnamon said. "But you have to dress me as well."

Arri dismissed Cinnamon's comment and strolled ahead of her.

Upon stepping onto the mirrored elevator, Arri pressed the button for the lobby.

"I almost forgot," Cinnamon said. "I met another guy from the paper today and I think it went pretty well."

"Aren't you afraid to meet these men?"

"I'm afraid that I won't like them, but not afraid of anyone hurting me. I've only met two and both meetings were in public places."

Once reaching the outside, they climbed into Arri's dusty Honda and waited for the car to warm. Cinnamon placed her finger on the power-window button.

"Don't even think about rolling down that window," Arri said. "So what happened on this date?"

"In some ways, he reminds me of Mitchell."

"Is that good or bad?" Arri asked.

"Their similarities have nothing to do with physical appearance. They're alike in that they're both kind and attentive."

"He's not ugly, is he?"

"No, he looks good. I mean, he's no Mitchell but he's okay."

Arri inched from the parking space and headed for the Tangeray pool hall on Halsted Street. While stopped by a red light, Arri powered on the radio. "Has he called you yet?"

"Who? Mitchell or Roman?"

"Both of them."

"Roman called me this afternoon and Mitchell called a couple of times but I have yet to call him back."

Arri circled the blocks near the pool hall four times, searching for a parking space, until finally she found one six blocks away.

Once inside, Cinnamon played one game of pool with Arri, then retired to the bar stool and observed Arri playing alone. Pool didn't provide that mental stimulation that Cinnamon liked and it bored her.

When they left the Tangeray, they convened at a nearby coffee house, a huge relief from the harsh wind.

Inside, the track lighting radiated onto the serene and warm atmosphere. This was the place to study, write, and read. Cinnamon and Arri seldom frequented this cozy establishment after being asked to leave on two occasions for talking loudly. But due to the almost freezing temperatures, they made an exception this evening.

They ordered cappuccino and found seating at the cherry wood table in the center of the room.

Directly to the right of them, a man sat alone reading. Arri nodded in his direction. "Cinnamon, look over there."

Cinnamon peered in his direction, then turned away. "So?"

"Don't you think he's cute?"

Cinnamon glanced at him again for all of two seconds. "He looks short."

Arri's eyes darted in his direction again. "Yeah, he is kind of short. Doesn't matter, he's gay anyway."

"Now how do you know that?"

"Look at him, he's sitting alone reading," Arri said, her voice elevating. "You wouldn't find a straight man alone in a coffee shop reading."

"Get over it. That doesn't mean anything," Cinnamon said in a whisper. "And if you don't lower your voice, they're going to throw us out of here. Again."

"I was right about Noel, wasn't I?"

"No."

Arri's voice elevated to a bellow. "What? I wasn't?"

"Will you lower your voice? It's embarrassing being asked to leave."

"What do you mean, asked to leave? Girl, we were thrown out."

They both burst into a belly laugh.

Seconds later, a short blond woman with glasses approached their table. "Excuse me, ladies, but could you keep it down. Some of the patrons here are studying."

"Of course," Cinnamon said. "Sorry."

As soon as the lady stepped away, Cinnamon said, "Maybe we should just leave now."

"No, I like it here. So anyway, you don't want to admit that Noel is gay, do you?"

"Let's just say I don't like to jump to conclusions," Cinnamon said. "I don't want to believe something about someone is true unless it is."

"Yeah, yeah, Ms. Philosopher." Arri added sugar to her cappuccino and stirred it. "I sure wish Eric would call me."

"I'm still surprised you haven't called him."

"I left a message. He never called me back."

"When?"

"Yesterday."

"Yesterday, huh? Not two hours ago you told me you hadn't tried to contact him."

"Did I say that?" Arri asked, her face oozing guilt.

"In other words, you lied," Cinnamon said. "It's okay though. I know you can't help yourself."

Arri rested her elbow on the table, her hand underneath her chin, and sighed. "I'm frustrated, Cinnamon. And depressed. Craving sex all the time."

"You're a natural born actress. You really are."

"I wish I could do the celibacy thing like you. How do you do it?"

"I don't think about it."

"It's been a week and I can't stand it."

"A week is not that long."

"For me it is. I think I miss the sex more than Eric."

"Now that I don't believe. I think you miss Eric. Now is your chance to go after that manager you're so crazy about."

"It's not like he's invited me out or anything. Besides, he probably wouldn't take a black woman seriously anyway."

"I thought we went over this already," Cinnamon said.

"Oh, and the other day he was explaining this document to me and instead of listening to what he was saying, I was admiring the hair on the back of his hand. Talk about a turn on. His name is Matthew, right, but I call him Matt."

"It's nice to hear you get excited about someone other than Eric."

"And you know what's funny? He's not that attractive or tall. As a matter of fact, he's an inch shorter than I am. But he's so beautiful to me." Arri folded her hands and closed her eyes as if lost in a rainbow. "I love it when he stands close to me because then I can smell his hot breath. I could hold that scent inside forever."

"You should hear yourself. You sound like you're having phone sex."

Arri opened her eyes and continued. "And he has this way of listening to me like he really wants to hear what I'm saying. I think I like him because I think he likes me. I can't be sure, but he has given me some clues."

"Like what?"

"Well, sometimes if I'm reading something, he'll ask what I'm reading."

"Is that the clue?"

"Oh, and one day after dropping off work at my desk, he told me he worked out in the gym too long and his back and arms were sore. What do you think about that?"

Cinnamon couldn't respond right away. She needed to convince herself that the person sitting across from her was not crazy.

CHAPTER TEN

"HE WAS JUST MAKING conversation, Arri."

"Yeah, but don't you think it's odd that he would share that kind of information with me? It's not like we're friends."

Cinnamon touched Arri's arm, peered into her eyes. "It's going be all right."

"Don't be sarcastic with me. I know a clue when I hear one. Oh, and I forgot. He also told me when his office door is closed, I don't have to knock, to just come on in. What do you think about that?"

"Oh, he likes you all right," Cinnamon said sarcastically. "I'm really shocked that someone other than Eric has you in such awe."

"Men are just so hard to figure out sometimes," Arri said. "You never know what's going on in their heads, either of them."

"No, you didn't say that."

"Oh, yes I did. And while we're on the subject, I think I might have to get one of those toys that you have."

Cinnamon almost gagged on her cappuccino, trying not to laugh. "What?"

"You heard me."

Cinnamon knew exactly what Arri referred to. She just couldn't believe Arri said it.

The next afternoon, while Cinnamon dusted her entertainment center and coffee table, the doorbell rang.

Wearing a t-shirt and socks, she hurried to the intercom and discovered it was Noel.

After buzzing him in, she flew into the bedroom and slapped on a pair of jeans.

When she opened the door, Noel bustled up on her, almost knocking her down and threw his arms around her.

"How is it that you always know when I'm home?" she asked.

"I just know these things." Noel stepped through the door and didn't waste time shedding his jacket. He buckled down on the sofa and crossed his legs, seemingly relaxed and in good spirits.

"What are you so happy about?" she asked.

"I'm happy to see you." He scanned the room from right to left and left to right. "Your place is gleaming as usual." Noel patted the sofa next to him, signaling Cinnamon. "Sit down next to me."

Cinnamon quickly joined him and smiled. "You just love stopping by without calling, don't you?"

"I wanted to surprise you. I left a couple of messages on your machine but never heard back from you. So what's up with that?"

"I was going to call you."

"Uh huh, you said that before."

Changing the subject, Cinnamon asked, "What have you been doing?"

"Calling you, mostly. How's your friend?"

"Who, Arri?"

"What other friends of yours do I know?"

"She's fine. I think she likes you."

"And what about you?"

"I like you too."

He stretched out his arms on the sofa. "That's hard to believe, you never call me."

Cinnamon meditated on how to word her sentence before she spoke. "I saw you one night at Lemar's Place."

"When? Why didn't you say anything?"

"You were with someone."

Noel stood, plucked a book from the bookshelf and returned to the sofa.

"So?" she questioned.

"So what?"

"Who was that guy you were talking to?"

"I have no idea who you're referring to," Noel said as he flipped through the pages of the book. "I'm sure I was talking to a lot of people that night. Who were you there with?"

Disregarding his question, she said, "My friend, Arri, hinted that. . ."

"Your friend hinted what?"

"That you might like more than just girls."

"She hinted?"

"Well, that's what she thinks."

He set the book on the coffee table and turned to her. "What do you think?"

"I don't know what to think. That's why I'm asking."

"I like women, Cinnamon. I like you."

"Does that mean you don't like men?"

"It means I like women."

"You're not answering my question, Noel."

Noel rose to his feet again, shoved the book back on the shelf and quickly grabbed another. "Exactly what is it that you are getting at?"

"I'm curious to know why you're interested in me."

"I like you," he said, joining her on the sofa. "You're a sweet person."

"Are you denying that you like men?"

"I'm saying that I like you."

Trying to land a straight answer from him was like extracting teeth. "Noel, it's okay if you do. I'm not asking so I can judge you. I'm asking out of curiosity."

"Would you be interested in me if I told you I did like men?"

"As a friend, I would."

"Just a friend?"

"Noel, we already went through this. We're friends. Just friends and it doesn't bother me if you happen to like men and women. You're still a cool person who I enjoy hanging out with."

"Okay. I do like men, but I also like women."

"I gathered that."

Even after suspecting Noel might be gay, Cinnamon was still stunned. Somehow hearing him confirm it made it more real to her.

"I have no prejudices against people who are that way," Cinnamon said. "But isn't that difficult for other people to accept?"

"Sometimes it is."

Intrigued by Noel's lifestyle, she asked, "Do you enjoy making love to men as much as women?"

"It's hard to say. They're both so different and yet the same."

Engrossed in the conversation, she fixed her gaze on him. "How so?"

"Well, it's the same in that both experiences are equally satisfying physically. Where they differ is mentally or emotionally if you will."

"Emotionally?" she asked.

"I don't experience the rush with women as I do with men."

"A rush? I don't understand."

"You know how you feel when you're really afraid or in a hurry or after a vigorous workout, like running, the energy you feel, the alertness?"

"I think so," Cinnamon said, captivated by his every word.

"Well, that same adrenalin high is what I experience when I'm wrapped in the arms of another man, cuddled tightly against his body, pinned down underneath his strength."

Never before did anyone come close to describing the physical connectedness as explicitly as did Noel.

"Why can't you experience that with a woman?" she asked.

"Probably because sex with men is different, opposite from the norm, a turn on in itself, at least for me anyway. It's an unbelievable experience, and I don't think I give true justice to it in my description."

"I do," she said, his words astonishing her.

"This should be a testament to how much I like you," Noel said. "Otherwise, I never would have shared that with you."

"Don't think I don't appreciate it," she said as she leaned in and kissed his cheek.

"I'll never wash this cheek again," he said, brushing his fingers against his cheek.

"Oh, shut up. Seriously though, Noel, after what you described, tell me what a woman can offer you?"

"Physically, I think I'm more turned on to a woman. Their physical stature, their hair, breasts, shapely legs. I get excited just thinking about it. I can't believe I'm telling you all of this."

"I'm glad that you are."

"And the fact that women are so smart, most of them anyway, that's one of the reasons I desire to connect with them."

"You think you'll ever choose?" she asked.

"Maybe someday, I don't know. Then again, why should I?"

"I won't even ask which it'll be. I already know the answer."

"Which do you think?" he asked.

"Men. Definitely men."

"We'll just have to wait and see, won't we?" Noel said.

Cinnamon stared into space, trying to conceive of the adrenalin high he spoke of.

"What about you?" Noel asked, displaying a curious smile.

"What do you mean what about me?"

"Do you ever wonder about women?"

"Do I think about making love to women?" she asked.

"Do you?"

"No, I don't think so."

"That means yes."

"No, it doesn't. I'm very much into men, always have been and always will be."

"You never told me who you were with the night you saw me."

"A guy I met at the Wild Hare. You don't know him."

"I'm sure I don't. Does this guy have a name?"

"Mitchell."

"Wait a minute. Is this the married man you told me about?"

"It is."

"I don't see you as that type."

"What type is that?" she asked, folding her arms..

"The type that would fool around with someone else's husband. You know, a home wrecker."

"I am not a home wrecker, and I'm not fooling around with someone else's husband. After I learned he was married, that was it."

"Oh, really?"

"Yes, really," Cinnamon snapped, tired of everyone reminding her of how wrong it was to date a married man, as if she couldn't make decisions for herself.

"I'm just asking," Noel said. "Don't bite my arm off."

She leaned back on the sofa and turned away from him.

"Are we still friends?" he asked.

"Of course."

Noel rose to his feet and said, "I'm going to go. You seem to be a little perturbed right about now."

"You don't have to go, I like talking to you."

She wanted him to stay just so long as he didn't thrash out about Mitchell.

"I don't know. You seem a little distant."

Holding out her hand to him, she said, "I want you to stay. You can go to the library with me."

After Noel and Cinnamon returned from the library, Noel left soon afterwards.

Two messages awaited Cinnamon on her answering machine. Following Roman's daily message was a message from Mitchell.

"Hi, Cinnamon. You are an impossible woman to catch up with. I've left you several messages, and I'm getting the feeling that you don't want to talk to me. Actually, I got that feeling a long time ago, but I just couldn't give up on you. I keep thinking about the day we met and I would love to talk to you again, maybe even see you again. Anyway, when you get ready to talk, if you get ready to talk, I'll be here. No questions asked. Bye."

Infatuated with Mitchell's voice, Cinnamon couldn't resist returning his call. She hurried into her bedroom and there it was. Mitchell's telephone number underneath a bottle of clear fingernail polish, exactly where she left it.

Upon dialing his number, the phone only rang twice before she panicked and hung up. As much as she ached to speak to him and hear his red-hot voice, she fought the urge.

He was married and that was the end of it.

Cinnamon listened to her Moondance CD by Van Morrison, snapping her fingers while she unwound on the sofa. With fresh air surging through the room, she skimmed her library book, basking in the moment when the phone rang.

"Is that Van Morrison you're listing to?" Roman asked.

"It is."

"I didn't know you liked that kind of music."

"Oh, I love me some Van Morrison."

"What are you wearing right now?"

"You always ask me that."

"That's because I always want to know. Come on, just tell me what colors you're wearing."

"Blue and white."

"Blue jeans and a white t-shirt."

"Very good."

"I'm looking forward to seeing you this Sunday. Are we still on?"

"Uh huh."

"I'd like to pick you up if that's okay?"

"Sure, that's fine."

"Think about me tonight," he said.

"I'll see what I can drum up."

Roman was a great guy. He was the guy she could show off to her parents, but not the guy she fantasized about making hot sizzling love to. But so what. Perhaps in due time she would grow to feel as passionately about him as she did for Mitchell.

Cinnamon just finished deep conditioning her hair when Arri popped by.

Arri shuffled through the front door, seemingly on some kind of natural high, as she performed a booty dance as if practicing for a Beyonce video.

"Ask me why I'm in such a good mood," Arri said.

"Why are you in such a good mood?"

"I think that prayer you said for me worked, girl."

Cinnamon's gaze enriched the room. "Really?"

"I saw my baby last night. All the other times I called, he was never at home, and all of sudden, last night, poof, he was home. I know it was that prayer. I just know it."

Astonished, Cinnamon relaxed on the sofa, certain nothing good or lasting would come from Arri's and Eric's reunion.

Arri continued with her eclectic dance, swaying her shoulders, hips and arms. "So do I look excited?"

"Honey, you couldn't be more excited. So tell me everything. What happened?"

Arri broke from her coat, hurled it over the sofa, bursting with enthusiasm. "He was so happy to hear from me. I think he really missed me."

"Details please."

"No, seriously, Cinnamon, I think Eric really loves me. He's just not in touch with his feelings," Arri said, continuing with her dance. "You know what I mean?"

"No, I don't. And will you stop all that moving around and sit down? You're making me nervous."

Arri posed, hands on hips. "No, I will not sit down. I'm in too good a mood to sit down."

"You better sit down, girl."

Arri dropped down on the sofa, slipped out of her shoes, and swung her feet up on the cushion. "Okay, so Eric comes by around eleven o'clock, right, no, no, it was later than that."

"Whatever," Cinnamon said.

"Do you want to hear this or not?" Arri asked.

"Yes."

"Anyway, we listened to some music for a while and talked. And laughed, you know that in-love laugh. Oh, and I gave him a massage." Arri's eyes sparkled. "Ooooh! We are such a perfect match. I thought I could fly last night, hell I was flying."

"That good, huh?" Cinnamon said, awaiting the rest of Arri's story, knowing that in a matter of just a week, Arri would be in tears. Again.

"I have so much energy this evening," Arri said as she jumped to her feet, stretching out her arms. "I feel like painting."

Cinnamon laughed.

"I'm serious. Give me a paint brush and some paint and I will paint the hell out of this apartment. And I think I'm going to join the gym. That's how good I feel."

"You didn't take anything, did you?" Cinnamon asked.

"Anything like what?"

"You know what I mean. Like speed. I'm used to your usual zest but you have me a little worried this evening."

"Of course not. I don't do drugs. At least not hard drugs anyway. I'm in love, Cinnamon," Arri said as she spun around. "And I just can't help myself."

"I'm going to write the Academy and ask them to please send you an Oscar for this evening's performance."

"This isn't a performance, Cinnamon. This is real. Real love. Real love flowing from me. I tried to stop it but I couldn't. I'm in love, Cinnamon."

"Arri, if you use the word love one more time, I'm going to scream."

"But I'm in love."

"AAAH," Cinnamon yelled at the top of her lungs.

"See," Arri said. "I'm so much in love, I'm not even affected by your screams. You know why?"

"Because you're in love," Cinnamon said in a sour voice.

"Who told you?" Arri giggled and hopped up on the sofa, trampling on it.

"Girl, if you don't get off my sofa. . ."

Arri leaped down to the floor, then scrunched down on the sofa next to Cinnamon. "I had my toes sucked, fingers licked, ass ate. Do you hear me?"

"You know you're losing your mind, don't you?"

"But am I feeling good? All this talk about last night is getting me all warm inside," Arri said as she wrapped her hands around her neck. "I need something to drink. Open some more windows, knock down a wall or throw some water on me."

Never before witnessing this much exuberance in Arri, Cinnamon figured Arri was surely setting herself up for a devastating fall.

Cinnamon moseyed into the kitchen for water, then returned to Arri.

"I don't want water," Arri said. "I want something else."

"That's all I have, Miss."

Arri reluctantly accepted the water and gulped it down.

"Are you okay?" Cinnamon asked.

"Just groovy."

"So where's Eric now?"

"He left this morning after breakfast. Oh, you haven't seen him since he grew his goatee. Girl, he looks good."

"What has it been? A week since you were with him last?" Cinnamon asked.

"It's been more than a week and a tough week at that, but you wouldn't know anything about that."

"Ha, ha," Cinnamon said as she snarled at Arri. "So are you two an item again?"

Suddenly, the mania on Arri's face vanished. "He thinks we shouldn't see so much of each other this time. That's why he felt crowded before."

"So are you back together or not?"

"Yes, and no," Arri said.

"Which is it?"

"It's kind of complicated."

"No, it's not."

"Well, we're both going to see other people, but we're only going to sleep with each other."

"And you believe that?"

"Yeah, why not?"

"Only Eric would even suggest such a thing," Cinnamon mumbled underneath her breath.

"What?" Arri asked.

"Nothing."

"No, tell me what's on your mind. What, you don't believe he can date other women without having sex with them?"

"Sure he can."

"You don't mean that," Arri declared.

"Arri, listen to me. I know I can be naive sometimes myself, but that's too gullible. What he's saying is 'I want to continue to screw you while I look for something better.'"

"I am not gullible. Besides, you're just jealous," Arri said as she stepped into her shoes.

"I am not jealous."

"Yes, you are."

"Why?" Cinnamon questioned. "Why would I be jealous?"

"Because I'm sexually involved with someone and you're not."

"I know you don't believe that."

Arri slipped into her coat and clenched her purse.

"Are you going to see other people?" Cinnamon asked.

"I don't plan to."

"Why not? That's what he's doing. Don't you see, Arri? That's what he wants. He wants to run around like a dusty old cat and have you to come home to so you can clean him up."

"Well, I don't see it like that," Arri said. "I've invested a lot of myself in this relationship and I am willing to compromise."

Arri stormed toward the door. Cinnamon scurried behind her, wishing she could take back what she said.

"Don't be mad, Arri. I'm sorry. Maybe I shouldn't have said those things."

"Too late now. Besides, you're welcome to your opinion."

"Arri don't leave upset. Let's talk about it."

"I'll see you later," Arri said, right before she slammed the door behind her.

Chapter Eleven

Cinnamon listened to the fierce winds whistling against the windows as she dolled herself up for her date.

She struggled not to ruminate over her argument with Arri, but she couldn't help it. Arri was her best friend and Cinnamon had tiptoed around voicing her opinion long enough.

Eric was playing Arri hard with his numerous head trips. And with Arri's blind-sighted view, Arri might not ever recognize it.

Cinnamon once suffered from the please-love-me syndrome herself and watching Arri was like reliving old times.

Never before seeing Arri this agitated before, Cinnamon felt it her duty to patch things up with her right away. But then in a wink of an eye, Cinnamon decided instead to let Arri cool off and work things out upon her return to Chicago.

For now, she would focus all of her attention on Roman.

Because she was due at Midway Airport for a flight to Los Angles that evening, her time with Roman would be limited.

She adorned herself with a suede dress that nearly reached the floor and her patent leather boots.

As she stood at the bathroom mirror, she picked out her hair. Because three weeks had gone by since her last haircut, her afro was losing its shape.

In need of fresh air, she raised the window. Soon the cold temperature would make it impossible to open her windows for the fresh air she treasured so much.

The cold air from outside seemed to induce a string of whimsical images.

What was Mitchell doing this evening?

Her first hunch was to call him, just to hear the sweltering voice that dazzled her spirit to the nth degree. But she couldn't, not unless she was ready to turn her back on what was right: staying clear of married men.

Glancing at her Fossil watch, ample time remained before Roman arrived. Though she planned to patch things up with Arri upon her return to Chicago, at the last minute, she changed her mind.

After dialing Arri's number, Cinnamon was transferred to Arri's voice mail. "Hey, it's me. I'm sorry if I upset you, Arri. I shouldn't have said those things. I know how important Eric is to you and it was insensitive of me to say what I said. You're still my best friend. Okay? I'll call you in a few days."

Now that Cinnamon made her peace with Arri, her date with Roman would be all that much sweeter.

The beautifully wrapped flowers were the first thing to awaken Cinnamon's attention when Roman stepped inside her apartment. Though she only knew him a short time, she trusted him, but more importantly, she trusted her instincts.

With a warm smile, he handed her the flowers.

"Thank you. This is so sweet of you." She held them against her chest like a new-found heirloom. "This is really sweet."

"Don't you want to open them?"

"They're beautiful just the way they are."

"They're even prettier inside," Roman said as he unbuttoned his coat and glanced over her apartment. "I like your apartment a lot. It's quiet, clean and orderly, a lot like my place."

Cinnamon carefully unwrapped the flowers and inside were six huge budded lilac tulips and a card that read: *You light up every little corner of my life.*

"What a sweet card. Thank you for the gorgeous flowers and the card. She raised the tulips to her nose and sniffed them. "Up until today, I never had a favorite flower."

"But you do now?"

"Oh, yes."

Cinnamon set the flowers down on the end table.

"Aren't you going to put them in water?" he asked.

"I will in a minute."

"I would have guessed that your apartment looked like this."

"Like what?" Cinnamon hung up his coat in the hall closet.

"So organized, yet stylish. You like a lot of black and white, don't you?"

"Yeah, black, white, and red. What can I say? I get fixated."

"I'll have to remember that." He eased down on the sofa, checking out Cinnamon from top to bottom. "I love that dress. And I can tell your hair is growing. It looks good."

Noticing Cinnamon's crammed bookshelf, Roman asked, "Are those all psychology books?"

"Just about. Some of them are Christian books." She stood against the wall, lightly pulling at her earlobe. "So are you ready to go?"

"We have a little time. I'd like to see the rest of your place. May I?" His lush sweater complimented his Kenneth Cole dark pants.

"There's not much to see."

"I'll be the judge of that."

After a quick tour, they left and rode down on the elevator.

While Cinnamon watched the numbers on the panel descend, Roman stepped to her and pulled her close, his eyes twinkling through his glasses. Avoiding eye contact with him, her gaze dropped to the floor. Gently, he uplifted her head and merged his lips with hers. With her eyes closed, for a moment, she envisioned Mitchell's face, light brown eyes, dark skin, innocent smile and she wondered what it felt like to be held in Mitchell's arms.

The spell was soon broken when the elevator door opened and their lips separated.

Roman was a pretty good kisser. However, considering she dreamed of someone else the entire time, she distrusted her assessment.

From where Roman parked his Volkswagen Jetta, they scurried several blocks to Lasiando's Restaurant. The brittle wind cut at Cinnamon's face, enough to bring tears to her eyes.

Once inside, a faint garlic smell seduced Cinnamon while the heat quickly warmed her face and fingers. After the pretty Mexican hostess escorted them to their candlelit table, Roman helped Cinnamon out of her coat, then pulled the chair back so she could sit down.

Not completely warm enough, Cinnamon folded her arms. "This is such a beautiful place." She slid her hand over the ruffled tablecloth that cloaked the octagon-shaped table.

"This is one of my favorite places," Roman said.

Cinnamon stared across the room at the eclectic oil paintings on the wall. "I'm still thinking about the flowers you brought me this evening."

"I'm sure you're used to having men do nice things for you all the time."

Cinnamon blushed as they scanned their menus by candlelight.

"You know what I've been wanting to ask you?" Roman asked as he leaned forward.

"What?"

"About the other men that responded to your ad."

"I told you before I didn't meet anyone else."

"Did you talk to anyone else?"

"You were the only person I called and the only person I met."

"Not to sound ungrateful, but why? Why just me?"

"Why not?"

"Weren't you just a little curious about the other men?"

Cinnamon hadn't planned on telling Roman about her date with Joseph, but she wanted him to understand her reluctance in meeting other people. "Well, before I wrote my ad. . ." She lowered her voice. "I answered a couple of ads myself."

He rubbed his chin as if studying her. "Did you meet any of them?"

"Unfortunately, yes. And he was nowhere near my ideal date."

"Switching to a great subject, let's talk about your ideal date," he said.

"You always ask me questions I'm not ready for."

"You need time to think about it?" he asked.

Cinnamon turned away from him, the conversation digging a little deeper than she wanted it to. She returned her focus to him and said, "Yes, I need time to think about it."

"Go ahead, think about it," he said. "Are you ready?"

"I don't know what my ideal date is."

"You know what you want, don't you?" He was making her nervous, the same way he did when they first met.

"Yes, I know what I want."

"Well, tell me about it then."

He sounded like a school teacher. After thinking about it, she said, "You're my ideal date."

"You don't expect me to accept that, do you?"

"What's wrong with that answer?"

He smiled and gently pinched her cheek. "That's too easy for you."

"Maybe you are my ideal date."

"I'm not disputing that."

"So you agree with me?" she asked as she tapped her fingers against the table.

"I didn't say that. I'm just saying if that's how you feel, tell me why."

"You're tall, which is always good," she said. "You're attentive, kind. And you're smart."

"I'm surprised you said all of that."

"I don't see why. It's all true. And for the sake of putting you on the spot for a change, let me ask you something."

"Anything. Shoot."

"Did you feel funny about meeting me through the paper?"

"No."

"You didn't?" she asked.

"Meeting through personal ads is no better or worse than meeting someone anywhere else. You're taking a chance with everyone you meet. There's always a chance it may or may not work out, no matter where you meet. Did it bother you?"

"I felt a little funny about it."

"Why?"

"Because most people don't meet this way," she said. "They meet at work, nightclubs, or through other people."

"Maybe more people connect through the personals than we know about."

His words always absorbed her. He seemed gifted in seeing both sides of the story.

"Did you think I would be unattractive because I placed an ad?" she asked.

"I knew it was a possibility you could be attractive or unattractive. I didn't think only unattractive women placed ads. So to answer your question, I was open-minded about the whole thing, knowing it could go either way."

"I like the way you think."

"I don't think I've been complimented quite that way before."

After dinner, the waiter cleared the table and brought over coffee and tea.

"You know, I answered a couple of other ads myself," Roman said.

"I thought you might have," she said as she added a half teaspoon of sugar to her tea.

"So you were curious?" he asked.

"I was a little curious."

"You want to hear about it?" he asked.

"No, not really. It's not my business," she said. "Tell me about you, the things you like to do."

"I play a little pool now and then. I love to read. I love basketball, to watch that is. I work out at the gym here and there and I love to write, which, by the way, you're welcome to check out any time you want. Just let me know."

Though she appreciated the offer, it would be a long time before she visited him at his place.

"So tell me about your book. What's it about?"

"I'll read you the one-sentence premise: For the first time in history, the WNBA and NBA compete against each other for the national championship."

"Really? That's what it's about?"

"That's what it's about."

"It sounds like a movie."

"It could be."

After leaving the restaurant, they retired back to Cinnamon's apartment until it was time for Roman to take her to the airport.

Cinnamon clicked on the hall light near the coat closet and closed the front door. Before she could remove her coat, the room went dark after Roman shut off the light. His abrupt action startled her until she realized he was about to kiss her again. She just hoped the garlic smell on her breath didn't turn him off. With her hands at her sides, she anticipated his next plan of action as her eyes adjusted to the darkness. She saw his eyeglasses resting on his pudgy nose and felt his breathing against her face. He wrapped his arms around her waist, then kissed her forehead, her cheek and her bottom lip.

"Are you trying to kiss me?" she asked.

He removed his glasses and devoured her mouth with his, easing his tongue between her lips. She wished to envelop him in her arms, but enjoyed playing the passive role instead. His warm breath sent a chill through her and for the first time she felt utterly aroused in his presence. And it felt so good.

Their lips parted and he nudged her against the wall. "You smell good," he said as he clicked on the light.

Cinnamon smiled to herself as she hung up their coats. "Is that something you planned to do on your way up here?"

He returned his glasses to his face. "Maybe."

"The remote is on top of the TV," she said. "I'll be out in a minute."

Cinnamon retreated to the bathroom, picked out her afro and brushed her teeth. When she returned to the front room, Roman had turned on the television and muted the sound. He skimmed through the books on the shelf. "You have a lot of good stuff here. I've read many of these myself."

"Which ones?"

"He read off the titles, *If Life Is A Game, These Are The Rules, Creative Visualization, Feel the Fear and Do It Anyway, The Power of Now, Excuse Me, Your Life Is Waiting.* These are all really good reads."

She found it odd and unusual that he would take an interest in self-improvement books, reasoning that most men found them to be a bunch of malarkey.

"I forget a lot of that stuff anyway after I read it."

Roman joined her on the sofa in front of the TV and gazed at her pantyhose.

"Are those pantyhose?" Roman asked as he caressed her legs.

"They're tights and you just wanted to touch my legs, didn't you?"

"I did. You know me well," he said with a friendly smile. "So what do you want for Christmas?"

"You don't have to get me anything for Christmas."

"I know I don't have to."

"I'll be working Christmas day anyway," she said.

"I'll get you something before then."

"I'm not really a Christmas person."

Growing up, Christmas was her favorite holiday, but since leaving home, the zeal faded. Though she hoped to rekindle the holiday joys of her past, she was doubtful.

"Come on, everyone loves Christmas." He eased closer to her and wrapped his arm around her. "I sure wish you didn't have to leave tonight."

She turned to him and asked, "Why do you like me so much, Roman?"

"Because you're different from women I have dated in the past. You're a good person with a good heart. And it doesn't hurt that you're beautiful and sexy. And you're independent. You're not looking for someone to take care of you, not that it's a bad thing for a man to take care of a woman. Actually, it's a good thing when it's the right time."

"You gathered all of that about me?" she asked.

"That's what I can tell so far." Abruptly, he hauled her into his lap. "Come here," then gently stroked her back. "You're so warm."

"You're so aggressive," she said.

"I have to be." He connected his lips with hers again and again.

As the light from the television shined on her face, she fantasized kissing Mitchell this way. And though she hated herself for what she was thinking, she couldn't help it.

In any event, she liked Roman, even enjoyed fooling around with him. Still she doubted their relationship would escalate past heavy petting, reason being: no magic. Perhaps if she met Roman first, before she set eyes on Mitchell, things might be different. Because after you meet *The Man*, anyone and everything after him falls short.

"I better start getting ready for work," she said as she attempted to ease up from his lap.

Restraining her, he said. "You have plenty of time."

"No sense in waiting until the last half-hour."

"I don't want you to go."

Again she tried to escape from his grasp but with no success. "I have to get ready, Roman."

Finally, he allowed her to break away.

Cinnamon headed for her bedroom, closed the door and changed into her uniform.

She believed in paying attention to people's behavior. People always left clues. And from what she gathered, Roman possessed all the makings of an aggressive and even an obsessive lover.

CHAPTER TWELVE

IT WAS SEVEN O'CLOCK in the morning when Cinnamon returned from her three-day trip to Los Angeles. Her weary feet longed for relaxation as she stepped through the lobby of her high-rise building. Before going upstairs, she checked her mailbox. Along with the usual cable and electric bills, she received a letter from Roman. In a hurry to open the pastel blue envelope, she ripped the paper inside.

December 10th

I dreamed about you last night. It was fall and we were in a cabin sitting near the fireplace. You were so beautiful, so sexy, so hot, and so sensuous.

I held your hand and touched your face. I kissed your lips and you kissed me back. I kneeled down on the floor and looked into your eyes as I rubbed your feet.

Then I lay on top of you so your heart could touch mine. I kissed your neck, I kissed your cheek, and I kissed your lips. I could taste your tongue as I inhaled the scent of your breath.

I loved you so much and when you kissed me, I knew you loved me too. A very special love, more special than I had ever known. You smiled at me.

Slowly, I caressed your breasts and stomach. I removed your panties and I liked what I could see and feel. Your scent was inviting. I kissed your thighs as you uttered a sigh of elation and when I awakened, I missed you.

Cinnamon beamed as she read every word. Rereading the last line, "And when I awakened, I missed you" sent a quiver through her.

This was indeed a sweet man.

Once inside her apartment, she showered and quickly dressed for bed. She then adjusted the volume on the stereo so it was loud enough to reach the bedroom, but at a level comfortable enough to sleep.

Rush hour traffic resounded from outside her frost-covered windows as she lay in bed with three pillows behind her head. With Roman's poem in hand, she dialed his number.

"Roman," she said.

"You're back. I knew you were in Chicago."

"How's that?"

"Because I woke up early this morning and I knew it was for a reason."

"Really?"

"I'm serious," Roman said. "I usually don't get up until seven o'clock, but I was up at five thirty this morning."

"I got your poem this morning. And I love it. Did you write it yourself?"

"Yes, I wrote it. No one could convey my feelings for you but me." He paused. "What are you wearing right now?"

"You're really into this phone sex thing, aren't you?"

"This is not phone sex, I just asked what you were wearing."

Cinnamon was silent.

"Are you going to tell me?" he asked.

"A t-shirt and socks. Not what you expected, huh?"

"I hadn't expected anything. Are the socks pulled up to your knees?"

"I don't do the knee thing, they're down at my ankles."

"What would you say to some early morning company?" he asked.

"I'm actually in bed, getting ready to take a nap."

"So am I welcome to come over?"

"What are you going to do while I'm asleep? Besides, what about work?"

"I was planning on taking the day off anyway."

"Oh, really and that's why you're up getting dressed?"

"No, seriously," he said. "I can bring some work with me. I'm going to come over, okay?"

Cinnamon didn't answer right away. Not sure it was a good idea, still she found it romantic that he desired to see her so early in the day.

"Okay," she said. "When?"

"In about thirty minutes. Can you stay awake that long?"

She laughed. "I'll see you when you get here."

Anxious about Roman's arrival, she fidgeted in bed, unable to feel at ease. She was now seeing him two, sometimes three times a week. Then it hit her. For the first time in a long time, Cinnamon had a boyfriend. And it was nice. What did concern her though was sex. It was bound to swing in that direction and she wasn't quite ready. But she would worry about that later. Right now, she would focus on the day.

For one mouth-watering minute, she imagined herself waiting for Mitchell to arrive as opposed to Roman, then realized it was wrong to continue her foolish fantasies.

It was Roman she chose. Not Mitchell.

Forty-five minutes passed before Roman arrived. He brought with him a box of Dunkin donuts and his designer briefcase.

Cinnamon put the kettle on the fire. "I only have tea and orange juice. Is that okay?"

"That's fine. You'll find that I'm not a difficult man to please."

"Have a seat," Cinnamon said as she grabbed two mugs from the kitchen cabinet.

Instead of sitting, Roman stood behind her, his body compressed against her back.

"Can I help you?" she asked as she turned to face him.

Roman wrapped his arms around her waist. "I sure hope so." He brushed his cheek against hers, then kissed her over and over again.

This was one affectionate man.

A long time passed since someone showed her this much attention and she reveled in it, remembering how much she needed it, even craved it.

Cinnamon gathered two salad plates from the cabinet and joined Roman at the kitchen table. She glowed as she reached for a glazed donut from the box.

This was what life was all about--having someone to come home to and share moments like this with.

"So what did you do about work?" she asked.

"I took a personal day. It's no big deal."

Cinnamon shook her head, smiling.

"Why are you smiling?" he asked.

"I'm just surprised, surprised that you called in just so you could come over here."

"Does that make you feel good?"

"I guess. A little." She bit into her donut.

"I brought some work for me to do while you're sleeping."

"Are you really going to work while I'm asleep?"

"I have to have something to do."

When the tea kettle reached a boil, Cinnamon prepared tea for them.

"I have something in my briefcase I think is yours," Roman said. He left the table, headed into the front room and returned with his briefcase. He then sat down and clicked open his briefcase.

Cinnamon watched him shuffle through his papers, wondering what it could be. Then she saw it. It was a Tiffany jewelry box wrapped with a red ribbon. Roman opened the box and lifted up a lovely bracelet with an attached heart-shaped charm.

"Is this yours?" he asked.

Pleasantly surprised, Cinnamon's eyes bloomed.

"I think it's yours," he said.

"Is that mine?"

"You tell me."

She reached for the bracelet, admiring it from every angle, then aligned it close to her cheek. "You have great taste."

"I chose you, didn't I?"

"Is this my Christmas present?"

"This is just a little something-something. Let's put it on and see how it looks. Shall we?"

He helped her lace it around her wrist.

"Thank you," she said as she kissed him.

"You're welcome."

"Why are you being so nice to me? What do you have planned for me?"

"I'll never tell."

"I knew it was something," she said, yawning. "Excuse me."

"Someone is getting sleepy. I've kept you up long enough."

"That's okay. I want to talk to you some more."

"We can talk after you've had your nap. Besides, I have work to do."

"Are you sure?"

"Most positively, categorically, and certainly, yes. I didn't come over here to keep you up, not today anyway."

"I am tired," she said, yawning again. "See you in a little bit."

Three hours passed and Cinnamon was still asleep in her room. Roman finished abstracting a sixty-five page deposition. After returning his papers to his briefcase, he opened the mini-blinds in the living room and cracked the window just a tad.

He then washed the few dishes in the sink and wiped down the kitchen table and counters. Glancing at his watch, he realized that in all the time Cinnamon slept, he had not once peeked in on her. Her having been asleep a long time, he missed her.

Quietly, he approached her bedroom, positioned his hand on the doorknob and slowly turned it. Once inside he tip-toed toward her bed, then marveled at her darling face, thick eyebrows and full lips. As he continued toward her, he longed to touch her, feel her, hold her and taste her.

He kneeled at her bedside, then gently caressed her face with his fingers. And he knew what he knew.

She was the one. And she was all his.

She possessed an innocence about her he adored, and he longed to always be there for her.

She was sweet.

She was pretty.

And she was his baby. It wasn't just that they shared the same beliefs, enjoyed the same books and movies that made her so special. What he admired most was her purity. She wasn't ruined by men like so many others. She was a clean slate he could mold into his own.

He longed to make love to her at that moment but he quickly suppressed the urge. With a woman like this, he wouldn't rush anything.

Cinnamon turned onto her back and mumbled some words under her breath. As she opened her eyes, he smiled at her. "I'm sorry if I woke you."

"How long have you been in here?"

"About two minutes. Are you thirsty?"

Cinnamon nodded.

Roman hurried into the kitchen for water and returned to her.

Cinnamon eased into a sitting position, her back against the brass headboard. She accepted the water from Roman. "What time is it?"

He scoped his watch. "One o'clock."

She polished off the water.

"Did you dream about me?" he asked.

"I could have." She set the glass on the night stand and moved to stand. "I'm starving."

"You don't have to get up," he said.

"I have housework to do."

Cinnamon stepped out of bed, then headed to the kitchen while Roman trailed behind.

"Were you able to get any work done?" she asked.

"Plenty."

She examined the kitchen with a warm glow. "You washed the dishes. Thank you. And put them away. You do it all, don't you?"

"The question is not what will I do for you, Cinnamon, it's what won't I do for you."

He could tell by the alarm in her eyes that his statement frightened her. But it was okay. Sometimes people needed a little fear to help them understand.

"I'm going to take a shower," she said. "I'm sure you won't have any trouble entertaining yourself."

Delighted just to know Cinnamon was in the next room, Roman crashed on the sofa, patiently waiting for her. After five minutes, he approached the bathroom door and knocked.

"Who is it?" she asked as if she didn't know.

"It's the plumber. I need to fix your shower."

She laughed, amused. "There's nothing wrong with my shower, Mr. Plumber."

"Do you need any company in there? I'm great with my hands."

"I'm sure you are, but I have everything under control in here, Mr. Plumber. But thank you."

"Are you sure? I come highly recommended."

"Yes, I'm sure. Now go sit down."

Shortly afterwards, Cinnamon appeared from the bedroom wearing her navy leggings and gold sweat shirt.

"Boy do you look sexy," Roman said, approaching her. "Good enough to eat. Literally."

"I'm going to pretend you didn't even say that."

"I'm sorry," he said. "I shouldn't have said that."

"It's okay. You're just being a man."

"Why do you keep your blinds closed?" Roman asked. "The room is much brighter and warmer with them open."

"It's more private that way." She paused and changed the subject. "Tell me about the other women you met through the paper."

"I thought you didn't want to know about that. I thought that was none of your business."

"Well . . . I changed my mind."

"I just spoke to a few women on the phone. I never went out with any of them."

They both collapsed on the sofa.

"Not even to see what they looked like?" she asked.

"They all wrote interesting ads, but it was what I found out on the phone that turned me off."

"Like what?"

"Had no interest in anything other than dating, not interested in doing anything with their lives, four and five kids. Now one or two children I can handle, but not four and five."

"But you do like children, don't you?"

"I love children, plan on having children myself."

"Me too," Cinnamon said. "Did it matter what size they were? I mean do you have a certain type you go for?"

"Beauty comes in all shapes and sizes."

Roman slithered his hand over hers. "See how compatible we are?"

"If you say so."

"I do say so." Roman paused. "I knew I'd like you, Cinnamon, when we first talked on the phone."

"Why?"

"Because I fell in love with your voice."

Cinnamon smiled, then kissed him. Roman was that special person she longed for an intimate friendship with. And she found him. But she didn't want to celebrate too soon. The relationship was still new and the future would not reveal itself until she arrived there.

Cinnamon awakened the next morning feeling refreshed after having slept nine hours.

Her spirits were in high gear. Her relationship with Roman was blossoming. She enjoyed his humor, his wit and his kindness. And in time, she trusted that her passion for Mitchell would disappear, making way for her to fully bond with Roman. And with that thought in mind, she concluded one thing. Life was good.

CHAPTER THIRTEEN

CINNAMON SPENT A LARGE part of the day organizing her closets, and mopping and buffing her hardwood floors.

Twice a year she searched through her closets and dresser drawers for clothing she failed to wear in a year's time and donated them to the Goodwill.

As she collected the trash from the waste baskets in the bedroom and bathroom, she realized she had not heard from Arri since their falling out, which meant only one thing. Arri was still pissed.

Already having apologized once, Cinnamon would have to apologize again especially since it was Cinnamon's blunt words that stirred the argument to begin with.

Hopeful a birthday card and leather-bound journal might win Arri's forgiveness, Cinnamon planned to deliver them that evening.

Cinnamon reached for the phone to call Arri. "You're not still mad at me, are you?"

"There's nothing to be mad about," Arri said.

Cinnamon sensed Arri's indifferent attitude. It was a rare day to hear Arri speak without her usual zest.

"Did you get the voice mail message I left you?" Cinnamon asked.

"Nope."

Cinnamon knew differently but it was okay. Arri was just being Arri.

"Would it be all right if I came over after work?"

"Do whatever you want."

Later that evening, Cinnamon arrived at Arri's apartment bearing Arri's favorite dishes--Pepper Steak and Shrimp Fried

Rice. Arri wore a mauve and white striped dress which made her appear even taller and leaner.

"I brought you some dinner," Cinnamon said.

Arri didn't flinch, didn't say a word.

"Aren't you going to let me in?" Cinnamon asked.

Arri stepped aside so that Cinnamon could enter. "I was just running a bath so I can only talk a minute."

Cinnamon set the Chinese food down on the coffee table, then sat down in the chair across from the futon.

Arri leaned against the wall, her arms folded.

"Will you sit down, please?" Cinnamon said. "You're making me nervous."

Arri dropped down on the cluttered futon and crossed her legs, her arms still folded.

"You're not going to make this easy, are you?" Cinnamon asked.

"I don't know what you're talking about."

"You know what I'm talking about. I know you got the message I left you."

"What message?"

"The message I left you a few days ago, saying I was sorry for what I said."

"Oh, that message. I think I did get that."

"I'm sorry I said those things about Eric and the things I said about you. I think you were right when you said I was jealous. Maybe I am a little jealous of your sexual relationship with Eric."

Desperate to win Arri over, Cinnamon outright lied, but only because it was what Arri wished to hear, even needed to hear.

"I know you're jealous," Arri said.

"Well, anyway that's what I wanted to say. I'm not going to say anything negative about your relationship with Eric anymore. Okay?"

"Good."

"Are we friends again?"

"Maybe." Arri stood and collected the Chinese food from the coffee table and lifted it to her nose. "This smells good. Thank you."

"You're welcome."

Arri was puddy in Cinnamon's hands. All Cinnamon needed to do was sugar up to Arri with a gift, baby her a little, make her feel special and presto. Cinnamon was forgiven.

Arri headed into the kitchen, packed her plate with Shrimp Fried Rice and Pepper Steak, and then returned to the living room.

"Where's Eric and Lyles?" Cinnamon asked.

"They're hiding around here somewhere. They don't like you."

"Since when?"

"Since you said all those mean things about me."

"Okay, now. I thought that was over."

"I'm just playing," Arri said as she stepped out of her dress. "You don't mind if I take this off, do you?"

"Whatever you like."

Wearing matching plum panties and bra, Arri dropped down to the floor and gobbled down her food at the coffee table.

While Arri stuffed her face, Cinnamon set Arri's gift bag containing a journal and card on the floor. "I got this for you when I was in Los Angeles."

Arri rested her jaws for a moment to check out her gift. Pulling the leather-bound journal and card from the bag, she smiled. "I love this journal. Thank you." Arri read the card and returned them both to the bag.

"Of course, I wanted to get you a purple one, but no such luck. They only had black and tan."

"This is just fine."

"Don't you have bath water running?"

"Oh, shoot, I almost forgot." Arri pushed herself off the floor and fled into the bathroom, then soon returned.

Arri quickly resumed her position on the floor and finished her food. "It's still hard for me to believe you're still seeing someone you met through the paper."

"Especially after you said the personals were for losers."

"Yeah, yeah, yeah. I didn't really mean that though," Arri said.

"All right then, prove it."

"Prove it?" Arri questioned.

"Yes, prove it. Place an ad yourself."

"Now that's not going to happen."

"I didn't think so."

"Well, it's just that I have someone already. I have Eric."

"Arri, you don't have to explain. Forget about it."

Cinnamon stretched out her arm, showing off her silver bracelet. "Check out the bracelet Roman gave to me."

"A Tiffany bracelet. Do you know how much those things cost? Close to two hundred dollars."

"Who cares? I think it's gorgeous regardless of how much it costs. And just think, I never would have met him if I had allowed Joseph to scare me off."

"That's true."

All smiles, Cinnamon continued. "He took a personal day yesterday just so he could spend the morning with me. Isn't he sweet?"

"What did you do for him?"

"Not much."

"I know that's right."

"I'll just pretend you didn't say that."

"Are you going to have sex with him?"

"Eventually I will."

"No, you're not."

"I am too," Cinnamon declared.

"Does he talk about sex much?"

"Not really. He did send me this erotic poem though."

"He writes poetry?"

"And he's working on a novel. So anyway, back to you. What are you planning this weekend for your birthday?"

"Actually, Eric and I are going shopping tomorrow."

"Eric is taking you shopping? That's a first."

"He's going to buy me something for my birthday with his first check in January."

"I thought you said you were going shopping tomorrow."

"We are. I'm going to get him a new coat because the one he's wearing now has had it."

Cinnamon stared at Arri, waiting for Arri's words to stick. "Wait, let me get this straight. You're taking him shopping and it's your birthday?"

"No, I'm just helping him out. He's taking me shopping for my birthday, just not tomorrow."

Cinnamon nodded like she understood, knowing she didn't. But not wishing to unsettle Arri again, she dropped the subject.

Arri rose to her feet and carried her plate into the kitchen. When she returned, she said, "I'm going to take my bath now. You don't mind, do you?"

"I'm leaving anyway."

"No, don't go. I want to talk to you. I haven't talked to you in a few days. You can read some of my trashy magazines or something. I won't be long."

Ten minutes passed.

Cinnamon sat at Arri's butcher block kitchen table, drinking tea while she thumbed through the pages of *Star* magazine.

From the bathroom, Arri called out. "Cinnamon, can you come in here?"

Cinnamon approached the bathroom and stood at the door. "What's up?"

Enwrapped in bubbles, Arri relaxed in the tub. "Sit down. I want to tell you something funny."

Cinnamon closed the toilet lid and took a seat.

"Remember that manager at my office I told you about?" Arri asked.

"The one you call Matt?"

"Yeah him," Arri said as she soaped her arms and shoulders. "I took him a letter to sign the other day, and I found myself looking at his pants, actually the center of his pants."

Cinnamon threw her head back and laughed.

"Only for a second though," Arri said. "I didn't want him to know what I was doing."

"You're a funny woman."

"And I know you're going to think this is so gross, but the other day when Matt was explaining this presentation to me, I was looking at his finger as he pointed to a particular paragraph on the page, right. And as I looked at his finger, I wondered. . . ." Arri couldn't stop giggling. "Well, let me say this first. You know how a man has to pull his thing out when he goes to the bathroom?"

"Must we go there?"

"Well, I have to tell you this first so you'll understand."

"Okay, Arri. Continue."

"You know how a man has to pull his thing out when he goes to pee?"

"Yes, Arri."

"Well. As I looked at his finger, I wondered if that was the finger he used when he touched his thing."

Cinnamon's eyes widened, shocked to the third degree. "Oh . . . That is so gross. Where do you get these thoughts?"

Arri laughed out loud. "I told you you would think it was gross, but I think about stuff like that. Think about it though, a man touches his thing every time he goes to the bathroom, right?"

"And?"

"And that was probably the finger that touched it. He's right-handed."

"So what are you saying?" Cinnamon asked.

"I'm not saying anything, just that the thought of it excited me." Arri wrung out her face towel and wiped her face.

"You are probably the only person in this world who has thoughts like that."

"No, I'm not. Other people are just afraid to say it."

"You have it bad for this guy, don't you," Cinnamon asked.

"I think I do. And his voice." Arri sighed. "Oooooooooooooh. I love the sound of his voice. It's subdued. And soft." Arri sailed down into the tub, leaving only her head and knees above water. "Anyway, enough about me and my over-sexed imagination. I've been wanting to tell you something for a while."

"What?" Cinnamon asked.

"Remember when you spent the night with me about a month ago?"

"I remember."

"Well, that night when you were asleep, I guess you were asleep, you wrapped your legs around me."

"I wrapped my legs around you?"

"Yes, while you were asleep. I'm serious. I'm not making this up."

"No, I didn't."

"I didn't say anything because it was no big deal. I just thought I should tell you though."

"What did you do when I supposedly did this?"

"I moved away a little, but you just moved right with me."

"Maybe I put one leg on top of yours unconsciously or something like that."

"No, Cinnamon. Both legs and with a grip."

"Well, even if I did. So what."

"It didn't bother me or anything. I just wanted to tell you. I figured you were unaware of it."

Cinnamon nibbled on her fingernails, wondering if any truth existed in Arri's words.

"Are you trying to say it meant something?" Cinnamon asked.

"I don't know. Maybe you're just a little horny. It has been awhile."

"I'm going to wait for you in the living room," Cinnamon said before her swift exit.

In the living room, Cinnamon stood at the window, staring out at the slush covered walks, thinking only of Arri's accusation when suddenly one of Arri's cats leaped onto the futon, startling Cinnamon to a near heart attack.

When Cinnamon heard Arri opening the bathroom door, she quickly hurled herself onto the futon and grabbed *Soap Opera Digest* from the floor. Arri's cat sat snug beside her.

Arri entered wearing a knee-length bathrobe and sat in the chair across from Cinnamon. She unclasped her ponytail ring and her brown hair splashed against her shoulders. "You and Lyles look pretty friendly."

Cinnamon studied the magazine, pretending not to hear Arri.

"Cinnamon, don't let what I said upset you. I'm sure it didn't mean anything."

"I'm not upset."

"Since when do you read *Soap Opera Digest*? You hate soap operas."

"I was just browsing through it."

"The way you're all crouched down into that magazine, someone might think you were studying for a test."

Cinnamon set the magazine on the table and stood up. "I'm going to go on home."

"I should never have told you that."

"Girl, I'm not thinking about that. You're the one who keeps bringing it up."

The more Cinnamon tried to convince Arri she wasn't upset, the more upset she became.

"I think you are," Arri said. "You just don't want me to know it. I know you, Cinnamon. I've known you for a long, long time. I know how secretive you can be."

"Well, I don't care what you think."

"Oh, it's like that, huh?"

"It's like nothing." Cinnamon headed toward the door, slipping into her coat.

"You want me to come with you?" Arri asked.

Cinnamon plastered a fake smile on her face. "Don't be silly. You just got out of the tub. I'm fine."

Back at Cinnamon's apartment, still wearing her coat, she stood with her back against the front door, staring at the floor. Over and over, Arri's accusations rang in her head. She just felt so embarrassed about the whole thing. And it bothered her. A lot.

A cup of tea later, she attempted to ease her unsettling emotions by calling Roman. When she reached for the phone, she saw her message light blinking.

It was a message from Arri, which could not have come at a more perfect time.

Arri recited her message to the Oscar Mayer tune. "My best friend has a first name. It's C-i-n-n-a-m-o-n. My best friend has a second name, it's B-r-o-w-n. Oh, I love her so much, yes, I do. Why? Because she's so sweet to me. Because Cinnamon Brown is my very best friend in the world."

Arri's message brought a smile to Cinnamon's face and helped her to realize it really was no big deal if what Arri alleged was true or not. Surely Arri didn't think anything of it.

After rewinding the tape, Cinnamon called Roman.

"Hey you," Roman said. "I was just about to call you. Why don't you come over? I'll pick you up."

"Tonight?"

"Yes, tonight. Is tonight not good?"

"I don't know."

"You don't know if tonight is good or you don't know if you want to?"

"It's too late," she said.

"Eight o'clock is not late. Come on, you've never been over here."

"Roman, I don't want to come to your apartment. It's too soon."

Abruptly, Roman altered the subject as if not to create a stir. "You like the bracelet I gave to you?"

Slightly irritated, she switched the phone to the other ear. "Of course, I do. I told you I did."

"Do I detect an attitude?"

"I'm sorry. I didn't mean to snap at you. I just have a couple of things on my mind."

"Anything you want to talk about?"

"No, not really. So how are you?"

"I'm great, would be even better if I could see you, but I'm not going to pressure you. You can visit me whenever you're ready."

"Thank you."

"Are we still on for tomorrow?" he asked.

"Yes, we are."

Her conversation with Roman failed to relieve her stress as she hoped. While on the phone with him, she realized she had nothing to say. Though she appreciated him, his eagerness to lure her to his apartment was a definite sign of things to come. And as much as she enjoyed his company, she possessed no desire to be compressed to his nakedness.

Ten minutes after she hung up from Roman, the phone rang. It was Noel.

"Hey, stranger," Noel said.

Right away, his voice made her smile and boosted her spirit.

He exposed her to a whole different world, and she felt lucky to know him.

"I haven't heard from you," Noel said. "Have you forgotten about me?"

"Not at all. I'm glad you called."

"So my timing is good?"

She picked at the fingernail polish on her nails. "I met someone, Noel."

"Is he cute?"

"Why?"

"He just might be my type."

"Don't even try it," she said playfully.

"What happened to the married man?"

"He's history, I told you."

"Just checking."

Already she felt her dark mood fading.

"You want to meet for coffee tomorrow?" he asked.

"I have plans tomorrow. Roman's coming over after work."

"I want to see you, Cinnamon. I can meet you tomorrow afternoon way before your friend comes over. Or shall I say boyfriend?"

"What time?"

"One o'clock, at the same place we met. It'll be like an anniversary date."

Noel was an original. In fact, it was because of Noel that she indirectly met Mitchell.

CHAPTER FOURTEEN

Slush overlaid Cinnamon's ankle boots as she treaded through the melting snow.

En route to Café Classico to meet Noel, Arri's accusations crept to mind again. That topped with Roman's attempt to entice her to his apartment concluded what she has known all along. Life was a series of ups and downs. Her world wasn't as enlivened as usual and the grey sky dulled her mood even more. Even the two barking German Shepherds annoyed her as she bypassed them, leading her to believe she might have been better off staying at home.

Arriving at Café Classico, Noel was nowhere in sight.

Cinnamon took a seat near the door so as to locate him upon his arrival. *New City* newspaper lay on the table just underneath her fingertips.

Ten minutes late, Noel strolled through the door. His leather jacket collar was pulled up to his neck, and his wavy black hair was neatly slicked back. "Sorry I'm late."

Happy to see him, her smile broadened. "It's about time."

"Let's get something to drink," Noel said as he led Cinnamon toward the counter.

After ordering hot chocolate, they convened at a table in the back.

To Cinnamon's delight, the milk chocolate aroma from the hot chocolate eased the negative spirits brought on by the desolate day.

Noel straddled the chair and faced Cinnamon. "You're looking good as ever."

"I can say the same thing about you," Cinnamon said. "I have never seen a man with such perfect skin, not one mark."

"Thank you." He threw his head back as if showing off. "I'm quite proud of it myself."

She noticed the diamond earring in his ear. "You're wearing a different earring. Nice."

"It was a gift."

"Oh? From whom?"

"A friend."

She sipped her steaming hot chocolate, wanting to gulp it down because of its luscious flavor. "You seem to have a lot of time on your hands," she said. "What days do you actually work?"

"It varies. Sometimes I'm working every day non-stop and then sometimes weeks go by without anything."

"I assume you work on an on-call basis. Does that work for you? I mean does it work financially? And what about that new Intrepid you drive?"

"Well, the car isn't mine, it's Aaron's, and he takes care of most of the bills."

"Why would he do that?"

"Because I have it like that. And we're friends."

"I have friends too, but they don't pay my bills, though I wish they would."

"We're close like that."

She suspected Aaron might be more than a friend, but she didn't want to assume anything. "What do you do for Aaron?"

Noel didn't answer right away, then said, "I spank him."

Having just ingested her hot chocolate, Cinnamon coughed, causing the hot chocolate to drool from her mouth. Quickly, she grabbed a napkin and dabbed her mouth and table.

"Excuse me. What did you say? You spank him?"

"I spank him. You heard me."

In a daze, perverted illusions raced through Cinnamon's mind. Of all the weird things she heard, that one took the medal. "Why? Why would you spank him?"

"Because that's what he likes."

Cinnamon blew out a long breath and scratched her head. "Wouldn't he rather have sex?"

"Guess not."

"I don't believe I'm hearing this." She laughed. "You spank him?"

"You don't believe me?"

"I guess I have to. I don't think anyone would make up a story like that." She leaned toward him and lowered her voice. "What do you spank him with?"

"A lot of things. Paddle, leather switch, belt, shoe, a lot of stuff."

For a half minute, low-key shrieks wailed from Cinnamon's uncontrollable laughter. With her hand on her stomach, she thought she might pass out before she stopped.

"Am I that funny?" he asked.

"Never have I heard anything like this."

"This is really amusing to you, isn't it?"

"I just don't believe you're telling me this. How old is this guy?"

"Forty-nine."

"Forty-nine? I take it he's gay."

"I don't know."

"You don't know? How can you not know?"

"I never asked. Okay, yeah, he's gay."

She moved her hot chocolate to the side and rested her arms on the table. "Okay, Noel, enough with the jokes. What's really going on with you and Aaron?"

"I told you. He takes care of me and I spank him."

Trying very hard to compose herself, she looked away for a moment then returned her focus to him. "I'm sorry for my reaction. It's just I have never heard anything . . ."

"Let's talk about this new man in your life. Where did you meet him?"

Cinnamon blew out a short breath. "Through the personals."

"Really. I think that is so cool."

"That's very open-minded of you," she said.

"Why shouldn't I be? It's a great way to meet people. So is he your boyfriend?"

"I guess you could say that. We do see a lot of each other."

"What makes him so much better than me?" Noel asked.

"Didn't we go through this? We're friends."

"You and him or you and me?"

"Us. You and me. Noel and Cinnamon. Besides you have enough on your plate with your Sugar Daddy taking care of you anyway. What do you care?"

Noel seemed to meditate on her words before responding. "Does he look better than I do?"

"Is this the reason you invited me out? To drill me?"

"No, but I do like the way you said that."

"Oh, please, don't even try it."

"I just want to understand why you wouldn't have a relationship with me, but you'll have one with this guy."

"Didn't we discuss this already?"

"No, we didn't. You avoided talking about it."

Cinnamon laughed. Noel was a bigger baby than Art. "I told you I wouldn't feel comfortable involved with a bi-person."

"What? A bi-person?"

"You know what I mean."

"It's okay to say bisexual, Cinnamon. It's not a vulgar word."

"Whatever."

"It's better than dating a married man."

"I'm not dating a married man. That is so over." Cinnamon paused. "Jesus!"

"You know what, you're right," Noel said. "I'm sorry. I know you're not dating a married man. I just feel a little rejected, that's all."

"Rejected by whom?"

"By you."

"By me? Because I'm dating this other guy?"

"Well, I did meet you first."

Cinnamon slid her hand across the table and glided it on top of Noel's hand. "I'm flattered that you wanted something special with me. I really am."

"Flattered enough to do something about it?" Noel asked, smiling.

"No. But let's just keep things the way they are. We have a great friendship. Now why go and ruin that?"

Cinnamon couldn't understand why Noel was so dead set on pursuing a relationship with her when he was swinging from both sides of the fence. But more importantly, she hoped this drawn out issue was once and for all finally resolved.

After Cinnamon's meeting with Noel, she lost her enthusiasm to see Roman and was inclined to cancel, but decided to play it through anyhow.

Maybe a hot shower would relax her and rescue her from her dull mood.

After a quick shower, she slipped into her tights and a long t-shirt.

At six o'clock, a long box wrapped with a pink ribbon and small decorative gift bag which read Merry Christmas rested in Roman's hand as he entered Cinnamon's apartment.

"Presents already," Cinnamon said, her face glowing.

He handed the box and the gift bag to her.

"Thank you."

"You'll get your other present in January."

"What other present?"

"You'll see."

Cinnamon headed into the living room and set the gift bag down on the sofa. Roman followed her and removed his coat.

She opened the box and inside lay six hot red tulips. "These are gorgeous, just like the others."

"There's a card inside," he said.

She pulled out the tangerine orange card which read, *'There's a special place within my heart that only you can fill.'*

"That's so sweet." She quickly turned to him and kissed his lips. "Thank you again."

"You're welcome again."

She set the tulips down on the table, anxious to see inside the gift bag. "What's in the bag?"

"I don't know. They were just giving them away on the street."

She laughed, then stuck her hand into the bag and pulled out silk pajamas, imprinted with burgundy leaves. Though she hated anything print or flowery, she graciously accepted his gift, then placed the pajamas back into the bag.

"That was very sweet, Roman. Now I feel guilty. I didn't get anything for you."

"Don't worry about it."

Cinnamon slouched down on the sofa and Roman joined her, scooting very close. He wrapped his arm around her and stroked her back.

For minutes, they sat next to each other not exchanging words. Then out of nowhere, she watched him fling his glasses from his face and set them on the table. He leaned back and pulled her on top of him, so they were face to face. "I've been thinking about you all day," he said, then kissed her, consuming her mouth with his tongue.

Finally, the time had come. He would probably try to undress her, and she wasn't exactly sure what she would do if he did.

Their lips parted and she opened her eyes. Roman continued to knead her neck with his mouth, piercing her skin between his teeth. Tremors rolled through her and she remembered what it was like to make love. But she didn't want to remember. Not yet anyway. He pulled her closer. And as she soaked up his warm breath, she felt numb, not sure if she were inclined or reluctant to continue with him. During this quiet moment, she heard fading police sirens outside her window, all the while Roman's breathing growing slower and deeper.

"I want to make love to you, Cinnamon."

Cinnamon swallowed hard and said nothing. She liked him a lot but not that way, her body failing to yearn for him as it should.

"Cinnamon? Did you hear me?"

Silence. Silence. And more silence.

He peered into her eyes. "Don't you want to make love to me?"

She tried to pull away from him, but he resisted. "I can't, Roman. Not now."

"Why not?"

"I just can't. Will you let me up?"

"No, I don't want you to get up. I want to make love to you."

"Let me up, Roman," she pleaded, ignoring his request.

"No," he said overpowering her with kisses.

Abruptly, with all her strength, she freed herself from his grasp and stood up. "Do you want something to drink?" she asked as if nothing happened.

"No, I don't want something to drink."

His tone intimidated her and she swallowed the saliva in her throat. She could only imagine the ideas that lurked in his mind.

"What's wrong?" he asked.

"Nothing is wrong."

"Why are you acting like this then?"

"I'm just thirsty."

She scurried into the kitchen and returned with two bottled waters. She handed one to Roman.

"I told you I didn't want any water." He stared at her, as if studying her.

"Why are you staring at me like that?" she asked.

"I'm trying to figure you out."

She twisted off the cap, gulped down the water, then turned on the stereo.

"Cinnamon, will you turn the music off? I would like to talk to you if you could turn off this act of yours if only for a moment."

"I'll turn it down low."

Before she could lower the volume, he yelled. "Cinnamon, turn it off."

She cringed at his thunderous voice. "You don't have to get ugly about it. My goodness."

"I'm sorry. I shouldn't have raised my voice. Will you turn the music off and sit down so I can talk to you? Please."

Though she knew she was driving him bonkers, she couldn't help it. She wasn't ready to graduate to a physical relationship with him just yet and this was her way of expressing it. She sat beside him and gulped down the rest of her water, her eyes deflecting in every direction but Roman's.

"Look at me, Cinnamon."

She turned to face him.

"Why are you acting like this?"

"Acting like what?"

"Cinnamon. You're twenty-nine years old. You know what I'm talking about. It's as if you're running from me. Are you running from me?"

She didn't have an answer for him.

"Are you going to answer me?"

"I don't have any answers, Roman, and I'm sorry."

"I want to make love to you and you know that. There's only so far we can go with conversation."

"I happen to like things the way they are."

"So do I, but that's no reason not to go forward."

"I still think it's too soon."

"Then why did you let things go as far as they did? Aren't you attracted to me?"

She set the empty water bottle on the table. "I never said I wasn't attracted to you."

"It's a secret to me."

"What is?"

"You, Cinnamon. You." He stood and straightened his shirt and pants. "I should probably get going."

"You don't have to go. Why don't you stay awhile? We can talk some more."

"I don't want to talk," he said as he moved toward the hall closet, "unless you have something specific you want to say."

Riddled with sadness, she listened but did not speak.

"I'm glad you liked your presents," he said as he buttoned his coat. "But I'm going to go now."

The disappointment in his voice oppressed her heart even more.

"Goodnight, Cinnamon."

As soon as the door closed, her eyes welled up with tears. She'd hurt him and she'd hurt him bad.

Into her bedroom she hurried, wiping her tears along the way. Reaching for the phone to call Arri, her teary eyes blurred her vision so much she could barely see the numbers on the dial.

"Hey, it's me," Cinnamon said with a sniffle.

"Do you have a cold?" Arri asked. "Or are you crying?"

"I'm not crying."

"Are you sure?"

Cinnamon sniffled again, making it impossible to hide her disposition. "Roman is upset with me."

"What happened?" Arri asked in a warm voice.

"I think he wanted to make love to me."

"You think he wanted to?"

"I know he wanted to. And I really upset him when I wouldn't. And he left."

"That's not what you wanted though, is it?"

"I like things the way they are." Cinnamon grabbed a tissue from her night stand. "Everything was going fine in our relationship."

"He just wants to advance the relationship."

"I suppose."

"He's a man, Cinnamon. He wants a physical relationship like everyone else. You really can't blame him."

"Maybe I just need more time." Cinnamon lay back on the bed and stared at the ceiling. "I really like Roman."

"I know you do, but you know what I think? I think your heart is not into Roman because you still have your eye on Mitchell."

"I thought about that too." Cinnamon paused. "What should I do then?"

"I don't know what to tell you. You're going to have to figure this one out for yourself."

Cinnamon felt better after hanging up. But she still needed to make a decision.

What was she to do about Roman? And Mitchell?

She stared at the ceiling, hoping the answers would come to her. Though no ideas flourished, her blue mood continued to fade with each passing breath.

The loud television from the apartment next to hers miffed her. She closed her eyes and envisioned Roman's naked body pancaked against hers, and she frowned. She felt his weight, heard his voice, and pictured his body and she grimaced. She and Roman shared a special relationship, but it lacked something. Something she couldn't quite put her finger on.

Without delay, she erased the visions of Roman from her mind and daydreamed about Mitchell. And oh, what a treat it was. She replayed the memories of when they first met, how kind, sweet and adorable Mitchell was.

Several weeks passed since she first met Mitchell and though she only met him once, she dreamed of him often.

He would forever occupy a sacred place in her heart.

CHAPTER FIFTEEN

JANUARY 2ND. The holidays were over.

Cinnamon met with her dentist of twenty years for her six-month cleaning appointment, usually booking it months in advance.

After leaving Dr. Sherie Criswell's office, located in the Water Tower Place, Cinnamon made a stop at Marshall Field's, her store of choice.

In a prosperous mood, she purchased a pair of silver hoop earrings, Fashion Fair press power and a new shade of Urban Ice lipstick.

Returning home, she gathered her jeans and dark shirts from the hamper and loaded them into the laundry bag. Usually, she chose to do her wash in the evening, electing to reserve her daytime hours for activities outside her apartment but today decided otherwise, wanting to be done with it.

When the doorbell rang, she suspected it might be Arri.

"I was just about to go downstairs and do the laundry," Cinnamon said.

"I'll go with you."

To the basement of Cinnamon's building, she and Arri fled, Cinnamon toting her laundry bag, Tide detergent and fabric softener.

After removing her coat, Arri hopped up onto the washer while Cinnamon dumped her clothes into the machine.

"I guess Eric has you all to himself now," Cinnamon said as she inserted four quarters in the slot.

"Girl, that is so over. I met somebody else."

"What happened to Eric? I thought you were back together."

"We were for a while until he acted like an ass."

"But he's always been an ass."

"Well, until he acted like an even bigger one," Arri said before inhaling a long breath. "That mother sucker showed up at my apartment with coochie on his breath."

Flabbergasted, Cinnamon froze, literally froze, her mouth hanging open. "No way. Did he really?"

"I only wish I was making this up."

"Not even Eric would do that. You are making this up, right?"

"I wish I could be so creative."

"What happened?" Cinnamon asked.

"He stopped by unexpectedly as usual."

"Yeah?"

"I hadn't seen him for a few days. Anyway, he was watching a Bulls' game and when the commercial came on, he told me he hadn't kissed me all evening. I didn't think anything of it. So I gave him a quick kiss on the lips and I swear to God, I smelled coochie on his breath."

Cinnamon burst into a roaring laugh. Almost a minute would pass before she composed herself. "What did you say to him?" Cinnamon asked.

"I told him I smelled pussy on his breath."

"And what did he say?"

"He denied it, of course, said he hadn't brushed his teeth. At that point, I was through. That was it for me."

"Even for Eric that's hard to believe and you know I don't have anything good to say about him."

"And you know he'll go to his grave denying it, don't you," Arri said.

"Let me see if I have this straight. He was with some woman and wasn't smart enough to brush his teeth, chew some gum or something?"

"Nope."

"That's so gross. Isn't that gross? What was he thinking?"

"That's just it," Arri said as she stepped out of her boots and lifted her feet upon the washer. "He wasn't thinking. Anyway, I don't ever want to see him again."

"Never?"

"I said never."

"Never is a long time, Arri."

Arri thought about it and then said, "Okay, well, not for a while anyway. I just hope that whoever that woman was, he messes up her life the way he messed up mine."

"Eric hasn't messed up your life," Cinnamon said as she hoisted her body up on the washer next to Arri.

"Oh, yes he has. I know I'm crazy about him and all that, but enough is more than enough. What is it with men and the truth anyway? They seem to be so far from it. Like this guy I met, Tony. Nice looking guy, nice body, intelligent, but a liar. Trying to impress."

"What do you mean?"

"I met him at the DMV when I had my drivers' license renewed, right? He's a little short for me but he's muscular though, big arms like I like."

"Will you get to the point please?"

"He told me he was a manager at Boston Market, right?"

"Yeah?"

"Girl, I went to his job. He's a cashier."

Cinnamon laughed. "Did he see you?"

"No, but it doesn't matter anyway. He'll only lie about it."

"Maybe he was helping out that day."

"Don't defend him, Cinnamon. Managers and cashiers wear different uniforms as if working as a manager at any fast food restaurant is impressive anyway."

"Actually, it is a little better than working as a cashier," Cinnamon said.

"I guess. But the way I see it, if you're going to lie and try to impress me, you would do a lot better than saying you were a manager at a fast food shack."

"I would have thought that after your little incident with Eric that you'd be. . . kind of in the dumps, but you seem like you're doing okay."

"What Eric did was downright disgusting," Arri said.

"You're not going to get an argument from me. So did you have sex with this guy?"

"Huh?"

"You heard me."

"Yeah. I slept with him. I know I'm a tramp, but you should see this guy. He's really cute."

"Aren't they all?"

"No, they are not. Anyhow, Eric has me completely dumbstruck right about now after the way he played me."

"You'll forgive him."

"No, I won't. If it wasn't for the sex, I wouldn't even have a man in my life."

"I wouldn't say all of that."

"I would," Arri said, then paused. "And did I tell you Eric wouldn't even leave that night? I tried to put him out but he wouldn't leave."

"You mean you didn't want him to leave."

"No, he wouldn't go. I asked him to leave but instead he just got into my bed and went to sleep."

"Where did you sleep?"

"I didn't sleep with him. And for the record, I have no intention of seeing him again after that stunt."

Cinnamon found it hard to believe that Arri would never again see Eric. Though she hoped this was the end of the Eric and Arri saga, she suspected it wasn't.

An hour later, still in the laundry room, Arri helped Cinnamon fold the clothes from the dryer.

"I still have the hots for that manager at work," Arri said. "I have this fantasy that I go into his office, knock him down and just take him."

Cinnamon laughed. "You'd probably do it too."

"You think I wouldn't?"

"I know you would. You have just the right amount of nerve to pull it off."

"As a matter of fact, he loaned me one of his novels."

"How did that come about?"

"On his way out one evening, I noticed a novel he was reading and I asked him about it, and if I could borrow it when he was done."

"But you only read romance and trashy magazine stuff."

"I know that. And you know that, but he doesn't know that. I really just wanted to see if he would loan it to me."

"Are you going to read it?"

"I tried to. It bored the hell out of me."

"What if he asks you about it when you return it, are you going to lie?"

"No. I'll just tell him I couldn't get into it. I think I have it here in my bag." Arri dug into her bag and pulled out a five-hundred page novel, *The Chief of Police*. She turned it over, rubbed her fingers across the back. "His hands were once where mine are right now."

"Oh, stop. Please. You couldn't possibly be that excited about a book that he once held in his hand."

"I like him," Arri said with conviction.

"What is it about this man that has you on such a high?"

"I think it's because he's white and I just love white men. And then, he has the most darling green eyes. He's not very tall, though, but I can tell he has a big one."

Cinnamon smirked, peering into Arri's eyes. "What?"

"You heard me."

"I thought you said size didn't matter."

"It doesn't. I'm just making an observation."

"You say that, but you don't mean it. You want him, don't you?"

"I do. I do. I do. I do." Arri blew a short breath from her mouth. "I'm attracted to his spirit."

"I say go for it," Cinnamon said.

"What can I do? I can't ask him out."

"No. You can't do that," Cinnamon said sarcastically

The glow on Arri's face suddenly turned to gloom. "If he hasn't asked me out by now, he probably never will."

"Not necessarily."

Cinnamon and Arri finished the folding, gathered their things and headed upstairs.

"Did I tell you Roman paid my rent for this month?" Cinnamon asked. "It was part of my Christmas present."

"You know what that means, don't you?"

"What does it mean?"

"It means you have to give it up."

"No, it doesn't. Besides, I wouldn't accept it."

"You never give money back, Cinnamon."

"Oh, yes you do if you don't want the strings attached. I'm not going to be intimidated into having sex with him. He's either going to wait or walk."

"You haven't been to his apartment yet, have you?"

"No way. You know there's an unwritten rule that says if you go to a man's apartment, you're consenting to sex."

"There is no such rule. You can visit a man and not have sex with him."

"I know you don't have to have sex, but he thinks it will happen. And I'm not going over there until I'm good and ready."

Comfortably wearing a sweat suit, Cinnamon stood at her kitchen counter preparing a spaghetti dinner. Usually, she could make it through the week on cereal, sandwiches, hotdogs and tuna fish, but this afternoon she was feeling good and chose to take advantage of her sunny disposition.

While boiling water for the spaghetti, she cut up onions and green peppers, then seasoned the green peas while they simmered on the stove.

When the phone rang, she quickly snatched the receiver from the wall.

"What are you doing?" Roman asked.

"Cooking."

Two weeks passed since he contacted her and she was surprised and delighted to hear his voice, especially considering their sexual relationship still hung in the balance.

"What are you cooking?"

"Spaghetti."

"So does that ruin my plans to bring pizza over after work?"

Preferring pizza over spaghetti any day, she said, "No, not at all."

"Does that mean I'm welcome to come over?"

"That's what it means and just in case you were wondering what I'm wearing, I'm not telling you."

"I guess I'll have to wait until I see you then, huh?"

"So it would seem."

"I'll see you after five."

With Roman bringing over pizza, Cinnamon stashed her spaghetti dinner into the refrigerator, reserving it for another day.

The butterflies flew rampant inside her stomach when she ended her call, wiping out her appetite all together. As much as she wished to see Roman, she was still reluctant to advance the relationship. She just hoped this visit would prove less stressful than his last one.

Bearing a Giordano's sausage and green pepper pizza and a bottle of white wine, Roman arrived at Cinnamon's apartment at a little after five o'clock.

At the kitchen table, they dined underneath the luminous track lighting.

Cinnamon bit into her pizza, careful not to burn her tongue. "I thought you were mad at me, Roman."

"I admit I was a little disappointed, but it was unfair of me to put pressure on you. Am I forgiven?"

"No, you're not."

"I'm not?"

Smiling, she swallowed the pizza in her mouth. "Of course, you're forgiven."

Twelve minutes later, Roman dumped his leftover pizza crust into the garbage. "I'll take care of the dishes."

"No, that's okay," Cinnamon said. "You don't have to do that."

"I don't mind."

"You're so helpful, Roman."

"I'm glad you think so."

Cinnamon was about to head into the front room and turn on some music when Roman stopped her. "Don't leave. Stay in here and talk to me."

He rolled up his sleeves and prepared the dishwater.

Still wearing her sweat suit, she dropped down into the chair. "I know what I wanted to ask you, Roman."

"Yes, I'll marry you."

"Very funny. Are you planning to go to law school?"

"I doubt it. Why? You have a thing for lawyers?"

"No, nothing like that, just curious. Four years of law school is a long time."

"Not really, but law school is only three years."

"I thought it was four years like medical school."

"No, just three. Now it's my turn to ask you something. Did you ever meet anyone else from your personal ad?"

"You always ask me about that."

"Well . . ."

"No, Roman. I didn't meet anyone else."

"May I ask why? I'm not suggesting that you should have. I just want to know."

"After I met you, I wasn't interested in meeting anyone else."

He cleared his throat as if to make a statement. "That makes me feel good."

Once Roman finished drying the dishes and putting them away, he filled two champagne glasses with white wine. He and Cinnamon then retired to the front room and cozied up on the sectional sofa. The eloquent sounds of Pat Metheny resounded from the stereo while a brisk breeze from the opened window flowed through.

"Let's make a toast," Roman said. "Shall we?"

"We shall," she said as she held up her glass. "What should we drink to?"

"To possibilities."

"To possibilities," Cinnamon said.

Just a shimmer of light shined through from the street lights as they clacked their glasses.

Cinnamon guzzled down her wine like a pro. "This is good."

"You don't play around, do you?"

"Not when it comes to good wine."

Roman set his glass on the table, then sensuously massaged her arm. . . up and down and round and round.

Anticipation rocketed through her, knowing what was soon to follow.

Being in his presence sometimes brought back memories of her teenage years when she was scared and unsure of herself.

As Roman continued to knead her arms ever so sweetly, she said, "That feels nice."

"You like that?"

"I do."

"Cinnamon?" he whispered.

"Hum?" she responded calmly, preparing herself for the sex question.

"I have a friend who's interested in applying with the airlines. Do you have the address and name of the person he would send his resume to?"

Her eye lids opened, relief sweeping through her. "Is that what you wanted to ask me?"

"That's all."

"I'll get it for you before you leave."

"Could you get it now?"

"I guess I can. Since you're such a nice guy and all."

Cinnamon forced herself to move from her snug position on the sofa and moseyed into the bedroom.

On her top closet shelf lay a manilla envelope where she kept important papers.

After reaching for it, she lounged on the perfectly-made bed and shuffled through the envelope in search of the Human Resources Address for ATA.

Only a minute passed before she glanced up and saw Roman standing in the doorway, already having removed his glasses.

She watched him. And he watched her.

"Hi," he said.

"What are you doing in here?"

"I wanted to see what your bedroom looked like."

"But you've already seen my bedroom, more than once."

"That's right, I have, haven't I? Did you find the address?"

"I did. I'll write it down for you."

As she scribbled down the address, he approached her and buckled down next to her.

After she handed him the folded piece of paper, he gently placed it on the edge of the bed. "Thank you," he said, then seized the folder from her lap and laid it on the bed as well.

With lust in his eyes, she watched him lift her fingers to his mouth, kissing and sucking each one slowly and methodically.

Engrossed in the moment, she didn't utter a word.

Suddenly, he guided her into a standing position, desire gaping from his eyes in rare form. As his face steered closer to hers, raspy breaths escaped from his mouth, intensifying with each exhale.

Wrapping his arms firmly around her waist, his lips coupled with hers, his tongue probed inside her mouth, slowly and then at top speed.

He gently squeezed her fingers together, and her heart raced with apprehension. She being the timid person she was, she said nothing and did nothing.

As he continued to search inside her mouth with his tongue, his hot breath channeled a rush up her spine. Only seconds elapsed with a break for air.

Standing perfectly still with her hands at her sides, playing the passive role, she hoped he would say something. But he said nothing. Instead, he mangled his body to hers, just enough to nudge her backwards onto the bed. Upon lowering his body onto hers, he knocked the manilla folder to the floor, scattering everything inside.

His belt buckle poked at her hip as his moistened lips kissed hers again, again, and again.

How would she talk her way out of it this time?

CHAPTER SIXTEEN

PELVIS TO PELVIS AND cheek to cheek, Roman mounted his body on top of Cinnamon's. As she lay pinned underneath his weight, the beaming ceiling light cast down on her face. His hot breath heaved against her ear as perspiration crinkles trailed down her forehead.

Hesitant to say anything, she shifted her body away from him.

"I've wanted to make love to you for so long," Roman said.

"Roman? I don't think we should."

He sidestepped her comment and kissed her, his tongue pulsating deep inside her mouth. "Let me make love to you, Cinnamon. Please baby."

Before Cinnamon could respond, he hoisted her arms above her head, her hands connecting with the cold brass headboard.

Immediately returning her hands to her sides, she said, "I'm not ready to make love, Roman."

He touched her face, exploring her lips with his finger. "I'm ready. I am so ready. I love you."

"But I can't. Not yet."

"You love me, don't you?" he asked.

Silence. Silence. And more silence.

"Do you love me?" he questioned.

Evading his question, she said, "I want to get up."

"Will you answer my question first?"

"I don't know if I love you, Roman. I just don't know."

"I think you do." He scaled his cheek against her mouth. "I'm aching for you, Sweetheart."

She struggled to break free of his clutches, but Roman resisted for all of fifteen seconds before releasing her.

Filled with conflicting emotions, Cinnamon climbed off the bed and pulled down her sweat shirt. "You had me a little scared there for a minute. I wasn't sure what you were going to do."

He arched his body forward. "I scared you? What exactly scared you, Cinnamon?"

"You. You scared me."

"Well you know something? You scared me because I don't know what's going on in that brain of yours. Why should me wanting to make love to you scare you?" His explosive tone alarmed her. "Why do you do this?" he asked. "Why do you play this game?"

"I'm not playing any game," she said as she collected the papers from the floor.

"You're a tease, Cinnamon, a genuine board-certified tease."

"That's not true."

"It is true. Is it a power thing with you?" he asked, his face flushed. "Is that it?"

"No, it's nothing like that. I like being close to you, it's just. It's just I'm not ready to take the next step. What's so hard to understand about that?"

"Why can't you understand that I need you? Do you understand what I'm saying? I lie awake at night craving the scent of your body."

Slowly, Roman rose to his feet and moved up on Cinnamon, enveloping her into his arms. "I can't wait any longer. Please, baby, don't make me beg."

Cinnamon absorbed his every word, then slid her hands up his shoulders. "You're right, Roman. I have made you wait long enough. And I am going to make love to you. . . but not tonight. Very, very soon though. And I mean that from the bottom of my heart."

Roman dropped down on the bed, his hands on his knees and his head down.

Cinnamon kneeled down in front of him. "You believe me, don't you?"

"I believe you. I know you wouldn't say it if you didn't mean it."

"I'm sorry for all of this, but I will make it up to you. I promise."

A few days passed with not one call or visit from Roman. With everything he endured, Cinnamon could hardly blame him.

On her way in from the barber, she collected her mail. Along with the phone bill was a pastel blue envelope from Roman. Inside was a poem that read.

What If

I think of you and I sometimes wonder, what if . . .
What if you were with me now,
What if we were a twosome and you were always by my side, could you fill the void deep within my heart, could you accept the affection I crave so much to give,
Could you comfort me,
Could I console you,
Would you love me if I loved you,
Could you warm my spirit and make me whimper,
Could you warm my body and make me moan,
There's so much I want to say, I can't say,
There's so much I want to do, I can't do,
The way is barred,
To really know want is to be without,
To really know passion is to have and grasp
My actions I sometimes can't interpret, but what I can reveal is true,
Listen to what I say to you today, because today is most important.
I love you.

The words leaped from the paper and grazed her heart. And for the first time, she believed he truly loved her. After everything she put him through, he could still conjure up such beautiful sentiments.

His words conveyed the same emotions she held in her heart for Mitchell. She regretted not returning Mitchell's calls, but it was only because she was bewitched by him.

Since the first day she laid eyes on Mitchell, she was spellbound with a passion that would not die. And not a day went by that she didn't daydream of him.

Cinnamon's eyes danced as she contemplated directing the poem to Mitchell. Of course, she would have to rewrite it on her own paper, but the message would be the same.

From underneath the fingernail polish on her bureau, she seized Mitchell's telephone number and called him. Mitchell's voice mail picked up, and Cinnamon left a message for him to call.

Later that evening, Mitchell returned Cinnamon's call.

"I wasn't sure you would call me back," Cinnamon said.

"And I didn't think I would ever hear from you. I met you in--what was it? November? And it's now February and I'm just now getting a call from you."

"I've thought about you a lot," Cinnamon said.

"Was today the first time?"

"No."

"What can I do for you, Cinnamon, or shall I say, what would you like to do for me?"

Cinnamon coughed up a large dose of shock, not sure she heard him correctly. "What?"

"I think you heard me. I'm glad to hear from you, but I didn't think it would take three months to see you again."

"I apologize for that. Do you think I could talk to you about something?"

"Of course."

"Nothing major, just something I need to say."

"Well, you want to meet me somewhere?"

"I was thinking you could come over here if that's all right with you."

"That's even better. So when is all of this going to transpire?"

"Can you come over tomorrow?"

"I can come over right now."

Mitchell's eager response jolted her, and she was flattered. "Tonight?" Cinnamon asked.

"Yeah, I want to see you. I want to see your pretty face."

Smitten by him to the first degree, she smiled to herself and said nothing.

"Cinnamon, are you still there?"

"Yes, I'm here."

"So I'll see you tomorrow then, okay?"

The more Cinnamon entertained the idea of coming face-to-face with the man who remained in her thoughts day after day, the more she realized that tomorrow was just too far off.

"Now that I think about it, this evening would be better," she said. "What time should I expect you?"

"In about forty-five minutes."

Immediately after hanging up, Cinnamon rewrote Roman's poem and signed her name, leaving out the last line which read *I love you.* So what if she didn't create it herself. It was the emotion it conveyed that was most important.

The doorbell rang and the butterflies in Cinnamon's stomach did a tap dance. She sprinted to the intercom, could hardly wait to see him, his ebony complexion, beautiful eyes and adorable smile.

For certain, his presence would dazzle her once again.

Mitchell strutted through the door. He wore a tan leather jacket and black jeans.

Only one question leaped to mind.

What would she have to do to get into those pants?

"Hello," Cinnamon said with a warm smile.

"Hey."

Cinnamon led the way into the front room.

"You have such a prissy walk," Mitchell said.

Cinnamon laughed. "I do not."

"You do too." Mitchell mimicked Cinnamon's walk with an exaggerated, heavy switch in his hips from left to right.

"I do not walk like that," Cinnamon said, cracking up at his over-the-top impersonation.

"Yes, you do. One day I'll have to videotape you so you can see for yourself."

"Can I get you anything?"

Mitchell eased down on the sofa, checking out the place. "You have any beer?"

"No. That I don't have."

"What do you have?"

"Water, tea and coffee."

"I'll pass."

Cinnamon joined him on the sofa, glowing as if she entertained a celebrity. "So?"

"So what made you call me after all this time?" he asked.

Cinnamon fixed her gaze on Mitchell's cheeks, the kind she could kiss all day. And all night. "I thought about you."

"I'd given up hope that you'd ever return my call. I said, this girl is never going to call me."

Cinnamon turned toward him and folded her hands. "I need to tell you something."

"You have my attention."

Unnerved, Cinnamon excused herself to the kitchen, returned with a bottle of water and then guzzled it down.

"Am I making you nervous?" Mitchell asked.

"No, I'm just thirsty. Okay, this is what I want to tell you, which you already know, but I feel compelled to say again. I can't involve myself with someone who's married."

"You told me that already. I know that. You've been afraid of me ever since we met."

"Well, if you knew. . ."

Mitchell leaned back on the sofa, a curt smile on his face. "Because I like you Cinnamon. I really like you and I love a challenge."

"What does that mean?"

"It means exactly what you think it means. You're a nice looking girl, Cinnamon and no matter what happens, I'm glad we met. You have that untouched look about you that I just can't get enough of."

For a moment time stood still as she tuned everything out, hearing only the sexy words that dropped from Mitchell's lips.

"Tell me some more about this untouched look," Cinnamon said.

"You know, clean and wholesome."

"I wouldn't go that far."

"I would. I always want what I've never had."

"I'm not sure how I should take that," Cinnamon said.

"I think you know how to take it. I mean exactly what I said."

Cinnamon enjoyed Mitchell's mannish exterior, the way he carried himself and his impeccable confidence.

"Well, we know you're not suffering from any self esteem issues."

"That's for sure. So what were you doing alone the night I met you?"

"Hanging out, just curious."

"About what?"

"About a lot of things."

"You know, observation will only take you so far and then you need experience."

Cinnamon heard herself swallow. "What do you mean?"

"I think you know what I mean."

"No, I don't. Tell me."

"You like hearing me talk about this, don't you? I can tell you do."

"But I don't know what you're talking about," she said, flat out lying.

"Okay, Cinnamon, if you say so."

"Oh, I almost forgot. I have something for you." Cinnamon stood and hustled into the next room.

Moments later, she returned holding a neatly folded piece of paper.

"What is it?" Mitchell asked.

"You'll see. Read it."

As Mitchell read the poem, Cinnamon picked at her fingernails.

After reading the poem, Mitchell asked, "You wrote this for me?"

"Do you like it?"

"Yes, it's very nice but it's also very confusing."

"Well, look at it this way. Regardless of your married situation and my reluctance to involve myself with you, I still have a special place in my heart for you. Does that make sense?"

"Yes, it does."

After Mitchell left, Cinnamon lay snug in her bed underneath the covers, reliving the short time she spent with Mitchell, savoring the joyful memories. Suddenly, her joy turned to sorrow as she concluded she and Mitchell could never be together. Turning and tossing, an uneasiness gnawed at her as she inhaled two drawn out breaths. She rubbed her sweaty palms against the sheets, wondering if her feelings for Mitchell would ever fade. Random ideas of constantly wanting him and never having him rummaged through her mind until the peak of exhaustion hit.

As the days passed, Roman and Mitchell left several messages for her. And she avoided them both.

CHAPTER SEVENTEEN

THE FLASHING RED LIGHT on Cinnamon's answering machine blinked once as she stepped into her living room.

Upon pressing the play button, she found a message from Noel awaiting her. "Cinnamon, this is Noel. Call me as soon as you get in. It's urgent."

At five o'clock that evening, Noel carried three pieces of matching luggage through the front door of Cinnamon's apartment. "I really appreciate you letting me stay here," he said as he set his luggage against the wall.

"No problem," Cinnamon said.

"Where should I put these?"

"I'll put them in the bedroom for now and you can just take what you need as you go along."

After stashing his luggage in her bedroom, Cinnamon joined Noel in the living room.

In front of the television, Noel slouched, flipping the channels via remote.

"Thanks for being such a cool friend," Noel said. "I couldn't go to my mother's house."

"Your mother knew you were living with Aaron?"

"And she didn't like it. She would have been too eager to give me a lecture that I probably need but am not in the mood for."

"What would she lecture you about?"

"About allowing someone to take care of me. I'm just so glad I'm here instead."

"You want to tell me what happened now?"

"He jumped on me."

"What do you mean?"

"Just what I said. He kicked my butt."

With every fiber in her body, Cinnamon tried to resist laughing but she couldn't.

Noel bummed out on the sofa, watching her. "You can laugh. I know it's funny."

"It's not that." Cinnamon's voice screeched with laughter, her hand on her stomach. "It's just the way you said it."

Noel stared at the TV as if his heart sang the blues.

The sadder his expression, the funnier it seemed and Cinnamon couldn't hold back the laughter.

"I'm sorry Noel. I didn't mean to laugh at you."

"That's okay," Noel said in a sour tone.

It was uncommon to see him exhibit such a desolate spirit.

"He hit you?" Cinnamon asked, snickering.

"Among other things."

"Has he ever hit you before?"

"All the time, especially when he drinks. That's usually when it happens."

With her hand on her stomach, bent over, Cinnamon broke into a deafening belly laugh. Though it was not her intention to make him feel worse, she couldn't help herself. "Why did he jump on you this time?" she asked.

"He thought I was messing around."

"Were you?"

"No, I was talking to this guy on the phone about a job. Aaron thought I was making a date and threw a cereal box at me."

Noel's last remark was all that was needed for Cinnamon to burst into another thunderous laugh. "I'm sorry, Noel. I am really trying my best to be serious about this and not laugh but you make it so hard."

"It's okay. I don't mind. One day when I'm not pissed, I'm sure I'll be able to see the humor in it myself."

Noel picked up a book from the coffee table and flipped through the pages as if giving himself something to do. "He doesn't like me hanging around people my own age."

"I forgot," Cinnamon said. "He is in his fifties."

"I'm ready to be on my own anyway," Noel said as he slammed the book shut.

"You're going to get your own apartment?"

"That's exactly what I'm going to do."

"Well, you're welcome to stay here for as long as you like. It's the least I can do especially since I laughed at you the way that I did."

"I knew I could count on you. What about your boyfriend? Will he have a problem with that?"

"You let me worry about him. Anyway, what about your other stuff?" Cinnamon asked. "Is he going to let you pick up the rest of your things?"

"What other things? Everything I own is with me right now."

Again Cinnamon erupted into a hearty laugh, at the brink of tears. "I'm sorry, Noel, but it's you. Why do you have to say everything so sadly?"

"Can't help it. That's the way I talk."

"The only things you own are clothes?"

"And my CD player and a few CDs."

"That's it?"

"Yep. Aaron bought everything else. Let me give you some advice, Cinnamon. Don't ever let anyone take care of you because I promise you, they will think they own you and make your life a living hell."

"And you say you guys weren't sleeping together?"

"No, we weren't and if you saw him, you'd see why."

"Why? What's wrong with him?"

"Let's just say it would take three six-packs to get me stoned enough to make love to him."

"He can't be that bad."

"Why can't he?"

"Are you sure you don't want to call him and patch things up?"

"I'm not calling him. He's drunk now anyway," Noel said as he rose to his feet. "I'm hungry."

"Help yourself to whatever you like."

In the kitchen, Noel collected the white bread, turkey slices and Miracle Whip from the refrigerator. "Are you sure me staying here will be okay with your boyfriend?"

"Roman doesn't pay any bills here. Besides, Roman and I aren't on the best of terms right now."

"So my timing is perfect then."

"Perfect as perfect can be."

"Maybe we should take advantage of this situation then," Noel said with raised eyebrows.

"What situation?"

"You know. You and me."

With a piercing stare, Cinnamon said, "Look, don't get evicted twice in one day."

Two days passed and it was time for Cinnamon to return to the skies.

She stood at the bathroom mirror picking out her afro when she called out to Noel. "Could you come in here, please?"

Wearing yellow briefs, Noel approached the doorway. "Yes, Your Majesty."

"Cut that out," she said, checking out his briefs. "You have no shame, do you? You just let it all hang out, don't you?"

"What? My briefs turning you on," he questioned.

"I don't have time for your games this morning, Noel. I didn't sleep well last night."

"Gees, I was just playing. What's got you so crabby this morning?"

"Like I said, I don't have time to play. And I don't like being called things I'm not."

"Excuse me."

"Anyway, first rule while I'm away. Number One: Please check the stove before leaving the apartment."

"I'm not going to leave the stove on, Cinnamon."

"Number Two: Please don't answer the phone. I haven't told anyone that you're staying here yet and I'd rather tell them myself."

"Okay, I got it. Should I stay in and lock all the doors and windows?"

"You're walking on delicate ground, Noel."

"Okay. . . I was just playing. I hope you're in a better mood when you get back. Is this one of those female days for you?"

Ignoring his comment, she rolled her eyes at him and headed toward the hall closet. Noel followed close behind.

"One more thing," Cinnamon said. "No company either."

"Is there anything else?"

She ignored his question. "I'll give you a call tomorrow."

Days later Cinnamon returned to Chicago.

She made a pit stop at Arri's place, wanting to fill her in on Noel's temporary living arrangement. She and Arri picked up an extra large pizza from Renaldi's and retreated to Cinnamon's apartment.

Loud music from the television vibrated into the hallway as Cinnamon and Arri made their way down the hall.

As Cinnamon lugged her tote bag through the front door, Noel stood as if expecting her. "I'm so glad you brought food. I'm starved."

"Hi, Noel," Arri said as she whisked past him.

"Are you deaf, Noel? Turn that TV down," Cinnamon said. "I could hear that music from the hallway."

Noel quickly lowered the volume on the television.

As Cinnamon embarked upon the living room, she saw a blanket and sheet bunched up across the sofa, three empty glasses on the coffee table, along with a dirty plate and scattered copies of the *Chicago Sun-Times* and the *Chicago Tribune* blanketing the floor.

"I don't believe you have my apartment looking like this. Clean this mess up."

"I see you're still in that foul mood," Noel said.

Ignoring his comment, Cinnamon rolled her eyes at him. "And open a window, it's stuffy in here."

As instructed, Noel opened a window, folded the linens on the sofa and trashed the newspaper from the floor.

Only one thing could explain Cinnamon's irritable mood. Her life was not perfect. Her relationship with Roman was going downhill and despite her yearning heart, she was avoiding Mitchell. The reality of it all set in and she was having problems accepting it.

Cinnamon delivered her tote into her bedroom and then joined Arri and Noel at the kitchen table.

Noel collected six pizza slices from the box. "Arri, did Cinnamon tell you we were shacking?"

"Ignore him, Arri. He's about to be put out real soon."

Noel leaned across the table and kissed Cinnamon's cheek. "You're just saying that. You wouldn't put a helpless man on the street, would you?"

"I most definitely would," Cinnamon said as she bit into her pizza. "Noel, will you get the napkins from the top cabinet, please? Thank you."

"You're just ordering him around like you're some queen or something," Arri said.

"No, I'm not. I just asked him to do me a favor."

Noel nabbed the napkins from the cabinet and returned to his seat.

Cinnamon turned to Noel. "Am I ordering you around?"

"Hell, yeah, but that's okay. I don't mind."

"Told you," Arri said.

"Did Cinnamon tell you all of my business yet," Noel asked.

Before Arri could make a comment, Cinnamon interrupted. "I didn't tell your business."

"So Arri has no idea why I'm here?"

"I told her a couple of things," Cinnamon said.

Noel collected two more slices from the box. "It's okay. I don't care. I have no secrets."

"Have you talked to him since you moved out?" Arri asked.

"I talked to him today. He wants me to come back, of course."

"You don't want to?" Arri asked.

"I'm moving on to better things. I've gotten as much out of that relationship as I can." He paused. "So, Arri, are you dating anyone these days?"

"Why do you ask?"

"How do you feel about bisexual men?" he asked.

Knowing where this conversation was headed, Cinnamon laughed.

"What do you mean how do I feel about them?" Arri asked.

He swallowed his pizza and leaned back in his chair. "Would you date a bisexual man?"

"I don't think so."

Cinnamon wiped her mouth. "Noel . . . Knock it off."

"Would you get a grip?" Arri said. "He was just asking me a question."

"Thank you, Arri. She's been in a funky mood lately. I think she's PMSing."

"I am not PMSing," Cinnamon yelled.

Arri shrugged and projected her attention to Noel. "Never mind her. You're a man, right?"

Noel glanced down into his lap. "That I am. At least I was the last time I checked."

"Arri, you're not going to get any serious answers from him."

"No, seriously, what is it you wanted to ask me?" he asked.

"Why can't men be happy with one woman?"

"They can."

"Please," Cinnamon said.

"Why do they cheat then?" Arri asked.

"If a man's needs are satisfied--"

Arri interrupted. "What needs?"

"His ego. His sexual needs."

"Excuse me while I disagree," Cinnamon said.

"For example," Noel said. "If Cinnamon and I were together?"

"Must you use me as an example?"

"Forget her, Noel."

"As I was saying before I was so hastily interrupted. If I was involved with Cinnamon, I wouldn't have an interest in any other women."

Cinnamon cleared her throat, signaling her disbelief.

Arri swallowed the food in her mouth. "So you're saying if a man is satisfied in his relationship and another woman comes along with the same qualities, he won't look her way?"

"Now that's another story." Noel stood and grabbed the Pepsi from the refrigerator.

"What are you saying then?" Arri asked. "You just said if he's happy, the temptation is small."

"I said it was small, but it's not non-existent. If a woman throws herself at a man, he's not going to back down." Noel filled three glasses with pop and then dropped down into his chair.

"So the answer is no," Arri said. "Nothing can keep a man from straying."

"I'm not saying that either."

"What are you saying then, Noel?" Arri asked.

"Yeah, what are you saying?" Cinnamon asked. "Arri, he doesn't even know what he's saying."

"What I'm saying is that if he's satisfied, he won't go out looking for it, but if it should come his way, that's a whole different scenario."

"You are so full of it," Cinnamon said, smiling.

"You know what I admire about women?"

Arri guzzled down her pop. "What?"

"They can go without sex for long periods of time. Men can't do that."

"Women are just as sexually driven as men," Arri said.

"No, they're not."

"Yes, they are too," Arri said with conviction.

Cinnamon alternated her gaze from Arri to Noel.

"A perfect example," Noel said. "No matter how sexually driven, as you call it, a woman might be, she still maintains a certain amount of discrimination toward men. Whereas, men don't necessarily discriminate when it comes to their sexual needs."

"Yeah, I guess, but that doesn't mean women don't crave sex the same," Arri said. "They may discriminate against certain partners but the need is the same."

"No, it's not. A man's sexual need is dire, more desperate."

"What do you think, Cinnamon?" Arri asked with a sneaky snicker. "I'm sorry, I'm asking the wrong person. Cinnamon doesn't have those needs."

"Is that true, Cinnamon?" Noel asked.

Cinnamon turned her nose up at Arri. "Forget you."

"Cinnamon is just waiting for Mister Right," Arri said. "Right, Cinnamon?"

"Yeah, right." Cinnamon stood and gathered the dishes from the table. "You guys can go on in the living room. I'll straighten up in here."

While Cinnamon washed the dishes and wiped down the table, Arri and Noel retired to the front room and found a Janet Jackson song on the radio.

When Cinnamon entered the living room, Arri and Noel danced in the middle of the room, their feet sweeping against the floor.

"You guys are noisy," Cinnamon said as she buckled down on the sofa.

"Maybe you can come out with me sometime," Noel said to Arri.

"I don't think so. I heard about those clubs you like to hang out at."

"That damn Cinnamon," Noel said playfully. "She's always telling my fucking business."

"Don't blame Cinnamon."

"It'll be fun, Arri. I'll be your date."

"You might as well forget it, Noel. She's not going to go."

"So Noel," Arri said in a whisper. "How can a woman keep her man monogamous?"

"What are you two over there whispering about?" Cinnamon asked.

Arri turned to Cinnamon. "Believe it or not, everything in this world doesn't concern you."

Arri returned her focus to Noel. "Now what were you saying?"

"Well, it's really not up to the woman. A man decides for himself whether or not he's going to cheat. It really has very little to do with the woman."

"Well, that's nice to know," Arri said sarcastically.

"What I'm saying is, if it's in his nature to cheat, something that he wants to do, then there's really very little a woman can do to prevent him from doing so."

"That doesn't give women much control."

"Sure it does."

"How?"

"A woman controls a relationship by what she will and will not tolerate. In other words, a man will try and get away with as much as he can. It's up to the woman to accept it or not."

The Janet Jackson song ended and Arri and Noel joined Cinnamon on the sectional sofa.

"So if a man really cares for you," Arri asked. "And he knows he will lose you if he cheats on you, that's motivation for him to remain faithful?"

"Exactly."

"But that contradicts what you said earlier," Arri said.

"I told you, Arri," Cinnamon said. "He doesn't know what he's talking about."

"Oh, you be quiet," Arri said.

"For the most part, in my opinion," his eyes shot to Cinnamon. "In my opinion, a woman cannot control whether or not a man will remain unfaithful or not. If he wants to cheat, he's going to and there's nothing a woman can do except not accept it. Period."

"That's really interesting," Arri said. "I like talking to you, Noel."

"As I you."

"What makes you such an expert," Cinnamon asked.

"I'm a man. Give me credit for that."

"Why are you so hard on him?" Arri asked. "I think Noel knows a lot about women. And relationships."

"Thank you, Arri. It's nice to know someone around here appreciates me."

"Okay, well answer this for me," Cinnamon said. "Why is it that sometimes when a man has sex with a woman, he never wants to see her again?"

"Oh, that's an easy one."

"Wait a minute," Arri said as she leaped from the sofa, dashed over to the stereo and powered it off. In one swoop, she returned to the sofa. "Okay now," Arri said. "What were you saying?"

Noel captured their full attention.

"When a man has sex with a woman and he never wants to see her after that, it's because he never liked her to begin with. As a matter of fact, he disliked her from the beginning, but didn't mind having sex with her, especially if she was pretty."

"Really?" Arri questioned curiously.

"And you know this how?" Cinnamon asked.

"I'm a man, Cinnamon."

Arri changed the subject. "So Noel, do you plan on having children one day?"

"I might if I find the right person," he said, peering in Cinnamon's direction. "You know what I mean, Cinnamon?"

"No, I don't."

"What about you, Arri?" Noel asked.

Arri shook her head. "No way would I bring a child into this terrible world, all the racism, murder, poverty and violence. I wouldn't do that to my child."

Cinnamon and Noel elapsed into silence.

As dark, depressing and dreary as Arri's words may have been, they were also very true.

CHAPTER EIGHTEEN

NOEL FROLICKED AT THE stove, wearing neon green hot pants as he prepared a cheese omelet.

In extended meditation, Cinnamon tossed down her chilled lemon tea while she stared at the edge of the table, mulling over her ambiguous feelings for Roman.

"You know what I wish, Noel?"

"That I was your man?"

"I wish that I wanted Roman the way he wanted me. Roman is a wonderful guy, has everything going for him. He's smart, intelligent, witty, ambitious and he's a writer. He's everything I could ever want in a man. But there's no sizzle."

"I hate to break it to you, honey, but if it's not there, it's just not there."

"I know but why can't I like someone who's so great?"

"You know the answer to that as well as I do. Your heart is still set on that married man."

Cinnamon nodded in agreement. "That could be it."

"That is it and there's no question about it. As a matter of fact, if it weren't for this married man, you would feel so different about Roman."

"You think?"

"Not think. Know."

Noel turned off the stove and joined Cinnamon at the table. "Where did you go this morning?" Noel asked.

"Why? I don't ask you where you're going every time you leave."

"That's because I always tell you."

"I just took a walk." Cinnamon set her coffee mug down. "I'm sorry I haven't been the best roommate to you. It's just. . ."

"Just what?" he asked as he stuffed his mouth with a piece of his omelet.

"It's a lot of things. For starters, I'm having problems sleeping at night."

"What do you want me to do about it?"

Noel managed to snare a smile from her, the first of the day. "I'm not asking you to do anything. I'm just telling you. But for the sake of educating myself, what could you do about it?"

Noel wiped his mouth with a napkin. "I could help you relax, release some of that tension inside, rid you of that attitude of yours."

"Excuse me, but I don't have an attitude."

"Oh, yeah? Well, what's that coming out of your mouth now?"

As much as she hated to admit it, Noel was absolutely right.

"Forgive me, Noel, if I've been rude or insensitive to you."

"You're asking for an awful lot. If you want me to forgive you for everything, it's going to cost you."

"Cost what?"

"Fifty *I love yous*, thirty *you are the ones* and twenty-five *I want you babys*."

"Where do you come up with this stuff?"

"I don't know, it just comes off the top of my head."

Cinnamon smiled and looked warmly into Noel's eyes. "Can I share something with you?"

"You can share anything you like."

"I invited Mitchell over here one day before you moved in."

"I'm not surprised. So what happened?"

"I really like this guy. You know I find myself thinking about him when I'm with Roman. That's how bad I have it for him."

"I'll ask again. What happened?"

"Nothing much. We just talked and I told him I couldn't get involved with a married man period."

"So nothing happened?"

"Absolutely nothing."

"But you wanted something to happen though, didn't you?"

"If I had my way, it would still be happening right now."

"You nasty little girl, you. I didn't realize you had so much fire inside."

"Well, now you know."

"I'm realizing there's a lot about you I don't know," Noel said.

"There's a lot about you I don't know."

"Does Roman know about Mitchell?"

"No way," Cinnamon said. "It's not his business."

"So when can I meet this Mitchell guy. I have to see the person who has you all in knots."

"No way," Cinnamon said. "What am I going to do? Invite him here so you can gawk at him?"

"What's wrong with that?"

"No."

"I'll be on my best behavior."

Cinnamon pondered his words for all of three seconds, then stood up. "But how would I explain you?"

"You can say I'm your cousin or something."

Noel scrolled her from top to bottom. "Look at you," he said. "Got two men chasing after you."

"It's not like that."

"Oh, yes it is. I don't have a chance."

"Don't start that again."

"Have you and Roman done the do?" he asked in a whisper.

"Why are you whispering?"

"Because this is a very delicate subject."

"Yeah, but there's no one here but us."

"You really know how to steal the juice out of something, don't you?"

She gazed at him, confused. "I don't even know what that means."

"So have you? Have you and Roman done it?"

"Not that it's any of your business, but no, we haven't."

Noel emptied the scraps from his plate into the trash. "Invite him over."

"No . . ."

"Come on. I want to see him. I won't be able to rest until I meet the man who has your nose wide open."

Gleaming with delight, Cinnamon smiled as she entertained the idea. "You really want to meet him?"

"Call him," Noel said. "You know you want to."

"I don't know. He's at work now anyway. Maybe I'll call him later."

"You're stalling. Listen, everything else aside, I want to thank you again for letting me stay here."

"I've enjoyed having you when you're not working my nerves."

"Well, I'll be out of your hair in a day or so anyway. I was going to tell you yesterday."

"Why? Are you leaving?"

"I'm moving back in with Aaron."

"You said you were through with that. I thought you were going to get your own place."

"Trust me, there's a method to my madness. I'm just going to be there for a while, just until I can get my finances in order and most of all to get my things. I'm giving myself two months tops and I'm out of there."

"Well, if it doesn't work out, you're always welcome here."

To distance herself from the loud TV Noel watched in the front room, Cinnamon slammed her bedroom door shut. But it did little good. Still the cackles from the TV sitcom blared through loud and clear.

Slightly ruffled, Cinnamon trotted into the living room. "Hey, Noel. Could you turn that down a little, please?"

"Sure, no problem," Noel said as he lowered the volume.

Once back in her room, she realized now would be as good a time as any to call Mitchell.

"Hi, Mitchell, it's me, Cinnamon."

"Cinnamon who?"

Cinnamon laughed. "Cinnamon Brown."

"Now you decide to call. I've been calling you and calling you."

"I know and I'm sorry."

"So what's your story? Just too busy to return my calls?"

Cinnamon twiddled with the telephone cord, basking in the sound of his words.

"Cinnamon?" Mitchell said. "Are you still there?"

"I'm still here."

"Say something," Mitchell said.

Though probably a mistake to invite him over, she craved to see him all the same.

"I was going to ask you if you wanted to stop by this evening?"

"Why? What do you want to do to me?"

"I just want to see you."

"If I come over, will it be another month before I hear from you again?"

"No."

"You wrote me this beautiful poem and then disappeared," Mitchell said.

"Are you going to come?" Cinnamon asked timidly.

"How can I refuse such a pretty voice?"

Cinnamon ended the call, seeping enthusiasm as she raced into the living room. "I just got off the phone with Mitchell. He's on his way over."

Cinnamon quickly gathered the blanket and sheets from the sofa and rammed them into the closet. "I don't want him to know you're staying here, so you'll have to put on some more clothes."

"Does that include shoes too?" Noel asked.

"Please, if you don't mind."

Noel slipped into the bedroom.

Cinnamon opened a window so the fresh air could breeze through, then deodorized the apartment with powder-fresh air freshener.

Noel returned from the bedroom wearing boots, a skull cap, and leather gloves.

"Is this enough clothes for you?"

Cinnamon fell over in one swoop, holding her stomach, trying desperately to contain the laugher. "Oh, so you want to be a comedian?"

"Is this too much?"

"Yes. I think so. You can lose the cap, gloves and boots. Oh, and don't forget to put your bag in the bedroom."

"Yes, Ma'am. One would think you were expecting the President."

Cinnamon gauged her watch every so many minutes.

She danced in front of the bathroom mirror, picking out her afro, then applied blush and lipstick.

Shortly afterwards, Mitchell arrived, carrying a big brown paper bag.

"Hi," he said. "I could hear your television in the hall."

"Yeah, I know. I think my cousin has a hearing problem."

"Your cousin?"

"My cousin, Noel, is visiting." Mitchell stepped inside and Cinnamon closed the door.

"Noel, can you turn it down?" Cinnamon shouted.

"What?" Noel asked.

"The TV, turn it down."

Noel lowered the volume and rose from the sofa.

Cinnamon led Mitchell into the front room. "Mitchell, I'd like you to meet my cousin. Mitchell, this is Noel. Noel, this is Mitchell."

"Hello," Mitchell said.

"I've heard a lot about you," Noel said.

"Oh, really? Wonderful things, I know." Mitchell looked at Cinnamon. "I brought some beer since you couldn't offer me any last time I was here."

"I'll take your coat," Cinnamon said.

After Cinnamon hung up Mitchell's coat, they all three relaxed on the sofa, Cinnamon sitting between them.

"I've seen you before," Noel said.

"Maybe." Mitchell pulled the six-pack from the bag and set it on the coffee table.

"You look really familiar," Noel said. "I'm sure I've seen you at one of the clubs."

"I have that look," Mitchell said with confidence. "Have one, Noel?"

"Yes, I will." Noel separated a beer from the pack.

"I think I'll have one myself," Cinnamon said right before she nabbed a beer for herself. Though Cinnamon never drank beer because of its repulsive flavor, this evening it seemed the cordial thing to do.

For thirty minutes, they watched MTV, not saying much of anything as Cinnamon soaked up Mitchell's presence in all its wonder.

Mitchell turned toward Cinnamon and asked in a subtle tone. "Can I talk to you for a minute?"

"Sure. We'll be right back, Noel."

Cinnamon placed her beer on the table before she and Mitchell headed toward the front door.

"What's up?" Cinnamon asked.

"Will you step into the hallway with me?"

"Sure."

They stepped into the hallway, closing the door behind them.

"When you invited me over," Mitchell said, "I had no idea your cousin would be here. I thought you wanted to see me."

"I did want to see you. He just happened to be passing through."

"Anyway, I'm going to go."

"You just got here."

"Next time invite me over when you're alone. Tell Noel he can have the rest of that beer."

Cinnamon studied Mitchell's lips as if she waited for them to perform. "I don't want you to go," she said.

"I'll come back again."

Stepping back inside her apartment, Mitchell asked, "May I have my coat?"

"Of course," she said as she moved to collect his coat from the hall closet.

"You can walk me to the elevator if you like," Mitchell said.

"Noel, I'll be right back. I'm walking Mitchell to the elevator."

"It was nice meeting you, Noel," Mitchell said.

"Same here."

Cinnamon and Mitchell wandered down the dim hallway across the psychedelic carpet.

"Too bad you can't stay awhile," Cinnamon said.

"I came to see you, not your cousin. Who knows when I will see you again? It's not like you call me every day."

Cinnamon was about to ring for the elevator when Mitchell stopped her. He clenched her body against his, groped her behind and kissed her.

Powerless to stop him, she kissed him back, his pillow-soft lips merging perfectly with hers. The smell of his breath sent tremors throughout her body and she felt breezy and light-headed.

This kiss being a long time coming, Cinnamon welcomed him with open arms and mouth. She dreamed about this kiss, fantasized about this kiss, since the first day she met him. She liked this man and parting from him was not something she ever wanted to do. Not ever.

It was wrong to kiss a married man but she was paralyzed at the lips. She could have been permanently glued to this man forever and she would not have cared.

Mitchell slowly pulled away. "I want you to be my rose, Cinnamon."

Cinnamon's head spun as the sweltering feelings for Mitchell brewed inside her. A little embarrassed, she couldn't keep from smiling. "I've never heard that expression before."

"But you know what it means, don't you?" he asked as he rang for the elevator.

"I guess."

When the elevator door opened, Mitchell stepped on. "Think about it," he said, just as the door closed.

After yielding to temptation, Cinnamon's life would never be the same. And as much as she treasured being wrapped in Mitchell's arms and locking lips with him, it could never happen again. Determined not to do the wrong thing, she would work overtime to release Mitchell from her heart.

With a sensuous glow surging through her, Cinnamon sprinted back inside her apartment. Noel waited by the front door as if he had been listening. "What was that all about?" he asked.

"He left," she answered as she closed the door.

"I can see that."

"I don't think he felt comfortable around both of us."

"You mean me."

"Probably."

She headed to the bathroom mirror and picked out her afro. After just kissing a prince, she studied herself in the mirror. She didn't look any different, but she was different. Finally, she had made a connection with Mitchell, something she needed to have experienced if only for the experience itself.

Noel watched her with an eagle eye. "You like him, don't you?"

"I never said I didn't." Cinnamon turned to Noel, radiating happiness. "He wants me to be his rose."

"Oh, that. I used to use that one too."

"What are you talking about?"

"Girl, he wants you to be his freak momma."

Cinnamon laughed. "That's not what it means. Does it?"

"Look, you're talking to a man who's been around the block, up the block and down the block."

"You ought to stay off that block."

Noel stood behind Cinnamon, watching her reflection in the mirror. "I was watching you when he was here, the way you looked at him like he was a piece of bread."

"Did I?"

"Yes, you did."

Noel didn't say anything right away, then he said, "He kissed you, didn't he?"

Cinnamon continued picking out her afro. "How can you tell?"

"You have that I'm-going-to-get-me-some look."

"Would you stop? It's not like that."

"Why are you fixing your hair then? He's already gone."

"I don't know. I just feel like fixing my hair."

"Feeling energetic, are we?"

"Yeah. I guess I am."

"Classic symptom."

"Classic symptom of what?"

"Honey, you're in love."

Noel was right. She was in love with Mitchell Maine.

Cinnamon lay in bed determined to silence her passions for this man, knowing exactly what was required--move closer to Roman. It was the only way.

Elated to have experienced such a special man as Mitchell, she was also saddened because what transpired earlier would never come about again.

With that in mind, she dialed Roman's number.

"Hi, honey," Cinnamon said.

"Cinnamon? Finally. Where have you been? Did you get the mail I sent you?"

"I got it. It was very sweet. Thank you."

"So no explanation? I started to drop by there."

"I'm surprised you didn't."

"You haven't answered my question," Roman said. "Why didn't you return my calls?"

"Well. . . I don't know."

"I think you do."

"I don't have any answers for you now, Roman, but I do need to talk to you about something really serious, in person though."

"Is it going to make me happy?"

"I hope so."

"Why don't you just tell me now?"

"I'd prefer to tell you in person."

"Do you want me to come over?"

"No, tomorrow. I'd like to come over there if that's okay. Am I still welcome?"

Hopefully, going to his apartment would signify her change in attitude.

"You're going to come over here? I've invited you over here several times. This must be bad news."

"It's not. Really, it's not."

"Should I pick you up?"

"No, that won't be necessary."

"I don't know if I can wait until tomorrow," Roman said.

"You'll have to. I'll see you around seven-thirty, okay?"

Making love to Roman would be awkward but even more challenging would be building up the drive to begin.

Chapter Nineteen

Noel moved back in with his roommate the next morning. Cinnamon hated to see him go. She grew accustomed to having him around, matching wits with him and most of all bickering with him. They exhibited a unique and awesome friendship, above all others.

Later that evening, Cinnamon prepared for her engagement with Roman, which began with a long hot shower. After that, she moisturized her skin, then sprinkled Johnson's baby powder over her chest, stomach and thighs. As she pulled her lace panties up on her hips, fear wavered inside her. Images of her and Roman intertwined induced a queasy sensation, causing her to question her plans. But she was committed to her decision and there was no turning back.

Out of the blue, an uncomfortable thought came to mind. She might have to change her telephone number to avoid Mitchell in the future, but it was too soon to worry about such trivial concerns. Now was the time to focus on Roman and only Roman.

Before trucking off to Roman's place, she dropped in on Arri.

Arri munched on hot corn chips as she bummed out in front of her bedroom television, watching a love story classic, *The Way We Were.*

"Guess where I'm going tonight?" Cinnamon said.

"Where?"

"The 6000 block of Lake Shore Drive."

"What's over there?"

"Roman."

"I thought you said you didn't want to visit him because you didn't want to give him the wrong idea."

"That was before."

Arri aimed the remote control at the television, lowering the volume. "Before what?"

Cinnamon witnessed a bewildered look on Arri's face.

"Things are different now," Cinnamon said.

"Different how?"

"I'm ready to be with him now. And I do mean that in the biblical sense."

Arri closed the bag of chips and set them beside her. "Wait a minute. What happened?"

Choosing not to let on about Mitchell, Cinnamon led Arri astray. "Nothing happened."

"Everything happens for a reason, Cinnamon. You're always telling me that. Something must have happened to get you to change your whole attitude."

"I just thought about it and made a decision."

"So one night you're sleeping and poof, you wake up and decide you're going to let Roman make love to you?"

"Not exactly like that."

Cinnamon would forever hold in her heart the memory of the kiss she and Mitchell shared. And it was a secret she would not yet reveal, not even to Arri.

Arri seemingly studied Cinnamon, trying to figure her out. "So tell me what really happened?"

Cinnamon raised her shoulders. "I told you, I just made a decision to sleep with Roman."

"So you're going to have sex with Roman?"

Cinnamon avoided answering. Instead, she stared down at the neon purple blanket covering the bed.

"You don't look too happy about it," Arri said.

"I am," Cinnamon said, lifting her head.

"I won't believe this until I hear about it. I still think something happened though. You just don't want to tell me. Have you talked to Mitchell at all?"

"Why do you ask?" Cinnamon asked. "Why bring him up?"

"Just asking. So was Roman surprised when you told him you were coming over?"

"Uh huh."

"Is this what you really want to do? Because if not, I don't think you should."

"But I do want to."

"Don't do this for him," Arri said. "I've had my share of experiences trying to please men. I tried to make Eric happy.

Look where it got me. I just hope I never have to see him again."

"Well, I'll believe that when I don't hear about him," Cinnamon said.

"And you won't hear about him either. I'm done with both Eric and Tony. I'm doing the solo act like you or like you used to, if you pull this off."

Glancing at the dirty clothes on the floor, Cinnamon realized she left her personal items at home. "I'm going to have to go back home."

"For what?"

"My toothbrush for starters," Cinnamon said as she climbed off the bed.

Arri's eyes gleamed. "What do you have planned for Roman?"

"Not that, nasty. But I do have to go back home."

"You're just stalling. You don't really want to go over there, do you?"

It was as if Arri could read Cinnamon's mind. "Yes, I do."

"Okay, but I want to know everything. Every blink of the eyes, every position, every leg here, leg there, every--"

"Okay, I got it."

Cinnamon swung through the front door, gathered her toothbrush, body wash, baby powder, deodorant, lotion and dumped them into her overnight bag. It was already 7:20 p.m. and Roman was expecting her at 7:30 p.m.

Just as she was about to head back out, the phone rang and she wasn't sure whether or not she should answer. Though she would have liked to talk to Mitchell, it was best if she didn't. Even still, the suspense continued to eat away at her.

Without examining it any further, she answered. "Hello," she said in a sexy tone.

No one responded, and for a moment she suspected it might be Joseph.

Suddenly, she heard this deep sumptuous voice. "You're not busy, are you?" Mitchell asked.

"Hi, Mitchell. I was just on my way out."

"I wanted to apologize for what happened the other day."

"Apologize for what?"

"For kissing you."

"You don't have to apologize. I forgot all about that."

That was a lie. That was all she thought about.

"Well, I want to apologize anyway. Do you mind if I stop by, I'll only stay a minute."

Cinnamon longed to say yes.

"I'm right around the corner," Mitchell said. "I can be there in five minutes."

Unable to resist, Cinnamon said, "Okay."

Cinnamon scanned her watch. It was now 7:30 p.m. and she was already late for Roman. But she couldn't help herself. Once again she yielded to temptation, unable to pass up the opportunity to see Mitchell, if only for the last time.

Not once did Mitchell inquire why Cinnamon failed to return his calls. Instead he seemed interested only in talking to her, giving her just cause to like him even more.

She contemplated informing Roman that she was running behind, then decided not to.

Like a kid waiting for Santa Claus, Cinnamon stood at the window watching for Mitchell. She knew she was tempting fate by having Mitchell over again, especially after what happened the last time, but it was too late now. He was already on his way.

Minutes later, the phone rang again.

Was it Roman?

Or was it Mitchell calling to say he changed his mind?

Hoping it was Mitchell, she answered. "I thought you were coming over," Roman said. "I'm waiting for you. I ordered out and everything."

"I'm on my way out the door right now."

Cinnamon didn't know what else to say to him. She couldn't very well tell him she was waiting for the love of her life.

Mitchell arrived within five minutes as promised. He stepped through the door, his bald head shining. He wore cowboys boots, dark jeans and a blazer.

Quiet as a couple of church mice, they nestled on the sofa while a Paul Hardcastle CD resounded from the disc player. After a drawn out silence, Mitchell dug into his jacket pocket. "Since you wrote me such a wonderful poem, I got something for you."

"What is it?"

Mitchell pulled out a tiny fuchsia bag, big enough to hold about twenty quarters. He then handed it to Cinnamon. "I want you to keep an open-mind about this. This is something that you have probably never received before and probably nothing you will ever receive again."

"Can I open it now?"

"As you open it, I'm going to tell you what the gentleman told me who sold this to me."

Cinnamon opened the suede pouch and inside were ten beautiful fuchsia colored rocks, which she poured into her hand. Her eyes illuminated the room as she studied them as if they were priceless jewelry. "These are so cute. What are they for?"

"Okay, this is what he said. These are magical love rocks. Supposedly, they bring true everlasting love into your life."

"Seriously?"

"You are to put them somewhere where you can see them every day. This is what he told me, and he truly believes in their power. He went on to say that sometimes the love can become so overwhelming that if that happens, you are to remove one of the rocks from the bag."

"That will never happen," Cinnamon said.

"Don't be so sure."

Cinnamon's eyes sparkled with enthusiasm as she inhaled elongated breaths. "I think I'm absolutely mesmerized." She kissed Mitchell's cheek. "This is the best present I have ever received. . . in my life."

"That's a little extreme."

"Maybe, but true."

"So you like them?" Mitchell asked.

"Do I like them? I adore them." She set them on the coffee table, forcing herself to turn away. "You have made my day, my night, my week. No, my year."

"Like I said on the phone, I wanted to apologize for what happened last time I was here."

"Don't worry about that. I enjoyed kissing you and you didn't do anything wrong."

"Anyway, I don't blame you for not returning my calls."

This was too weird. Though Cinnamon avoided Mitchell's calls, Mitchell was the one apologizing. It was unreal. If anyone needed to apologize, it was Cinnamon.

"So that's all settled, right?" Mitchell asked.

"Yes."

"I know you said you were on your way out so I won't keep you."

"That's okay. I have a few minutes. Can I get you something to drink?"

"Sure."

As Cinnamon and Mitchell headed toward the kitchen, the phone rang. It was Roman again no doubt, but so what. She was with Mitchell now.

Right as Cinnamon reached for a glass from the kitchen cabinet, she felt Mitchell standing directly behind her, pressing into her, his magic wand fully alert. Her heart thumped as she stood motionless. She wanted to turn around but was afraid of what might happen if she did. Perspiring in all the right places, she swallowed hard and wondered what Mitchell would do next.

How would she escape Mitchell's presence without Mitchell witnessing the dumbfounded expression on her face? Hesitating no more, Cinnamon swept around, leaning back against the counter, Mitchell's body sandwiched against hers. "Am I keeping you from something?" Mitchell asked.

"No, not at all. I'm supposed to meet someone but he can wait."

"Your boyfriend?"

"Something like that but you don't have to leave."

"Are you planning on taking me with you?" Mitchell asked sarcastically.

"Now there's an idea."

How could Cinnamon go to Roman's place and at the same time stay at her place with Mitchell? She smiled to herself, knowing she was just being silly.

"Since we're just standing here," he said as he stepped back from her. "And you have someone waiting for you, I'm going to go, but I'd like you to call me later, even if it's super late. Will you call me?"

"I'll try."

"I can't ask for more than that."

Cinnamon raced into her bathroom immediately after Mitchell left. She stood before the mirror, wanting to see the face of a woman in l-o-v-e. Though she hated to admit it, she was positively on fire for this man with little she could do about it except run the other way.

She treasured the beautiful love rocks given to her and decided to keep them on her coffee table, wishing to see them every time she entered her apartment.

In such a good mood, she preferred not to spoil it by going to Roman's. But she had to go. She promised and it was too late to renege now. After all, he was expecting her, ordering out and everything. Maybe the exuberance she held in her heart at this moment was exactly what she needed to overcome her hurdle with Roman. Who knows? She might even enjoy it.

After all this time, today would be the day. The day she and Roman did the do. In honor of the special occasion, she decided to wear something sexy and quickly changed. She now sported a navy miniskirt, a low-cut blouse and no pantyhose.

Having just been mildly seduced, she was now heading to Roman's apartment for sex.

She was living the life. The life of adventure and excitement. She toyed with both Roman and Mitchell, not being totally honest with either of them, and definitely not committing to either as well.

Though she was having fun, she frowned on her behavior. She was a tease and she didn't like herself for it. But maybe just maybe this day would change everything.

She would sever all ties with Mitchell and at the speed of light fast forward to Roman. And that was it, no ifs, ands or buts. She made her decision and she was sticking to it all the way.

As she headed out the door, she doubled backed and called Mitchell, hoping to reach his voice mail. And she did. "Hi, Mitchell, it's Cinnamon. I really enjoyed seeing you this evening. It's very difficult for me to say this so I'm just going to come right out and say it. I apologize for giving you mixed messages. I really have no excuse except for the fact that I really like you. But. . . I won't be able to talk to you or see you anymore. I hope you understand."

Cinnamon hung up and closed her eyes.

Had she made a mistake in leaving Mitchell that message?

At this point, it really didn't matter because it was too late to do anything about it.

All the way to Roman's apartment, the knots in her stomach grew tighter and tighter as if maybe she was doing the wrong thing. But when the taxi dropped her off at

Roman's building, her stomach settled instantaneously. Then she knew for sure.

This was the right thing to do.

Roman awaited her at his front door and gifted her with an enchanting smile.

"What took you so long?" he asked. "I was starting to worry."

She stepped inside and set her overnight bag on the floor.

"I'm sorry." She waltzed her arms up his shoulders and hugged him. "The important thing is that I'm here now."

He buried his face in her neck. "You smell good. Is that a new perfume?"

Cinnamon lifted her blouse to her nose. "I don't think so." She purposely neglected to mention that the distinct aroma he smelled was possibly a combination of her chemistry and Mitchell's.

Roman remarked her overnight bag. "What's that?"

"Just some personal items I might need."

With his place cold enough to store meat, she hugged her arms as she examined the condominium, noting the floor-to-ceiling windows that overlooked Lake Shore Drive.

Though Cinnamon favored a chilled environment, Roman had taken it to a new level. She felt as though she switched places with Arri, since Arri was the one always too cold when she visited.

"Is the heat on?" Cinnamon asked.

"I'll turn it up."

His apartment was furnished with an Asian flavor, embellished in red and black with oriental paintings mounted on the walls. Even the sofa was blanketed with a rich red cover inscribed with Chinese lettering.

"You weren't kidding about the red and black, were you?" she asked.

"I was not."

"Where's your bedroom? Can I see it?"

"Right this way, Madam," he said, eagerly leading the way.

Once inside he clicked on the ceiling light. The fire-engine red comforter neatly folded on the platform bed was the first thing she noticed. Everything in his room rested in its own place, from the coins in the oriental glass container to the CDs in the decorative rack.

"What's with the oriental fetish?" she asked.

"Most of it came from my mother. She was really into oriental art, and I sort of inherited a lot of it when she passed."

"Oh, I'm sorry, Roman. I never knew that."

"Don't worry about it. It happened a long time ago."

"Did you know that red and black were two of my favorite colors?" she asked.

"I did and you should feel right at home."

"As a matter of fact, I do," she said as she dropped down on the bed like it was hers.

"You're awfully relaxed this evening," he said as he eased down next to her. "First you agree to come to my apartment, something I have wanted you to do forever. And now here you are in my bedroom, sitting on my bed like you own the place."

She caressed his cheek with her fingers and smiled. "I like you, Roman, and maybe I haven't been adept at showing you that. But I'd like to change all of that now."

"Did anything happen that I should know about?"

"Not at all." She scooted into his lap and wrapped her arms around him. "If you still want me, I'd like to stay here with you tonight."

"Tonight?" he questioned as he kissed her. "You can stay here forever."

He kissed her for moments on end, exploring her mouth with his lips and tongue. It seemed he might kiss her forever.

When their lips parted, Roman said, "I'm glad you came."

He rotated her body off his lap and onto the bed. He lay rammed on top of her, his erectness in full bloom as the bright light shined on her face. "Are you going to turn off that light?" she asked.

"Why would I want to do that? It's not often I have such a beautiful creature in my apartment and in my bed."

"Well, since you put it that way. No seriously, Roman, could you turn off that light?"

Roman clicked on the lamp by the bed and then turned out the ceiling light. He then resumed his position on top of Cinnamon, caressing her hair and face, before kissing her. . . kissing her. . . rough. . . hard. She worried she might collapse from exhaustion, and the main event was still to come. All she could think about was when he would undress her. Suddenly, Roman snaked his hand up her skirt inside her lace panties, probing every crevice with his fingers.

"Let's go into the kitchen," he said.

Though his suggestion seemed odd, she followed his lead.

Once in the kitchen, Roman hoisted her up on the counter top, then slithered his hand up her thighs.

And it suddenly hit her. Roman was a freak. But because of her two-year celibacy, he was just what she required.

He clasped his lips with hers and worked his hand inside her moist panties.

The lights beamed across her face, even brighter than the bedroom lights. But not wanting to suspend the moment, she said nothing. She had made Roman wait a long time and she was anxious to play it through to the finish line. Tonight was his night. His night to do things his way.

With a delicate ease, he spread her legs farther apart and slithered his finger inside her, prodding deeper and deeper. Drenched in his eroticism, she soaked up his hot breath. Quivering in the magical minute, she found herself utterly aroused, more so than she imagined. Parts of her body lay dormant up until this point. And for the first time, she desired him, almost needed him. And she was elated.

This relationship could work out after all.

Cinnamon leaned back on the counter, saturated in their body heat, every part of her screaming for the finale. After months of denied pleasure, she felt herself ready to explode. Roman seemed to pick up on her potent vibes because once he unbuckled his pants and dropped them to the floor, it was lights, camera and action!

CHAPTER TWENTY

CINNAMON STARED INTO SPACE while Roman lay sound asleep. She inspected her body. Every muscle ached, but it was a good ache. Underneath the comforter, they lay cuddled, Roman still clutching her hand.

It was over. The moment she dreaded ended and she was glad to have taken the dare. This being her first sexual experience in a long time, her body gave Roman a marvelous welcome. Though at times painful, it was bearable. She characterized the episode as neither good nor bad. But somewhere in the middle, wherever that might be.

She enjoyed parts of it, especially the foreplay. Actually, she appreciated everything up until the great moment. That was where mediocrity set in. Not that Roman was lacking in some way, in fact, he was quite good. She just didn't favor the evening's highlight as much as everything else. In fact, it was a little humdrum and she couldn't figure out if it was Roman or just the sex itself. Though while in the moment her body possessed a grand desire for him, once the activity was underway, the desire seemed to vanish. And she just couldn't understand it. She longed for the day when she would speak as highly of sex as did Arri.

Her sexual encounter with Roman would certainly clue her in on her true feelings, which proved what she knew all along. As nice and wonderful as Roman may have been, he was not the one for her.

Roman and Cinnamon's erotic encounter seemed to have induced a snowstorm.

Cinnamon watched the falling snow and icicles forming on the windows. She liked to believe that everything she noticed with wonder held meaning, and she understood the falling snow as a symbol of the beginning or end of something.

After musing over the manifestation even further, she realized that the falling snow was the beginning and end of their sexual relationship. Though she planned to stay the night, if she did, she would not sleep well. But she couldn't leave, especially since it was their first time together. She would appear cold and insensitive and she was neither.

She had just made a sticky situation even stickier. Now Roman was certain to believe their relationship had progressed. But from where Cinnamon stood, their relationship failed to progress at all. But instead regressed.

Careful not to wake Roman, Cinnamon eased from his arms and climbed out of bed.

Standing in the shower, she turned on the water and leaned against the wall. She remained perfectly still as she relived the evening's events, from the time Mitchell visited with her, all the way to this very moment. Everything seemed to happen so fast and she needed more time to digest it all. As she lathered her body with the liquid soap, she was startled when Roman pulled open the shower curtain and stepped inside. "I thought you might like some company. I missed you."

"How could you miss me, I just left your side?"

"That should tell you something, then," he said as he saddled his hands on her shoulders and kissed her.

She turned to face the water, allowing it to cascade down her face. Roman wrapped his arms around her, his chest locked against her back. "I love you, Cinnamon."

Though his words did not shock her, she was too numb to respond.

"Aren't you going to say you love me back?" he asked.

Cinnamon hesitated for a moment, then turned to face him. "I don't know if I love you, Roman."

"That's okay. It'll come."

There was no question in her mind. Roman was here to stay.

Wearing her navy uniform, Cinnamon stood on the packed Orange line train, en route to Midway Airport. She ceased reflecting on her first time with Roman. Instead, her thoughts lay elsewhere. With Mitchell.

What was it about this man that made Cinnamon so gaga?

Despite everything, she could not and would not ever see Mitchell again. And not just because she was involved with Roman but because of something much more deadly. She was in love. In love with Mitchell Maine.

In Albuquerque, New Mexico, Cinnamon sipped on Chamomile tea while she conversed with Arri over the phone.

"I did it," Cinnamon said.

Arri screamed. "You didn't."

Cinnamon shifted the receiver from one ear to the other. "Will you calm down?"

"How was it? Did he hurt you? Did you like it?"

"Calm down, Missy. It was okay, nothing special."

"Was it big?"

"I don't know," Cinnamon said. "I didn't look at it."

"Well, did it feel big?"

"It felt normal. That's all I can tell you."

"Did you do that thing?"

"What thing?"

"That thing that men like so much."

"Most certainly not."

"Did he do you?"

"I'm not going to tell you."

"Why not?"

"'Cause it's none of your business."

"Everything you do is my business," Arri said. "I just can't grasp you having sex with anyone."

"I have done it before, you know. It wasn't like it was my first time."

"But that was years ago."

"It's not like I could forget. It's not like anyone could forget."

"I know. I know. I'm just so happy for you," Arri said. "Is this going to be an ongoing thing now?"

"Maybe."

"Oh, no," Arri said, her exuberance fading. "You're going to break up with him, aren't you?"

"I didn't say that."

"You didn't have to. I heard it in your voice."

"Just because we slept together doesn't mean we're perfect for each other."

"You're going to run away from him," Arri said.

"I'm not going to run away from him."

"Will you at least give him a chance before you break up with him?"

"I'm not going to break up with him, at least not right away anyway."

Cinnamon was supposed to call Roman immediately upon her return to Chicago, but decided not to. She needed some time to herself and to catch up on Arri's drama.

In the midst of another crisis with Eric, Arri began smoking again, this time more than ever. Her new ploy of easing her heartache was to give away her cats that bore Eric's first and last name. And Arri insisted Cinnamon be a part of it all.

Arri backed her Honda into a parking space across from the Anti-Cruelty Society. She stubbed out her cigarette and took hold of the two pet carrying cases from the back seat. Inside the carriages were Eric and Lyles.

"Will you grab my purse for me?" Arri asked.

Cinnamon grabbed Arri's purse from the front seat. She and Arri exited the car and headed across the street to the Anti-Cruelty Society on Grand Avenue.

"I really think you should think about this some more, Arri."

"I have thought about it. I thought about it all last night."

"But if you change your mind, they won't be here when you come back."

"I know what I'm doing, Cinnamon. Trust me."

Inside the Anti-Cruelty Society, they approached a cheerful woman in her sixties at the counter. "May I help you?"

Arri placed the carriages on the counter. "I have two male cats for the shelter."

"Are they sick?" the woman asked.

"No. I just can't take care of them anymore."

The woman handed Arri a form to fill out.

"You're going to give these cute things away," Cinnamon questioned.

"Why don't you take them then?"

"I can't. I'd have cat hair everywhere."

Cinnamon pulled the cat from the carrier and positioned his face in front of Arri's. "Are you sure you want to give this cute face away?"

Arri turned away and continued filling out the form.

"See, you can't even look at him," Cinnamon said.

Cinnamon placed the cat back into the carrier. The sixty-year-old woman then carried them both away.

"Goodbye, Eric, goodbye Lyles," Cinnamon said, waving to the cats.

"Come on, let's get out of here."

"It's not too late, Arri. If you want to change your mind, now is the time."

"I'm not going to change my mind."

As soon as they reached the outside, Arri lit a Virginia Slims cigarette.

"You don't have to give those cats away, Arri. You can always change their names."

"I don't want to change their names. Besides, even if I did, they would still remind me too much of Eric."

Inside Arri's Honda, Cinnamon and Arri sat while Arri started the engine.

Arri was about to light another cigarette when she realized she already held one in her mouth. "Eric was my last chance at romance and now it's not going to happen."

"Are you planning on dying soon or something?"

"No, it's just that my opportunity for love has passed me by."

Arri could not have been more dramatic if she were Susan Lucci herself.

"Are you saying Eric is the only man in the world who you can have a relationship with?"

"No, I'm not saying that," Arri said as she pulled from the parking space. "He's the only man I wanted to have a relationship with."

"What about that manager at your office?"

"He doesn't count. He's just a fantasy."

Arri and Cinnamon relaxed in the lotus position on Cinnamon's living room floor with their eyes closed and hands in their laps. Arri recently persuaded Cinnamon to take up meditation, promising it would encourage clarity, enabling them to make better decisions.

Five minutes passed. Cinnamon sighed. "I'm sorry Arri, but I'm not getting it."

With her eyes still closed, Arri said, "It takes practice."

Cinnamon opened her eyes, pushed herself up from the floor and eased down on the sofa. After a short silence, she said, "I like Roman a lot, but I don't think I love him. Arri, have you ever been with someone who was so perfect for you, yet you didn't love him?"

Arri remained silent.

"Arri, are you listening to me? I'm talking to you. This is important."

"I'm listening. I just have my eyes closed."

"Well, open your eyes."

Arri opened her eyes, peered up at Cinnamon. "I heard every word you said. You like Roman a lot, but you don't love him."

As Arri pulled a cigarette from her purse and lit it, Cinnamon frowned. "I don't have any ashtrays, and I refuse to condone this disgusting habit of yours in any way."

"What happened to that beautiful ashtray from Universal Studios?"

"I got rid of it when I quit smoking."

"I'll just put my ashes out on your floor then."

"Okay, try it."

Arri left the room, then returned with a piece of aluminum foil. "See how creative I can be," Arri said. "Now what were you saying about the perfect person?"

"Never mind. I forgot who I was asking."

"What's that supposed to mean?"

"It means that the only person you ever thought was perfect for you was Eric and that manager at your office, Matt."

"I never thought Matt was perfect for me." Arri blew smoke from her mouth. "I just wanted to fuck him."

Cinnamon studied the cigarette between Arri's fingers. "Why are you still smoking those darn cigarettes?"

"We had this conversation already."

"Can we have it again, please? Because this smoking has got to go."

"Smoking helps me."

Cinnamon's forehead creased with confusion. "How?"

"It just does. Okay. It helps me cope."

"Whatever."

"What's got you so irritable?" Arri asked.

"I think it was a mistake for me to have sex with Roman. Now he thinks our relationship is going to soar."

"How do you know what he thinks?"

"Why wouldn't he think that? And if I break up with him, he's going to think I'm a nut."

"But you are."

"Very funny."

"I wouldn't worry too much about the sex thing. It's bound to get better. I didn't always enjoy having sex with Eric. It took awhile."

"How long are we talking about?"

"About a month."

"That's too long."

"What else can you do?" Arri asked.

"I don't know."

"Just be patient. Roman may very well be the One, which reminds me, when do I get a chance to meet him?"

"You'll meet him soon enough."

Arri was right.

Cinnamon failed to give Roman a chance. It was too soon to tell whether or not their relationship would work. It needed time to prosper.

In an effort to prove to herself she was giving Roman a fair chance, she surprised him by showing up at his office for lunch. This would be the first time she saw him since their night together and she felt a little weird. Though she was only a year from turning thirty, she felt like a teenager when it came to sex.

In Roman's office, she sat across from him, her legs crossed.

Roman picked up the phone and made a call. "Simon? Roman. Can we do lunch tomorrow? I need to take care of something this afternoon. Sounds good."

"You didn't have to break your lunch date for me," Cinnamon said.

Roman grabbed his coat from the back of the door. "What is it going to take for you to realize that you are first in my life?"

Cinnamon and Roman dined at a stuffy restaurant on Randolph Street.

"I've been offered a promotion at work," Roman said. "That's what that business lunch was about today."

"That's wonderful. Are you excited?"

"It's going to mean a lot of long hours and a lot more responsibility."

"I have complete confidence in you. You're a smart man and you can do anything."

Roman crept his hand on top of hers, fondling her fingers. "You ever think about getting a regular job?"

"I have a regular job."

"I mean a job with regular hours, one where you could stay in the city and I can see you more often."

"No. I don't think about that. I like my job just the way it is."

Cinnamon watched Roman eye an older woman of about fifty at the next table, seemingly captivated by her.

"Do you know her?" Cinnamon asked.

"No. She just reminds me of my mother, that's all." Quickly changing the subject, he said, "Here's what I have planned for us this evening."

"I'm listening," she said with a warm smile.

"I'm going to pick you up around six and we're going to take a long walk by the lake."

"But it's freezing outside."

"That's okay. When we get back to my place, I'll warm you up. Do you have any plans this afternoon?"

"No, why?"

Roman's eyes sparkled. "Let's go to my place. Now."

"Now?"

"Yes, now."

She hesitated for a moment. "I have to do my laundry and stuff and catch up on my housework."

"You can do that any time."

"But I want to do it today."

"Okay, but I will see you tonight."

"I was actually thinking maybe we should slow it down a bit," Cinnamon said.

"Why would you think that?"

"Because," she said.

"Because what?"

"Because it feels like we're moving too fast."

"Did you enjoy making love to me the other night?" he asked.

"I thought it was the other way around."

"It was that too," he said. "Did you enjoy it?"

"Yes, but--"

"No, buts. It's settled."

That evening Cinnamon and Roman returned to his apartment after their long stroll. To avoid having sex with him, she pretended to be on her cycle. She hated lying to him, but she didn't know what else to do, especially since he was so adamant about everything.

In the morning, she would leave for work, and she was eager to get away. She felt trapped by the way Roman demanded her time, not to mention how he insisted he be the first person she call upon her return to the city. Though his attention was flattering, it was also draining.

Three days later, Cinnamon passed over his request to call him upon her immediate return. Instead, she reorganized her closets, dusted her furniture and cleaned her refrigerator. After she finished, she folded the freshly-washed linens, categorizing the towels, sheets and pillow cases.

When the doorbell rang, she soon learned it was Roman, which marked the second time he showed up unannounced. After buzzing him in, she left the front door ajar and returned to folding her linen.

When she heard his footsteps across the threshold, she said, "I'm in here, Roman."

He approached her and kissed her cheek. "I thought I told you to call me when you got back."

Ignoring his statement, she continued folding the linen.

"So why didn't you call?"

Having no answer for him, she raised her shoulders.

He dropped down on the bed, seemingly lax and assured. "Is that an answer?"

"I don't know, Roman. All right."

"Sorry if I come on a little strong. It's only because I miss you when you're away."

"I miss you too," she said out of obligation.

She was about to leave the room when the phone rang. She watched in astonishment as Roman reached for her phone, her mouth hanging open.

No, he didn't.

"Hello. . .Yes, she's here. Who is this? Who?"

Roman didn't hesitate to hand her the phone. "I think it's your boyfriend."

"What boyfriend?" Cinnamon asked. "Hello . . . I'm kind of busy right now. . . No, you shouldn't call here anymore."

Cinnamon hung up the phone and her eyes immediately shot to Roman. She could only imagine what circulated through his mind. If he was the jealous type, which every man was, she was sure to find out now.

"Who's your boyfriend?" he asked playfully, as he pivoted over to her.

She disregarded his question and headed toward the door. "You're not going to tell me?"

"That was Joseph. I met him right around the time I met you."

"Why is he calling you now?"

"I don't know. I just heard from him today."

"Really? Well, I'd rather he not call here."

"Whatever, Roman. I have to get the rest of my laundry."

Roman followed her to the laundry room. He watched her empty the clothes from the dryer into the wicker laundry basket. From the pile of clothes, Roman plucked out a pair of sunlight yellow mens' briefs. "What the hell is this?"

Cinnamon noted the briefs, laughing on the inside but displaying nonchalance on the outside.

"Are these Joseph's?" Roman asked.

After thinking about it for a moment, she found it somewhat funny because she knew they belonged to Noel. But what she couldn't figure out was how they got there.

"Okay," she said, still laughing on the inside. "This is what happened. Those belong to a friend of mine, Noel, and I guess they got mixed up with my laundry when he was staying here."

"Why was Noel staying with you?"

"He was having some problems at home, and I let him stay with me for a while."

"When did this happen?"

"Awhile ago."

After Cinnamon finished her laundry, she stood in the kitchen, still amused after finding Noel's underwear in her wash. She smiled to herself as she poured herself a glass of water.

Moments later, Roman entered. "You think this is funny, don't you?" he asked, obviously witnessing the zany expression on her face.

She tried to keep from smiling but she couldn't. "No, I don't."

"I'm not going to tolerate any other men, Cinnamon. You know that, don't you?"

"Noel is just a friend, Roman."

"I don't care. I won't be second in your life."

He stepped to her, gripped her buttocks and pulled her close. He united his lips with hers and kissed her over and over. It seemed his jealousy somehow shifted to lust.

When the phone rang, she pulled away but he resisted, keeping her close. She opened her mouth to speak but he quickly enveloped it with his lips.

One thing was for sure. Her relationship with Roman was on borrowed time.

CHAPTER TWENTY-ONE

Harris Bank.

Cinnamon stepped off the elevator where Arri worked and bypassed the four handsome businessmen conversing in the reception area. She jaunted across the wheat colored carpet, down the corridor until she reached Arri's desk, which was the epitome of disarray. Stacks and stacks of paper rested on every corner of the desk. While the sweet sounds of Nora Jones resounded on the desk radio, Cinnamon watched Arri finish up a call. "And your number?" Arri scribbled down a quick message. "I'll let him know."

Arri hung up the phone and looked up to Cinnamon. "Hey."

"Ready?" Cinnamon asked.

"Just as soon as I deliver this message."

Arri delivered the phone message into the corner office, then returned to her desk. Cinnamon's gaze circled the office. "Where's the famous Matt?"

"In his office probably. You want to see him?"

"Only if I can tell him you've been fantasizing about him."

"Be my guest. What, you think I'm ashamed?"

"I know you have no shame."

Arri garnered her purse from the desk drawer, and just as she and Cinnamon were about to leave, a gentleman approached. It was Matthew Murphy. He looked to be in his early thirties but possessed a youthful air. He wore a tired dark suit and was nearly bald.

"Arri, could you fax this before you leave, please?" Matthew asked.

"Sure, Matt." Arri accepted the document from him.

Matt turned to Cinnamon and gifted her with a smile. "Hello."

"Hello," Cinnamon said.

As soon as Matthew stepped away, Arri looked to Cinnamon, bubbling with enthusiasm. "That was him."

They both laughed.

"What do you think?" Arri asked.

"He looks so young but he seems like a really nice guy. I can see why you like him."

Cinnamon and Arri originally planned to lunch at a new Mexican restaurant on Adams Street but because of the crowd, they bought McDonald's instead.

Returning to Arri's office, Arri located an unoccupied conference room where she and Cinnamon could eat in private.

In this windowless conference room, Arri and Cinnamon dined at the long, shiny table, large enough to seat ten people.

"I had such a disturbing dream last night," Arri said as she unwrapped her cheeseburger. "I dreamed I sold everything I owned, withdrew all my money from the bank and showed up at this love booth. I was trying to buy love, but I didn't have enough money. I pleaded with the lady, Lana was her name. I explained to her that all I had was in my hand but she wouldn't listen, didn't even care."

"You're making this up, right?"

"No, I really dreamed that."

While Cinnamon munched on her French fries, her pager beeped.

"What the hell is that?" Arri asked.

Cinnamon dug into her purse and pulled out her pager, then browsed the number. It could only be Roman, seeing he was the only person with the number.

"Since when do you carry a pager?"

"Since Roman became paranoid that other men were out to steal me away from him."

Cinnamon never took well to the pager idea to begin with, but she agreed anyhow, striving to be the nice and accommodating girlfriend. But it wasn't until that first page that she realized it was not a good idea.

Cinnamon returned the pager to her purse.

"Aren't you going to call him?" Arri asked.

"He'll page me again." Cinnamon bit into her Big Mac. "There's a side to Roman I am just now beginning to see."

"Like what?"

"Well, for starters, he has this thing with mixing passion and aggression."

"Oh, really? Tell me more."

"You get off on stuff like this, don't you?"

"What can I say but yes."

Arri finished her lunch, then grabbed an ashtray from the side table and lit a cigarette.

"You can't smoke in here, Arri."

"Why can't I? The executives and their clients do it all the time."

"If you say so."

Arri took a long drag from her cigarette. "So tell me some more about this passion-aggression thing."

"He'll be angry with me one minute, and the next minute he'll want to make love."

"Sounds kinky."

"It's not. And this whole pager thing, I don't like that either."

"So break up with him then."

"I can't, remember. You told me to give him a chance."

"Why would you listen to me?"

"That's a good question. Why would I listen to you?" Cinnamon paused. "I guess I'm just waiting for the right time."

"You mean you're scared."

"That too."

Cinnamon wiped her mouth and stuffed her food wrappers into the McDonald's bag.

Today being the first time Cinnamon felt ready to disclose her true feelings about Mitchell to Arri, she said, "Listen. I have to tell you something that I probably should have told you before."

Arri's face reeked of concern. "You're pregnant."

"No, Arri, I'm not pregnant."

"What kind of protection did you and Roman use?"

"If you must know, Nosy, we used a condom."

"Eric doesn't like those."

Annoyed, Cinnamon held up her hand. "Can we talk about me for a second, here?"

"Well, excuse. . . me," Arri said as she took another drag from her cigarette."

"I think I'm in love."

"With whom? Not Roman."

"Not Roman. It's someone you don't know."

Arri's forehead creased with wonder. "That married man...What's his name? Mitchell. Why didn't you tell me?"

"I'm telling you now."

"You know what I mean."

"You know how private and secretive I can be sometimes."

"You're in love with him?" Arri asked. "What? How? When?"

"I saw him a couple of times and he kissed me."

Arri stubbed out her cigarette and jolted forward. "You two kissed?"

Cinnamon smiled, basking in her memories. "And it was great. It was one of those kisses where it's like having sex."

"That's one hell of a kiss."

"That's what I'm trying to tell you."

"And now you're in love with him. That's why your heart isn't in it for Roman, you're all wrapped up with this married man."

"Even though I have no intentions of seeing him again, I think about him all the time."

"I don't know how that's going to work, you and this married man."

"You speak as if I'm planning my life with him. I just told you I'm not going to see him again, much less establish a relationship."

"Your situation reminds me of this book I just finished. The main character is so much like you, it's scary. It's entitled *Single Black Female* by this new author, Carrie Carr. You have to read this book."

"A novel?"

"I know novels are not your thing, but you and the main character are both going through the same exact thing. As a matter of fact, you two could be twins. Trust me, you have to read this book. I'll loan you my copy."

Arri was about to say something, then didn't. Cinnamon witnessed the concern on her face.

"What?" Cinnamon asked.

"I was just wondering. Did you sleep with this guy?"

"NO! Not that I didn't want to but no, I didn't."

"Just checking. You speak so highly of him, I was just wondering."

"Well, wonder no more."

After lunch, Cinnamon and Arri sauntered to Borders Books on Michigan and State.

Feng Shui was Arri's latest craze, certain it would change her life, especially her love life. After Arri purchased two books on the subject, she and Cinnamon headed back to Arri's office.

On State Street, they waited for the light to change before entering the crosswalk. Though the sun was bright, the air was frigid and damp.

Cinnamon pulled her leather gloves from her coat pocket and quickly slid them on. From a distance, Cinnamon was certain she saw Eric and a woman exiting Marshall Field's department store.

"Is that Eric?" Cinnamon asked.

"Where?"

"In the dark coat."

Cinnamon pointed in Eric's direction and Arri's eyes followed. "Hell, yeah, that's him. He's wearing the coat I bought him. And who is she?"

Most women might have judged Eric as attractive, but not Cinnamon. She disapproved of his politics toward Arri so much that it was difficult for her to recognize anything positive about him. He was well buffed, actually too buffed with an oversized body hovering over his slim bottom. He was as light as Halle Berry and possessed a slick head like Michael Jordan. These days it seemed every other black man was bald, as if it were a symbol of some sort.

When Arri headed toward him, Cinnamon yanked Arri's arm. "Where do you think you're going?"

"I'm going to go talk to him. I want to see who that girl is."

"And say what?"

"I'll just say hi."

"No, you'll say more than that."

"I'll be cool," Arri said as she continued to ogle Eric from a distance.

"At this moment, you don't even know how to spell cool."

Cinnamon witnessed an agitated Arri before and knew better than to allow Arri to confront Eric in a flustered state of mind. It would only end in disaster and possibly even an arrest.

Arri snatched her arm away from Cinnamon. "I know what I'm doing."

The light turned green but Arri and Cinnamon remained at the edge of the crosswalk, the harsh wind clamoring past them.

"Arri, please don't. I know you. Approaching him will only upset you."

"No, it won't."

"Yes, it will. And it will be ugly, too ugly for me to witness."

Arri hesitated, then stomped her foot. "Well, what am I supposed to do?"

"There's nothing you can do. If he's with someone else, there's nothing you can do."

Arri stared into space, seemingly oblivious to her surroundings.

Cinnamon connected her hand with Arri's and led her across the street.

"I feel a depression coming on," Arri said as she dragged her feet. "I don't think I want to go back to work."

"You only have a few more hours. I'll drop back at five and we can do something fun."

"I don't want to have any fun. I just want to medicate myself and cry."

Though Cinnamon may have convinced Arri to keep her cool for now, it was far from over.

As promised, Cinnamon met Arri at five and they headed to Arri's apartment.

With numerous runs in her pantyhose, Arri crashed on the futon, her body slumped over as if someone died.

Many times Cinnamon witnessed a saddened Arri but nothing like this. Cinnamon stood in front of her, looking down at the top of Arri's head. "You want to talk about it?"

Arri shook her head.

"Can I light a cigarette for you?"

Again, Arri shook her head.

Though Cinnamon didn't condone Arri's smoking habit, at that moment, she would have done anything to pull Arri from her pit of despair.

"Can I make you some coffee? Or maybe we could watch some *Martin* reruns? That always cheers you up."

Arri remained silent, her body still slumped over.

Cinnamon kneeled down in front of Arri so that they were eye to eye. "I'm sorry, honey that you saw Eric with someone else."

"Why are you sorry? It's not your fault."

"I just hate to see you in so much pain."

"I think I might become a lesbian, Cinnamon. They're not all masculine, you know."

"You would never make it as a lesbian."

"Why? Do I have to take a test or something?"

They both burst into laughter.

"Are you feeling any better?" Cinnamon asked.

"Not really," Arri said as she rose from the futon. "But I have dishes to do."

"That's my girl."

As Arri headed into the kitchen, Cinnamon's pager beeped. She glanced at the number and saw that Roman was calling from his apartment. For a moment, she considered throwing it against the wall, but decided to toss it back into her purse instead. She couldn't believe she agreed to carry a pager just to feed his ego, but it really didn't matter anymore because things were about to change. And soon.

Cinnamon joined Arri in the kitchen. On the kitchen counter was a beautiful multi-colored flower arrangement.

"Those are lovely," Cinnamon said. "Who sent you those?"

"My mother." Arri wiped down the kitchen table, then set the flower vase in the center. "She knew how upset I was about my breakup with Eric." Arri paused. "I know what you are about to say. So don't say it."

Cinnamon eased down in the chair. "Don't say what?"

"How I should call my mother more."

"I wasn't going to say anything about that. I'm the one who needs to call my mother more often."

Seemingly in serious thought, Arri washed the coffee mugs and silverware.

"Who do you think that girl was?" Arri asked.

"Could have been anyone. A friend, a relative."

"It couldn't have been a relative, not the way she was hanging on his arm. You think it was his girlfriend?"

"Who knows?" Cinnamon said. "Who cares?"

"I care," Arri shouted.

"I'm sorry, you're right. That was insensitive of me."

Arri dashed out of the kitchen, darted into the bedroom and slammed the door.

Cinnamon was about to go after her when her pager beeped again. She blew a irritating breath from her mouth and decided to return his call, if only to gain a sense of peace.

"Where are you?" Roman asked.

"I'm at Arri's. She's upset, Roman, and I'm going to stay with her for a while."

"What about us?"

"I can still meet with you later. Okay?"

"No, it's not okay."

"Well, what do you want me to do, just leave now?"

"How long will you be over there?"

"I don't know. Awhile. I'll call you when I'm on my way home."

She didn't bother waiting for his reply. Instead, she hung up, then hurried to Arri's bedroom.

"Arri, are you okay?" Cinnamon called out as she knocked on the bedroom door.

Arri didn't reply and Cinnamon knocked again. "Arri?" Cinnamon opened the door and saw Arri sitting against the wall, her head down, bawling to the high heavens.

Cinnamon stooped beside Arri and gently lifted Arri's head. "Don't cry, honey. I'm sure that woman with Eric was nobody."

"I must have really done something terrible to Eric for him to hurt me like this."

"You did nothing. It's him. He's the problem. Not you. He doesn't deserve you anyway. And I know you find that hard to believe but it's true."

Arri wiped the ripples from her face, then pushed herself off the floor and dropped down on the edge of the bed. "How do I make it go away, Cinnamon? How do I make it stop?"

"Make what stop?"

"The hurt, the pain. I feel like this too often and I want it to stop."

Cinnamon wasn't sure if she should answer or not because Arri was certain not to agree with her response. Cinnamon stood up, still debating whether to answer Arri's question, then decided to go for it. "If you really want to help yourself feel better, Arri, you have to forgive Eric. For everything."

Arri wiped her face, smearing her blush into her cheeks. "That's crazy. Why would I forgive him after what he did?"

"It will help you more than it will help him."

"I'm not doing that. That would be like saying it was okay for him to do what he did."

"Will you at least think about it?"

"No, because I'm not doing that."

Cinnamon said what she needed to say and now the rest was on Arri. "I'm meeting Roman at my apartment so I'm going to head on home. Will you be okay?"

"You go, I'll be fine," Arri said. "I have to write some things in my journal anyway."

"Call me later if you need to."

Over and over, Cinnamon rehearsed her words for Roman as she walked home. Her words would be a mixture of firmness and kindness.

As soon as Roman entered her apartment and before he removed his coat, Cinnamon handed him the pager. "I don't want this anymore. Any of it."

"Any of what?"

"This relationship. Or the pager."

"You want to end this relationship because of a pager?"

"No, it's not just that." Cinnamon swallowed hard, then continued. "I made a mistake and I don't think we should be together."

"What? Why?"

"I'm just not happy. You have this need to be with me all the time, this need for me to call you all the time. And I didn't sign up for that. I'm sorry, Roman but it's just not working."

With beer on his breath, he nudged her against the wall and brushed his face against hers. "I'm not going to let you leave me because of a pager, because of my desire to be with you. You're going to have to come better than that."

"Who says? If I don't want to be with you anymore, I don't need your permission. This is not a request I'm making."

"Don't I have a say in this matter?" Roman asked.

She avoided his question. "Roman, I don't want to be with you anymore, and if my explanation is not good enough for you, then I'm sorry but that doesn't change how I feel."

"Let's be rational now and really think about this."

"I have thought about it and I want out."

"But your reasoning makes no sense. Okay, maybe I do love you too much, but--"

"Maybe I don't want to be loved like that," Cinnamon said. "I don't."

She hated being so cold but he left her no choice.

Roman eased down on the sofa, not uttering a word as if in a trance-like state. "Don't do this. Please. If you don't want to carry the pager anymore, that's fine, but don't do this to me. Please, honey."

Cinnamon stood motionless, absorbing the despondent air in the room as well as Roman's pain. She knew the anguish of unrequited love well. But it still didn't change the way she felt.

Roman approached her, clutched her arms and tried to kiss her, but Cinnamon resisted and turned her head. "I don't want to do this anymore. I'm sorry."

"I know you don't mean that. You're just upset."

"I can mean it and I do. Look, Roman, I care about you a lot. I really do. But it's not meant to be. It's not."

"Just tell me what you want and I'll give it to you."

"You can't. You can't stop being who you are because of me. And I accept that. I also accept the fact that this relationship is over and I want you to accept that too."

"What do you think, that I'm this way with everyone? Well, do you?"

"I don't know."

"Well, I'm not," he said. "I love you. I'm not some obsessed man. I'm this way because of my love for you."

"Well, I'm sorry," she said as she wrestled her arms away from him. "I'm sorry if I've made you into something you're not."

"Don't apologize. I love you for it."

"It's still not going to work."

"It will."

"It won't."

"Yes, it will."

Exhausted, she threw her hands up. "I want to be with somebody else."

Roman's aggressive demeanor quickly vanished. His mouth hung open but nothing came out.

"I'm sorry, Roman."

"There's someone else?" he questioned.

She nodded. "I'm sorry. I really am."

"Well, I guess that's that then, isn't it?" He headed toward the door and before she could blink an eye, he was gone.

She felt horrible saying what she said. But she only said what needed to be heard.

What else could she do?

She kidded herself into believing she could make herself love Roman. It was time to wake up from this fantasy world she lived in and face the facts about who it was her heart cried out for, and Roman was not him. Letting him go was the best thing for all considered, an opportunity for the both of them to find true love. And at that moment, her greatest wish was that Roman find his perfect love.

CHAPTER TWENTY-TWO

NOEL GREEN.

Cinnamon neglected to talk to him since he settled back in with his lover. Concerned for his safety, she called him.

"Just calling to make sure Aaron isn't beating up on you again," Cinnamon said.

"You should have called yesterday then."

Cinnamon laughed. "You guys still fighting?"

"Of course. Did you think it would stop just because I came back?"

"Was it a cereal box this time?"

"The remote control. He threw it at me."

Cinnamon chuckled, forever gurgling whenever she conversed with him. Noel could build a comedic routine solely on his love life.

"But you're okay though?" she asked.

"I'm all right. I would have called you but I've been getting a lot of hours with this temporary agency."

"Secretarial work?"

"I like the term administrative worker better," Noel said with a twang.

"Well, you know you can always move back in here if you need to. I enjoy having you around."

"The way you were always bitching at me."

"That's because I love you. My bitching is a sign of affection."

"Well, next time, don't love me so much."

"Listen, let's get together real soon," she said.

"You bet."

"Since I know you're okay, I can put my fears to rest."

"Thanks, Cinnamon."

"Sure, and you tell Aaron that Cinnamon said to watch his back because I'll "F" him up."

Noel laughed. "I'll tell him."

Today was Cinnamon's day to relax.

Between Roman's obsession and Arri's weekly crisis, little time remained for herself. But things had already begun to change. She ended her relationship with Roman, and Arri was an amazing work in progress. Eventually Arri would conquer her self-worth issues, opening herself up to promising love relationships. In the meantime though, all Cinnamon could do was hold Arri's hand along the way.

Now if only Cinnamon could forget about Mitchell, her life would be perfect, well not quite, but close.

Cinnamon luxuriated in a warm raspberry bubble bath. She reveled in the fruity scent, the stillness and quiet of the moment. The novel, *Single Black Female*, which Arri loaned to her, rested on the fluffy rug near the tub. Careful not to wet the pages, she lifted the book from the floor and flipped to the first chapter.

While she soaked in the tub, she listened to an old, old Van Morrison tune, "Someone Like You." It was a slow melodramatic tune with soft piano music, similar to a melody heard at the end of an uplifting love story. It was a tune she loved for many years and for which she planned to dedicate to that special person who touched her life like no other. When that unique individual showed up, she'd set out to sing him praises through Van Morrison.

Forty minutes into the novel, a chill swept through her as she turned each page. The novel paralleled her life to a tee, evoking a sense of *a-ha*. It was an absolute surreal experience and she couldn't wait to see how it would end.

Unexpectedly, the incessant doorbell ringing thrust Cinnamon's attention away from her enchanting novel.

All she could think about was that someone must have died.

Ring! Ring! Ring! Ring! Ring! Ring! Ring!

Cinnamon tore herself away from the novel, leaped from the tub and grabbed her bathrobe from behind the door. The unrelenting ringing echoed throughout her apartment before she could reach the intercom.

It was Arri and she was on her way up.

Cinnamon wished to prepare herself, but with Arri, it was impossible.

Arri stumbled inside the door, seemingly intoxicated but cheerful. Her hair was pulled back into what used to be a ponytail without anything to keep it together. Her wrinkled skirt inside her opened coat appeared to have been taken from a clothes hamper and she was wearing no pantyhose with her boots.

"You look terrible," Cinnamon said.

"Thank you." Arri dropped her purse to the floor.

"What happened to you?"

"Life happened to me." Giggly and full of life, Arri broke out of her coat and tossed it to the floor. She then fumbled toward the bathroom, staggering along the way.

Cinnamon trailed behind, watching and wondering.

Arri took the Tylenol from the medicine cabinet. She then popped three down her throat, cupped the water from the faucet into her hands, and threw her head back.

Cinnamon had seen Arri perform before but not like this. "Are you okay?"

"Nope." Still wearing her boots, Arri teetered into the bedroom and climbed upon the bed.

Cinnamon quickly unzipped Arri's boots, stripped them from her feet and watched Arri twist her body into a fetal position.

Cinnamon lay on the bed beside her. "I called your office today."

"I wasn't there."

"No kidding," Cinnamon said, repulsed by the pungent alcohol smell on Arri's breath. "Have you been drinking all day?"

"Not all day, just most of it."

Cinnamon recognized Arri's condition for what it was. Heartache at its finest.

"So this is what it has come to, huh? This is how you get over Eric, by drinking yourself into a stupor."

"What other choice do I have?" Arri combed her fingers through her hair. "My hair is all messed up, my clothes are dirty and I need a new pair of boots."

"Anything else?" Cinnamon asked.

"Ah yeah, I need to clean my apartment."

"Where did you go today?"

Arri closed her eyes and said nothing.

"Arri, where were you today?" Cinnamon marked the tears streaming down Arri's face. "Did you see Eric?"

For several moments, Arri said nothing, then said, "I think he raped me."

"You mean you had sex with him."

"No. He raped me."

Playing Arri's game, Cinnamon asked, "Did you call the police?"

"No," Arri said.

"Why not?"

Arri smiled to herself and looked to Cinnamon. "Okay, he didn't really rape me."

"I didn't think so. So what were you doing at Eric's house?"

"He invited me."

"I guess that's as good a reason as any. So tell me something. How long is this going to go on? This drinking and acting out?"

"I don't know. Ask Eric."

"Did you find out who that girl was he was with?"

"His new girlfriend."

"So why were you over there?"

Arri wiped the tears from her face and raised her shoulders. "I guess I'm just stupid."

"You are not stupid."

"How else do you explain it then?"

"You just want someone to love you, honey, that's all. And there's nothing wrong with that. I must say though you picked a real winner with Eric."

Arri sat up as if revitalized by a bolt of energy. "You're right . . . You are so right. He's egotistical, dirty, selfish, sleazy, mannish. He can't be trusted."

Cinnamon watched Arri try to convince herself.

"He's confused," Arri continued. "Doesn't know what he wants. A bonafide dog."

"You still want to be with him, don't you?" Cinnamon asked.

"I sure do." Arri flopped back on the bed, resuming her fetal position. "I sure do."

"I know you do. Getting over someone is not an easy thing."

"How would you know?"

"I've been in love before. I know all about the agonies of unrequited love." Cinnamon took Arri's hand into hers, gripping it firmly. "Listen, I know you are in a lot a pain. Believe me, I feel for you, but you have a choice to make."

"You think I should kill myself?" Arri questioned.

"No, that's not one of the choices."

"What else is there?"

"Very funny, Arri. You have to decide what to do about it."

"I'm doing it already. I'm doing it right now."

"I mean after you're done acting out, what are you going to do?"

"I don't know," Arri said. "What options do I have?"

"I'm sure you can think of a few."

Arri climbed off the bed and stood in front of the mirror, studying herself. "I could stop crying over him."

"That's a good place to start."

Arri continued ruminating over Cinnamon's suggestion. "But what else?"

"Don't worry about anything else, just concentrate on what you just said. And I don't think you should drive in your condition, so how about I put you in a cab or drive you home myself?"

Arri flopped down on the bed, her face grimaced with worry. "I don't want to go home. Are you're putting me out?"

"No, I'm not putting you out, Soap Opera Queen."

"Good, because there's no one there. The cats are gone, Eric is gone. My next door neighbor is back in rehab."

After they both shared a long belly laugh, Cinnamon said, "Okay, then, you stay here tonight."

The next morning, Cinnamon and Arri hailed a taxi to Sacramento Street. In Arri's inebriated condition, she parked her car in a tow zone and to reclaim it from the auto pound was one hundred and sixty-five dollars, not including another fifty for the ticket.

Heartache was expensive.

Afterwards, Arri drove Cinnamon back to her apartment, Arri still wearing her clothes from the previous day.

"I appreciate you coming with me to get my car," Arri said.

"That's what I'm here for."

Arri breathed powerfully, as if centering herself. "I thought a lot about myself this morning--who I am, and you know what?"

"I sure hope you'll tell me."

"I'm tired of being me."

"What?"

"The person I am, the person I have become--crying all the time, whining, pining for Eric and most of all chasing a man who could not care less whether I live or die."

Impressed, Cinnamon looked past Arri, could barely believe her ears.

Arri touched Cinnamon's arm and gently shook her. "Are you still with me?"

Cinnamon snapped from her momentary trace. "Excuse me, it's just that it's so wonderful to hear you say these things."

"And you will be proud to know that I said a prayer last night for Eric. And I forgave him."

Now Cinnamon knew for sure Arri was on the road to recovery. "Now don't you feel better?" Cinnamon asked.

"I'm still hurt but I do feel more in control of the situation."

"Good for you."

"I'm just so tired of things being the way that they are. You know what I mean?"

"I know what you mean. So what about work? Are you taking off again?"

"No, I'm going. I'm just going in a little late."

Arri pulled up to Cinnamon's high-rise, shifted the gear into park. "With Roman out of the way, I guess you can see Mitchell now, huh?"

"What makes you think that?"

"I just figured."

"You just figured what?"

"Don't get upset, it was just a comment. I just thought since Roman was out of the way, there would be no reason for you not to. . ."

"Not to what?"

"Not to be with Mitchell."

"I admit, I do love him, but he's married, Arri. You know that as well as I do."

"Yeah, but I kind of got the impression he was the one, like you two might be meant for each other."

"I don't think so." Cinnamon opened the door and stepped out. "Call me later. And please stay away from Eric."

Cinnamon relived her conversation with Arri as she trolleyed down her hallway toward her apartment.

With Roman out of the picture, what was to stop her from pursuing the person she yearned for so desperately?

Upon reaching her apartment, she made a beeline to the love rocks on her coffee table. She picked up the tiny pouch, emptied the rocks into her hand, weighing the pros and cons of following her heart's craving. Excitement churned inside and she smiled. But she needed to talk to someone first, someone sensitive to her feelings, someone who had perhaps maybe traveled the same road as she.

Only two names sprung to mind. Noel Green.

Chapter Twenty-Three

ON THE SEVENTH FLOOR of the Harold Washington Library, Cinnamon arranged to meet Noel. Eager to begin writing a self-improvement book, she chose the literature department as their meeting place so as to obtain information for her book proposal.

Underneath the bright lights, she casually skimmed the book titles, immersing herself in the vintage aroma of old books. She loved the feeling of libraries, the high ceilings, the mountainous collection of books and the concentrated silence.

Noel soon arrived.

Though the temperature outside was below zero, Noel still sported his leather jacket, the collar pulled up to his neck and his hair slicked back.

He slunk toward Cinnamon and presented a brilliant smile. "My bud, Cinnamon."

She hugged him, having missed him more than she realized. "So how's life?" Cinnamon asked.

"Life is good. What about you?"

"Good. Now that we've exchanged pleasantries, let's get down to business."

"Let's," Noel said.

"You know I almost got into trouble because of those yellow briefs you left at my place."

"So that's what happened to them."

Cinnamon laughed. "It's so good to see you. You're still just as cute as ever."

"I could say the same thing about you."

"Well, then say it," Cinnamon said.

Noel stepped back from her, checked her out from top to bottom. "You look fabulous!"

Cinnamon bowed. "Thank you, thank you."

Out of nowhere, a tall woman with short extension braids flung from around the corner. "Excuse me, but could you keep it down?" she said before she dashed away.

"Oh, no she didn't."

"We were getting kind of loud," Cinnamon said.

"So?"

Cinnamon grasped Noel's hand and led him to the aisle at the end.

She quickly assumed a comfortable position on the floor but Noel seemed to be on the lookout for that tall woman. "Where is that bitch?"

"Noel, will you forget about her? I have something really important to talk to you about."

Noel slumped down to the floor and removed his coat. "Okay, shoot."

Cinnamon surveyed the area and made certain no one was around, then whispered. "Have you ever wanted to do something so badly but you knew it was wrong?"

"Every day of my life."

"I'm serious, Noel."

"I'm serious too. Everything I want to do is wrong. Well, just about. What exactly are we talking about here?"

Cinnamon opened her mouth, but nothing came out, then she tried again. "There's this guy, Mitchell."

"Say no more."

"But you don't even know what I'm about to say."

"Oh, yes I do," Noel said. "You want to know if it's okay for you to be with a married man, Mitchell, namely."

Cinnamon flashed him a look of wonder. "How did you know that?"

"Because I went through the same thing myself."

"You?"

"Yes, me. I do have some morals."

"So what did you do?"

"Well--"

Before Noel could complete his sentence, the tall woman approached again. "Is it possible you two could go elsewhere and have your conversation? I'm trying to study. This is the library."

Noel leaped from the floor and lifted his knee. "And this is my knee soon to be going up your ass."

To prevent Noel from retaliating any further, Cinnamon covered Noel's mouth. "We apologize and we'll try to keep it down."

The woman rolled her eyes at Noel, then jetted away.

"Why did you stop me?" Noel asked. "I was about to tell that heifer off."

"She is trying to study, and we were disturbing her."

"So?"

"Noel, just squash it with that woman. Okay? Please."

Noel exhaled, seemingly trying to calm down. "Okay, but only because I'm a gentleman."

"Now, finish what you were saying."

"Are you sure it's safe to talk here?" he asked in a bitter voice.

"Come on, let's go to another floor."

After taking the escalators up to the eighth floor, they found an isolated aisle against the wall toward the back.

"I was going to say--," Noel said. "What was I going to say?"

"About how you went through a similar situation."

"Right. I struggled with a very similar dilemma, wasn't sure if I should continue seeing this particular person. After wrestling with myself, I decided since I couldn't figure out for sure what was right, I would just do what I wanted. That narrowed my options and made the decision a whole lot easier."

"Just like that?" she asked.

"Just like that. You have to ask yourself, 'What does Cinnamon want?'"

Cinnamon sparked him the most zealous smile she could evoke. "Cinnamon wants to always have a friend like you."

Cinnamon raced home.

She had come face-to-face with the darkest hour, the depths of her spirit and the essence of who she really was. There could be no more pretending, her passion being too intense to be denied because of a passed-down belief.

It was time to rekindle what once was and nothing else mattered. It was wrong to pursue a married man but she couldn't deny her love any longer.

Even before removing her coat, she called Mitchell and left a message for him to call her ASAP. What she planned to say to Mitchell, she had to say in person and she had to say it now before she lost her nerve.

Two days passed and not a word from Mitchell.

Cinnamon couldn't blame him after dodging him the way that she did. Though Mitchell had ample reason to stay away, Cinnamon wasn't giving up. She didn't know exactly how, where or when, but for certain she would inevitably make contact with Mitchell Maine.

It was a promise she made to herself.

With Cinnamon's book project in the making for two years, she was finally ready to create an outline. The tentative title was *Teach Me How to Live*.

After skimming through the books she checked out of the library, she outlined her table of contents. The list encompassed the finer points from her favorite books, including the lesson she recently learned from Noel about making difficult decisions.

Making the best decision

Gratitude attitude

Life happens perfectly

Affirmations for all occasions

Intention rules

Change – Your best source of power

Trust God

Praise yourself often

Written visualizations

Worry: A slow death

Now all she needed was a chapter for each heading and voila! She would have a book.

After another two days passed of leaving messages for Mitchell with no success, Cinnamon decided to take drastic measures. Because she had no idea where Mitchell lived, she was forced to cruise the nightclubs until she found him. Her difficult task could take days, weeks, even months, but what other choice did she have? She had to do what she had to do.

For her mission, she rented a metallic blue Dodge for the weekend. Friday night came and her first stop was the Wild Hare, but to Cinnamon's disappointment, Mitchell was nowhere in sight. Then Saturday evening came and Cinnamon had high hopes. She dolled herself up and hit the road again, making another appearance at the Wild Hare. But luck was not on her side.

Two more weekends of cruising the Wild Hare in search of Mitchell would pass with no success whatsoever.

Then on the following Saturday, Cinnamon remembered Lemar's Place, which drew an even bigger crowd on Saturdays than the Wild Hare. Just as she pulled up to the busy establishment, she sighted Mitchell leaving the club. And he was alone. All Cinnamon could think about was that if she arrived one minute later, she would have missed him.

Cinnamon frantically searched for a parking space to no avail. When her eyes spotted a driveway, she swerved into it, threw the gear into park, clicked on the hazard lights and lunged from the car. By this time, Mitchell was halfway down the street. Cinnamon sprinted up behind him and tapped him on the shoulder.

Mitchell turned around.

Out of breath, Cinnamon panted. "Hey, you." At this moment of connection, the flame inside her heart was indescribable.

"Cinnamon," Mitchell said, surprised. "Are you okay?"

Desperate to catch her breath, Cinnamon said, "Yeah, I'm okay. Will you come with me to my car? I don't want to get towed."

"Sure."

Cinnamon led the way and Mitchell followed.

Upon reaching the Dodge, Cinnamon opened the passenger side and let Mitchell in, then quickly raced to the other side and jumped in.

After waiting for Mitchell to return her calls, seeking him out at the nightclubs and chasing him down like he stole something, the moment arrived when he was once again in her presence. And it felt amazing.

For all her trouble, he was worth it all. Her only wish was that she not die before she locked lips with this man one more time.

Still a little out of breath, Cinnamon turned on the motor and turned up the heat. "I don't blame you for not returning my calls."

"That's mighty big of you," Mitchell said.

Cinnamon smiled as if she had just met a famous person. "I've been looking for you."

"Well, you found me."

"Yes, I did. I came here to tell you something, something I have wanted to tell you for weeks now. I'm just going to say it and then I'll let you go and you can think about it later."

"Fair enough."

Suddenly, an incredible urge overpowered Cinnamon. And without pause, she opened herself up to her instincts, leaned over and kissed Mitchell, slowly and with all the hunger in her heart and soul. Again and again, she kissed him, and she didn't want to stop, not ever. She would remember this superb moment forever.

Mitchell gently pulled away. "Is that what you wanted to tell me?"

"From the day you met me," Cinnamon said. "From the day I met you, I have put you off and pulled you back, over and over. I have no excuse but I do apologize for everything, even the crazy and sometimes confusing messages I left you."

Silence. Silence. And more silence.

"You had a lot to say," he said.

"Do you forgive me?"

"I'll think about it."

After a long walloping breath and with fire in her eyes, Cinnamon said, "I want to be with you, Mitchell. I mean really be with you in every way, if you still want me."

"But you said you couldn't be with a married man."

"Forget about what I said," Cinnamon said sharply. "Listen to what I say today, because today is most important."

Cinnamon had come a long way. She arrived at a place where she could admit her true feelings and, most importantly, what it was she truly desired. Several times she blinked her eyes, hoping this wasn't another fantasy.

"I think I love you, Mitchell. That night you invited me to your apartment, it took a pound of willpower not to go home with you because I really wanted to."

"Now that I didn't know. I'd love to be with you, Cinnamon. It's what I wanted from the start."

Cinnamon burst with enthusiasm. "Let's celebrate. Let's go to Orlando."

"What's in Orlando?"

"Universal Studios and it is the place to be."

"When do you want to do this?"

"This week, my treat," she said with zealous.

For seconds on end, Mitchell's eyes beamed with a fervent glow that sent Cinnamon's heart ablaze.

"I'd like that," he said.

A long time passed since Cinnamon first attempted to bury her affections for Mitchell. And for all her struggles, in the end she pursued him with an insatiable fervor despite everything and everybody. And at any price.

En route to her apartment, Cinnamon traveled down Clark Street, Mitchell trailing right behind her in his shiny ten-year-old Jeep. Though the night was cold, her heart was in flames, in flames for this man. So many nights she dreamed of the day she and Mitchell would come together and at last that day befell her.

She continued to monitor her rearview mirror, checking to make sure he was still behind her. The night air from the opened window sent shrills of lust through her. All she could think about was having Mitchell stay with her for the night.

After months of coveting him from afar, she lusted for him and ached for him. Having put him off for several weeks, they were already behind schedule. But still she couldn't sleep with him just yet. And as much as she desired to rip his clothes off and pounce on him, she resolved to control herself no matter what.

Arriving at the front of her building, Cinnamon crept into the driveway and watched from her rearview mirror as Mitchell pulled up behind her. She turned off the motor and eagerly awaited his arrival. Moments later, Mitchell opened the door on the passenger side and stepped inside.

"Well, well, here we are," Mitchell said.

"Yes, we are. What do you want to do now?"

"What do you want to do?"

"Would you like to come upstairs?" Cinnamon couldn't believe what she said. After just making a pact with herself not to rush things, her natural instincts kicked in and she couldn't restrain herself.

"I would love to come upstairs," Mitchell said. "But I can't."

Cinnamon tried to hide her disappointment but she couldn't. "Why not?"

"I just can't, not tonight."

"That's too bad. I really wanted you to come."

"I really wanted to come too."

Cinnamon smiled, wondering if they were talking about the same thing because what she had in mind had a dual meaning.

"I'm so glad you came out tonight to find me," Mitchell said.

"I just wish I'd done it sooner."

Slowly Mitchell leaned in, moving his hand up her shoulder and kissed her lightly on the lips once, twice, then three times. As he pulled away, she reveled at his hazel eyes, wanting to lock lips with him again and again.

"So are you serious about Orlando?" he asked.

"Most definitely. Can you get a few days off?"

"I'll take them whether I can or not."

"Are you sure you don't want to come upstairs?"

"I'm sure I want to but I can't." He kissed her again before stepping out of the car. "I'll call you."

After Mitchell returned to his Jeep, Cinnamon circled the block, desperate for a parking space. In the end, she paid to park at a Broadway lot about a mile from where she lived.

When Cinnamon reached the inside of her apartment, she stood against the door, not moving, not hearing, not seeing. She wanted to soak up the remarkable evening and burn it into her memory for all time to come.

With her escapade to Orlando approaching fast, she had much planning to do. First thing Sunday morning, she reserved two standby seats with American Trans Air for herself and Mitchell.

Once all reservations were made, she yawned from sleep deprivation. Throughout the night, she replayed her meeting with Mitchell over and over again to the point of exhaustion.

They were scheduled for a seven o'clock non-stop flight to Orlando that evening. Universal Studios being her favorite vacation spot, she anticipated sharing the experience with Mitchell with much excitement.

Hoping she and Mitchell could unite earlier in the day, Cinnamon tried to reach him on his cell but with no such success. On his voice mail, she conveyed all the details of their excursion and left word for him to call.

Two hours later, Cinnamon stuffed her suitcase with jeans, t-shirts and underwear. When she heard the phone ring, it was like a bolt of electricity surging through her. It had to be Mitchell because what she experienced inside felt so good. It was p-a-s-s-i-o-n.

"Did you get the information I left you?" Cinnamon asked.

"Yes, I did, thank you very much. I'll pick you up around four-thirty. That's enough time, isn't it?"

"That's fine but I was kind of hoping I would see you before that."

"I'd love to but I have a lot to take care of before I leave, seeing as we won't be back until Friday."

"I guess, but that doesn't mean I like it."

"That's my girl. I'll see you this afternoon."

Before Cinnamon could say another word, Mitchell disconnected. Disappointed that she would not see him until later that afternoon, she blocked it from her mind. What else could she do? He was unavailable and that was that. She wondered if he might be involved with someone else, namely his wife, then quickly erased those horrors from her mind. Surely if he were involved with someone else, he wouldn't be heading off to Florida with her, or would he?

After she finished her packing and washing the coffee mugs and spoons in the sink, she could relax the rest of the day, watching movies and reading until Mitchell came for her.

Instead of informing Arri that she was heading out of town with her new beau, she decided to shake her up with a call from their Orlando hotel.

Cinnamon opened the window so fresh air could course through the living room as she listened to her favorite Bob Marley song, "Is this Love." Excited and on top of the world, she found herself singing along with Bob. "I want to love you and treat you right. I want to love you, every day and every night."

The romantic lyrics sent her on a trip down memory lane. She relived the first time she lay eyes on Mitchell and how she resisted him for so long. . . and lost. Even after making peace with her decision to pursue Mitchell, a tiny grain of doubt lurked in the back of her head, but she snubbed it. She had to. After everything she endured to land at this point, she continued full speed ahead.

At four-thirty that evening, right on schedule, Mitchell buzzed the doorbell. With her tote and overnight bag, she headed downstairs. When she exited the building, Mitchell stepped from his black Jeep. He was wearing black jeans, a baby blue shirt and no coat. "Hey you," Mitchell said. "Let me help you with those."

Mitchell collected Cinnamon's bags and placed them in the back while she stepped into the Jeep and patiently waited for him to join her.

Once inside Mitchell swayed his hand on the gear shift and turned to Cinnamon. "Are you sure about this?"

Without even giving it a second thought, Cinnamon leaned toward him and planted a big juicy kiss on his lips. "Very, very sure."

"You don't have to tell me more than once."

Mitchell quickly shifted gears and they were on their way. Nervous and excited at the same time, Cinnamon couldn't remember if she brought everything she needed. Though they would only be gone for a few days, this was a very unique trip, and she wanted everything to be perfect, if at all possible.

"So have you given any thought to what we would do in Florida?" Mitchell asked.

"You mean besides Universal Studios?"

"Yes, besides that."

"Oh, yes, I've thought a lot about that."

"Just so you know, it's even better than you think," Mitchell said with a seductive smile.

"What?" she asked, trying to appear naive.

"You heard me."

Cinnamon couldn't help but blush. Was he referring to what she was thinking? She didn't want to heighten her expectations too much. Most men claimed to be all of that in bed so his statement really meant nothing. But boy did she hope he was right.

Mitchell eased his hand on hers, softly stroking the back of her hand and then caressing each finger.

Cinnamon smiled, lust pulsating through her. What could be better than this moment? Absolutely nothing except the moments to come.

Cinnamon found herself mesmerized by this venture as they entered Lake Shore Drive, going south. Immediately, traffic slowed. Obviously a traffic accident of some sort. Every lane was lined with cars and SUVs, and it wasn't long before they rolled to a complete stop. But it was okay because as long as they were together, they could be stalled forever.

"You like Bob Marley?" Mitchell asked.

"Do I?" I love me some Bob Marley."

"That makes two of us."

Mitchell popped a Bob Marley CD into the disk player and Cinnamon's favorite song, "Is This Love," played through.

Cinnamon smiled as the excitement shrieked from her voice. "I love this song."

With traffic moving again, Mitchell accelerated while he and Cinnamon sang the lyrics of the tune. "I want to love you and treat you right. I want to love you, every day and every night."

Their duet was soon interrupted by Mitchell's cell phone. Cinnamon watched him take the phone from his pocket, glance at the number before flipping the phone shut.

"I guess it wasn't too important," Cinnamon said.

"Not as important as being here with you."

"You are so sweet. Have I told you that yet?"

"No, you haven't. Why don't you tell me now?"

"You are so sweet," she said.

"You're pretty sweet yourself."

"Are you sure it's the real you?" Cinnamon asked.

"What do you mean?"

"Well, you know what they say? The real person doesn't come out until after the fact."

"After what fact?" he asked.

"You know what I mean? After your heart is involved, then the real person comes out."

"Well, you tell me," Mitchell said. "I see you as a warm, intelligent beautiful woman who I adore being with. Is that really you?"

"Yes, it's all me."

En route to Orlando, Florida, Cinnamon and Mitchell were seated in 13A and 13B. Eager to become airborne, Cinnamon fastened her seat belt as she gazed out the window, the man she loved sitting only inches away. She watched Mitchell read the newspaper, admiring everything about him, his shiny bald head, his Hershey skin complexion and his hypnotic hazel eyes. Smiling, she inhaled. Bewildered with joy, she closed her eyes and sat perfectly still. Her search for Mister Wonderful was over. And she yearned for the entire country to know.

As she sat relaxed, her head back, eyes closed, she found it interesting that personal ads were all about what people were in search of. Never did people mention who they found. And though Cinnamon did not meet Mitchell through a personal ad, she felt compelled to share with the world who she found in her search for love.

She pulled out her tiny notepad and composed her post for the world.

FOUND: Sexy black male, loving, affectionate, sweet as chocolate and every bit as dark. But don't bother responding, he's already taken.

Chapter Twenty-Four

THIRTY MINUTES INTO FLIGHT, Cinnamon drifted into a delicate sleep. When she awakened, she found Mitchell staring at her with a welcoming smile.

"How long have you been staring at me?" she asked.

"I don't know." He ran the tips of his fingers across the back of her neck, then behind her ears. Cinnamon closed her eyes, treasuring his touch.

"Have I told you lately just how beautiful you are to me?" he asked.

"Not lately you haven't. So why don't you tell me now?"

"You are so beautiful to me."

Cinnamon smiled to herself, then turned away, afraid of what she might reveal if she stared at him too long.

"You never did tell me what changed your mind about us," Mitchell said.

"No?" Cinnamon asked innocently.

"No, you didn't."

"Of course this may sound like a cliché, but life is short. And if a person is lucky enough to find someone who they connect with, who makes their heart go pitter patter--"

"Pitter patter?" Mitchell questioned playfully.

"Yes, pitter patter, then they have to grab hold of that person."

"Cinnamon, I had no idea you were so aggressive."

"You know what I mean," Cinnamon said. "I consider myself fortunate to have met you, and I'm not going to let you slip away for any reason."

"Even though I'm married?"

"You just had to remind me of that, didn't you," Cinnamon said jokingly.

"It's not like I can deny it, but we are separated, soon to be divorced."

Cinnamon kissed him. "That's all I need to hear."

All this marriage business induced a sense of imbalance within her. Already she made peace with herself for even dating a married man regardless of the possible detrimental effects it could have on her life. Now she doubted herself. Again.

Had she made the right choice?

Was she doing the right thing?

Over and over she wrestled with herself and enough was enough. Mitchell was her man. Case closed.

It was almost one o'clock in the morning by the time Cinnamon and Mitchell checked in at the Buena Vistas Suites hotel.

Once inside the chilly room, Cinnamon turned down the air conditioner, which was going full blast. She stepped across the peach carpeting, flopped down on the king-sized bed and kicked off her shoes. Right away, Mitchell headed to the bathroom after setting his suitcase by the bed.

Their suite was well furnished with everything they might need for their four-day stint in Orlando, including two televisions and a DVD player.

Exhausted from her travel, Cinnamon unpacked only her velvet dress and the toiletries she needed for the night. She would unpack the rest of her things in the morning.

When Mitchell came from the bathroom, Cinnamon collected her body wash, baby powder and nightie and headed for the shower. Her trip to Orlando did not exclusively revolve around Universal Studios. Other adventures awaited her exploration, Mitchell being one of them.

In the shower, she brushed her teeth, then lathered her body with the strawberry body wash, making sure to layer every crevice.

Out of the shower and smelling fruity fresh, she shrouded her body with cocoa butter until every inch of her skin was soft and moist.

As soon as Cinnamon slipped her silk nightie over her head, Mitchell knocked on the door.

"Yes," Cinnamon said warmly. "Who is it?"

"Open the door and find out."

Cinnamon opened the door and found Mitchell wearing just his pants and no shirt. "It's lonesome out here."

"You're so sweet."

"You're the sweet one," Mitchell said. "Are you all done in here?"

"I am."

Mitchell clutched her hand, led her into the other room and backed her against the wall. With hunger in her eyes, inhaling his hot breath, she watched him elevate her arms above her head. Mitchell kissed her cheek, then without warning, instilled his tongue into her mouth which she welcomed with much pleasure. If kissing him felt this majestic, what else was to follow? She exhaled a sigh of elation. All she could hear was the subtle humming of the air conditioner and Mitchell's strained breathing.

Just when Cinnamon was about to lose herself in the torrid moment, Mitchell pulled away. "I have to take a shower."

Cinnamon swallowed hard as if to say, okay.

When Mitchell escaped into the shower, Cinnamon crumbled in the center of the bed, trying to recover and catch her breath. She inhaled lengthy breaths, holding each breath in for as long as she could before exhaling. After a minute or so she felt herself winding down. Calmer. . . Calmer. . . Calm.

While waiting for Mitchell, she unpacked the rest of her things, placing them neatly into the dresser drawers. After unwrapping her three-inch pumps, she set them in the closet. By the time she finished unpacking her overnight bag, she heard the bathroom door open. Like a bat out of hell, she dove into the bed, clicked on the radio and switched the channels until she located a reggae station.

Moments later, she turned and witnessed Mitchell standing before her, ass out, butt naked with a condom in hand. Her heart skipped a beat as she peered at his gargantuan, erect wand.

Damn! Was he ready or what?

She wanted to devour it like a banana but she couldn't do that. She was a LADY.

It seemed she unwound for nothing because she was all roused up again, this time even more so. And it was now time. Time for Cinnamon to get her freak on.

Mitchell dimmed the lamp and lowered the volume on the radio. He then extended his hand to hers and guided her off the bed and down on the carpeted floor. This was different. Though a huge bed existed above them, Mitchell chose the floor and Cinnamon was all for it, following his direction every step of the way.

Mitchell lay on top of Cinnamon, grinding his upright member against her inner thigh. Caressing her shoulder continuously, she felt his hot breath sail across her neck. She released shallow breaths as Mitchell kissed her, seemingly sucking the breath from her body. Holding the top of his shiny head, she felt herself moistening just underneath him.

In a flash, he was wearing a condom and about to enter her when he spread her legs and slipped his finger inside her. A chill spiraled through her body. She tried not to swirl her hips but his finger gratified her too much to remain immobile.

With his finger still inside her, he kissed her, kissed her and kissed her some more.

"You like that, don't you?" Mitchell asked in a whisper.

Cinnamon said nothing but instead let her revolving pelvis speak for her. He seemed to know just what to do to hold her at his mercy.

She was hyperventilating, felt hot and lightheaded but in a strange, sensuous way. Her heart was beating faster and faster, and if he did not make love to her right away, she was going to shout out his name along with some nasty vulgarities that she might regret later.

Just when she expected him to enter her, he asked, "You want to make love to me?"

"Yes," Cinnamon said, out of breath. "Yes."

Mitchell was an erotic little devil. It wasn't enough what he was doing to her, but he discussed it as well. Desperately, Cinnamon wanted to feel him inside her, but she couldn't bring herself to make the first move. A half minute would pass before at last Mitchell was inside her, all eight inches of him. She thought she might struggle to accept all of him, but it turned out not to be much of a struggle, having been ready for him for so long. She embodied what she wanted, Mitchell inside of her in all his splendor.

The sweat from his slick head glistened underneath the dim light as he prodded inside her slowly and then at top speed. She worried she might pass out from an overdose of euphoria. She thought to say, "Scottie, beam me up! I can't take it anymore."

Mitchell brandished her with a level of ecstasy she didn't know existed.

Her pleasure was mounting. She wrapped her legs around his back, pulling him deeper and deeper inside her. She did not want to miss out on anything. And at the rate she was going, she definitely wouldn't because after all was said and done, she climaxed so hard she went into spasms.

Three hours later, Cinnamon awakened, her head against Mitchell's hairy chest. She planned to sleep through the night but her elation kept her awake. Inhaling a state of bliss, she blinked her eyes and smiled. This was as good as it got, waking up in the arms of the man she loved.

Where had Mitchell been all her life?

No man ever made her feel this good. And though they were just getting to know each other, this was more than just great sex. A marvelous chemistry lurked between them from the moment they met, steadily building with time.

Suddenly, out of the blue, it dawned on her that she neglected to inform Arri of the sensational news. Careful not to wake Mitchell, Cinnamon eased out of bed, then set way into the next room to use the phone. As she dialed Arri's telephone number, she glanced over at the clock. It was four forty-five in the morning and Arri would not be up. But so what. Cinnamon was on fire and it was imperative that she disclose her tidings to Arri right away.

"Hello," Arri said.

"It's me, Arri," Cinnamon said in a whisper. "Your best friend, Cinnamon."

"I know it's you. Did you get my message? I've been calling you."

"No, I didn't." Cinnamon squealed with excitement. "Guess where I am?"

"Cinnamon, I just looked at the clock. Are you aware that it's not even five o'clock?"

"Who cares? Guess where I am?"

"Obviously out of your mind."

"I'm in Orlando with Mitch."

"What? Did you say you were in Orlando with Mitchell?"

"Actually, I said Mitch."

"The married man?"

"I like to think of him as separated," Cinnamon said.

"He's still married."

"I know that," Cinnamon said. "And you know that."

"Yeah, but does his wife know?" Arri asked.

Cinnamon switched the receiver to the other ear and continued in a whisper. "What's that supposed to mean?"

"What if his wife doesn't know that they are separated?"

"Of course she knows," Cinnamon said. "They don't live together. He lives by himself."

"How do you know, have you been over there?"

"I just know. Okay? You really know how to take the 'J' out of joy, don't you?"

"I'm sorry. I just want you to know what you're doing."

"He's planning to file for his divorce sometime next month," Cinnamon said, outright lying.

"Oh, I didn't know that. Sorry for giving you such a hard time."

"I know your heart is in the right place," Cinnamon said. "I think."

"So tell me, where is he now?"

"He's asleep."

"So how was it?"

"How was it?" Cinnamon repeated, smiling. "Let me put it to you this way, if I died today, it would be okay because I would die a happy woman in love."

"Damn, he must have been good."

"Must have been is right," Cinnamon said.

"So you're in love?"

"That's right. I am in love."

"I guess I can't say I'm surprised. You have been carrying a torch for this man forever."

"And it was all worth it. This is the man of my dreams, Arri, and I'm not kidding. This man made me feel so good, I thought I zoomed off to another planet."

"What exactly did he do?"

"I don't kiss and tell."

"I'm not talking about the kissing."

"I don't do that and tell either."

"You know you want to tell it," Arri said.

Cinnamon laughed. "Okay, you got me."

Cinnamon shared with Arri the sordid details of her escapade with Mitchell, leaving very little to the imagination. After hanging up, Cinnamon climbed back into bed and snuggled up to her prince.

"My Cinnamon," Mitchell said as he kissed her hand.

Cinnamon smiled to herself, closed her eyes and underneath her breath said, "Thank you, God."

Life couldn't be any better than this.

Later that morning, Mitchell and Cinnamon showered and dressed. They ate breakfast in the hotel restaurant which was included in the price of their room. Famished from her late night workout, Cinnamon ordered the French toast, bacon and sausage, hash browns and a little orange juice to wash it down.

It was close to eleven by the time they made their way to Universal Studios.

It was a comfortable seventy-two degrees and it felt spectacular. They spent a dynamite day at Universal Studios and the Island of Adventure. Because it was February, the least busy season, the lines were not as long as usual.

Two years ago when Cinnamon accompanied her sister, Kim, to Universal, she fell in love with the theme park and from that point on it remained one of her much loved places. The entire park was a movie set, mostly where old black and white movies were filmed. They even checked out the house used in the movie "Psycho," one of Cinnamon's favorite movies of the past. But the main attraction was the virtual reality rides: "Back to the Future" and "Spider man" just to name a few. Of course their visit would not be complete without a visit to Twister, the living, breathing tornado, Earthquake and Jaws. Though it was Mitchell's first time visiting the park, he seemed to enjoy himself.

Later that evening, after walking miles and miles at the theme park, Cinnamon was drained by the time she and Mitchell returned to their room.

"I really had a nice time," Mitchell said. "I didn't think I would enjoy myself as much as I did."

"Sounds like someone has been bitten by the Universal Studios bug."

"Maybe."

Cinnamon slipped out of her shoes, her feet aching. After they showered and changed, they cuddled on the bed, facing each other while listening to the all-reggae station on the radio.

"I want you to know I have really enjoyed being here with you," Mitchell said.

Cinnamon gazed into his light brown eyes, not ever wanting to turn away. "Thank you for saying that."

"It's true."

Other than the fact that he was married, she knew little else about him. In realizing this she said, "So tell me about your work."

"You don't want to hear that. That is so boring."

"I hardly doubt that. Come on, Mitchell, I insist."

"Since you insist," he said.

"And I do."

"I place children in foster homes, which means it's my job to keep track of them and also to remove them when I have reason to believe they should be removed."

"Is it stressful?"

"It can be sometimes after I've placed a child and at three in the morning they call me to come pick up the child."

"They can do that?"

"Oh, yes, they can and they do. And then I have what you call home visits where I have to visit with each child and the family, which sometimes means going to the Projects."

"I wouldn't like that."

"Tell me about it," Mitchell said. "But it's not what I'm planning on doing much longer. Eventually I'd like to start some kind of business. Just as soon as I get the chance. What about you? What do you want to do?"

Cinnamon wrapped her arms around him and smothered him with kisses. "I'd like to stay here in Orlando with you forever."

"That would be nice. Seriously, though?"

"Seriously, I would like to finish my book and have it published."

"I'd be the first one in line to buy it."

Cinnamon chuckled, rolled onto her back. "Just listen to us, talking about our hopes and dreams."

"I know," Mitchell said. "It's disgusting, isn't it?"

"I think it's fabulous."

Could Mitchell actually be the one? All signs pointed in his direction. Not only was he intelligent, but he was fun, a first-rate conversationalist, affectionate and passionate beyond words.

What more could she ask for?

The next day Cinnamon and Mitchell shopped at a nearby mall. She planned to purchase a couple of gifts for Arri and Noel, and Borders Books was first on the list.

As Mitchell browsed the books in the barren History section, Cinnamon approached him pretending not to know him.

"Excuse me, Sir, but are you looking for a date this afternoon?" she asked, her hands on her hips, posing.

"As a matter of fact, I am," Mitchell said as he pivoted around her.

"What a coincidence. I had a special feeling about you the moment I walked through the door."

"Do you have this special feeling often?" he asked.

"Only when I run into special people."

Mitchell brushed up against her, exhaled an amorous breath and whispered. "I don't want to hear the word special anymore."

"Me either." Cinnamon stepped back, took in a bird's eye view of Mitchell from bottom to the top. "You know, you are one handsome man. As a matter of fact, I'd be willing to leave my husband and three children just to have coffee with you."

"I could say the same thing about you."

"Then say it."

"You are so beautiful," Mitchell said. "I would be willing to quit my job just so I would have the afternoon free to stand here and look at you."

"You don't have to quit, man, just take the afternoon off."

"No!" Mitchell declared. "I would have to quit."

"I think I know what you mean. Because I'd be willing to pay money just to stand next to you."

"I'd pay money just to run my fingers through your hair," Mitchell said.

Cinnamon scaled up on him, their lips almost touching. "I'd pay money just to run my tongue up and down and back and forth across your lips."

Mitchell clenched both of her hands into his. "I'd pay money just to suck your fingers, one, then the other, then the other."

Consumed by lust in an almost trance-like state, Cinnamon said, "Take me, Mitchell, take me now."

"Right now?"

Cinnamon flung herself into Mitchell's arms, kissing him, kissing him, kissing him. Seconds passed before Cinnamon realized she and Mitchell performed before an audience of three older men. Flushed with embarrassment, she and Mitchell bolted from the bookstore.

After four memorable days in Orlando, playing miniature golf, dining out, shopping and theme parks, it was time to head home and return to reality.

Cinnamon thought she might have a good time with Mitchell, she just didn't know how good *good* would be. The bond between them grew more powerful with each passing day. With that in mind, she couldn't help but theorize if their life back in the real world could live up to this one.

CHAPTER TWENTY-FIVE

ORLANDO AIRPORT INTERNATIONAL.

Cinnamon and Mitchell waited to board Flight 533 to Chicago after checking their luggage and going through security. It was 6:45 p.m. and their flight didn't leave until eight o'clock, giving them plenty of time to kill. While Mitchell read the day's paper, Cinnamon stared out the window, reliving the last four days as she listened to the distant conversation from the couple across from her. Suddenly, Mitchell's cell phone rang. Once again Cinnamon observed him glance at the number before flipping the phone shut. Having watched Mitchell flip his phone shut twice, Cinnamon was tempted to ask him about it. But she hesitated for fear of appearing nosy, though it would only be true.

As if Mitchell could read her mind, he turned to her. "It was nobody."

"'Nobody' as in 'nobody' or 'nobody' as in someone you don't want to talk to?"

"Nobody period," he snapped.

Startled by his tone, Cinnamon flinched, not ever having witnessed that side of him before. But she chose not to make a big deal about it. Nobody was always in a good mood. Even Cinnamon had days when she wasn't the most pleasant person to be around.

"Don't mind me, Cinnamon, I'm just not that anxious to get back home. That's all."

"Well, that's understandable."

"I'm sorry," he said as he folded the newspaper. "I shouldn't have snapped like that."

"Don't give it a second thought. Everything is cool between us."

Cinnamon excused herself to the ladies' room and upon her return the vibe between them somehow mysteriously changed. Mitchell seemed a million miles away, not reading, not writing, not doing anything.

"Hey," Cinnamon said as she sat next to him.

Seemingly in a daze, Mitchell did not respond. Either he was engrossed in his thoughts or purposely ignoring her. Very gently, Cinnamon tapped him on the shoulder. "Are you okay?"

"I'm fine," he said unconvincingly.

He displayed a distant and cold persona, not paying Cinnamon any mind at all. Either he was angry with her or Cinnamon was just plain paranoid. And she doubted it was the latter. Obviously, something bothered him. So much Cinnamon wanted to ask him about it, but she hesitated for fear he might snap on her again.

Unexpectedly, Mitchell rose to his feet. "I'll be back."

"You come right back now," she said playfully.

His eyes darted to her, oozing animosity. "Don't talk to me like I'm a kid," he said right before he dashed away.

Cinnamon's eyes reached upward in search of the answer to the unasked question. Had she become involved with Dr. Jekyll and Mr. Hyde? He seemed like a completely different person all of a sudden and it frightened her.

Fifteen minutes passed. And Mitchell had yet to return. As not to come off as some nervous girlfriend who freaks out when her man is away, she held out for as long as she could, nibbling on her fingernails. It would be another five minutes before she went looking for him.

Through the mass of eager airline travelers, Cinnamon wended her way toward the restrooms. Just as she embarked upon the men's room, she observed Mitchell, standing near the pay phone but talking on his cell.

Slowly, Cinnamon crept toward him and made immediate eye contact. She then patiently waited for him to end his call. But it didn't happen. Only a half minute would pass before Mitchell snatched his cell from his ear, his eyes pelting anger in Cinnamon's direction. "Do you mind?" Mitchell asked. "This is kind of personal."

Accustomed to his mood swings by now, she didn't say a word. Instead she calmly stepped away and returned to the waiting area.

Mitchell was just full of wonder. With each passing minute, their wonderful vacation was inexplicably transforming into its opposite.

While Cinnamon munched on her fingernails, the butterflies in her stomach reminded her that something was not right. And then there was the curiosity. Who was the mystery caller who put Mitchell in stitches?

Six eaten fingernails later, Mitchell returned, buckled down next to Cinnamon. "Sorry about that. I didn't mean to be rude but sometimes when I'm pushed to my limits, I'm not a nice person."

"Who was it?" Cinnamon asked.

Mitchell didn't speak right away, as if he wasn't sure he should, then said, "It was Valerie."

"Your wife?"

"Soon to be ex-wife."

Not being the type to remain silent for long, Cinnamon said, "Listen, Mitchell, I don't like to be in the dark about anything so if there's something going on between you and your wife, I would really like to know."

"There's nothing going on between us. If there was, I would tell you."

"Well, what was that conversation all about?"

Mitchell exhaled with a hint of annoyance. "It had nothing to do with you, Cinnamon."

"Does Valerie want to work things out with you?"

"I don't know," Mitchell said.

"You don't know? How can you not know?"

"I don't know what's in her mind."

"You just got off the phone with her. You should know something."

Mitchell straightened his shoulders and turned to her. "If you must know, our conversation was about money. She's wants more than she deserves. Okay?"

"You have to give her money?"

"The money is for my three-year-old daughter."

Cinnamon's eyes widened. This she had not expected. "I didn't know you had a daughter."

"Well, you know now."

"Did you purposely withhold that from me?"

"I don't have to purposely withhold anything from you. If I didn't tell you, it's because it never came up."

Cinnamon shifted her body back, taking a moment to regroup. "We had such a beautiful time in Orlando, and it seems now that everything is going south."

Mitchell wrapped his arm around her and gently nudged her against his shoulder. "I'm sorry if all of this upsets you, but it's upsetting to me too. We did have a great time in Orlando, so let's not let all of this ruin it."

"I don't see how it can't. You have a wife who may or may not want you back and now I learn that you have a daughter."

"What difference does it make whether I have a daughter or not? Are you saying you wouldn't have gone out with me if you knew I had a child?"

"No, I'm not saying that, but it's definitely something I would have liked to know about."

"Are you saying you don't want to see me anymore?" he questioned.

"No, I'm not saying that."

"Well, what's the problem?"

"I don't know." Cinnamon combed her hand through her hair, then stretched out her arms. "I'm just a little stressed right now."

"You're allowed. I'm sorry if I upset you. But I want you to know something. You are the one I want. And nothing is going to jeopardize that. Nothing."

Mitchell was king at knowing just the perfect thing to say at the right time.

"Thank you for saying that," she said, feeling a little more at ease.

"You're welcome."

Though not completely relaxed, one thing was for certain. Mitchell was her guy. And she resolved to do anything to maintain what they experienced in Orlando. Almost anything, that is.

In flight to Chicago, Cinnamon requested hot water for her peppermint tea. After having been on such a high in Orlando, she felt herself spiraling downward as they cruised closer to their destination. To break the agonizing circle of dread in her mind, she closed her eyes and reflected on a saying her mother declared long ago: What ventured upward, most certainly plummeted downward. Truer words were never uttered from her mother's mouth.

Waiting for the flight attendant to return with her water, she inhaled a long breath, then glanced over at Mitchell. She watched him seemingly engrossed in the day's newspaper.

"Anything exciting happening these days?" she asked.

"Not particularly."

"I never really cared much for the day's paper. It's so depressing."

"That's for sure."

Abruptly changing the subject, Cinnamon asked, "What's your daughter's name?"

"Tory."

"That's a pretty name. You like being a father?"

"I do. It's great."

For a minute, Cinnamon hesitated to inquire about his marriage, then ventured ahead anyhow. "Why did you and Valerie break up, if that's not too personal?"

Mitchell closed the newspaper, then eased back into the chair. "Irreconcilable differences. We couldn't get along anymore. I don't think she liked me. I mean I knew she loved me, but I don't think she liked me. Does that make any sense?"

"Yes, it does, but I can't see why anyone wouldn't like you."

"You might not say that after we've been together for a while."

"Well, we'll just see about that, won't we?"

"I guess we will," he said with a smile.

Back at Cinnamon's high-rise, Mitchell dropped her off before heading home himself. Though she welcomed the chance to spend another night with him especially since it was their first night back in Chicago, Mitchell didn't feel the same. But it was okay because she had much to do before returning to the skies anyway.

On her answering machine, four messages awaited her. The first two were from Arri. Next was a message from Noel informing her he was leaving town for a few weeks and would call her upon his return. The final message was from Roman.

"Hello, Cinnamon, it's Roman. I hope you haven't forgotten me already. Anyway, I just wanted to say hi, and hear about how well you're doing. No need to return my call unless you want to. Bye."

What a sweet message. Not expecting to ever hear from him again, it was quite a surprise. How could she not return his call? Not only was she a sucker for people who depicted humility, she very much wished to chat with him.

She planned to do right by Roman. Having already released him so that he might find someone to fill the void in his heart, all she could do now was continue to befriend him, which included being completely honest with him about her new-found relationship.

After saying her prayers, she sat on the edge of her bed and dialed Roman's number, which she still knew by rote.

"Good evening, Roman."

"Cinnamon, I didn't think you'd call."

"I hadn't expected to hear from you either."

"Well, I'm glad you did," he said.

"I'm glad you did too. And by the way, thank you for your nice message."

"You're very kind," he said.

"So are you." Cinnamon laughed. "You know, we could go on and on about who is the most kind and in the end, you would come out as the all-time champion."

"You think so, huh?"

"I know so," she said. "So how have you been?"

"Great. I received a huge raise at work to go along with that promotion."

"Really, how big? I'm just kidding."

"Seven thousand."

"That's pretty big. Well, you deserve it."

"So what about you?" he asked. "What's going on with you?"

Cinnamon hesitated to mention Mitchell for fear of spoiling the ambiance. "I've been good."

"Anything exciting happening?"

Roman was not making this easy. "Actually, I just got back from Florida, just tonight."

"Did you go with your boyfriend?"

Knowing the conversation was headed in that direction, Cinnamon responded in a unruffled tone. "I did."

"You two have a good time?"

"It was nice, very nice."

A small silence grounded them as Cinnamon searched for what to say next.

"I get the feeling you weren't going to tell me that if I hadn't asked," Roman said.

"Your feelings would be right. It's weird talking to you about other guys, Roman. Did you forget we used to date?"

"No, I could never forget that. And what do you mean used to?"

"Huh?" Cinnamon questioned.

Roman chuckled. "I'm just kidding with you, Cinnamon. I wish you and your friend all the best and I mean that sincerely."

"Thank you, Roman. You have a good heart."

"Yeah, yeah, yeah, that's what they keep telling me but what I want to know is, if I'm so wonderful, why am I still single?"

"Isn't that the title of a book?" Cinnamon asked.

"Probably."

"There are a lot of women out there on their knees every night begging for a husband. And I'm willing to bet there are even more than that who would move heaven and earth to be with you."

"And what about you?" he asked. "Are you one of those women?"

Completely taken by surprise and not sure how to respond, Cinnamon didn't answer right away, then said, "Yes, I'm one of those women."

"Oh, yeah, so why were you in Florida with someone else?"

Cinnamon switched the phone to the other ear, not sure how to squirm her way out of this one. "Because," she said.

"Because what?"

"Roman, I don't have an answer for you, okay? I'm sorry."

"I didn't know it was such a hard question for you."

"Well, it is."

Abruptly, Roman changed the subject. "Cinnamon, it's been great talking to you as always. I'm going to hang up now but let's keep in touch, okay?"

"For sure."

What a relief to end that call. For a moment, she was certain he had her back against the ropes. She couldn't reveal too much, especially the fact that her new boyfriend, Mitchell, made her heart sing like no other. But Roman just kept picking. He seemed exceptionally skilled at backing her into a corner until she spoke the truth whether she wanted to or not. All the same though, he was a blue-ribbon guy to have as a friend, provided he lay off the questions.

After washing two loads of laundry, picking up her uniforms from the cleaners and having new taps put on her shoes, Cinnamon headed to Jewel grocery store. Her grocery list consisted only of grapes and all the ingredients for her spaghetti dinner which she planned to cook that evening. As she headed home from the store, Mitchell entered her psyche. Having just separated from him yesterday, she missed him already. She considered calling him but then decided against it, not wanting to come off as needy. Besides, it was always better for him to call anyway. That way, she didn't have to worry about interrupting him.

Ideally, Cinnamon would have liked to stay in constant contact with him, even if it meant talking for one minute once a day, but her intuition told her it would not work that way with Mitchell. He seemed the type that required a lot of space and private time. It was okay though because what he lacked in that department, he made up with his singular wit, warm heart and illustrious sex.

Cinnamon dropped in on Arri, it being the first time Cinnamon visited with her since her rendezvous with Mitchell.

Arri sported a burgundy pants suit which was a true shocker, seeing that the color purple dominated her wardrobe. And an even bigger surprise was Arri's hair, Arri having chopped most of it off and now wore it in a blunt fade like a boy.

"What did you do to your hair?"

"You don't like it?"

"Are you kidding me?" Cinnamon asked. "I love it." Cinnamon swept her hand across Arri's sassy do. "It's cute."

Arri closed the door and they retreated into the living area. A lavender aroma infused Cinnamon's senses as she absorbed a relaxing and sanitized atmosphere.

"This place smells great."

"I'm into this aromatherapy these days. You like it?"

"Where can I get some?" Cinnamon asked. "And this place. . ."

Cinnamon stepped back and examined Arri's apartment from wall to wall. A new olive green cover draped her futon, and only two Essence magazines veiled the coffee table where once fifty lay scattered. And the hardwood floors loomed clean enough to eat on.

"This place looks fabulous. What happened to the rest of your magazines?"

"Oh, those. I threw a lot of that stuff out. I have de-cluttered you might say."

With admiration, Cinnamon perused every inch of Arri's transformed living space.

In the kitchen, sitting at the table, Cinnamon noticed the new garbage container as well as the freshly washed dishes.

"So have a seat and tell me what's going on," Cinnamon said.

Arri poured two glasses of lemonade, handed Cinnamon hers and then sat across from her. After taking a long gulp, Arri said, "I had to do something. I figured the way I was living just wasn't working so I tried something else."

"Which was?"

"Everything. I needed other interests besides men, and most of all I had to do something for me."

"Which explains the hair."

"You could call it a cleansing process, shedding the hair along with the crazy lifestyle that went with it."

This was a notable moment for Cinnamon to hear her best friend speak with so much spunk. "I am so proud of you, Arri. I knew all along it was in you."

"What? Stupidity?"

"No, greatness."

"I wouldn't go that far."

"I would. I couldn't be more proud of you than if you were my own child."

Arri laughed. "Will you stop it? You're embarrassing me."

"I can't help it."

"Well, try. Oh, I almost forgot." Arri pulled up her pants' leg and stretched out her leg. "Check it out."

On Arri's left ankle was a green shaded tattoo of a cat.

"It's nice." Cinnamon sailed her hand over the tattoo and inspected it with her fingers. "What is it, a cougar?"

"Exactly."

"When did you get it?"

"A few days ago. Remember how you wore your wedding band to signify a major change in your life? Well, this is something like that."

"Did it hurt?"

"Enough for a tear to fall from my eye."

"So does this change of yours mean you're not smoking anymore?"

"Well, I can't make any promises, but for now I'm not smoking."

Cinnamon peered across at Arri, enshrouded with admiration. "I have to say I'm a little envious of you right now."

"Why?" Arri asked.

"Because you transformed yourself, which is not an easy thing to do. It's just so refreshing to see something this wonderful happen right before me."

"Don't get all intense on me now. I only made a few changes."

"That's not what I'm talking about. I'm talking about the inner change in you. That's what really counts. I remember before I went to Orlando, you told me you were tired of being you and I don't think I got what you were saying at the time. But I get it now."

"That's right, I remember," Arri said, nodding her head. "I was tired of being me, tired of being Arri. And most of all, tired of crying all the time, whining and pining over a man who's not worth the price of coffee."

Cinnamon blinked and blinked and blinked and blinked. "Hello, did you just say Eric wasn't worth the price of coffee?"

"Yes, I did and I'm not ashamed."

"You shouldn't be because you're absolutely right."

"I'm not completely over Eric, though I wish I were."

"You will. The day will come. And soon." With her elbows on the table, Cinnamon rested her clasped hands underneath her chin. I even noticed that you're not wearing purple."

"Well, I still have a lot of purple in my wardrobe, but I'm no longer obsessed with it like before. Oh, I almost forget. I joined a gym."

"No."

"Oh, yes," Arri said with a sneaky smile.

Cinnamon pounded the table with her opened hand. "You took a stand, girl! A lot of people complain about their lives, but you did something about it. And for that, I salute you."

"Please don't."

"You know what I mean. You did a good thing."

"Yeah, after making a fool out of myself for years."

"It doesn't matter how long it took you to get there, just so long as you get there. You know what I mean?"

"I think I do," Arri said.

"I used to think of you as a beautiful work in progress and I was so right."

"Oh, come on now, don't get all touchy feely on me."

"I can't help it."

Arri rose to her feet and set the two empty glasses in the sink. "So you want to come to the gym with me?"

"No, not really. But I'll go anyway. See, your change is even having an effect on me."

"And you can tell me more about this new man of yours."

"That's right, I almost forgot," Cinnamon said, her eyes gleaming. "I got so wrapped up in hearing about you, I forgot all about my Mitchell."

For several weeks Mitchell consumed Cinnamon's daily thoughts, and she found it odd that she failed to reflect on him once while visiting with Arri.

And that was not a bad thing.

Chapter Twenty-Six

THE FAINT SCENT OF chlorine from the pool nestled in Cinnamon's nose as she and Arri stepped off the elevator at Bally's gym. Dance music echoed throughout the vast warehouse-like space, which consisted of at least forty treadmills, a juice bar and a retail shop that sold overpriced workout apparel. And that was just the main level.

As Arri's guest, Cinnamon submitted to a short sales pitch before she joined Arri in the locker room.

Girlie scented perfumes, deodorants, hair sprays and shampoos saturated the women's locker room while naked and half-dressed women rambled to and from the showers.

After Cinnamon and Arri disrobed and changed into their exercise clothes, they zeroed in on the treadmills. Across from the juice bar, they occupied the last two available treadmills, walking at the same swift pace. It being over a year since Cinnamon exercised in a gym, she was out of breath in just a matter of minutes.

"So tell me about Mitchell," Arri said.

"I told you most of it over the phone. What I didn't tell you was what I found out on the way back."

"Oh, no." Arri covered her mouth, her response outwardly premature.

"What do you mean *oh no*? I haven't said anything yet."

"I'm sorry. Continue please."

Cinnamon picked up speed, as if to run away from Arri. "I don't know if I want to tell you now."

"Come on, spit it out. You know you want to tell it."

"Well," Cinnamon said as she cut back on the treadmill. "He has a little girl."

"He's married and he has children?"

"It's not the worst thing in the world you know. It's not like he's a convict or something."

"I know. It's just that the child makes it even more complicated. Even after his divorce, he'll still be involved with his wife or ex-wife for that matter."

"I guess," Cinnamon said as she grasped the handles on the treadmill, staring straight ahead. "I hadn't really thought about it that far into the future. But still, I'm not going to stop seeing him just because he has a child."

"I didn't really think you would, but. . . what I want to know is why he didn't tell you this before."

"I asked him the same thing."

"And what did he say?"

"Something about it not coming up until now."

"Sounds like you have your hands full with this one, but as long as you're happy."

"I was until this conversation," Cinnamon said.

"I just want you to know what's in store for you. And just remember, you can get out of this relationship any time you want. You remember that."

"Will you cut it out?" Cinnamon said, smiling as she slicked the sweat from her forehead. "You're beginning to sound like me."

"I'll take that as a compliment."

Fifty-five minutes later Arri and Cinnamon worked up a heavy sweat on the treadmill, then revisited the locker room.

After stripping down to their panties, they trampled through the shower area, toward the swimming pool and ducked into the steam room. Having the sweltering room to themselves, Cinnamon and Arri stretched out on their backs. At opposite ends of the dank built-in ceramic bench, they fluffed the towels underneath their heads, their hands at their sides.

With much delight, Cinnamon consumed the eucalyptus fragrance as it relaxed and stimulated her senses. Immersed in the splashing sound of the hot vapors congesting the air, every muscle in Cinnamon's body loosened and unwound so much she could have easily fallen asleep.

"So you think this Mitchell guy is Mister Right?" Arri asked.

"I do. I really do." Cinnamon wiped the moisture from her forehead. "I'm telling you, Arri, this guy has me on fire sometimes."

"On fire, did you say?"

"In flames."

"You went such a long time without dating, not to mention how long you went without doing the you-know-what."

"It wasn't so bad," Cinnamon said as she closed her eyes. "Now, if you want to talk about a miracle, let's see how long *you* can go without dating or doing the you-know-what."

"Are you saying I can't do it?" Arri asked.

"I don't want to sound pessimistic but, no. I don't think you can do it."

"You care to put some money where your mouth is?"

"Without a doubt. How much?" Cinnamon asked.

"Now that I think about it," Arri rose to a sitting position. "Money is no good here. I have something else in mind."

"I'm listening," Cinnamon said, opening her eyes.

"If I manage to go thirty days without one date--"

Cinnamon interrupted. "No, thirty days is too short and I'm not talking about dating, I'm talking about the *Do*. Let's say you go sixty days without having sex and then we can talk."

"You're on." Arri lowed her body back onto the bench. "You must think I'm some nympho or something."

"In a one word--yes."

"Okay, smarty pants," Arri said. "Here's the deal. If you lose, you have to give up your fling with this married man."

"What?"

"You heard me. You have to give him up."

Inflamed that Arri would suggest such a thing, Cinnamon said, "No! That's not the deal."

"Well, if you're so certain you're going to win and I'm going to lose, then it should be no problem."

"What do I get if I win and you lose?" Cinnamon asked.

"Anything you want because I'm not going to lose."

Cinnamon rose to a standing position. "I don't like this deal." She wrapped the towel around her, her body drenched in moisture.

"Are you chickening out?" Arri asked.

"No, I just don't like the deal."

Who was Arri to dictate to her who she couldn't see? Cinnamon absolutely positively refused to base her decision on whether to see Mitchell on a bet, he being much too precious for that.

"Are you saying it's off?" Arri asked.

"Yes, it's off."

By the time Cinnamon returned home, she hoped to hear from Mitchell but to her disappointment, her wish was not granted. A call from him would pacify her, inducing a feeling of security in her and the relationship. And on the flip side, not hearing from him provoked questions.

After their glorious stay in Orlando, it would have been nice to hear from him to reassure her that their coupling wasn't just a fling.

When the phone rang, certain it was Mitchell, she lunged to the phone and snatched the receiver from the hook, nearly spraining her wrist. But to her dismay, it was not Mitchell.

"Oh, hey, Roman," she said in a less than enthusiastic tone.

"Is this a good time?"

Cinnamon hesitated for a moment, then said, "Yes, it's fine. What's up?"

She nibbled on her fingernails, thinking only of Mitchell.

"I need to ask you something," Roman said. "And I need you to be very truthful. Okay?"

"Okay."

"Is it at all possible that you and I could start over again. As a couple?"

Cinnamon's eyes expanded. This she had not anticipated. Their relationship ended weeks ago and she trusted Roman had accepted it, or at least she assumed he did. Either he never comprehended it to begin with or he refused to consent to it. With all the grace she could garner, she said, "Roman, I thought we went through this already."

"We did, but I have good feelings about us."

Cinnamon relinquished a frustrated breath. She was in no mood for this. In love with Mitchell, here Roman was asking for another chance. And as eager as she was to end this call and track down Mitchell, she wished to be kind. "Roman, I appreciate you suggesting that we start over and I am very flattered because you are a great guy."

Roman cut in. "But you're involved with someone else."

"That's right, I am. And I'm sorry."

She refused to give him false hope. It was only fair that she disclose her situation with Mitchell so that Roman might move on.

"Well, it was worth a shot," Roman said. "However, I do appreciate your honesty and I wish you well, Cinnamon, because you deserve it."

"Thank you."

"Good night, Cinnamon."

"Good night, Roman."

Positively and categorically, Roman touched her with his warm words and good wishes. As disappointed as he may have been, he wasn't bitter or mean because of it.

And she would always respect him for that.

After regrouping from her moving conversation with Roman, her thoughts immediately scurried toward Mitchell.

Where was he? Why had she not heard from him?

What was going on?

Were they still a couple?

Was it over?

The suspense of not knowing gnashed at her to an almost breaking point while the butterflies in her stomach ran rampant. She consumed deep breaths in an effort to calm herself. Inhale. . . exhale. . . inhale. . . exhale. . . Ten breaths later, Cinnamon felt herself settling down. Settled enough to know she needed to call Mitchell and could not dodge the idea any longer. Quickly, she dialed his number and he answered.

"Hey, Mitchell. It's Cinnamon."

"I'd know that delectable voice anywhere."

Cinnamon smiled, relieved to finally hear his voice and almost assured they were still a couple.

"I was planning on calling you earlier," Mitchell said. "But I was so busy trying to catch up on some unfinished business."

"What, paperwork?"

"No, just stuff, calls to make, people to see . . . So how are you?"

"I'm great now that I'm talking to you," she said, gleaming with joy.

"You really know how to push my buttons, don't you? Listen, can I call you right back?"

"Sure."

Cinnamon hung up the phone, her heart and soul dancing the dance of good cheer, making light of the fact that she distressed herself for nothing.

Cinnamon rested on her fluffy sofa, reading while she waited for Mitchell to return her call. Halfway through her new book, *The Prospering Power of Love*, she glanced over at the clock atop the television. An hour passed and Mitchell failed to return her call. Unable to deny her uneasiness, she checked to make sure the phone was properly on the hook. And it was.

So why hadn't he called?

Refusing to stress herself out again, she attempted to erase him from her mind and conjure up something else, anything else. But it was useless. Eventually he would call, but the question was when.

The book she read was a little more than a hundred pages and already she completed it, even taking time to highlight some of her favorite passages.

Again, her eyes flashed over at the clock: eleven fifteen. That meant more than an hour passed since Mitchell stated he would call back.

For seconds on end, she stood motionless in the center of her living room, thinking, pondering, wondering.

Should she call him again or shouldn't she?

This inconsistency of his annoyed her to the fullest. She envisioned all the places he could be gallivanting when the phone rang.

She delicately picked up, choosing not to sound anxious. "Hello."

"You weren't asleep, were you?" Mitchell asked.

"No, just finishing up some reading." She longed to scream at the top of her lungs, '*Where in the hell were you?*' but she kept it on the down low.

"Would you like some company?" he asked.

"Of course."

"I have something very important to talk to you about."

"As long as it's good news," she said.

"It is. The best. I'll see you in a bit."

What did he want to talk to her about? It couldn't be marriage because he was already married. She would just have to wait and see.

After quickly brushing her teeth and washing her face, she sprayed her hair with a light moisturizer and massaged her fingers through it. In preparation for the excitement Mitchell purged from her, she sprinkled baby powder inside her panties and underneath her arms.

At the window she watched for him, as if to speed his arrival. To rid her mind of the anticipation, she flipped on the television. But it did not work. All she fantasized about was how sexily he would strut through her front door and, most of all, what he would talk to her about.

On the Discovery Channel, she caught the tail end of *The New Detectives*. Just as she was about to learn the identity of the murderer, her doorbell rang. Without even asking who it was, she pressed the entry buzzer.

Eagerly she waited by the opened door and watched him step off the elevator. With a cocksure swagger, Mitchell coasted toward her, carrying a tiny gift bag.

"Hey," she said.

Unexpectedly, Mitchell grasped Cinnamon into his arms, lifted her off the floor and twirled her around as if it were New Year's Eve.

Surprised and enchanted by his gesture, she asked, "What was that for?"

"For being so sweet and so beautiful."

After releasing his grasp and lowering her back to the floor, they stepped inside. With joy in her heart, she closed the door and hung up his coat. He wore black designer dress pants and a grey turtle-neck sweater. He was appetizing enough to eat. And she meant that literally.

Cinnamon's attention drifted to the gift bag in his hand. "What's in the bag?"

"Oh, this, this is nothing. Just the keys to my heart."

"What are you talking about?" she asked playfully as she snatched the bag from him.

Inside the gift bag, Cinnamon plucked out a set of keys and dangled them. "So what is this you're saying?"

With a sincere expression on his face, Mitchell stood before her. "Those are the keys to my heart."

"Very funny."

"You don't believe me?"

"No, I don't."

He clutched her hands and moved up on her. "I want you to move in with me. Do you believe that?"

"Are you serious?"

"I am serious. You are my one and only, girl."

"Thank you."

"Thank you?" he questioned. "Is that all I get?"

"What did you have in mind?"

"What are you offering?"

"How about a kiss?" she asked.

"I'll take a kiss."

Cinnamon kissed him with all the affection she could muster.

Mitchell abruptly pulled away, out of breath. "I want you. Right now."

"Isn't that kind of forward?"

"What's forward about it? We spent four days in Orlando, doing everything under the sun. What's forward about wanting to make love to you now?"

"Since you put it that way," she said as she headed toward the bedroom.

Mitchell grabbed her arm and flung her back. "No, not in the bedroom. Right here."

"You are a kinky little devil, aren't you?"

"It takes one to know one. Isn't that right, Cinnamon?"

Ignoring his question, she said, "So tell me some more about this idea of me moving in with you? Where did that come from?"

"I'm crazy about you, Cinnamon. And I had the best time in Orlando."

"As did I."

"My concern is that with you traveling all the time, I won't be able to see you as much as I need to."

"Yeah, but moving in, that's a pretty big thing."

"I know and I'm ready to take that step with you."

Mitchell was highly talented with perfect responses.

"But we just started dating," Cinnamon said.

"Who's fault is that? I have been trying to get with you for months. Isn't that right?"

"Yeah, but--"

He feasted his mouth onto hers. "No buts. We connect, Cinnamon, and there is no denying that."

"I don't deny it."

"Well, then say you'll move in with me."

Cinnamon stepped away from him and sat on the edge of the sofa. "I have to really think about this, Mitchell. This is a very serious thing for me."

"It'll be great, Cinnamon. The days when you're in town, I'll have you one-hundred percent at my side."

"That does have a nice ring to it."

"And that's just the beginning. We'll have breakfast together, dinner together. We'll make love early in the morning and late at night. I'll rub your feet for you and give you massages, wash your back, everything."

"Okay, now, you better watch it or I'll try to move in with you tonight."

"That doesn't sound like a bad idea to me." Mitchell continued. "We'll do our laundry together and shop for groceries together. Then we'll snuggle underneath the covers and watch movies."

"You do make it sound tempting."

"Say yes, baby, please say yes."

"I have to think about it though. Just give me a day."

Mitchell and Cinnamon made love into the early morning hours.

Cinnamon awakened to find Mitchell laying across from her, peering into her eyes. If he weren't so damn fine, it could have been a startling experience.

"I love you, Cinnamon. I don't think I realized that until this very moment."

Cinnamon snuggled against him and kissed his cheek. "You are so sweet. I just want to squish you."

"You can do anything you want to me." He stroked the inside of her hand. "Move in with me, Cinnamon."

"You're really rushing this, aren't you?"

"Why shouldn't I?"

"What about my stuff?" Cinnamon asked.

"You can put it into storage."

"You have an answer for everything, don't you?"

"It will only be until we get married. I want you next to me every morning."

Cinnamon swallowed the saliva in her mouth and her jaw dropped. "What did you just say?"

"I want you next to me every morning."

"No, before that."

"Until we get married?"

"Yeah, that. Are you serious?"

He kissed her. "Yes, very serious. So will you do it?"

"I don't know, Mitchell. I have to really think about this."

Mitchell rolled on top of her and buried his head in her neck. "I love you, Cinnamon, and I want to marry you as soon as my divorce is final. You're everything to me, girl. Hell, I'd marry you today if I could."

His words sounded awfully good, but too much in shock to respond, she closed her eyes, soaking up everything that was transpiring at warp speed. If she gave him an answer at that very moment, it would have been an outright yes. But it wasn't like that. She had ample time for a well-thought-out answer and she was going to use every minute of it.

CHAPTER TWENTY-SEVEN

WITH SO MUCH ON the line, she needed to be absolutely sure.

She would have an answer for Mitchell upon her return from Texas. As not to do something she might regret later, she planned to mull it over with her head and her heart. No doubt, his desire to marry her naturally swayed her in his direction.

In the meantime, she packed her bag for her four-day run. Throughout her stay in Dallas, she relived her conversation with Mitchell. With an extraordinary sense of power, she restrained herself from calling him. She needed time to scrutinize his offer without any influence from him.

Back in Chicago, she needed to talk to someone, that someone being Arri or Noel, hoping they might cast some light on her situation and perhaps examine it from a different angle.

Cinnamon met Arri at Harris Bank. It was only four o'clock in the afternoon, and Arri did not finish work until five o'clock. But Cinnamon couldn't wait, needing to talk to Arri right away.

Arri and Cinnamon congregated in the lunchroom on the eighth floor and convened at a table in the back.

"You didn't call me while you were away. I was expecting to hear from you."

"I know. I didn't call anyone, not even Mitchell."

"What's up with that?"

"Mitchell wants me to move in with him *and* he wants to marry me as soon as his divorce is final."

"That's kind of sudden, isn't it? You two just started dating."

"I know. I'm just as surprised as you are."

"So are you going to move in with him?"

Cinnamon's eyes scanned upward, searching for the answer.

"You are, aren't you?" Arri said. "Otherwise, you would have said 'no' right out."

"Probably."

"No probablies to it. You have already decided."

"I guess maybe I have. You don't think it's a good idea?"

"Who am I to give advice?" Arri asked.

"I value your opinion. What's your take on all of this?"

"You want my honest opinion?"

Cinnamon nodded, wary of what Arri might say. "Yes, I do."

"I don't trust this guy," Arri said firmly. "I just don't."

"We're just two people who met and want to be together. What's wrong with that?"

"Nothing except for the fact that he's married, has a little girl and has all these plans and his divorce isn't even final."

"So? What's wrong with him making plans?"

"I don't know, Cinnamon," Arri smiled and folded her hands. "I know you have to follow your heart though so if you move in with him, and I know you're going to, I'll support you."

"Thank you for saying that. That means a lot. Do you think it would be okay if I had my mail forwarded to your place for a while?"

"Sure, but why not have it go to Mitchell's place?"

"I'd just rather not," Cinnamon said.

"Sounds like you're not planning to be there long."

"It's not that. It's just that it would be easier for me this way."

"Sure thing. It's not a problem at all. I just can't believe my girlfriend is about to shack up with her man."

"Well, believe it, 'cause it's happening."

"If Eric had asked me to move in with him, I would have taken the day off to do it."

"That's right, you would have."

Cinnamon yawned and covered her mouth. "Would you take him back if you could?"

"Absolutely not."

"No, did you say?"

"No is right. Eric caused me a lot of needless heartache and I've had all I can stand."

"Sounds like you are a transformed woman."

"A woman in progress is what I call it. Oh, you know what I meant to ask you? What about the lease on your apartment?"

"I forgot all about that. I guess I'll have to break it."

The next morning, Cinnamon awakened from a dazzling dream and she was all smiles. All smiles about her wondrous life to come. In her perfect dream, she greeted Mitchell every night with a savory meal before snuggling up in front of the television. After which they made love into the wee hours of the night, Mitchell constantly yammering about how special she was until she could barely stand it.

Ah, the fantasies.

The euphoric high from the dream seemed to carry over into reality because she was filled with zest as she stepped from the bed.

While she brewed coffee, she composed a list of all that needed to be done.

Disconnect electricity, phone and cable.

Schedule movers

Pick up boxes from U-haul

Have mail transferred

Update employee file with American Trans Air.

One thing that slipped her mind was her apartment lease, neglecting to inform the management office of her move. After having rented for five years, surely they would not make a stink about her moving out two months early. And even if they did, so what. Rare opportunities to share her life with a terrific guy befell on her and she wasn't about to let it fade away because of an apartment lease.

Before turning in the keys to her apartment, she cleaned it from top to bottom, choosing to return it in tip-top condition. As she rinsed the kitchen sink, it dawned on her that she hadn't spoken to Noel in weeks. And she missed him dearly. Upon calling his house, she learned he was still out of town and might return the following week. In her message to him, she left her telephone number at Mitchell's apartment.

Most of Cinnamon's things would go into storage, taking only her clothes, favorite CDs and books with her.

After Samson movers stockpiled her things into a storage unit on Broadway, they transported the rest of her things to Mitchell's place, now their place. Mitchell would not arrive until later, though it would have been splendid if he were there to welcome her.

Mitchell lived in a one-bedroom apartment on Roscoe, not far from where she and Arri lived. It was a four plus one unit, very modern, on a quiet street.

Having only visited Mitchell's apartment once, it exhibited a strange feel to it, knowing it was now her new home. Charcoal gray carpet shrouded the floors. Other than the leather couch in the living room, only a big screen television and sound system existed.

His place was messy. Clothes, shoes, books, a slew of CDs and unopened mail lay scattered everywhere. Then there was the subtle stench that pervaded the room, a combination of smoke and dirty socks. And it was F-O-U-L.

Right away she hauled butt to the nearby Jewel grocery store and purchased an Air Wick plug-in air freshener. In addition to that, she purchased some greens, chicken wings, Sweet Baby Ray barbeque sauce, Jiffy mix and sweet potatoes. For their first night together, she planned to surprise him with a delightful meal.

Upon her return, the phone rang and she hoped it might be Mitchell, but soon determined it was just a hang up.

Before Cinnamon could even think about preparing dinner, she would wash the day-old dirty dishes, wipe down the wooden kitchen table and run a mop over the grungy floor.

In an effort to organize his apartment and create order, she stacked his John Coltrane jazz CDs along with the other jazz artist CDs next to the big screen television. Next was the bedroom and bathroom, which she set out to tackle later.

While her chicken wings baked in the oven, she seasoned her greens with ham hocks, onions, salt, pepper, a splash of hot sauce and a snippet of sugar. Eagerly expecting to hear from Mitchell all day, she pondered why he failed to call. Obviously, he wasn't one to call on a systematic basis.

Preparing to wash the pots and pans, she filled the dishpan with hot water when again the phone rang. Optimistic it might be Mitchell, she sailed over to the phone, drying her hands on the dish towel. "Hello."

For seconds, Cinnamon heard nothing but silence, then a young woman asked, "Is this Cinnamon?"

"Yes, who's this?"

CLICK!

The disconnection inflamed Cinnamon's ear.

Now that was strange. Who was this mystery caller? Her first reasoning was that it might be Mitchell's ex-wife. Whoever it was, she obviously knew who Cinnamon was and probably that Cinnamon was living there. Not wanting the incident to botch up her mood on her first day in her new home, Cinnamon pushed it from her mind. She would query Mitchell about it later. But for now, she would resume her cooking and cleaning.

In Mitchell's bedroom, she took in the clutter and the unmade bed, which was minus a headboard. His bed was masked with girlie magazines, mail, clothes, and a single shoe. Housework was definitely not a priority for him. The floor was an exact replica of the bed, only worse, dishes, newspapers and more girlie magazines.

Twenty minutes later, order was restored, including crisp white cotton sheets on the bed.

Next was the bathroom, which really did not take long at all, it being the cleanest room in his apartment.

Now she could unpack some of her things. After she hung up her uniforms, pants and shirts, she stored her t-shirts, underwear, nighties and socks in the three drawers Mitchell reserved for her. For her miscellaneous items, she would need to purchase a storage unit from Target department store. Because she brought so few things with her, her new home felt more like a boarding house than anything else.

With everything neatly put away, she climbed up on the bed and stretched out on her back. Tonight would be their first night together in their apartment. She gazed up at the cracks in the ceiling, closed her eyes and a sadness fell over her. And she didn't know why. It was as if her intuition was communicating with her, forewarning her of unfavorable happenings to come.

CHAPTER TWENTY-EIGHT

SEVEN THIRTY THAT EVENING, a bubbly and full of life Mitchell wandered in, sporting jeans and a sweater. Considering he only worked until five, Cinnamon expected him earlier. But this was their first night together and she would not fret over it.

Mitchell's eyes searched the room. "Sorry about the mess but it looks like you did all right. All settled?"

"All settled. I didn't know you could wear jeans to work."

"I changed before I left," he said, as he suddenly hurled her into his arms, lifting her off the floor. "God, you feel good. And you smell good too. As a matter of fact, this whole place smells good."

"That's a great welcome. Can I expect this every night?"

"Every night and three times on Fridays." He oozed a fiery enthusiasm as he returned her to a standing position.

"What's got you in such a good mood?"

"It's you, Cinnamon. You have me in such a good mood. I'm off work at home with my girl in our place. What more can a man ask for?"

"Not much." Cinnamon helped him off with his coat. "I made us a little something in honor of our first night."

Mitchell extended his hand toward her and motioned her to come here. "Give me a kiss, you sweet thing." Without warning, he flung her into his arms. "I'm so glad you agreed to move in here with me."

"So am I."

All the tension that coursed through her earlier mysteriously vanished upon his arrival. And for the first time, she was confident she made the right decision moving in with him.

An hour later, they congregated in the kitchen underneath the bright ceiling light. Cinnamon fixed plates for both of them. She loaded his plate with greens, corn muffins, candied yams and barbequed chicken, then set it before him.

"Anything to drink?" Mitchell asked.

"Of course." She poured him a glass of iced tea, then sat across from him.

"This looks good. I didn't even know you could cook."

"I guess there's a lot we don't know about each other."

"That's what makes all of this so exciting," Mitchell said. Without further ado, Mitchell wolfed down his food, not taking his time about anything.

Cinnamon broke off a chunk of the corn muffin and put it into her mouth. "I received a strange call today. A lady called here, asked if I were Cinnamon, then hung up."

"It was probably Valerie," Mitchell stated with his mouth full.

"Why? Why would she do that?"

"Who knows? But you are here with me now and that's all that matters. You prepared this marvelous dinner and I don't want to ruin it by talking about her."

Cinnamon attempted to push the incident from her mind but with little success. It just didn't feel resolved. "Can I expect to hear from her again?"

Mitchell polished off the last bit of his corn muffin. "She's not going to call you again, but if it'll make you happy, I'll talk to her about it. Is it settled now?"

"It would put my mind at ease."

"Okay, then, it's settled.

"So how was your day?" she asked.

He gulped down his iced tea and returned the glass to the table. "My day was fine. These are the things that couples discuss, aren't they?"

"Some couples do," she said.

"Okay, well, we're not going to be one of those couples."

"Why not?" she asked playfully."

"Because it's boring. Need I say more?"

With Mitchell in a mellow mood, she asked, "So where did you go after work today?"

"What business is it of yours?" he said with a snap.

"Excuse me?"

"You heard me. I didn't stutter."

Cinnamon's mouth hung open but nothing came out.

"Don't look all shocked. Just because we live together doesn't mean I have to tell you my whereabouts twenty-four seven."

Losing her appetite, she pushed her plate away. "I didn't ask you to."

"It sounded like that to me."

"Don't you think you're overreacting just a little? I only asked you a question."

"And I answered it."

His defensiveness alarmed her.

Why had that one question roused so much emotion, negative emotion she might add?

"Why are you being so defensive?" she asked.

"Because I don't like being harassed."

"Who's harassing you? No one is harassing you."

"It sure feels like it."

"You're like a different person sometimes, you know that? You're in one mood one minute and then the next, you're somebody else."

"That's just your imagination," he said as he munched on the last chicken wing.

With venom in her eyes, she peered across the table and for less than five seconds she despised him. But she refused to foster such hostile emotions. She shook her head, hoping to slough off the animosity.

Maybe he was just having a bad day. Although she would have liked to believe that, she sensed it was much more serious.

After dinner, Cinnamon washed the dishes and ran the mop over the floor again. She could hear the television blaring from the front room where Mitchell watched the cable sports station.

As she wrung out the mop, an uneasiness wavered in the pit of her stomach and it would not fade. His outburst at dinner disturbed her and until it was resolved, she would not be herself. As surely as her name was Cinnamon, his whereabouts after work was the topic of a heavy discussion. Though she hesitated to bring it up again for fear it might ruffle his edges, she resolved not to live in fear.

Drying her hands on the dish towel, she stepped into the front room and waited for a commercial interruption in his program. "Hey. You got a minute?"

"Hold that thought," Mitchell said as he zipped away.

Two minutes later, Mitchell returned from the bedroom, closing the door behind him. Forging toward her, he flung her into his arms, lifting her off the floor.

He was just full of surprises. To say he was unpredictable would be a gross understatement.

"I'm sorry for the way I went off on you earlier."

Cinnamon displayed nonchalance, not knowing whether to be shocked or happy or shocked and happy.

He kissed her over and over again, then returned her to a standing position.

"What's that for?"

"For making such a fabulous dinner and for being the sweet person that you are."

"Thank you," she said still trying to figure him out.

"I shouldn't have gotten so upset with you before. Will you accept my apology?"

"Of course."

"I had to go to Cabrini Green today and didn't want to wear my suit. I was supposed to meet with this family at three o'clock but she rescheduled for six. That's why I was so late getting home."

"Well, I wasn't trying to be nosy or anything. I'm not going to be one of those women who tries to keep tabs on her man."

"I know you won't. And again, I'm sorry."

Cinnamon wrapped her arms around him. "You're forgiven."

At this moment, things seemed fine. But she wondered.

Were more outbursts of his to come? Having just moved in with him, right from the very beginning, they were off to a bad start. But things could change for the better or maybe even perhaps for the worst.

Hot baths bore magical healing powers. In a long, lemon-scented bubble bath, Cinnamon relaxed while Mitchell finished watching his sports program.

Tranquility was restored. She scooted down into the tub so only her head was above water as she inhaled the tart flavor of lemons. And at that moment, life was good. She met a marvelous man, was living in his apartment while he watched TV in the next room.

What could be better?

A knock at the door caused Cinnamon to break from her luxuriating daze. "Come in."

Mitchell stepped inside and rested on the edge of the tub.

"Is your program over?" she asked.

"It is." He paused. "You look so sexy in that tub. I just want to dive my head between your legs."

"Oh, Mitchell, you old dog, you."

"Ruff, ruff," Mitchell said. "Listen there's something I have to tell you. I guess I should have told you sooner but I didn't and to be honest, it's really not that big a deal."

"What is it?" Cinnamon asked as she eased up, knowing that whenever anyone said it wasn't a big deal, it surely was.

"I really like having you here," he said.

"Okay."

"And I want to be completely honest and up-front with you."

"Thank you. I appreciate that. Now what is it?"

"I want you to know that. . . sometimes I get high."

"Really? How?"

"Marijuana."

"Really?" she asked in a timid voice, hoping it wasn't true.

"It's not a big deal though. First of all, I seldom do it and second, it won't interfere with our relationship."

"It already has."

"Don't say that. You and I have a good thing here."

"But--"

He caressed his finger against her lips. "Shss. Nothing is going to ruin what we have. Nothing."

She wanted to believe him, even needed to believe him, but how could she? Her chances of having a prosperous relationship with a marijuana user were next to zero. But she didn't abandon all hope just yet. At least now she could explain his mood swings, and it was all beginning to make sense. Outside of his drug habit, Mitchell was a good guy, her guy and she would do her best to make their relationship work up until the very end.

At opposite ends of the leather couch, Mitchell and Cinnamon relaxed. While Mitchell watched the *Chappelle's Show*, Cinnamon began rereading her book, *The Prospering Power of Love*. Usually reading any of Catherine Ponder's books transformed Cinnamon's mood. But not this time. She was still numb from Mitchell's admission earlier and that was all that rummaged through her head.

Then it happened.

Mitchell's television program broke for a commercial. Cinnamon studied him as he reached underneath the sofa and slid out a tray filled with marijuana, two wooden pipes, a small piece of foil, two lighters and a book of matches. Everything an efficient drug user needed. Cinnamon witnessed a true pothead before her. And it was not a pretty sight.

From the corner of her eye, she observed Mitchell loading his pipe before taking a long, drawn out hit. He inhaled it like it was the last breath of his life and it made Cinnamon's stomach churn. Then slowly he blew the smoke from his mouth, polluting the air with a pungent aroma. Somehow seeing him actually get high was much more wicked than hearing about it.

After returning the paraphernalia to the tray, he leaned back, seemingly released from all his troubles.

Cinnamon closed her eyes, thinking she must be asleep. And dreaming. This moment could not be real.

Had she really given up her apartment for this, to live with a moody drug user?

She blinked and blinked and blinked until she concluded she was not dreaming. This was indeed her life in all its troubles. She could have screamed.

With her eyes closed, she lowered her head. She just couldn't conceive of a future with a drug user. It went against everything she believed in. Raised to do the right thing, pay her taxes, never cheat or steal, be kind and forgiving at all costs and even rate other people's feelings higher than hers, she just didn't get it.

How could that same person with those beliefs have been caught up in a relationship with a married man who uses drugs?

Was she really that stupid or was it just love? They say love is blind, but in her case, it was blind, deaf and dumb.

About to spiral downward into a black den of despair, she stopped herself. If she didn't snap out of her dismal train of melancholy immediately, she might not ever recover. With that in mind, she stood and headed into the bathroom, closing the door behind her. After shutting off the light, she dropped to the floor, her back against the door and her head between her knees.

When she first embarked on her search for the *Mister*, she met several men.

Joseph,

Noel,

Roman, and

Mitchell.

And with all the choices before her, she elected the married pothead. Looking back, even Joseph might have been a better prize with all his idiotic eccentricities. Captivated with Mitchell's impeccable looks and charm, she lost her sense of reasoning. Then Roman showed up in her life, who was everything she could have asked for and much more and yet she even let him slip away.

A plan of action was needed fast.

One thing was for certain. She wanted out and she wanted out now. But having just moved in, Mitchell would think she was crazy for giving up so quickly.

What was she going to do? She didn't want to stay but she couldn't go either.

Then a strange reflection hovered over her. Maybe she might be the one to assist him in kicking his terrible habit, then her being with him would prove to be a good thing after all.

Two hours later, Cinnamon shook her head in disgust as she bypassed Mitchell in the front room, still going at it full force. He seemed totally uninterested in anything but his pipe and the television before him. How could she compete with *Salle*, the name Cinnamon spontaneously gave Mitchell's drug.

While she boiled water for tea, midstream into her pessimism, she heard Mitchell call to her.

She stepped into the front room. "Yes?" she said with a fake smile.

"Come sit down next to your man."

Burdened with worry, she flopped down on the couch next to him, her hands in her lap. "Is your TV show off?"

"It just went off." He leaned over and kissed her. "I love you, Cinnamon. Did you know that?"

"Do you love me because you love me or do you love me because you're high?"

"I love you because I love you."

Not feeling the love at the moment, it was difficult for Cinnamon to pretend otherwise.

"What's wrong, Boo?" Mitchell asked. "Tell Daddy what's the matter?"

"Boo? Who's Boo?"

"You. You're my Boo."

"I don't like that name," she said, remarking his glossy eyes.

"Okay, then what about Cinne?"

"Why can't you just call me Cinnamon?" She turned from him, blew out a tainted breath. "I'm sorry if I'm not in the best mood. It's just that I'm still in shock after our conversation earlier."

"Are you still thinking about that?"

"Yes."

"I think you're trying to make it into something bigger than it is."

Suddenly, Cinnamon made a serious observation about Mitchell. When he was high, his tongue sometimes seemed glued to the roof of his mouth. Though it did not impair his speech, it looked weird.

"Somehow I thought our first night together would be special," Cinnamon said.

"It is special."

"You know what I mean, like maybe we would have done something special or something."

"We can."

Exuding discontent, Cinnamon glanced at her watch. "It's already eleven o'clock."

"What does that mean? The night is not over."

"If you say so."

"I have never seen you so blue before."

With every ounce of energy, she raised her shoulders. "So what do you want to do?"

"What do you want to do?" he asked. "Hey, Cinnamon, who's on first?"

"I don't know. You maybe." Mitchell chuckled as only a stoned man would chuckle, then tickled Cinnamon. "I'm not going to stop until I get you to smile."

Finally Cinnamon managed to pull a bogus smile from within. "Okay. Okay," she said. "I'm smiling."

"You want to go for a walk?" Mitchell said.

"As cold as it is?"

"We can make it a short walk then come back, snuggle up and drink hot chocolate," Mitchell said, his bloodshot eyes glowing. "How does that sound?"

Now that, she could go for.

Back from their long stroll along Lake Shore Drive, Cinnamon returned refreshed and high spirited. The cold air was truly what she needed to clear her head and change her focus. With an unstable sense of hope, she resolved not to bail out on Mitchell. A fine opportunity presented itself, a chance to help someone overcome an ugly habit. She planned to be his personal aide on the road to recovery if he so desired. And if not, at least she could say she gave it her best.

During her entire stay in New York City, Cinnamon vacillated between helping Mitchell vanquish his drug habit and simply abandoning ship. Despite the fact she intended to stick it out, she changed her mind. Again. Though it might be better to cut her losses, a fragment of her believed their relationship might flourish, but the other part, the essence of who she was, told her it was doomed to crumple. And at that point, she wasn't certain what to do.

At the airport, waiting to board her return flight to Chicago and in dire need of a sympathetic voice and ear, she called Arri.

"Mr. Murphy's office," Arri answered.

"Hey, it's me," Cinnamon said. "Can you talk?"

"Of course. How's married life?"

"I think I screwed up, Arri. Big time."

"It can't be that bad."

"It can't be that good either. I moved in with this guy entirely too soon, without even really knowing him. And I just don't see much of a future for us."

"Because?"

"Well, think about it," Cinnamon said. "He's still married, having yet to file for divorce, meaning in all likelihood, he and his wife could very well get back together."

"Yeah, but you knew that going into this. Didn't you?"

"I don't know, Arri. I just don't know. And then another thing bothers me. Mitchell and I never had one date. Other than the day I met him at the Wild Hare, he didn't take me out one time."

"What about Florida?"

"That was my treat. And he has never bought me flowers or a gift of any kind. All we did was. . ."

"Remember what you used to always tell me," Arri asked. "You have the power to change it all right now."

"Did I say that?" Cinnamon questioned, staring down at her pumps.

"Yes, you did. Of course, I never really took your advice but it was good advice."

"You picked a dandy time to share that with me."

"Why thank you."

"I didn't mean it as a compliment."

"I know you didn't." Arri paused. "You're going to move out, aren't you?"

"You can read my mind, can't you?"

"I can read pain."

Cinnamon switched the phone to the other ear. "I thought about leaving, but where would I go?"

"You could live with me. I would love to have you."

"I'll keep that in mind." Cinnamon paused, reflecting on her past. "You know the night before I moved in with Mitchell, I had the best dream. Our life was perfect in every way."

"Aren't dreams usually the opposite of reality?" Arri asked.

"That's right, they usually are, and yet I did it anyway."

"Listen, I have to go. Matt is just finishing up his call which means he'll be out here soon with a slew of things for me to do. I know everything is going to work out just fine. It always does."

Upon hanging up from Arri, Cinnamon silently thanked God for friends, not knowing what she would do without them.

Cinnamon's plane touched down at Midway Airport. On the Orange line, she traveled en route to downtown Chicago. Near a window, she sat next to a woman in her fifties. The automatic PA system echoed in the background, announcing the next approaching stops. In an attempt to pinpoint a clue she might have missed concerning Mitchell's drug use, she reflected on their relationship, and the only thing that stood out were his erratic mood swings. Knowing these things now certainly would not make much difference in the dilemma she faced, but it might bring peace to her psyche, if only just to understand.

From inside the "L" car on Monroe and Wabash, Cinnamon's eyes caught a glimpse of an interracial couple waiting for the train. Her focus immediately switched to Arri. It seemed she and Arri traded places, Arri having rid herself from the clutches of Eric and finally securing peace.

Where was Cinnamon's peace at this time?

It was as if Cinnamon picked up where Arri left off.

The excitement of living with Mitchell having completely worn off, Cinnamon dreaded returning to his apartment. Oh, how she wished for a place to retreat to on days like this one. If only she could turn back the hands of time, she never would have given up her apartment. Never. But there was no sense in playing the "I wish" game because she couldn't win.

Cinnamon hated to acknowledge regret. She preferred to view all of life's events as learning experiences. But this time she couldn't deny it. She had screwed up. And not just because of Mitchell's drug problem or his mood swings, but because of something much worse. From the start, she knew it was incorrect to date another woman's husband. And yet she did it anyway, that being her biggest downfall of all.

Chapter Twenty-Nine

The blaring television signified that Mitchell was home when Cinnamon inserted her key into the door. As she lugged her tote bag through the door, Mitchell didn't appear to notice her, seemingly more focused on his television program.

Cinnamon set her tote bag against the wall and stepped over to the sofa. "Hey."

Not looking in Cinnamon's direction, Mitchell nodded.

"Hello," Cinnamon said with a little twang in her voice.

"I heard you," he snapped.

Not tonight, she thought, as she shook her head in disgust.

"What's the attitude for?" she asked after having stressed out about him the entire time she was away.

"I don't have an attitude," he said. "Maybe it's you with the attitude."

With her flight into Chicago being delayed several hours, it was now close to midnight and she was exhausted. In no mood to match wits with him, she scurried into the bedroom and changed into her sweat suit.

Mitchell seemed deliberate in his attempt to pick a fight with her, but she refused to sink to his level.

As she unzipped her tote, she concluded Mitchell must have finished off his supply of *Salle* because his drug usually brought out the best in him. Before leaving the bedroom, Cinnamon shut her eyes and inhaled five elongated breaths before wholly extinguishing them. In an effort to rid herself of the day's stresses, she shifted her focus away from Mitchell. This way, she might perhaps experience a tranquil evening.

With her hand on the doorknob, she speculated that a little cordiality might alter Mitchell's rotten mood. For sure it was worth a try. Via that notion and with all the kindness she could dig up, she entered the front room and dropped down next to him on the couch. "What are you watching?" she asked as she planted her hand on his thigh.

He continued to view the television as if Cinnamon didn't exist.

"Did you hear me?" Cinnamon asked.

"No, I didn't hear you," Mitchell said, not looking at her. "I'm deaf."

Exasperated, she sucked her teeth. "What is your problem? All I asked was one funky question."

"A dumb, stupid question."

"Just because I asked what you were watching?"

"If you had any sense at all, you would see that I'm watching the game. Any idiot would know that."

Cinnamon turned to him, venom in her eyes. "Who are you calling an idiot?"

Mitchell didn't even look at her. Instead he raised the volume on the television via remote.

Cinnamon stood, leaned back, her head cocked to the side. "I don't have to deal with this crap. Do I look like some homeless person to you? I don't have to stay here and take this from a loser strung out on pot."

Mitchell lowered the volume on the television, apparently in shock from Cinnamon's words. "You're calling me a loser?"

Cinnamon stepped toward him, not backing down in any way. "You and your wife too."

A dark silence fell over them before Mitchell quietly and calmly left the room. Not knowing whether to grab her purse and leave or brew a pot of coffee, she waited on the edge of the sofa, watching for Mitchell's return. She found it interesting that for all the self-improvement books she read, she seemed to forget everything in a time of crisis.

Sitting perfectly still, Cinnamon rested her clasped hands between her thighs. About to pick up the phone and call Arri, she looked up to see Mitchell pelt from the bedroom, his arms filled with Cinnamon's underwear, uniforms and shoes. Before she could utter a word, Plop!, as Mitchell dispersed everything to the floor.

"What are you doing?" Cinnamon asked as she rose to her feet.

"You're getting the fuck out of here," Mitchell said. "That's what." He flaunted the two keys in his hand. "And don't worry about returning the keys, I already have them."

"You're putting me out? Why?"

"Because I don't want you here. And I don't need you here, not anymore anyway."

"What do you mean anymore?"

Mitchell grazed up on her with a faint smile on his face. "You don't even know, do you?"

"Know what?" she asked, her faced plagued with confusion.

Mitchell collapsed on the couch, stretched out and relaxed. "Pack the rest of your things and I might tell you."

"Where am I supposed to go?"

"That's not my problem."

"I can't believe you could be this cold." Cinnamon felt her eyes welling up with tears fast. "What are you so upset about?"

"Why is it so hard for you to believe that I don't want you here?" he asked, almost pleading.

"Because it doesn't make any sense. I just moved in and now you're asking me to leave."

"Not asking, telling. I don't want you here, Cinnamon. What part of that don't you understand?"

Her eyes shifted to him in disgust. This whole thing being totally out of control, Cinnamon wasn't ready for any of it. Though she planned to leave anyway, she never dreamed she would be asked to leave. This was more than a late night argument. Something else lurked over this relationship, and Cinnamon thirsted to know what it was.

Cinnamon bent down to collect her things from the floor, all the while sniffling and wiping the tear smudges from her face. "I know this isn't just about an argument."

Mitchell exhaled, seemingly irritated. "There's no way to shut you up, is there?" He paused. "Okay, Cinnamon, here's the deal."

Cinnamon's watery eyes shot to him in a flash. She flung her clothes over her arm and smeared the tears into her cheek. With every cell in her body, she listened with a meticulous ear.

Mitchell continued. "I only asked you to move in here so I could make my wife jealous."

With her face numb, she closed her eyes as she consumed his remark. She could almost see red as she gazed at him, her face oozing disbelief. "You couldn't have done that. No one could be that cruel."

"Well, I did do it and I still want you out."

"You asked me to give up my apartment, put my furniture in storage and move in with you just so you could make your wife jealous?"

Mitchell clapped his hands as if it was a hallelujah moment. "Yes, yes, I think you finally caught on."

Much too disturbed to continue the conversation, she gathered the rest of her things, utilizing every drop of energy in her. She calmly, without any emotion, stepped into the bedroom and locked the door behind her. On the edge of the bed, she rested for a moment, thinking, pondering, contemplating, her heart beating faster and faster.

Several minutes would pass before she could stand on her feet. Then suddenly she charged to the closet and hurled her two suitcases, tote and overnight bag to the floor and swung them open. After she yanked her clothes from the hangers, she tossed them into the suitcase along with the dresser drawer contents.

Before she continued, she picked up the phone, out of breath, and dialed Arri's number. Right away, she was transferred to Arri's voice mail. Not knowing Arri's whereabouts, she chose not to leave a message.

Noel being out of town ruled out her running to him, and calling on her parents was not an option. Her eviction was privileged information and she wasn't about to disclose all the nasty details to no one but a select few.

Upon frisking her mind for a place of refuge, her options looked pretty grim. Then it hit her. Her last hope--Roman Richardson. However, she wasn't completely certain about his telephone number. The last four digits were 1679. That she knew for sure. It was the prefixes, 728 and 784 that she couldn't straighten out. Not giving it any more thought, she tried them both. Moments later, a sense of relief swept through her when she heard Roman's sympathetic voice on the other end.

"Could this be Cinnamon calling me at such a late hour?"

"It is."

"This isn't a booty call is it?"

"Very funny," Cinnamon said, drawing a smile from inside. Roman was making this so easy.

"It's okay if it is a booty call," Roman said.

"It's not but I do need to ask a huge favor."

"Consider it done."

"But I haven't asked you yet."

"It doesn't matter. I can't think of anything I wouldn't do for you."

Her eyes watered as she struggled to resist crying. His kindness impressed her in a way that touched her right where she lived.

"Can I come over tonight?" she asked.

"Of course. Are you okay? Do you want me to pick you up?"

"No, I'm fine. I'll just meet you there in about thirty minutes. Okay?"

Off the phone, Cinnamon continued to overload her luggage until she ran out of space. Having thrown out all her moving boxes, she was forced to use garbage bags for the remainder of her things. Not knowing whether she would ever return, she left nothing behind, not even a coffee mug.

After piling all her things by the door, she grabbed her purse and ordered a Flash Taxi. In front of the television, Mitchell didn't move, seemingly oblivious to Cinnamon's presence. She hoped he might offer to help her with her bags, but that didn't happen. She was on her own. She hesitated to say anything before closing the door behind her, but so not to ignite his fuse, she opted to just leave.

It was after 1:00 a.m.

With all of Cinnamon's bags piled by the door in the lobby, she resembled a sophisticated bag lady.

Though it would have been helpful for Roman to pick her up, it was best that she depart from Mitchell's place alone.

She waited outside, on the lookout for a white taxi. She stuffed her hands into her pockets and lifted her coat collar. Her tears having dried, she felt numb and at the same time relieved to be out, out of Mitchell's life forever. Having composed herself and assembled her wits, she could see the event for what it was--an unfortunate experience that could have been a lot worse.

En route to Roman's place, seated in the back of the taxi, Cinnamon felt a little embarrassed having to share with Roman that the man she supposedly loved tossed her out like a pile of garbage.

But what else was she to do? In need of a place to stay and Roman willingly offering one, pride simply occupied no place in her life.

The taxi driver helped Cinnamon unload her bags into the lobby of Roman's building on the 6000 block of Lake Shore Drive.

Soon Roman approached and greeted her with a smile. "How much stuff did you bring with you?"

"It's an ugly story. I'll have to tell you all about it."

While Cinnamon hung up her coat in the hall closet, Roman lumped her bags in the corner of the living room floor. Not having visited Roman for some time, she checked out the oriental paintings on the wall as she hugged her arms.

"I'll turn up the heat," Roman said. "Can I get you anything? Some water, coffee, tea."

"Tea would be great."

In Roman's kitchen, Cinnamon sat across from him, her hands folded while the water boiled for tea.

Soft melodic sounds resounded from the stereo throughout his one-bedroom unit. She peered across the drop-leaf table at him in the dimly lit kitchen, the only light coming from the light fixture above the kitchen sink.

An extended silence dominated the room, seemingly both of them at a lost for words.

"So what's in all the bags?" Roman asked.

"A few of my personal things."

"A few of your personal things?"

"A lot of my personal things."

"Are you hungry?" he asked.

"Not really. But I do want to thank you for letting me come over here. That was very kind of you and I do appreciate it." With a solemn look on her face, she stared down at the table. "Sometimes I don't think I deserve a friend like you."

"Why would you say that?"

"After what I did to you? And instead of you punishing me for it, you rewarded me with your kindness."

Roman listened to her, but he did not speak.

"I'm sorry, Roman, for what I did."

"It's okay, Cinnamon," he said as he glided his hand on top of hers. "Just try not to think about it."

"Thank you for being so nice to me," she said with tears in her eyes. "And giving me a place to stay tonight."

"You're welcome, but please don't cry because I might start crying too."

A huge laugh burst from Cinnamon's mouth.

"I knew that would get you," he said, laughing.

"And you were right." She used her pinkie to blot the tears from the corners of her eyes. "I never told you this before, Roman, but the women in my family have been cursed never to become involved with married men."

"Cursed? How?"

"My two sisters both had tumultuous affairs with married men, which I thought would be enough to deter me from doing the same."

"This guy you were with was married?"

Cinnamon nodded, covered in shame. "And look at me now. He threw me out."

"I thought it might have been something like that."

"I had only lived there a few days too. But no one is at fault here but me. I saw the worm and I walked right upon him. I really believed that he was in the process of filing for a divorce and we might actually have a chance." Cinnamon paused for thought. "Boy, was I way off track."

"You think you're the only woman who has hoped a married man would leave his wife for her? Trust me, you're not alone on this one."

"Yeah, but I had ample reason to stay away from him, if only for the curse that haunts my family."

"You're not going to wallow in regret about this, are you?"

"I was kind of hoping to," she said, smiling.

"You don't want to do that," Roman said. "But somehow I get the feeling you're into self-punishment, aren't you?"

"How did you know?"

"We all are. At least sometimes anyway."

The tea kettle whistled and Roman prepared tea for them and handed Cinnamon hers. "Watch it now. It's pretty hot."

"Thank you," she said. "You're so kind, Roman. Anyone ever tell you that?"

"Only you. So what are you going to do?" he asked.

She blew on her tea, then tasted it. "About what?"

"About your apartment situation."

"Oh, that. Well, obviously, I don't have one of those anymore. I'll probably move in with Arri. It's not like I have a lot of choices."

While drinking her tea, Cinnamon experienced a mild buzz. "This is caffeinated, isn't it?"

"That's all I have."

"That's okay. A little caffeine never hurt anyone."

Right out of left field, Roman said, "You're welcome to stay here if you like."

"I couldn't impose on you like that."

"You wouldn't be imposing."

"Thanks, but I couldn't do that. Shoot, I almost forgot. I have to call Arri and let her know where I am."

After Cinnamon left word with Arri, she returned to the kitchen and slouched down into the chair. She then moved her tea cup to the center of the table and folded her hands in front of her. "Life is strange isn't it?"

"It can be."

"I mean you plan on things working out a certain way and, boom, it doesn't happen like that at all, doesn't even come close."

Roman leaned back as if collecting his thoughts. "When we first met, I was so sure we would be together forever."

"Really? You thought that when we first met?"

"I sure did. But then when we broke up a while ago, I just made peace with the fact that if we were meant to be together, we would."

"Now that's having a lot of faith."

"Did you ever think that maybe your getting together with this guy was the miracle needed to bring you to me?"

"Now that I never thought about."

"Think about it. It's after one in the morning. What are the chances that you would have come to visit me at this hour of the night unless what happened happened?"

"Not very good." Roman's words made the hair on the back of her neck leap to attention.

"Not good is right. I'm not saying that this is the beginning of something between us. I'm just saying this wonderful moment that we're sharing together is the result of your fiasco with this guy."

"Wow, that's pretty deep."

"Maybe, but you get where I'm coming from, don't you?"

She nodded in agreement. "We always did have the best conversations."

"Yes, we did."

Cinnamon insisted she sleep on Roman's sofa even after he offered his bed. Already having welcomed her into his home, she chose not to impede on his bed as well.

An early riser like Cinnamon, Roman was up and out by the time Cinnamon awakened. Because she continued to beat up on herself for giving up her apartment, she hardly slept at all. Though self-punishment wasn't the best thing to do, she was so good at it.

Still no word from Noel, Cinnamon once again tried him at home and to her surprise and much delight, Noel answered.

"I didn't think I would ever hear from you again," Cinnamon said.

"I called that number you left for me and this guy says you don't live there anymore. What's that all about?"

"Shambles," she said.

"How's that?"

"You heard me. Shambles. My life is in shambles."

"I hardly doubt that."

"Anyway, how are you?" she asked.

"Did you just change the subject on me?"

"I did. So how are you?"

"I'll let you get away from the subject for now. But anyway, I'm great. I missed you."

"Not as much as I missed you," Cinnamon said.

"No way. I bet I missed you more."

Cinnamon laughed, reveling in their dialogue. "Will you listen to us? We sound like high school seniors in love."

"I thought we were in love."

"We are but we're not in high school anymore," she said. "So where were you?"

"I was helping my friend rehab a property in Missouri, made over three thousand dollars in just the few weeks I was gone."

"You didn't have to kill anyone, did you?"

"Of course I did," Noel said. "I'm just kidding. I did some serious work though. And I must say I was not used to it."

"Used to working?" she questioned.

"Used to working for money." Noel paused. "Okay, time's up. What I want to know is who that guy was that you don't live with anymore."

"I'll tell you all about it tonight. Why don't you come by Arri's place and we can catch up."

"Are you talking about your fine tall friend?"

"Yes, that would be her."

"I'll be there. You two aren't going to try anything, are you?"

"Of course."

"Good, I was hoping you would."

It was so easy to flirt with Noel. It came so naturally because they were the best of friends. Her conversation with him revived her spirits and perked up her mood. And she was so thankful to have such good friends.

Before going about her day, Cinnamon voiced a special prayer. First she was grateful for Noel and Arri, and secondly, she released all negative energy she held for Mitchell, refusing to hold a grudge against him despite everything that happened.

Cinnamon prepared the bathroom, wanting it to be nice and toasty before stepping in the shower. For three minutes she would close off the bathroom, allowing the steam to warm the space before she disrobed. While she waited, she perused Roman's clothes closet, admiring his organization, his pants and shirts separated by color.

Unable to resist nosing around in his chest of drawers, she peaked inside, beginning with the top drawer. Nothing out of the ordinary stood out, just dress socks neatly folded. The drawer underneath was the underwear drawer with a slew of plaid boxer shorts. Just as she was about to close the drawer, a folded piece of paper lodged toward the back caught her eye. She reached for it, having to discern more. Upon unfolding it, she saw it was a typed poem, entitled *The Night You Left Me*. After examining it for a name and not finding one, she eased down on the bed and read it.

The Night You Left Me

I remember when your presence took me to a warm and delightful place
My spirit was alive and vibrant
My heart danced, my eyes glistened, and my smile sang the song of joy
But now, no more. Alone, I am, so without
My heart stings with desire
I want, I want, I want, but I cannot have

I can feel the longings in my arms and fingers
When you're not on my mind, you are
When I'm not wanting you, I am
When I'm not sad, I really am, like today
I close my eyes, I can see you, feel you, smell you
Your presence surrounds me, bombards me
Muddled and locked up
Locked in a dark hole with no one to talk to but misery and despair
No way out, not even a flicker of light
Darkness wavers over me and I can't shake it
The woe in my heart weighs me down,
And I ask my myself
Oh, I ask myself
How much more will I suffer before I shed my last tear.

CHAPTER THIRTY

A PART OF CINNAMON suspected Roman wrote that poem for her. But she wouldn't know for sure unless she confronted him, which would mean admitting she was snooping through his things. But so what. The curiosity of it all simmered inside her and probably wouldn't die down until she learned the particulars. Not able to postpone it any longer, she picked up the phone and called Roman.

"I've been a bad girl, Roman."

"Oh, really? How bad?"

"Well, I feel a little embarrassed admitting this to you, but I'm going to do it anyway. I was going through your dresser drawers and came across one of your poems."

"Is that right?"

"I'm sorry," she said, knowing he had already forgiven her. "I know I shouldn't have done that, especially since you were so nice about letting me stay here last night."

"I don't know, Cinnamon," he said in a playful tone. "What you just told me is pretty serious. What do you think we should do about this?"

"You could forgive me," she said in a child-like tone.

"Forgive you? I don't know, Cinnamon. I'm going to have to think about this."

She enjoyed playing along with him. "Come on, Roman. I said I was sorry."

"Okay. You talked me into it."

"That was easy. And since you're in such a good mood and everything, might I ask you who wrote that poem?"

"You can ask but that doesn't mean I'm going to tell you."

Not sure if she should pursue it any further, she said, "Okay, well, I'll see you when you get home."

"I wrote it for you, Cinnamon, the day you left me or I should say the night you left me."

"Really?" she asked, trying not to let on how happy he made her. "But you never gave it to me."

"No, I didn't. It was probably best that I didn't."

A prolonged silence sailed over them. "Thank you for everything, Roman, for your kindness, your warm heart, the poem you never gave me and most of all for your forgiveness."

"You are most welcome."

Roman did it again. He managed to kindle her spirit with his impeccable eminence. And if she were to learn anything about building character, Roman would be the one to teach her.

It would be several hours before Roman could relocate her things to Arri's. In an effort to make good use of her time, she began work on her book in progress. Already having prepared a table of contents, she was remiss in composing an outline, much less a first chapter. Her first chapter would address the power of words, bringing to mind a favorite affirmation she planned to practice. *Everything always works out fine.*

After over an hour of compiling material for her book, she strolled to the video store and rented one of her favorite love stories of the past, *An Officer and a Gentleman.* Two hours later, Cinnamon's eyes were filled with tears. Though she viewed the movie umpteen times, it still possessed the power to make her cry. Character played a huge factor in her choice of movies. It was not so much what happened in a movie, but more about what the character made happen. She liked to envision herself as a character who grew and changed and most of all who reached out her hand to help someone else. That was who she longed to be.

All settled in at Arri's apartment, Cinnamon and Arri drank lemonade in the kitchen while they waited for their pizza delivery. A sweet green apple scent coursed through the apartment, even making its way into the kitchen.

"So much has changed with us in such a short time," Cinnamon said. "You're no longer chasing Eric."

Arri interrupted. "And you're no longer ga-ga over Mitchell, the man you fancied as *all that.*"

"And I'm homeless."

"You're not homeless. You're living here with me."

"Yeah, I know." Cinnamon inhaled a skimpy breath and crossed her legs. "Okay, enough of this joyless talk. What kind of pizza did you order?"

"One half cheese and the other sausage. Extra large of course. What time will Noel be over?"

"Around seven," Cinnamon said. "You ever notice that when something is happening to you or when you are going through something, it seems like time stands still, but then you blink once and it's all over?"

"I'm not following you."

"Just think," Cinnamon said. "Not two weeks ago, I was living on Lake Shore Drive in my own comfortable, wish-I-had-it-back one-bedroom apartment. Now look at me. I'm living out of garbage bags."

Arri laughed. "I guess when you put it like that."

"I used to pull my underwear and pantyhose from my dresser drawer, now where is it? I don't know. Maybe it's in my tote, my suitcase, laundry bag or one of the three garbage bags I brought with me."

"Will you stop it?" Arri said as she continued to laugh. "You'll have your own place again soon."

"I'm just reminiscing and reflecting," Cinnamon said in a docile voice.

"Well maybe you shouldn't if it's going to have you talking like this."

Cinnamon stood and composed herself. "You're right. I have to wipe this sadness off. Right now."

"That's right, girl, wipe it off."

Cinnamon slid her hands down her sweater, then flung the imaginary sadness into the air. "There, it's gone. I wiped it off."

Still reflecting, Cinnamon dropped down into the chair. "You know what I think? I think I may be in love with Roman."

Flushed, Arri ogled Cinnamon. "What happened at his place last night that I don't know about?"

"Nothing. He was a perfect gentleman."

"Not too perfect I hope."

"Yes, a perfect gentleman," Cinnamon said. "Will you get your head out of the gutter? Roman was great to me last night, a perfect friend even after I broke up with him to be with someone else. Still, he showed me nothing but warmth and kindness."

"He is quite a guy."

"So why didn't I know that before?" Cinnamon asked, angry with herself.

"You did know. Your heart was just somewhere else."

"Do you think you could show kindness to someone who had broken up with you for someone else?" Cinnamon asked.

"I don't think so. Roman is a unique individual."

"You can say that again."

"Roman is a unique individual."

Cinnamon laughed, amused with Arri's bland sense of humor. "You have to be a comedian, don't you?"

"Well, you walked right into that one. You want to know what I think," Arri asked. "I think Roman loves you too."

"You think?"

"Without a doubt, the way he allowed you to stay with him last night knowing you had just been with another man. It's love in the first degree."

"I sure hope you're right."

"What I want to know is," Arri said, "how this fight with you and Mitchell started."

"He came home in a foul mood, then just snapped. The next thing I knew, he had thrown my clothes on the floor."

Arri laughed as if she heard the story before. "And I thought he was just your average guy who happened to be married."

"You wouldn't believe how easily his mood would change from peaceful to hostility."

"Oh, I would believe. I dated a pothead before and it was bad. He went from the sweetest man in the world to the meanest devil."

"Sounds like we're talking about the same person."

Noel arrived at Arri's apartment wearing tight jeans and a tan shirt.

"There's my girl," Noel said as he bear-hugged Cinnamon." The hug went on and on and Cinnamon didn't think he would ever let go.

"You look good," Cinnamon said.

"Thank you. Thank you."

Arri approached Noel at the doorway. "Hello, Noel."

"I am loving your hair," Noel said, pivoting around Arri. "Loving it a lot."

"Thank you," Arri said, extending her hand. "It's nice to see you again."

Noel shrugged and sucked his teeth. "What's with this shaking hands stuff?" He moved up on Arri, wrapped his arms around her and leaned into her. "Now, that's how you greet someone."

Arri smiled. "You better be careful. Don't start nothing you can't finish."

"Oh, honey, I always finish." Noel snapped his fingers. "Snap. snap."

"Okay, Arri, did you get that?" Cinnamon asked.

In the kitchen, they all gathered around the table. Cinnamon grabbed a handful of napkins from the counter and relaxed in a seat next to Noel.

Arri flipped open the huge pizza box and slouched down in her chair.

"Smells good," Noel said. "Is all of this for me?"

"All for you," Cinnamon said sarcastically.

"So Cinnamon, tell me everything," Noel said. "And don't leave out any of the filth."

"Basically," Cinnamon said with her mouth full. "I had an affair that led to disaster and that's pretty much it."

"The married man, right?" Noel asked.

Cinnamon nodded and swallowed her pizza.

"You must have really liked this guy if you gave up your apartment for him."

"I was lost and turned out."

Noel broke into a song. "Lost and turned ouuuuut, lost and turned ouuuuut."

Arri held up her hand as if in school. "No singing, please."

"Maybe later, huh?" Noel said as he loaded his plate with six pieces of pizza.

"Much later," Arri stated.

Cinnamon stood and filled three glasses with lemonade, then returned to her seat.

"Thank you," Noel said. "It's so hard to find good help these days."

"Okay, now," Cinnamon said.

"So tell me some more about this real estate stuff, Noel."

"Oh, yeah, my cousin just got into the real estate business and I helped him rehab one of his properties."

"What did you have to do?" Cinnamon asked.

"All kinds of stuff, paint, I helped him refinish the floors, replant flowers."

"You planted flowers?" Cinnamon asked with a chuckle.

"Yes, I did."

"I was just trying to picture you planting flowers."

"Make sure you picture right. Anyway, I'm seriously thinking of getting into this rehab business myself. It's a great way to make some real money." Noel wiped the pizza sauce from his mouth. "So what about you, Arri? You've been sitting there not saying much."

Arri finished her lemonade. "There's not much to say except I finally stopped chasing Eric."

Noel scooted closer to Arri and leaned toward her. "So uh, you're looking for a replacement?"

"You know someone?"

"As a matter of fact, I do."

"Noel, will you knock it off?" Cinnamon said playfully.

"No, I will not knock it off. A man has got to do what a man has to do."

"What the heck are you talking about?" Cinnamon asked.

"I don't know, it sounded good at the moment."

Cinnamon and Arri burst into laugher.

"You know what you are, Noel?" Cinnamon asked.

"I'm sure you'll tell me."

"You are one-hundred percent personality."

"One-hundred percent?"

"That's right. There isn't a cell in your body that does not have personality."

"I'll take that as a compliment. So, Arri, back to you. Since you're not dating these days, does that mean you're climbing the walls?"

"How did you know?"

"It's the look in your eye."

"You two are so full of it," Cinnamon said.

"I almost forgot," Arri said, turning to Cinnamon. "Remember that manager at my office I was so crazy for?"

"Of course."

"He's leaving the company."

Before Cinnamon could respond, Noel slunk his hand on top of Arri's. "Don't worry, Arri, I'll step in to take his place."

"How are you going to do that?"

"You can be crazy for me if you like. I won't mine at all."

Arri casually released her hand from Noel's. "Thanks, Noel, for the offer, but I'll pass."

"That's what you say now but what about in a couple of weeks?"

"Well, let's worry about that in a couple of weeks," Arri said. "So, Noel, any interesting stories to share with us?"

Noel seemed to meditate on her question before answering. "Not that I can think of. I did get into a fight with a homeless man, but other than that, not much to tell."

"Wait a minute," Cinnamon said. "A fight with a homeless man?"

"Yeah, I told him I didn't have any money to buy his Streetwise paper so he follows me into the store and proves me wrong."

Arri and Cinnamon laughed to no end.

"And you know me," Noel said. "I had to put him in his place. But then the store manager asked us both to leave and this guy tells him we're old friends."

"No, he didn't," Arri said.

"Yes, he did."

"Only you, Noel, only you," Cinnamon said.

After dinner, Arri, Cinnamon and Noel retired to the front room. All clumped together on the futon, they watched the movie, *Threesome,* a movie Noel insisted they see, insinuating that one day the three of them could be the same trio in the movie. And to Cinnamon's surprise, the movie proved quite entertaining.

When the credits rolled, Noel stood up as if inspired by the movie. "I have the best idea."

"Well, let's hear it," Arri said.

Noel turned to Cinnamon. "Why don't you and I get an apartment together?"

Cinnamon smiled, the bell inside her head going ding-dong. "I didn't even think about that. That's a fabulous idea."

"Sounds like a winner to me except for one thing," Arri said. "I'm jealous. I want to live with the two of you too."

"I'm not surprised," Noel said, returning to a sitting position. "I do have that effect on people."

"Arri," Cinnamon said. "You know you'll always be welcome to stay with us as often as you like."

"That's right," Noel added. "And there will be no sleeping on the sofa. Oh, no. You'll sleep with Cinnamon and me in our bed."

Arri laughed. "That's so nice of you, Noel. Does Cinnamon know you and she will be sharing a bed?"

Cinnamon's eyes shot to Noel and she smirked. "No, Cinnamon doesn't know."

"Okay, okay, you got me. I know we'll have separate beds."

"That's right, Noel," Cinnamon said. "And don't forget it."

"I'm not making any promises."

"So what's your friend going to say about you moving out?" Arri asked.

"Nothing," Noel said. "Because I'm not going to tell him. One day I'll leave and never come back."

"That's how you do it," Arri said, giving Noel the high-five.

"I don't think that's right, Noel," Cinnamon said. "You should at least tell him. "You know I'm a firm believer in karma."

"You can't be that much concerned with karma after dating that married man," Noel said. "Especially after the tragedy your sisters endured."

Noel's words seemed to capture even Arri's attention. "You know, I forgot all about that."

"I was a fool, okay? I have no excuse."

"Well, we can understand that," Arri said. "Can't we, Noel?"

"Most definitely. We all have at one time or another done something we knew was wrong."

"Yeah that may be true," Cinnamon cut in. "But from this day forward--"

"No need to make any theatrical speeches, Cinnamon," Noel said.

"I know, but still," Cinnamon said. "I want to say this. From this day forward, I will listen to my intuition to the fullest extent."

Noel shifted his ear to Cinnamon's cheek. "What? I hear your intuition saying something now. It's saying that I should stay here tonight with you girls."

"I don't hear anything," Cinnamon said.

"Neither do I."

"That's because you two don't have the kind of hearing that I have."

"Noel, we would love to have you stay over, but it's my first night here since my eviction and we girls have a lot to talk about."

"I understand. No men allowed."

"How about we have you over next weekend?" Arri asked.

"That sounds like a great idea," Cinnamon said.

"I guess. Maybe. If I'm free."

"Oh, you'll be free or else," Cinnamon said.

"Are you threatening me, Cinnamon Brown? 'Cause if you are. . . I like it."

Cinnamon laughed. "I bet you hit on women in your sleep, don't you?"

"Of course. It's how I perfect my skills."

Always a treat to be around, Cinnamon hated to see Noel leave later that evening. Thrilled with the idea of them sharing an apartment, she planned to hop to it right away. Having so much fun when he lived with her before, she didn't believe it could possibly be any better.

CHAPTER THIRTY-ONE

LIFE WAS JUST SO unpredictable, Cinnamon thought as she stood in front of the bathroom mirror, brushing her teeth. Twenty-four hours ago she was with Roman at his condominium. And just twenty-four hours prior to that, she was with Mitchell. Now this night made the third night she slept in a home not her own. Though it was always nice to stay at Arri's, she preferred her decision be based on want and not need.

After rinsing her mouth with Scope, she clicked out the light and headed for the bedroom. Already in bed, Arri wrote in her journal while Cinnamon climbed into bed and slid underneath the covers.

"What are you writing?" Cinnamon asked.

"Just talking about how great it was to have you and Noel here tonight."

"He is great, isn't he?"

"You and him are going to have so much fun living together. It should be a sin."

"Yes, we are." Cinnamon paused, then changed the subject. "So how are you holding up with your boss leaving and all?"

"I'm a little bummed out about it, but I'm happy for him."

"I think being on your own for a while has been really good for you. You seem so much more secure in yourself."

"I wouldn't say that," Arri said.

"I would," Cinnamon said, staring into space. "While you were finding your strength, I was cohabitating with a married man, as if there weren't enough single men to choose from."

"Yeah, but there's only one Mitchell."

Cinnamon clasped her hands. "Thank God for that. And I have to tell you something, Arri. I have my eye on Roman. Big time."

"I know, you told me before. You really think you love him, huh?"

"I do."

"So what's the problem?" Arri asked.

"He would never have me now after what I did to him."

"Are you kidding me? Of course he would. Roman is just as crazy about you as you are about him. He's been crazy about you from the first."

"I know, but that was before I broke his heart."

Cinnamon really hoped Arri's words were true.

"Let me tell you something about men," Arri said. "They don't hold on to stuff like women do. I'm not saying they always forgive, but they are more forgiving than women."

Cinnamon nibbled on her fingernails.

Did she really have a chance with Roman?

"Even if he did forgive me, it's not going to make him forget what I did."

"Who says he has to forget? I'm telling you Roman wants to be with you. Tell him how you feel and he'll lie down for you."

Cinnamon halfheartedly considered Arri's proposal for all of ten seconds. "Maybe I will tell him how I feel. But I'm scared."

"What's the worse thing that can happen?"

"He can tell me where to get off, that's what."

"So what? Isn't it worth the risk? The only thing is when you tell him, you have to tell him exactly what you want."

"What do I want?" Cinnamon asked, confused.

"You know what you want, don't you?"

Cinnamon shook her head. "No I don't."

"You want someone to be your friend. You want someone to date. You want someone to spend weekends and holidays with. Right?"

"Yeah."

"And what else?" Arri asked.

"I want us to be together exclusively until we decide to marry or not to marry."

"Great. Tell him that."

While away in Los Angeles, Cinnamon reflected on everything that happened to her in the last few weeks, concluding that Susan Jeffers, one of her favorite authors, was right. Something good could many times be found in something bad, if you knew where to look.

Something good indeed came from her turbulent experience with Mitchell. Not only did she find a great roommate in Noel, but she also learned to always trust her intuition. And the biggest prize of all was finding Mister Right in a place she was not likely to look.

Right in front of her.

By the time Cinnamon returned to Arri's apartment, she was gung-ho about her quest for Roman. With all the sincerity in her heart, she would express to Roman how she felt. Having gone through hail and rain in search of love and romance, there was no sense in pulling back now.

It was four-thirty in the afternoon, and Arri had yet to arrive home from work.

While Cinnamon stood in the bathroom washing her hands and face, she heard Arri come through the front door.

"Cinnamon," Arri yelled. "Are you here?"

Cinnamon stepped from the bathroom, pat drying her face. "What's up?"

"You will never guess who I had lunch with today!" Arri burst with zeal and before Cinnamon could respond, she performed a soft-shoe dance and blurted out, "Matt. And guess what else?"

"You're going to have his baby?"

"Close. He asked me out this weekend."

"Really? How did this come about?"

Arri broke from her coat and flung it into the chair. "I don't know. He called me into his office this morning and invited me to lunch and it wasn't until we were at the restaurant that he asked me out."

"That's great. You think it has anything to do with him leaving the company?"

"I asked him the same thing, but he said it didn't."

"Who cares anyway?" Cinnamon threw up her hands in praise. "This is great news, girl."

"You should have seen me at the restaurant. When he invited me out, I was all calm and cool, my hands folded, but what was really going on was--" Arri reached her hands skyward. "Yaaaaaay! Matt invited me out. Yay! Yay! Yay!" Arri composed herself. "But I didn't let him see *that*. I kept it all inside."

Cinnamon laughed. "I'm so glad."

"I'm going to take it really slow this time, Cinnamon. I'm not going to rush anything."

"Good for you. Now all I have to do is tell Roman how I feel and we'll both have someone."

"When? When are you going to tell him?"

"Tonight," Cinnamon said sensuously. "I'm going to make my surprise visit around seven."

Cinnamon showered and coordinated the sexiest outfit she owned. She adorned her body with an ebony suede miniskirt, low-cut red blouse, DKNY tights and her shiny come-get-me boots.

After a quick dab of Cool Water Woman perfume to her neck and arms, she proceeded with her mission.

It was a little after seven o'clock when she arrived at Roman's place, but to her dismay he was not there. Filled with disappointment, Cinnamon quickly returned home. After finally building up the nerve to admit her feelings to him, her heart was crushed. And she almost crumbled. She should have phoned first, but choosing to surprise him, she ended up surprising herself.

Back at Arri's apartment and massively disappointed, Cinnamon expected Arri to bolt from her bedroom, wishing to know all the details of her visit to Roman's. But instead Arri sat on the floor in her bedroom, immersed in an intense telephone conversation.

Cinnamon changed into a cotton nightgown and prepared a cup of peppermint tea. A gush of uneasiness rollicked inside her. Earlier, she was self-assured about confronting Roman, but now she wasn't so sure anymore. It concerned her that if she didn't do it tonight, she might not ever build up the courage to do it again. Adhering to that thought, she called him.

"I was just at your place a few minutes ago," Cinnamon said.

"I'm sorry I missed you. I would have called you at your friend's place, but I wanted you to get settled first."

"That's okay. I was just glad you were there for me when I needed you."

"So are you coming back over?"

"No, I don't think so," she said, the letdown still rampaging through her. "It wasn't that important."

"It had to be something," Roman said, "if you came over here to surprise me."

"No, seriously," Cinnamon said, lying through her teeth. "It was nothing."

"So how are things going with you and Arri?"

"Great. I am a lucky woman to have such great friends."

"Yes, you are."

With little else to say, she said, "Okay, well I guess I'll talk to you soon."

"So was there a reason for this call?" he asked.

"No, not really."

"Just wanted to call and see if I was home?"

"Something like that."

"Okay, Cinnamon, I know there's more to this, but I won't force you to talk about it. We'll talk soon."

Roman left a hole in the pit of her stomach. She yearned to tell him how she felt, but the fear enveloped in her again and this time she couldn't conquer it.

How would she deal with the pain of Roman rejecting her?

Disappointed things didn't go according to plan, she was faced with a few options.

One, she could forget the whole thing.

Two, she could tell him over the phone or

Three, she could return to his place.

And it was the third choice that frightened her most.

CHAPTER THIRTY-TWO

IT MIGHT BE BETTER to tell Roman over the phone, Cinnamon thought as she blew on her peppermint tea. But before she made the call, she needed to mull it over some more. In the midst of her heavy contemplation, Arri danced into the kitchen.

"Guess who I just got off the phone with?"

"Let me guess."

"Matt," Arri blurted out before Cinnamon could answer.

"I kind of figured that."

With so much energy exuding from Arri, she seemingly couldn't stand still. Then without warning she dropped down in the chair across from Cinnamon. "So did you have your talk with Roman?"

Cinnamon shook her head in discontent. "He wasn't home."

"Oh, that's too bad."

"Then, as soon as I returned home, I called and sure enough he was there."

"Well, what's the problem? Take your butt back over there," Arri said as she prepared the dishwater.

"I'm not feeling it right now, Arri, and to be honest with you, I'm not even sure anymore about the whole thing."

"You just have cold feet. That's all this is."

"Cold feet, cold hands, cold everything."

"You're not going to be happy until you play this thing through. I know you, Cinnamon. This is going to haunt you every time you think about that man. You'll always wonder what if."

"Will you stop?" Cinnamon said playfully, knowing Arri was absolutely right. "I'm under enough pressure."

"Obviously you're not if you're willing to let him get away from you."

Cinnamon sighed, then exhaled a long-winded breath. "Maybe I'll tell him over the phone, then if he's not interested, he won't have to witness the gloom on my face."

"Yeah, but if you do it in person, he'll know you're really serious."

"Will you give me a break? The phone is the best I can offer right now."

"Okay, okay. I hope you get together with this man soon so you won't be so crabby."

"I'm not crabby. I'm stressed."

"Same thing."

Cinnamon rose to her feet and closed her eyes. "I'm going to do it. I'm going to call him. Right now and I'll use the phone in your room."

Cinnamon stepped forward, then stopped. "I don't know, Arri. What if he doesn't want to be with me?"

"What if he does?"

With a twisted mouth, Cinnamon rolled her eyes at Arri. "You're no help at all."

Cinnamon sat in Arri's bedroom on the edge of the bed. With butterflies in her stomach, she dialed Roman's number. "Hey, Roman, it's me again."

"Cinnamon, so nice to hear from you. So did you figure out what you wanted to tell me?"

"I did." She paused. "What I wanted to say was," she said, hesitating again, "that I really like you."

"As I you."

"And I think you're a terrific guy, a really terrific guy." Feeling like a sixteen-year-old, she wiped the sweat from her brow. "What I'm trying to say is. . . I think we have something truly unique and I'd like a second chance. But only if you want to. Only if you want to."

"It's not a matter of me wanting to. My concern resides more with the fact that you've just broken up with your boyfriend. And I have to be frank with you, this may be a little too soon for you."

"I see your point."

"How do I know this isn't a rebound yearning?"

Cinnamon nodded in agreement, knowing he was probably right.

"Is this a rebound thing?" he asked.

"I don't think it is."

"That's not good enough, Cinnamon. I need to know that you're totally over your ex-boyfriend before I involve myself in something like this. Do you understand what I'm saying?"

"I do." Though she understood, it did nothing for the ache in her heart.

"I appreciate you sharing this with me because it means a lot," Roman said. "And I know it wasn't easy for you to say it."

"No, it wasn't, but I appreciate your honesty as well." With a teardrop in the crack of her eye, she flopped back on the bed.

After a brief silence, Roman said, "I'd love to have a friendship with you though if that's possible."

"Of course." She agreed quickly as not to let on just how completely devastated she was.

"If you want to talk some more," Roman said. "Give me a call. Okay?"

"Okay, thanks."

Cinnamon stared at the ceiling and didn't move for a long time. Never before did she experience such woe in the center of her soul. And not just because he rejected her but because she once had a chance with him and she blew it. Big time.

In her heart, she knew he was right to feel as he did. Still, it offered little solace because she yearned for this man, wanting a life with him. And nothing, absolutely nothing else would suffice.

With Cinnamon in mourning, nothing else mattered. She called off work the next two days, the despondency too overwhelming to pacify customers on a crowded airplane. Instead, she tended to her own trials.

Though she planned to go apartment shopping with Noel, her enthusiasm was next to nil and she cancelled.

Later that evening, Cinnamon lay on her side in Arri's made bed. Having yet to shower or brush her teeth, she wore a long bathrobe and white socks, her hair matted together like a jacked up hairpiece.

She watched Arri enter the room with the broom and begin sweeping. In a trance-like state, Cinnamon stared at the stack of romance novels against the wall until it became just one blur.

"I ordered some pizza," Arri said.

"I don't care. I'm not eating anymore. I'm going to starve myself until I die."

Arri chuckled. "Whatever you say, Cinnamon. After you starve yourself, what should I do with the body?"

"I don't care what you do with it."

"You could just slit your wrists and be done with it."

"That's not funny, Arri."

Arri set the broom against the wall, flopped down on the bed and faced Cinnamon.

"Poor little Cinnamon."

"Oh, shut up."

"So tell me. How long is this going to go on?"

"I don't know what you're talking about," Cinnamon said unconvincingly.

"Oh, yes you do. This pouting and moping, not eating."

"What else can I do?"

"You can go to him and tell him how you feel."

"I did tell him how I felt and then he told me how he felt."

"Yeah, but you didn't tell him in person."

"Arri, give it up. I can't go through this anymore. I won't go through this anymore."

Arri dropped to her knees so her face was directly in Cinnamon's. "Will you listen to yourself? And you said I was dramatic."

"Love does strange things to you," Cinnamon said as she turned away from Arri. "Tell me something, did you take the day off just so you could harass me?"

"I most certainly did," Arri said. "What did you think? That I took the day off for nothing?"

Arri shifted to the other side so she was once again face to face with Cinnamon, and attempted to run her fingers through Cinnamon's hair. "And what is with this hair? You have to do something about this."

"I'm in pain, Arri, can't you see that?" Cinnamon said, trying not to laugh. Unable to hold it in any longer, Cinnamon burst into laugher, and Arri immediately joined her.

"Okay." Cinnamon flipped onto her back. "I may have laughed, but I am still in pain, Arri, and I don't know how to make it stop."

"I do."

"And how would I do that?"

"Get up, eat something, take a shower, brush your teeth, do something with your hair, then go to Roman and tell him what you want from him."

"Arri, I'm not doing that anymore. Besides he's at work."

"Even better. If you show up at his office, he'll know for sure you mean business."

"Or am desperate, whichever comes first."

Arri stood and finished sweeping. "Okay, sit around with messed up hair, moping, hoping and wishing."

Cinnamon rolled onto her side, facing the books and magazines against the wall. "Thank you, because that's exactly what I plan to do."

"That's fine with me," Arri said, before disappearing into the other room.

Just when Cinnamon expected Arri to leave her to her misery, Arri soon returned. "Cinnamon, what's this? I found these in the garbage."

Cinnamon lifted her head long enough to see what Arri was talking about. It was the pouch of fuchsia love rocks Mitchell gave to her.

"Oh, those. Make sure you put them back where you found them."

"But what are they?"

"Mitchell gave them to me. Supposedly they were to bring true love into my life. Need I say more?"

"That's what he said?" Arri asked as her face creased with doubt.

"That's what he said."

Arri opened the suede bag and dropped the rocks into her hand. "What's funny is that I saw these same rocks at the Pleasure Chest about a month ago, same color, same suede bag and everything."

Cinnamon sat up, suspicious. "Really?"

"And trust me if he got them from the Pleasure Chest, they are not love rocks, that's for sure, especially since they only cost three dollars."

"Three dollars? Are you saying he made it up?"

"What do you think?" Arri asked sarcastically.

"He never was a big spender."

"Do you mind if I keep them?"

"Just so long as I don't have to see them."

"All right, I'll leave you to your misery now."

"You said that before."

"Well, excuse me." Arri faded into the next room.

Returning her focus to the stacks of books against the wall, one book in particular caught Cinnamon's eye. *Thirty Years of Learning.* Instantly, Cinnamon climbed off the bed, slid the book from the stack, and flipped to the table of contents. She understood why it looked so familiar. It was her book.

The title fascinated her and she wasn't exactly sure why until it hit her. She would turn thirty in a few months. And she had to read this book. It was a must.

Cinnamon rushed into the other room with the book in hand and interrupted Arri as Arri watched the cable channel E.

"Arri, is this my book?"

Arri glanced over the title. "Yep, I forgot to return it to you."

Cinnamon flipped through the pages, admiring the context. "Did you read it?"

"I'm sure I didn't."

"I don't think I ever read it either, and I can't understand why."

"It's good to know that the only thing that can get you out of bed is a damn book."

Exploding with enthusiasm, Cinnamon returned to the bedroom, flopped down on the bed and skimmed the book, knowing why she purchased it in the first place. It discussed some of her favorite subjects.

God

Forgiveness

Surrender

Prosperity

And love. It spoke a lot about love.

Why she failed to read it before remained a mystery to her.

Forty minutes into the book, she stumbled upon a statement that struck a nerve, *Sometimes the thing you want the most is wanting you back.*

Could there be any truth in that statement?

Was it possible Roman was longing for her the way she longed for him?

An hour later she completed the one hundred and sixty-one page book, her spirits livened with a miraculous sense of hope. This was the reason she loved books so much. They held the power to transform her mood instantly.

The next day Cinnamon awakened cheerful and inspired. She beamed with optimism as she stepped out of bed after resolving not to give up on Roman. For the second time, she would confront Roman, conveying to him in her own special way just how much he meant to her. Meeting with him in person would affirm her true sentiments. And this time she was not without a backup plan. If after her face-to-face engagement with Roman, he still proved unreceptive, she would make peace with the outcome, concluding that it was not meant to be. She could breathe easily, knowing she did all she could. It was her new attitude that paved the way for a momentous encounter with no added stress.

This time Cinnamon would not doll herself up like before, trying to manipulate him with her feminine wiles. She intended to speak from the heart. No need to show off anything else. As added ammunition, Cinnamon took with her a portable CD player, along with her Van Morrison CD, which included one of her favorite tracks, "Someone Like You," a song she planned to dedicate to Roman.

Cinnamon rode the 151 Sheridan bus downtown to Roman's office and walked three blocks over to LaSalle Street.

On the twenty-first floor, she stepped off the elevator, expecting to be nervous but, surprisingly, she wasn't. After having released all her expectations, she would come out a winner no matter what happened.

Endowed with confidence and finesse, she sauntered over to reception like she owned the place. She wore flare legged jeans, a hot pink shirt and her short wool coat.

After asking for Roman, she waited in the reception area, her legs crossed, not reading, not thinking, or hoping. Just being. This was going to be a glorious day. That was her affirmation and she clung to it.

Less than a minute later, Roman greeted her with a smile. "This is a treat."

Cinnamon rose to her feet and smiled. "Can we talk?"

In Roman's office, Cinnamon sat across from him, on the edge of the chair, not bothering to remove her coat.

"You look so serious," Roman said.

"That's because I have serious stuff to say."

Roman eased back, seemingly relaxed, as he waited.

"I have a song I want you to listen to."

"What's this song about?"

"It's about you," she said as she dug into her bag and pulled out her portable CD player. "It's all about you."

"I can't wait to hear it."

She fast forwarded to track number seven, stepped around to Roman's desk and slid the earphones over his head.

"Before you press the play button, I have three things I want to say. The first being, I love you."

She watched him blush as he has never blushed before and then she continued. "The second is this. I mean every word on this track. And third, despite everything we talked about, I want to be your girl, Roman, and never go another day without having you in my life."

Seemingly somewhat enchanted, Roman listened but he did not speak. Though Cinnamon always planned to dedicate the song, "Someone Like You," to that special person, it was not until this very day she realized Roman was that person. Never did she imagine that the lyrics, "searching a long time for someone like you," that those words, those beautiful heartfelt words would be addressed to Roman Richardson.

Cinnamon observed him from across the room while he listened to the song. He didn't move an inch, as if hypnotized by the words. Less than two minutes later, Roman removed the headphones and his eyes fell shut as if he was still in the moment.

Cinnamon waited for him to speak, but he said nothing.

Several seconds would elapse before a word uttered from his lips. Then it happened. Roman opened his eyes and his body shifted back. "I'm without words, Cinnamon, simply aroused by your grand gesture."

"And I meant every word."

Roman rose to his feet, stepped around the desk and helped Cinnamon into a standing position. He smoothed his hand across her face and then sensuously past her lips. "From the very start, you tugged at my heart strings and stole my heart." He wrapped his arms around her and gripped her by the waist. Not a speck of air dwelled between them.

Cinnamon peered at him through his round glasses and smiled. "Love touches us in the most beautiful ways. And you've done that to me, Roman."

He kissed her eyelids, then her forehead and both sides of her face. "Do you know how much I love you, Cinnamon Brown?" he asked in a whisper.

His question made her feel so special and she couldn't hide it. "I know I wanted you to love me."

Enraptured in the moment, she kissed him gently, over and over, her heart pounding as he gazed back at her. She smiled with a glow that could start a fire. "Will you be my guy, Roman Richardson, be with me on weekends and holidays and be my greatest friend until we decide to marry or not to marry?"

"Oh, yes. Most positively, categorically, and certainly, yes."

The author welcomes your comments and questions. She can be reached at carriecarr3@yahoo.com.

WITH MUCH GRATITUDE

A very warm thank you to Kevon at Culture Plus Books who is not only a savvy businessman but also a good person. May you continue to be blessed.

A special thanks to Wale at Afrocentric Book Store in Chicago who was one of the first persons in the business to steer me in the right direction. Thank you, Wale.

To my husband, Philip, who has encouraged me throughout this entire endeavor. You are the best.

Hats off to Cindy Salmon, Theresa Conner, Pam Preston, Linda King, Melissa Green, Sherry Washington and Jamie McGhee. Thanks guys for everything.

A warm thanks to Pamela Bolden at Rawsistaz Reviewers and T. Rhythm Knight at APOOO Book Club for their glowing reviews.

And finally a warm hug and kiss to my wonderful mother and father, Thelma and Herman Coleman, my beautiful sisters, Kim and Valerie, and my witty brother, Trint. I love you all.